CUT OFF AT THE THROAT

OISÍN MCGANN

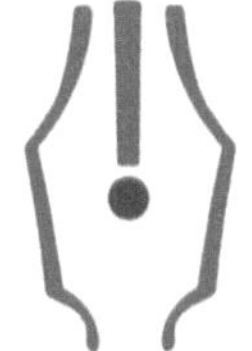

Also by Oisín McGann

Novels from Open Road Books (US)

Ancient Appetites: The Wildenstern Saga – Book 1

The Wisdom of Dead Men: The Wildenstern Saga – Book 2

Merciless Reason: The Wildenstern Saga – Book 3

Strangled Silence

Rat Runners

Novellas from Open Road Books (US)

The Vile Desire to Scream: A Companion to

The Wisdom of Dead Men

The Need for Fear: A Companion to *Strangled Silence*

Spoil the Kill: A Companion to *Rat Runners*

Novels from Penguin Random House (UK)

Ancient Appetites: The Wildenstern Saga – Book 1

The Wisdom of Dead Men: The Wildenstern Saga – Book 2

Merciless Reason: The Wildenstern Saga – Book 3

Strangled Silence

Rat Runners

Small-Minded Giants

Kings of the Realm: War's Harvest

Kings of the Realm: Cruel Salvation

Novels from The O'Brien Press (Ireland)

The Gods and Their Machines

The Harvest Tide Project: The Archisan Tales – Book 1

Under Fragile Stone: The Archisan Tales – Book 2

Race the Atlantic Wind

Non-fiction from Little Island (Ireland)

A Short, Hopeful Guide to Climate Change

For a full bibliography of his work, please visit his website at:

oisinmcgann.com

Praise for Oisín's Books

'A sinister, shadowy world of conspiracy theorists, political double-dealing and media distortion. McGann, in his most accomplished young adult novel to date, handles all of these (and more) with an excellent pace and occasional flashes of ironic humour. The result is an impressive and highly intelligent political thriller.'
Robert Dunbar *The Irish Times Weekend Review* for *Strangled Silence*

'Richard Morgan blasted on to the bookshelves with his hard-hitting tech-noir *Altered Carbon*, a book so in yer face you could smell its toothpaste. Oisín McGann has done the same thing in young adult form with *Small-Minded Giants*, a debut novel so powerful it all but explodes off the page . . . What's astonishing is the confidence with which McGann describes his world, from the workings of the mammoth machinery powering the city to his evocative descriptions. Acts of terrorism give the plot a *V For Vendetta* feel and the tone is just as uncompromising. In short, this book isn't content to sit on your shelf; it's too busy screaming at you to pick it up and **READ IT!**'
Jayne Nelson, *SFX Magazine*
(gives *Small-Minded Giants* five stars out of five)

'The internal turmoil of this multi-generational family is intense and resembles the powerful Russian sagas written by Fyodor Dostoyevsky and Leo Tolstoy. Thankfully, the spunky characters, accessible dialogue, and nonstop action make this novel enjoyable for contemporary teens who already enjoy the [steampunk] genre and are willing to tackle a dense and complex story.
Sunnie Lovelace, *School Library Journal* for *Ancient Appetites*

'Four criminally inclined teenagers in future London are on the run in this fantastic dystopian thriller . . . Teens will relish McGann's nonstop action, full of intrigue and heart-pounding excitement. Fans of Cory Doctorow, particularly the Orwellian surveillance-themed *Little Brother* (2008), will find a lot to love here.'
Stacey Comfort, *Booklist* (Reviews journal for American Library Association) for *Rat Runners*

'This excellent novel is a fantasy, yet every word of it has direct and understated relevance for our own political world ... The novel is chiefly a fast-paced, tense and highly convincing thriller. But McGann's impeccably fair-minded and intelligent hints at parallels with Israel and Palestine, or America and the Middle East, or the secular west and Islam, are impossible to

miss, and his even-handed narrative is all the more effective in consequence. Exciting as fantasy adventure, thoughtful in present-day relevance, the book is a fine achievement and is strongly recommended.'
Peter Hollindale, *The School Librarian* magazine
for *The Gods and Their Machines*

'With this book, Oisín McGann has contributed a compelling and complex work about people who have suffered and been scarred by the war attempting to use the airplanes that were once instruments of war in a way that will inspire instead of destroy . . . McGann offers a view of humanity as something that is flawed, ingenious, passionate, wounded, terrifying, and ultimately, hopeful that it might be possible to change.'
Tony Flynn, *Inis Magazine* for *Race the Atlantic Wind*

Pronounced 'Uh-Sheen' – Biography

Oisín McGann was born in 1973 in Dublin, Ireland, and grew up there and in Drogheda, County Louth. He studied at Ballyfermot Senior College and then Dun Laoghaire School of Art and Design, before going on to work in illustration, design and film animation, later moving to London to work as an art director and copy writer in advertising.

He has since become one of Ireland's most prolific and best-known writer-illustrators, and has produced dozens of books for all levels of reader, including thirteen novels.

Oisín is a winner of the European Science Fiction Society Award, Children's Books Ireland's Children's Choice Award and has been shortlisted for numerous other awards, including the Waterstones Children's Book Prize in the UK, le Grand Prix de l'Imaginaire in France and Locus Magazine's Best First Novel Award in the US.

He is married with three children, two dogs and a cat, and lives somewhere in the Irish countryside, where he won't be heard shouting at his computer.

Chapter One
Opening with a Bang

Hurled backwards by scorching heat as hammers thump into my ears. The ground lurches up and hits me, a bone-bending thud, driving my left shoulder hard into the gravel and rasping my face like a cheese-grater. My brain sways in my skull as I roll over and lift my head to look up. An explosion. The monastery's on fire. Flames surge through the collapsing roof, rising from inside the broken blocky stone walls, crackling, tangling and churning upwards into thick gritty smoke that glows a deep burnt orange against the sullen evening clouds. Its pungent tang fills my nostrils and I feel the heat of the inferno on my scraped face. There are sounds around me, voices, but they're dull, muted as if my ears are full of water, and it's hard to hear or think anything over the piercing whine my throbbing eardrums are transmitting through my head.

The mon is on fire. What the f– *(deleted)*, how the f– *(deleted)*, what stupid b– *(deleted)*. Wait . . . wait, what's happening to my text? . . . Oh, right. Right. The censor chip in my head. I forgot, we can't *swear* now either. *Another* thing I can't say. I'm trying to talk about how our *home* is on fire and I can't even swear in my journal. Like Noon says: "you can record your thoughts, Billy, but you can't speak your mind". So . . . here I am, stretched out on the ground, the muscles of my back, shoulders and neck like strips of pain over my bones. Watching our most important building burn. And I *need* to swear because without the monastery, this whole island is f– *(deleted)*.

* * * *

It's a surprise to wake up, partly because I hadn't realized I'd passed out and partly because this isn't my room. This is the room of someone who thinks stylish décor is a human right and expects the world to provide her with the best in life – because that's how you treat someone who's going to be in charge of that world when she's older. She's sitting on a stool beside me, perceptive green eyes glazed in distracted thought until she snaps back to the here and now as she notices I'm awake. We call her Duchess, or Dutch for short, even though she doesn't like that much. Duchess has the flawless bronze skin of someone with all the best genes privilege can bestow. She's smart, gorgeous and all sorts of other social-climbing, high-achiever clichés you'd expect to find in the alpha female of a bunch of teenage students. But she's a practical type too, and can do the mothering bit for her subjects, particularly the girls, when we need it. Like now, as I try to sit up and my mind seems to roll like a boat hit side-on by a big wave

'Sit back, moron,' she says warmly, placing a manicured hand on my forehead and pushing me gently back down to the couch. 'You just got knocked out by an explosion.'

This couch has embroidered decorative cushions as well as its own cushions that you actually sit on, and is draped with a

12

'throw', which is basically just the word for a blanket you put on furniture instead of people. It's dark outside the wide window in the wall beyond the end of the sofa. Still the middle of the night. There's a faint breeze and I see that the glass has been almost entirely blasted from the window. Her villa is one of those closest to the monastery. Shards of glass lie all over the floor, but the worst of it has been swept in against the walls.

My living-room is the same size and shape as Dutch's, but mine looks like what it is, a seventeen-year-old's chill-out pad. Despite the fact that she has the same furniture, Duchess's is like a penthouse suite in a high-end development – apart from the blasted-out windows.

'Your brain has been bounced around your skull, Billy,' she adds. 'You've probably got a concussion.'

That's what they named *me* when I came here: 'Billy' – as in Billy Goat. Me being a picture of elegance and all that. With my head lying still, I can really appreciate the bass drum beat of pain contained within it, focussed around my ears, which seem to be emitting a mosquito whine all on their own. I woozily wonder if Duchess can hear it too.

'How long have I been out?'

'More than half an hour. I was about to call Karava again.'

'No, don't. I'll be fine.'

Karava's the island's doctor, a soft-mannered ferret of a man, but good at his job. I just need to lie down for a bit. The rest of my body takes this opportunity to make itself felt – and it feels as if it was stamped on by a bunch of football hooligans. I groan and close my eyes, before opening them again to gaze up into Dutch's film star face. Somehow, she doesn't look or smell right. Her boho casual white top and long apricot skirt are scuffed and dirty. Whatever that fruity, rose petal perfume is that she normally wears during the day is cloaked by the nostril-twitching itch of smoke fumes. There's a grey smudge of ash on her right cheek, quite fetching in the way it renders her imperfect, not quite hidden by a lock of black hair tinted a cinnamon colour. The smile she's giving me looks dislodged, a bad fit on her face. It finally occurs to me to ask about the others.

'What happened to the mon?' I ask, my voice feeling rough in my throat. 'Is everyone okay?'

'They think it was a gas explosion,' she replies, brushing the loose lock of hair out of her face and fiddling with the bun that binds her thick waves onto the back of her head. When Duchess is anxious, she needs to do things with her fingers. 'Everyone's fine.'

The hands come down into her lap, then they take my hand, not clasping, just in a girls-chatting kind of way, but her face suddenly falls slack and she blurts out a trembling sob and then just as quickly composes herself, as if that's all the loss of control she can allow.

'Actually . . . actually, they're not,' she says shakily, letting out a long breath. 'Valtere was hurt. Burned . . . I saw him, just for a few seconds, before they covered him up. He was really badly burned. They don't know if he'll survive.'

I can see it in the slight lack of focus in her eyes; she's in shock. The image of the man's charred injuries must have imprinted itself upon her mind and yet she couldn't tell me at first. She's still processing it – has probably been thinking of nothing else while she sat here waiting for me to wake up. I know that's how I'd be, if I was left alone after seeing that.

I remember something from the moments before I must have blacked out. A figure standing in the side entrance to the mon, silhouetted in the flame and smoke that burst through the doorway with the suddenness of a gun's muzzle flash. The figure's flesh almost seeming to spray out as the blast hit. A little gasp escapes from my mouth at the memory, my body reacting to the horror of it even as I get my head around what's happened. Brother Valtere's one of the decent guys; one of the few guardians who doesn't keep that emotional distance from us studes. We all liked him. I mean *like* . . . we all *like* him.

'F–,' *(deleted)* I try to say, before the censor chip cuts me off. The tiny microchip in my head that monitors what I say and stops me saying the wrong thing. It's like your parents having a mute button that controls your mouth. The interruption of my much-needed profanity makes me grimace and it takes me a couple of seconds to get my thoughts back on track. My throat is painfully dry too, so I'm croaking a little too.

'I should go and see him. What about all the rest?'

'Yes, the others are all okay – at least everyone we'd accounted for when we brought you in here. I didn't get to check on everyone and some of the oldies are still dealing with the fire. Anyway, you'll see them yourself when we can get you back on your feet.' She gives a grim smile as she wipes a tear from under her eyelid. 'Buckley's called a meeting.'

'Oh, of course.'

This is not news. Brother Buckley is the leader of our little community and he's a fiend for the meetings. It's not that he loves the sound of his own voice – he's not an especially egotistical man – but in making pains to keep things as 'democratic' as possible, there's no mundane task he can't prolong with the addition of several hours of exploratory discussion. This is the first time a building has ever blown up in the village, so it's likely that Buckley is already scheduling a f–(deleted) . . . a frickin' week-long conference.

Duchess hasn't asked me what I was doing out near the mon at that hour of the morning, but Buckley and the other guardians have to be wondering. It's only a matter of time before someone puts the question to me.

As I screw up my face at the idea, I notice for the first time that there are thinner, sharper lines of pain on my left cheek. I sit up now, my brain not reeling as much as it did before, and look over the back of the mulberry-coloured couch at the ivory painted wall, where there's a wide mirror with an ornate gold frame, a *real* gold frame, that Dutch must have brought here, because it certainly didn't come with the villas that are provided for us.

If you ever see me in photos, my brown-skinned face never seems to take the same form twice, as if my tangled thoughts are constantly tugging on the strings of my facial muscles. Most of the time my dark chestnut eyes are too large, too sincerely intent, like those of a gormless child. They combine with my baby's button nose and a mouth that's too wide for my face to give people the impression I'm a bit naïve, childishly innocent, even though I've had the least pampered life of all the studes on the island.

My hair is almost exactly the same colour as my eyes, shoulder-length and usually left in a natural afro, but tied back nice and tight to stop it bouncing around for when I want to run. And now I'm scratched all down the left side of my face, clawed by the gravel after the explosion. The bleeding has stopped and I think Duchess must have dabbed the grazes clean, but it seems the blast has left its marks, inside and out.

'I can give you some cream to stop those from scarring,' Duchess says helpfully.

'What about the stores?' I ask her, my eyes shifting from my reflection to hers. 'Did we lose much?'

'The stores,' she sighs and her face sets in the firm, resolute expression that tells you her defences just went up. It must be bad. 'Yes, we lost . . . well . . . we lost pretty much *everything*.'

Chapter Two
A Fascination with Destruction

I figure people might want to read about what happened with the blast; I could probably get this published as an article or a blog or something later on. An explosion is news wherever it happens and there are plenty of people who take a particular interest in this place. If you've downloaded this and you *have* just started reading from here, I'll try and make what follows as complete as possible, that way you don't have to read back over my whole journal.

Oh . . . what I *should* tell you, in case you don't know, is that this text is being recorded on my censor chip, which is one of the chip's more useful and less insidious functions. I can write just by thinking and then download the text into my folder on the Hub later. It's pretty excellent, really. Keeps things nice and immediate, helped along by the whole first person, present tense deal. The one drawback – and it's a real *teeth-grinder* of a drawback – is that the same things that are censored in my speech, are also censored in my journal too. I can't talk about why we're all here on this island – though I'm sure you must know already – I can't discuss religion, people's nationality, or get too specific about politics. The only exception is when we're in history, geography or civics class, when the ban on those topics is put on pause.

Since the new ban that came in around the time of the hurricane, I can't use anything but the mildest swearwords or insults, which is driving me nuts. I *like* swearing. There are a few other forbidden files too, but those are the main ones.

The chip monitors the language centres in the brain and, apart from the swearing, it doesn't prevent you from using particular words, it's watching for *meaning*. The little sh–*(deleted)* uses your own brain against you. If you try to say something, or even write something down that you *know* you're not supposed to say, it cuts you off, and if you really push at it, you lose your train of thought and completely forget what you wanted to say.

So I swear, I'm not *trying* to be an unreliable narrator, it's being forced upon me.

Every student on the island has one of these chips in their head, their settings controlled by Brother Buckley. I find myself lingering around our responsible adults, the guardians, more than I should, keeping my ears open, because even though there are thoughts of my own I can't write down, I *am* allowed to record anything *anyone else says*. If it's said out loud, I can convert it to text there and then.

Okay, so that's the info-dump out of the way. Normal storytelling service shall now be resumed.

It's the middle of the night, my censor chip tells me it's three forty-five in the morning, and the fire is almost out. The guardians have done their best to control it, but we have no fire service here, only fat hoses, extinguishers and other basic equipment. We're supposed to have this state-of-the-art fire prevention tech, so I'm wondering what's gone wrong. Over the last half hour, the focus has been on containing the inferno to this one building and letting the blaze run out of fuel. I can hear popping and cracking sounds that could be bullets going off in the weapons locker or exploding tins of food.

Some of the guardians have finished, and now they're sitting exhausted on the ground, their skin and short-sleeved fern-green shirts and khaki trousers charcoaled in grime and ash, blackened by smoke. They gaze back warily at the slain beast with watering eyes, gagging and coughing up the burnt particles that fill the air around the scene, clouds of the near-weightless soot slowly sinking to render every surface below in monotone.

Off to my right, Sister Adeyemi walks past, carrying the mangled body of one of our cats. A tabby; probably Tex, judging by the markings, but most of its head and one of its legs is missing, so it's hard to tell. I put my fingers to my mouth, feeling a rising nausea. Bloody hell. I immediately peer around to see if I can spot any others. There were always two or three cats hanging around the mon. Chances are, Tex wasn't the only one we lost.

You do have to wonder about humans' fascination with destruction. Even as Duchess and I make our way towards the green, the central lawn in front of the mon where Buckley has asked us to congregate, I can't help gazing at the smoking ruins of the building in awe, taking in the exposed details of its carcass with no small sense of relish. This is something that has never happened here before, a dramatic, monumental level of damage that even the recent hurricane could not match. The mon had stood against that storm, as it did for all the others over the centuries. What the full violence of the weather could not achieve in days of high wind and flooding, our methane-fuelled, back-up heating system managed in seconds. I am shocked about it, of course, and worry and pity for Valtere churn in my gut and tighten my lungs, but on an island where we go to great lengths to contrive variety in our days, this is a monster event and I can feel the crackle of excitement as I walk towards the people gathering on the green. The studes are buzzing on this.

The oldies have taken a big hit. It's not just about the damage that's been done to the structure. The bulk of our food and medical supplies was in there, and if Duchess is right, we've lost the lot. The guardians will *have* to take us off the island now, at least for a short while. It's been too long since my parents' last visit and I feel an overpowering longing to see them again; to smell Mum's skin and hair when I hug her, to hear Dad's childish giggle in real life, instead of over a video link. I want to go for a walk in the hills near our house, some place where I can smell the woods, but not the ever-present sea. That familiar hollow in my chest is back, the void that can only be filled by being home.

I wish Noon was here now. Of all the guardians, she's the only one I feel completely comfortable around; she helps keep me sane and I'm missing her like crazy now, but she's out on the boat and won't be back for a couple of days.

The monastery was the anchor building in the village, by far the largest and most important structure. This architectural mongrel served as the headquarters for the oldies, housing their offices, as well as an assembly hall, the infirmary, the library, kitchen and canteen and the lab for our science classes. The classrooms were in there too, though we took many of our lessons outside on the grass or in other spots around the village. The main section was a stone church and out-buildings that had been here for over two hundred years. Their cave-like, metre-thick walls of lumpy stone were left natural and bare to contrast with the newer materials of the extension that tripled the building's size, constructed when the island was chosen for the mission.

That rock must have become shrapnel in the explosion, broken fists of it punching through the concrete and wood-frame structures that made up the more modern wing, smashing through walls, floors and ceilings. Pieces of that stone and shards of concrete, wood and adobe roof tile had rained down all over the village, sharing the monastery's mortal remains among all the buildings close to it. The thickest sections of the original walls are still standing, tenuously-linked individuals now, rather than part of a whole, missing their tops and their roof, but enduring, as if to say: 'We were here when you arrived and we'll still be here long after you leave.'

It's only as I stare up at the ruin, that I see the long steel radio mast lying at an awkward diagonal, thrown from the roof and now leaning against the front wall, off to my left. The radio. For crack's sake. I'd forgotten about the *f–(deleted)* radio. That was in there too. Ever since the satellite link stopped working, the radio has been our only means of contacting the outside world. Without the sat-link, we could only communicate with ships or planes that came within range. And most of those are supposed to keep clear of the island. We're too far from other land masses, too far round the curve of the Earth, to make contact directly without satellite. I know there's a spare radio at the air base, but will it work without the mast?

All the other buildings in the village are modern residences, built for purpose from the ground up, like our squat, adobe-tiled, white-walled villas, or functional structures like the gym, the sauna, the swimming pool, the pump-house for the pool, the solar panels and wind turbines, or the boathouses down at the dock. Even some of these have been affected, just as a gruesome accident damages the lives of all those around the victim. Every building within fifty metres of the mon has had its windows blown out. I wonder how many of the studes are feeling similar effects.

The guardians had only recently finished clearing up after the hurricane that passed through a few weeks ago. That ripped the roof off one of the boathouses, wrecked our biggest boat, tore the rest of the place up a bit and left debris all over the roads, lawns and courts. The village was barely back on its feet after that and now we've slammed into the canvas for a second time. All the studes must be wondering if this is the knock-out blow and, despite the loss we've all suffered, there is a thrill of anticipation. Surely now, we'll get to go home for a few weeks. Given the communications problems we've been having since the storm, the only question is when.

Duchess and I walk among the others, looking for somewhere to sit down on the lawn in front of the shattered remains of the building. I settle down gingerly beside Smood and Gemmy, who are sitting on the grass near the Fractal Fountain. Gemmy's cuddling another one of the cats, Cassie, who looks properly freaked, huddled into him as his fingers stroke through her fur. Fragments of ash, delicate as moth's wings have billowed out from the fire, swirled in the gentle night breeze and floated down all over the area. The fountain's water, muddied with grey particles, lies still in its splaying arrangement of circular, white-concrete-walled pools. Smood offers up his hand in support, but I don't take it. I'm not a cripple; I can still get my backside down to the ground without help. Duchess sits on the opposite side of me to Smood and I wonder if their 'ship is on or off at the moment; I can never keep up. She runs out of patience with him every two or three weeks. But she's like me trying to quit sugar; she keeps going back.

Not that she's got a wide selection to choose from. There are sixteen studes on the island, including me; nine boys, three of whom she's dated while she's been here, and subsequently rejected. Some are either too young for her to consider, being below her cut-off age of sixteen years; others just don't come close to meeting her standards. She's had a fling with a couple of the girls too. That's it, though. If she wants to look further afield, there's only the guardians left, which is against the rules and, frankly, just too far off the reservation for our society girl. We all have the same problem. We're a pretty tight group, but it can get very claustrophobic at times. I've dated two guys since I arrived and I'm growing increasingly suspicious that word has gone round that I'm too weird to bother with.

It probably wouldn't help if any of them found out I was keeping a journal in my head. As far as I know, nobody else has thought to do it and they might not be too keen on hanging round someone who's writing down what they do and say. Which is why I've never mentioned it.

Smood has the blond beach bum thing right down; sapphire blue eyes that I *do* like gazing into, hair that looks like he doesn't give a damn about it, but takes ten minutes in the morning to mess just right, careless stubble over sculpted features atop an athlete's frame. While his laid-back manner comes from the confidence that his success in life is assured, he also has an easy smile that you can't help liking. He's a brat too, though he's never really nasty with it.

When he first arrived on the island 'smood' was his word for cool – he used it all the time. In that mildly mocking way that these labels are applied, it's what everyone started calling him. He doesn't use it for cool any more.

He's leaning back on his elbows, his legs stretched out in front of him, white skin tanned and muscled, his shorts riding a little high up on the thigh. He looks at me, with just a touch of that expression that always appears on his face when he's talking to a girl, like you're being measured on a scale, but his concern is real as he asks:

'Hey, Billy Goat, how you doin'? You gave us a bit of scare there.'

I'm one of the younger ones in the group, and one of the smallest, so they occasionally treat me like I'm a baby or something. Sometimes it's patronising, sometimes it's sweet. I'm feeling like five kilos of crap in a three-kilo bag, so I'll take sweet tonight.

'I'm okay. You?'

'Yeah, yeah. Me and a couple of the guys tried to help with the fire, but they wouldn't let us.'

'Can't risk damaging the merchandise,' I told him.

'That's a pity,' Duchess snorts softly.

So . . . the relationship's off at the moment then.

Chapter Three
A Cruel Blow

There are murmurs of conversation all around us as we sprawl on the carefully trimmed lawn and wait to hear what the oldies have to tell us. We can see Brother Buckley off to our left, standing on the gravel drive, near what was once the back door into the kitchen. He stares at the last few stubbornly surviving flames that flicker in the gutted windows, then his balding head, the colour of cooked chicken skin, sinks down to his chest. He's either fixed his eyes on the white gravel or he has them closed in thought – I can't tell. The weight of tonight's events press down heavily on his shoulders. The responsibility of his role has aged him, and this tragedy will add depth to the furrows on his face. However close we might be to Valtere, Buckley worked with him in the Order for years. Although our principal would never be a man who inspired pity, for once, I find myself feeling sorry for Buckley. Not only has his friend been burnt to the edge of death, but this incident will almost certainly mark the end of the principal's career. The Council will be calling him back as soon word reaches them.

'Look at him,' Smood whispers. 'He's lost it. They *have* to let us go home now.'

Duchess doesn't reply, though like the others around me,

she nods in agreement. This is it. We're getting off the island. Even in the midst of this disaster, I feel my heart lift with hope.

All the studes have gathered, along with many of the guardians, who stand or sit solemnly on our flanks. I don't know if this formation is deliberate or not. The members of the Order see themselves sometimes as our 'shepherds', both protective and controlling. It's another reason I get on so well with Noon. She doesn't give off that vibe. When we're together, she acts like she doesn't give a damn about what I do.

Buckley rouses himself from his thoughts and walks over slowly to address us. His demeanour is enough to end the chatter. The hurt is evident, washed-out blue eyes surveying us for a moment before he speaks. Buckley's face is like a fence, broad and formed of vertical lines, all seemingly held in place by a few strong horizontal ones around his brow, eyes and mouth. A leathery white guy weathered by island living, he is a blocky figure, square and broad-chested. He holds himself upright at all times when he speaks to you, as if setting an example, urging you to stand strong.

He brushes his fingertips over his bald head, a mannerism of his when he's unsettled, then casts his eyes over us again, fixing a reassuring expression on his face.

'We have been dealt a cruel blow,' he begins. 'One that will test all of us in the coming weeks.'

Eh? What does he mean, 'in the coming weeks'? I blink at

that, glancing at Duchess, who shrugs dismissively, shaking her head. I'm piqued now, though. How long does he seriously expect us to stay on an island with no f–*(deleted)* food? Man, we are *outta here* as soon as our parents hear what's happened.

'Let me first assure you that we are doing everything we can for Brother Valtere, but his burns are severe and his body has suffered other injuries from the blast too; broken bones and internal bleeding. We don't think he will survive long without major surgery. Doctor Karava has treated the most urgent of these injuries, but he is limited in what he can with the resources we have available. We have lost most of our painkilling medication, including all of our anaesthetic. If Valtere is not airlifted to a hospital ship within the next day or two, it's unlikely he will survive.'

No proper painkillers for a guy in his condition. F–*(deleted)*! Several of us wince at that. Buckley pauses, taking in a deep breath, letting that news sink in, because we know what's coming next. He gestures at the fallen radio mast, now tangled in cables, its top bent against the ground, its lower section leaning up against the wall, amputated at the ankles, its feet presumably torn off where they had been bolted to the monastery roof. The steel framework is ten metres long and could almost be a square-framed ladder that's been used to rescue someone from the burning building. I mean, if a fireman's ladder came equipped with a few random broken antenna and satellite dishes.

Without the sat-link, this twisted piece of metalwork was our means of reaching out to the world beyond the island. They'll have to sort that out before we can go anywhere. Three of the guardians are already working to cut the mast free from the wreckage, with others standing by, ready to catch the thing when it slides down.

'As you can see, the radio mast is damaged and the radio, and the Hub itself, have been destroyed. Even while they were operational, we have had no contact with anyone over the last week.' Buckley notices that he is kneading his hands together in an anxious manner and, instead, clasps them firmly in front of him. 'Given the island's position, that in itself hasn't been a cause for concern up till now. We're isolated for a reason, after all. But combined with the loss of the satellite link and now this new emergency, it is vital that we repair the mast and bring up the spare radio from the air base. Once that's done, we can only hope that someone comes within range and can relay our distress call to the mainland.'

'How did this happen?' Duchess demands to know.

'We haven't ascertained the cause as yet,' he tells her. 'We'll investigate the crime scene properly once it's safe to do so. It's unfortunate that we do not have the benefit of Sister Noon's expertise at the moment, but we'll keep the site intact until she returns.'

'What about the stores?' Smood calls out.

'Yes, I was coming to that,' Buckley replies. His features set themselves in a grim expression. 'Everything in the monastery stores was destroyed. The only food we have left is whatever we have in the villas. We still have the well and the collector tanks, so water is not an issue. The emergency generator is gone too, but most of the solar panels, the wind turbines and batteries are undamaged and will supply us with all the power we need. As of now, however, we must take stock of what food we have and begin rationing.'

'*Rationing?*' Smood exclaims, springing to his feet, fists bunched, and is quickly followed by some of the others around us. 'Are you kidding? How long are we going to be stuck here without *food?*

'You can't keep us here under these conditions!' Duchess pipes up. She's up now too, so I find getting to my feet because everyone else is looming over me. Being one of the smallest in the group doesn't help. Dutch points a finger at Buckley, as if she's going to stab him with it – or target him with an armour-piercing lawyer. 'You have to let us go home!'

'That's not my decision to make, as you well know,' Buckley responds in an even voice, raising his hands in a placatory gesture. 'Nor do I have the means to get you home, until an aircraft or support ship arrives. In the meantime, we have to deal with the circumstances in which we find ourselves. We are very low on supplies and cannot contact the mainland, so we must control our consumption as much as possible, to make the most of what we have. We don't know for how long, but it's not likely to be more than a week or two. We can still keep fishing, for what it's worth, and we can also investigate the possibilities of hunting and foraging.'

'Foraging?' Gemmy bursts out a laugh, his husky voice high in indignation. His thin brown hands stiffen like talons around the cat, who thrashes out of his grip and leaps from his arms. Gemmy's childlike, boxy face, topped by spiky black hair, is a caricature of disbelief. '*Foraging?* What? I mean, what are we . . . wombats? You want us crawling through the woods looking for nuts and berries?'

'You'd be lucky to find berries this time of year!' I call out.

My irate observation on the local flora sounds a little pernickety when I hear it out loud, but I wanted my voice to be heard and I think it's a very valid point. Despite his protests, I can't help thinking that Gemmy's anticipating the impending lack of food with a certain miserable relief. It'll mean less for him to throw up after meals, and misery loves company.

'I understand it's hard to take,' Buckley says to our small crowd, his voice louder, firmer now, his authoritative tone trying to suppress further objections. 'However, we have to consider our resources. In the effort to make the stay here as pleasant as possible, poisons and engineered diseases were released years ago to clear the place of rats, mice and cut down on insects, which were a problem on the island. It worked . . . but the measures also wiped out most of the small animals, many of the species of birds and some of the plant life. The environment here will provide little in the way of food, so we have to–.'

'Can we see Valtere?' I ask. 'Is he conscious?'

'Now would not be a good time. Doctor Karava is still treating his wounds. Valtere is . . . he's in a very bad state. It might be upsetting for you to see him.'

'We'd still like to–,' I begin, but I'm cut off by another voice.

'Wasn't he supposed to be on *watch* tonight?'

We all fall silent. I don't see who posed the question, but it sounded like Noddy's clipped, angular accent. He's standing on the far end of the crowd from me. It's as hard as ever to read the towering Norseman's sallow, long-boned face. You do your best to gauge his emotions by the expressive tilts of his head – hence his name. His neck does more moving than his face. Right now he seems stern. Tipping his head toward the ruins, he adds:

'For the explosion to have been so big, the building must have completely filled with gas. Where was Valtere while this was going on? How could he not notice the smell?'

Noddy's not trying to be cruel – he's just, well . . . a bit socially inept. And he's voicing what we're all thinking. We want to know how this has happened, but it must come across as callous to Buckley. Noddy stops short of making a direct accusation. Smood pushes that little bit further. Though he doesn't say it loudly, everyone hears it all the same:

'Was he drunk again?'

There's a real awkwardness in the air now. It's something we all want to know, if only we could get past the bit where we feel like insensitive as–*(deleted)* . . . sphincters for wondering about it.

'I can't yet say,' Buckley replies curtly. While Valtere's drinking problem is supposed to be a secret, it's a small island. 'As I've already–.'

'Brother, you have to be considering it yourself. Look, this has screwed everyone, including you,' Gemmy says, wincing even as he speaks, and slowing down towards the end of his question, his voice faltering as he meets Buckely's glare. 'Could Valtere have . . . could he have done something to . . . eh, to cause the, um . . . the explosion?'

The muscles of Buckley's jaw are clenching. His gaze sweeps across us, I can almost feel the heat of it on my skin. When he finally replies, his voice is trembling with restrained emotion. He's as close as I've ever seen to losing his composure.

'Brother Valtere is *dying*. He was never been anything but decent and encouraging to all of you and you will show the man *proper respect* in his last hours, *is that clear*?' A look of pain flickers across his face, a quick decision is made and he growls: 'Mark this: As of now, there will be no more talk about Brother Valtere. Until further notice, you are not to discuss him.'

And that's it. The chip in Brother Buckley's controls all of ours. With a thought, he activates the ban, and from this point on, none of us can mention V–*(deleted)*. It's not specific words that are forbidden, it's *meaning*. The chip uses your own brain against you. Now that *you know* the topic is banned, your own brain activity alerts the chip if you try and say something you shouldn't. You can't even talk around the subject, to try and be sneaky about it, like saying –*(deleted)*, or generalise in any way that will enable people to understand what you're talking about, like asking –*(deleted)*. It's the end of the discussion, pure and simple.

Welcome to our world.

'We will all have to pull together to get through this – but we *will*,' Buckley continues. 'Now, my staff and I normally cater for all your needs here, but these are extraordinary circumstances, so let me make this very clear, in case any of you little princes and princesses think this is not your problem. We're facing *severe hunger* on an island with nothing but a thousand kilometres of empty ocean in every direction and we have no communications. Either pitch in and help, or ask yourself how hungry you have to get before you start eating the *grass*.'

Chapter Four
Forbidden Subjects

Everyone's a little shaken after the shout-down and the new ban from Buckley, though we're all giving it loads, mouthing off about him once he's walked away, as if we're not scared of him. We rarely see this side of him; the guy's normally such a professor, it's easy to forget he was some hardcore colonel in the special forces before he got this gig. That's part of why we're never supposed to talk about the reason we're here. It *(deleted)* . . . we *(deleted)* . . . what was I saying? Ah f-*(deleted)*! Frickin', baboon-butt, dung-eating, thought controlling little c-*(deleted)*.

The block on discussing it helps you forget, that's all I'm trying to say. It helps make our existence more *bearable*, pretending everything's normal by not talking about it. That's the reason the doctors gave me in the beginning, when they were inserting the chip into my brain.

'The way the satellites have gone quiet . . . and there's been no ships or planes recently,' Duchess says in a hushed voice, raising her eyes to the sky. 'Do you think it's . . .' She blinks and twitches her head, tutting to herself. A blank moment. She's hit a block, because she's veering into forbidden subjects. It's not often you see Dutch getting caught out by her chip; she's normally so aware of what she says. She finally manages:

'Has something *happened*, do you think?'

She hasn't directed the question at anyone in particular. She's just letting it out. In fact, if any of us knew, it would most likely be her. She's the one who pays the most attention to what's going on in the world. Nobody answers her.

We wish she'd kept her mouth shut.

It's after four in the morning and sleep holds no appeal for any of us. The sun will be cracking the darkness over the horizon so, by mutual assent, all the studes set out for the Perch. We have to walk up a stretch of the main road illuminated by gentle blue sensor-lights that brighten as we pass under them, before cutting up the side of the hill, through the trees to the cliff. Before we take a left turn off the road, the headlights of a car appear on the crest of the hill ahead of us, electric white piercing the gloom, the muscular, battery-powered motor barely audible until it's only a few metres from us. The wide tyres humming on the road make more noise. We glimpse the driver behind the lights as the SUV goes past; a hatchet-chopped block of a face, dark tan with a wild black beard. Brother Earnest, on his way to the scene.

'Wonder what took him so long?' Smood sniffs.

He lives a few kilometres east along the coast, little more than a ten-minute drive away.

'Maybe he was asleep,' Gemmy grunts. 'Everyone else was.'

Not me, I think, but I'm glad no one says it out loud. I

really could do without them asking what I was doing so close to the scene of the explosion. Their minds are on Earnest anyway. Nothing is said, but you can tell. The man keeps himself separate from the rest of the community; speaking only to the guardians, never the studes. We don't talk to him either. It's not a block on our speech, just a rule – one that we all obey. He's not like the other guardians, and we're never allowed to forget it.

We're climbing the hill along a foot-beaten trail that winds between the trees; the sky visible through the shadowy, interlacing foliage is tinted a pale indigo by the first colours of sunrise. We're all walking by the light of the torches on our phones – phones provided by the guardians, that have never made a call beyond this island. I cast my eyes back and out to my left, peering down at the village, red-roofed buildings in a leisurely spread as if a piece of wealthy suburbia had washed up on the shoreline of this small hump of wilderness in the middle of the Atlantic. The new brightness along the rim of the world throws an even darker shadow over the land, east-facing edges outlined with faint pink highlights. I can see Earnest's truck parked on the gravel within the curving verge that skirts the mon. He's there beneath one of the sensor-lights, talking to Brother Buckley. They both turn and climb into the SUV. Its headlights switch on to harsh high-beam and sweep round through the darkness as it turns back out onto the main road, the sensor-lights looking dim by comparison, their blue-white illumination reflecting along the vehicle's polished red bonnet and roof as it passes under each one.

I know where those men are going. And I want to go too.

Chapter Five
Wild Terrain

It's not that I'm nosey – I mean, I know when to mind my own business, mostly. I just think curiosity is an essential quality if you want to be a journalist, which I do.

When I first came to this island, my head wasn't in a good place. I knew I was going to be here for three years and I got a little weirded out. I'd agreed to this, but I was more traumatised than I'd expected, being taken so far from my family. I'd never considered myself a homebird, but ever since I came here, there's been a hurt in my heart that never quite goes away. So when we landed on that first day, as soon as I got the chance, I took off into the woods and they couldn't find me for hours, and when they did find me, they couldn't catch me. I was now the responsibility of the Order and the guardians were worried that I was going to fall off a cliff and break a leg or my neck or something, but physically I was fine. I've hiked and camped out in all sorts of places with my family.

Hills like these are my natural habitat. I can run faster and further over rough ground than I can on any tame, boring running track. The hills suit my legs. The other studes got a great laugh out of seeing the guardians searching the woods trying to chase down this feral child who'd escaped into the wild. Brother Valtere eventually had to climb up a tree after me and talk me down. By the time the oldies brought me back to the village, Smood was demanding that the studes name me 'Goat', but Duchess tweaked it to 'Billy' and it stuck. Every stude who comes here gets an island name and their real ones are rarely used.

It takes about fifteen minutes to drive along the looping main road to the air base, which lies to the west. Both the base and the village are situated on the south coast of the island. I set off at a run, quickly out-distancing the rest of the group. Passing the small plateau we call the Perch, I shift into five-kay race-pace. From the Perch, I can run along the cliff path, nearly a straight line to the base, in less than twenty minutes.

There's not a whole lot of level ground on the island. The first mountain got erupted out of the ocean as a volcano a few million years ago, piling molten rock around it, with surrounding pimples of smaller hills that spewed up to the north and west in the upheavals that followed, forming a kind of rounded triangle of low peaks on the surface of the sea. The south-east side is where the biggest and best hills are, and most of the trees. It's the pretty side of the island. The prettiness disintegrates towards the north, where the bare volcanic rock hunches up in raked ridges of black and grey, petrified lava flows and cinder cones, those weather-worn dormant craters. That exposed face of the bedrock is all jagged and bitter at being ugly, scaring off the greenery with its harsh demeanour. I love its fierceness almost as much as I do the peace of the wooded hills.

The air base is a desolate, post-apocalyptic scene in the horizontal glow of mauve light that stretches out from the top curve of the sun. The base occupies the largest spread of flat land, where the south-west side of the island slopes down into the ocean, but these days, the wide, weed-strewn runway is regularly invaded by the breaking waves and is slowly crumbling away, cracks creeping like the seaweed across it, barnacles clustering around its eroded edges. Our changing climate has lifted the sea, consuming large sections of the coast and flooding the remaining low areas at every high tide. That's one reason the village wasn't built here, the other being that the bunker-strength buildings on the hillside overlooking the airstrip would be so hard to demolish, it wasn't worth the hassle.

My route brings me in away from the shoreline to the steep scree bank, thinly carpeted with bristly grass, that drops towards those hulking concrete bunkers. By the time Earnest's truck rolls in along the road below me, I'm jogging down the precarious path of loose stone, buzzing on the endorphins flushed through my body from the run, breathing hard and loving the burn in the muscles of my legs as the sea breeze cools the sweat coating my skin. Although my headache is still lingering a bit, the mosquito's still whining in my ears, I can hardly feel the pattern of aches the explosion stamped across my body.

The two men are climbing out of the SUV and don't look too pleased to see me, but they don't shout at me to go back, waiting instead for me to make my way down and join them on the road. The guardians give us a pretty free rein of the island, for the simple reason that we're easier to manage that way.

'If it isn't our intrepid reporter,' Buckley sighs. He shows none of the hostility we witnessed earlier. 'Just the facts, right Billy?'

He can monitor everything on my censor chip, so he knows about my journal. All of the guardians do, but none of the students.

'Just the facts I'm allowed to *record*, Brother Buckley,' I chirp back. I have to retain what little journalistic integrity I have left, after all. 'You're here for the spare radio, right? Are there any more food stores?'

These old bunkers are our back-up. In the unlikely event of the village being wiped out in a hurricane, say, or a freak explosion, the whole idea is that there will still be emergency supplies and equipment stored in a secure location, somewhere else on the island.

'We had already moved all the extra food stores up to the monastery, after the supply ship was forced to turn back,' he says in a subdued voice. 'As I'm sure you know.'

That was the other thing about our recent hurricane. Our regular supply ship was damaged on its way out to us, battered by monster waves, and had to turn back. We were already running low on some basic goods before the storm hit. That was no big deal, because there should have been enough of the essentials to see us through another three months or more. Another ship was surely on its way.

Then, less than a month later, with no sign of a relief ship, those back-up stores got blown up by our back-up heating system. Someone's gonna catch hell for this mess when word gets to the Council. Mostly Buckley, I imagine.

He pulls a bunch of keys from his pocket and Earnest and I follow him up a concrete walkway to the drab, military-crude, single-storey, architectural slabs that jut from the hillside like worn down teeth. The door to the nearest building is in the far wall, facing away from the corrosive Atlantic weather. The original door, which probably resembled the indestructible kind you find in the bulkhead of a submarine, was replaced years ago with a normal, solid wooden one. It's not like we do war here, and there's no point having emergency supplies that you can't get at if you lose the key.

When we walk round the corner and see the door, Buckley instantly holds out a hand to me, making me stop and wait where I am. I go to speak but he does the zip across the mouth gesture, then puts a finger to his lips. I notice he and Earnest don't even look at each other; it's as if their bodies have switched to a different mode. They move lightly, silently, positioning themselves so that Earnest takes the lead, but

Buckley is behind and to the side, so he can see past the younger man and still back him up. Their hands lift up, a cautious guard stance, as if they're expecting a fight.

The door has been forced open, probably with a crowbar. The green-painted wood of the frame has been dug out and splintered around the lock, the latch prised away from the striking plate until the door could be shoved inwards. It stands ajar, but the gap is too narrow for me to see past it into the darkness. Buckley has made a fist with his right hand around his keys so that the steel tips protrude between his fingers like a makeshift knuckleduster. Earnest has opened the blade on a large utility knife and is holding it at chest level, the other hand up at the height of his throat, the stance of an experienced knife-fighter.

Earnest whips the door open and leaps in, immediately checking either side of him. Buckley rushes in after him. They disappear and for a minute, there's no sound. The lights go on. I'm standing there, a few metres from the busted door, stupidly holding my breath, every muscle tense. I exhale shakily and bend forwards to see past the doorframe.

'Clear,' Earnest says from inside.

'Billy, you can come in,' Buckley calls out.

I find myself trembling and it doesn't subside once I hear the building's safe inside. There's a chill beneath my skin and I can feel the bruised stiffness caused by the explosion tightening across my body. Perhaps it's shock finally setting in after the blast, or the violence done to the doorframe, the way that piece of butchered wood hints at much worse within, just as you can follow a small, neat bullet hole through to find massive internal damage. This break-in is the footprint of an enemy, a defiler of the peace on our island.

Our house was broken into years ago, before Dad got all the security he has now. Once your home has been invaded, it leaves you feeling violated, like you'll never feel safe in this place again. Now, for me, this new blow triggers a creeping decay of the secure life I thought I had here. It was so easy to keep believing everything was normal.

I shuffle slowly towards the doorway, hating my hesitation, but trying to delay the discoveries I'll make inside. Buckley delivers the worst of the news before I can even look into the room.

'The radio's gone,' he announces. 'All the hard drives in the back-up servers too.'

He emerges from the building, pushing past me, his face expressionless, all business, pulling his short-range handset from the pouch on his belt. These are how the guardians talk to each other across the island, low-watt devices that have nothing like the range of the VHF unit we use for transmitting offshore.

'Nguyen, this is Buckley, come in please.'

'Nguyen here,' the reply comes back almost immediately.

'We have a hostile. Identity and location unknown. Go to

Status Orange. Gather all the students, make sure you account for everyone. I'll be back there in twenty minutes. Buckley, out.

'You can help us here, or wait in the truck,' he grunts to me. 'Don't go running off. As of now, you're all grounded.'

'You make it sound like one of *us* did this!' I snap at him, dismayed that my voice sounds querulous, weak. 'This could have been anyone! What makes you so sure it was a *student?*'

He throws a scolding glance at me, as if I'm smart enough to know better, clearly not willing to dignify my question with a response. I bloody hate it when they treat us like this. Noon never does this patronising crap, but she's one of the few. Yet again, I find myself wishing she was here. Still, I want to know what's going on, so I join the two men inside. The doorway opens into a corridor that runs down the middle of the building, with a rectangular open space, like an atrium, to the left as you come in, then three doors down the left side and four down the longer, right wall.

There are weapons cabinets in the atrium, all still securely locked. With sober fascination, I regard the contents behind the metal grills, taking a mental inventory. Everything I can see would be categorised as 'non-lethal': shock batons, tasers, tear gas, stun grenades. They all still look like they'd really, *really* hurt. There are helmets and light body armour too, and handcuffs. There's a gun cabinet with no guns in it. Before I can ask Buckley if they've been stolen, he sees me staring and answers:

'They were all moved up to the monastery a couple of years ago.'

Which presumably means they've been destroyed too. It's only then that it dawns on me and my mouth drops open. Damn it, I'm dense sometimes. The explosion – *it wasn't an accident.* Maybe Valtere was drunk and maybe he wasn't but . . . I suffer another shift in my reality right there, hugging myself as the realization comes over me. If somebody broke in here to steal the radio, they must have caused the blast at the mon too. This whole disaster was a deliberate act. And whoever this was, they're prepared to *kill* to do whatever it is they're trying to do. Holy sh–*(deleted)*.

I need to get busy with something or I'm going to start freaking out. Earnest is coming out of a room at the bottom of the corridor carrying a tall stack of pots and pans.

'What do you want me to do?' I ask him as he passes.

'You know the rules, Billy,' he says gruffly. 'We don't talk. Ask Buckley.'

Buckley's moving stuff around in one of the rooms down the corridor. The walls of most of the spaces are lined with either heavy duty racks, smaller shelves, drawers, lockers or cabinets. Everything is light grey or olive drab or mid grey or dull khaki or dark grey and it all looks like it could take a beating and stay standing. What the military lacks in colour palettes and feng shui, it more than makes up for with stuff that soldiers almost can't break. Everything contained on the shelves or in the cupboards is compactly packaged for long-term storage and clearly labelled: antiseptic, waterproof clothing, assorted nuts and bolts, containers of water, gel packs for warming your hands, sunscreen, rat poison, socks . . . Absolutely nothing at all that you can eat, as far as I can see.

The last two rooms on either side offer little of interest, only empty racks that used to hold our ill-fated emergency food supplies. I've only been in here once before, during my orientation, and it hasn't changed at all apart from the front door and the tech room. This is the third door on the right, furnished with some desks and chairs, along with drawers of spare parts, wall racks of tools and banks of unidentified electronics. There's an olive drab desk tucked in to the left that has a dinner-tray-sized rectangle of dust where the radio used to be. The black, skeletal tower racks beside the desk that hold the back-up servers for the Hub are missing their hard drives, which is a bit weird, because they're not used for communication . . .

'Why did they take those?' I wonder aloud.

'Because they contain information,' Buckley replies from behind me. 'Petabytes of newsfeed and intelligence reports that we get from all over the globe. If we had a chance to look through it, there might be something going on back in the world that would tip us off to who did this. That's why they had to destroy the Hub too. Something's happened out there that means trouble for someone here, and this bastard's covering their tracks.'

I shudder. It's like knowing there's a venomous spider in your bedroom, but you can't see it. The island still has one more VHF radio, though it's currently out at sea. Noon and two of the other guardians took our remaining big boat out a couple of days ago to try some fishing and see if she could reach anyone beyond the horizon. Anxious now, and reaching out for some reassurance, I gesture towards the radio-shaped void in the dust on the desk.

'Sister Noon still has the radio on the boat, right? She'll be back in a day or two.'

'Yes she does, and yes she will. Here, take these out to the truck.'

He hands me a plastic box the size of a microwave oven. Peering through the clear plastic lid, I can see bags of different kinds of seeds, all marked with printed labels; potato, aubergine, cabbage and others. I frown, smile a little.

'What are . . . Can we eat these?'

'No, we can grow vegetables from them,' he says.

I give him an incredulous look and blurt out a little laugh.

'What? How long does it take to *grow vegetables*? I mean, that must be . . . I don't know, weeks . . . even months.'

I actually have no idea how long it takes. Don't get me wrong, I'm not a complete ignoramus; I know you plant seeds and they'll grow. I've spent enough time in the garden at home. But I haven't a clue about growing stuff to *eat*; what season to plant, when to harvest, what fertiliser you'd use, or compost or pesticides . . . y'know . . . *farming*. And now I have this slightly manic grin stretching across my face.

'Seriously . . . how long do you think we're going to be stuck here without food?'

I'm speaking hesitantly, waiting to be interrupted because surely I have the wrong idea. I let slip another childish chuckle, though I'm not sure why, because this wasn't funny to start with and Buckley's expression is dimming the last glimmer of light in the situation.

'Brother Buckley?'

'Just take those to the truck.'

I'm staring straight ahead of me, conscious that I'm already feeling hungry – I've been up all night and it's getting close to breakfast time. That demanding little hollow in the pit of my belly has a sickening, disturbing quality to it, as if something in my head has started making the connection between the hunger I feel now and the seeds I'm holding in my arms. Seeds that, even if we can manage to germinate them, won't grow into something we can eat for longer than I can bear to think about. It's like I'm holding the threat of time, miserable weeks of hunger right here in my hands and it's all starting to feel very real.

I stretch my eyes open, willing myself to snap out of the funk. The sky blue packages on the shelf right in front of me are flat and oblong and the shapes are familiar. I put the box down on the desk and walk closer, tilting my head to read the label: 'Bright white cartridge, A4, 100gsm. 500 sheets.' It's paper – reams of it. There are other boxes lying beside these packages, labelled as pens, pencils and erasers. We never use the stuff, not even in our art classes; we do all our work on screens, but I'm thinking technology might not be all that reliable any more, so I add a few of each package to the top of the seeds box. It feels comforting; I figure writers have been working on paper, like, forever, so maybe this will do me good. I head out to the truck with my load. Earnest is hefting a large black kit bag into the back. It's obviously heavy, and from the sound it makes as he places it down, there are long metal and solid plastic objects inside. I glance back as Buckley closes over the broken door, wedging it shut. Just before it closes, I get a quick look at the weapons lockers and see that more of them are empty now.

Chapter Six
Saboteur

Dawn has spread its light across the village and damage that was hidden by the gloom is becoming visible. The ground is littered with ash and burnt debris; scorched, blackened lumps of solid material or feathery remains that bristle gently like dead birds in the morning breeze that breathes in off the ocean. The origins of some are identifiable: a fork, the frame of a chair, a piece of an amethyst wind-chime; the fronds of a potted plant; the body of an old ship's compass that had nestled in its cradle in the library. For the most part though, the burnt things are amorphous, reformed by the heat or the shockwave, cooling into alien, unrecognisable forms. I pick up a clump of fanned, charred sheets that look like crêpe paper. Yesterday, this was a book. Now, I can't make out a single word of it.

A weak shroud of smoke still hangs over the ruins of the mon and the air is filled with the stink of it, heavy but sharp. When you're downwind of it, it stings your eyes. A half-melted piece of slag sits on the gravel not far from the mon, the size and shape of a tumble-dryer, its grey, sculpted plastic cowling has been almost entirely burnt off, exposing a buckled metal frame holding mangled circuitry and other electronic components. It's the Hub, or at least what's left of it. To my amazement, I see Brother Mthembu inserting his long, black, sensitive fingers into one section, as if trying to connect two scorched pieces together. Surely, after what happened, the server is just a lump of shattered, fused-together parts?

When I thought the explosion had been an accident, I had considered the disaster finished, that it only remained to clear up and move on. Now that I know it was a deliberate act – some of the studes are already using the word 'terrorism' – I'm seeing things differently. We all are. People are scared in a way they weren't earlier. And with that fear has come suspicion. Though the fire has been put out, the disaster persists. This is getting surreal. Our parents must know something is badly wrong by now. The ever-present drones must have witnessed what happened, watching from overhead, unseen, thousands of metres up. Aren't they still patrolling the skies? In fact, why haven't we seen any other aircraft? There hasn't been so much as a jet trail in the sky for weeks. Mum and Dad must be going out of their minds with worry – *all* our parents have to be feeling the same way – so what are they *doing* about it? What the hell is going on out there?

There's another meeting on the green, the studes gathered once more to hear Buckley report. This time, however, our leader's benevolent concern has hardened into the resolve of a law enforcer. Though there might be a criminal among us, we are still his responsibility. He must tread with care. His tone is authoritative, measured, with a just touch of menace.

'For those of you who haven't heard yet, the radio at the air base has been stolen, along with the back-up hard drives,' he begins. 'There can be no doubt now, that the explosion was deliberate. The target was our communications gear; whether the saboteur meant to blow up the entire building as well is unclear and, to be quite blunt, largely irrelevant. Once they committed to this action, once they chose violence to achieve their goal, they became a criminal and a traitor. An enemy to every other person on this island. There's good reason to believe that something has happened out there that this person doesn't want us to know about. And there is every possibility they will resort to violence again to further that goal.

'I know what some of you must be thinking. You're afraid. Because of the loss of the satellites, because of the lack of contact by radio, you're afraid that something has happened out there that might affect you. I remind you that this island is kept isolated for a *reason*, for the *greater good*. The exclusion zone around the island keeps ships and aircraft away, so it's hardly a surprise that there has been no radio contact. I don't know why the Council haven't sent a bird to check on us before this, but they must have their reasons. And because we are equipped for this isolation, this loss of contact is not a sign that we've been forgotten. If something *is* going on out there – and that's a big "if" – it could very well be that we've been kept out of it for a reason, that the Council is waiting until the issue is resolved before they contact us again.

'If they know how bad things are here now, they will already be sending out a plane to make contact and to drop supplies ahead of the arrival of a support ship. If they are still unaware, it's only a matter of letting them know. Let me assure you, that we have received *no* emergency broadcast regarding any of you, or your parents, and *no* new orders from the mainland. The loss of communication, in itself, is no reason to be afraid.'

He stops to swing his gaze across us, a lighthouse look that serves as a signal as much as an attempt to see. The stare that tries to convince you your guilt can't be hidden, that, when caught in the right light, it can be read on your face.

'But fear would be understandable in this situation, and maybe it's because of that fear that one of you has committed these acts.' He pauses again, to let those words sink in. 'If that's the case, then this is *your one and only chance* to admit it. If you step forward now, you have my word that there will be no punishment. After this, you'll be caught, arrested and tried as a criminal. This is your one chance to avoid that, here and now.'

He gives us a good minute to respond. A sickly chill settles across the group of students; each of us is looking at the others, curious, suspicious, each of us waiting to see if someone will step forward. Seeing the expressions on the faces of my friends, I feel the first burns of an ulcerous guilt for the way Buckley's words have divided us so easily. I thought we were better than this. Every one of us came to this island from a different part of the world, but once here, we'd bonded into a comfortable, if slightly snarky gang. This one accusation is like that damaged entrance to the bunker. Having had our door smashed in, we've lost all trust in what lies beyond.

'I don't get it, what good does it do anyone?' Smood asks abruptly, the breaking of that tense silence coming as a relief to all of us. 'Taking out the radios, I mean. The sat-link will be back up at some point, right? Or someone will come and check on us. We're all still stuck here until then. What was this bonehead trying to achieve? It's not like they can get off the island, so what was the point?'

'We don't know,' Buckley replies. 'Maybe they were just buying time. Maybe they didn't have a plan. Or maybe this is only the start and they're not done yet. We just don't know.'

'Only the start of *what*?' Gemmy calls out.

'Why are you so sure this was a student?' Duchess presses Buckley. 'Maybe this is part of some bigger play – a strategic move to get us *all* off the island, or . . . or to cut off our communications before someone launches an attack. You know how important this place is. Can you vouch for the motives of every single guardian? How sure are you of their loyalty? You're certain none of them could be *bought*? How can you even be sure that we're alone here? It's possible this saboteur is someone new, maybe even part of a team that's come ashore without you knowing.'

'Our security measures would have picked up any new people on the island,' Buckley assures her, though there is hint of scorn in his voice. 'And while one can never completely discount *conspiracy theories*, I find the simplest answer is normally the correct one.' He gestures at the ruins behind him. 'Someone here has acted out of fear and has made a disastrous misjudgement. In my experience, that's the cause of most of the harm that's done in the world and I'm quite sure it's what has happened here.

'But you do have a point; we can't exclude the guardians from suspicion, if only out of a need to cover every angle. Which brings me to another matter that we have to deal with. Before this new development, I was willing let you volunteer any food you had in your villas. Now that we have a crime to investigate, we will have to search every building anyway. So we will be combing through every centimetre of this village and while we're at it, we will be collecting every item of food and drink.'

There are instant cries of outrage, along with many a swearword cut short as the censor chips are cranked into overdrive by sixteen anxious teenagers facing the threat of major embarrassment. This is a step too far. We have to share so much on the island, having been separated from our families and removed from the outside world, the villas are supposed to be our personal space, the last places where we can claim any individual privacy.

I'm experiencing some almighty, buttock-clenching dread of the humiliation I now know is coming. They're going to find my shrine. Oh, holy f–*(deleted)* and a half, they're going to find my shrine. I close my eyes and a barely audible moan of pain issues from my lips. Not this. *Not this!* Sh–*(deleted)*!

After the outcry, some of the studes immediately turn to start heading back to the residences, no doubt intent on getting rid of the various compromising items secreted away in their lodgings, but Buckley's bark pulls them back.

'Everyone will *stay on the green* while the searches are carried out!' he declares. 'We're going to do this out here in the open, to keep everything above board.' He holds his hand up to quell the protests that ignite even before he can finish. 'I will lead the searches, along with one other guardian, whom I will let you choose. I will also let you choose two students who will act as witnesses during the searches, to avoid any accusations of unfair treatment. Enough of the chatter! The quicker we get this done, the sooner your "torment" will be over.'

It's a smart move, letting us choose the other guardian and two student representatives. It distracts us from the ugliness of what's coming and throws some responsibility back on us. Challenged with this task, the discussion among the studes quickly becomes heated. We settle on Dr Karava as the second guardian to carry out the search – we've all been through extensive check-ups with him over the years, so the thought of him poking around our personal stuff isn't likely to be any more humiliating than peeing into a container or having your boobs or scrotum checked for suspicious lumps.

Then it comes to picking the two studes. It's no surprise when Duchess takes an early lead and is voted in first. Not everyone trusts her – she's often accused of being manipulative – but while Smood is as popular, we can't count on him to take this seriously enough. Dutch is the most respected in our agitated little group, she's methodical in how she goes about things and we all figure she has the nerve to call foul if she sees the guardians trying to pull a fast one. The second choice comes as a much bigger shock to me, because . . . well, because it's *me*. Listening to my name being bounced back and forth among the gang as one of the options, my unease increases to quaking proportions as it appears increasingly likely that I'll be chosen. When it finally happens, I put my face in my hands and groan.

The reasons I'm everybody's second choice for acting as a witness are, apparently: a) I don't stand out enough for anyone to hate me; b) I'm used to poking my nose around where it doesn't belong; c) I'm considered too gormless to be a saboteur; d) It's unlikely that the explosion could have been caused by someone who has consistently scored the lowest grades in her chemistry class and; e) I was nearly killed myself in the blast. Smood points out that I *should* be a suspect for *exactly the same reasons*, but it's only a half-hearted objection.

We are going to be searching every residence, guardians'

and students'. It'll take most of the day, so Buckley has another task for everyone else being forced to cool their heels on the green. It can wait until after we've had something to eat though. A makeshift breakfast is served, packet meals from the store in the remaining boathouse. Meant for use as emergency rations at sea, they're small and taste pretty much like those protein bars fitness fanatics buy in bulk – a kind of bland and grainy pulp infused with sugar and artificial flavourings that don't match the textures on your tongue. But they feed the hunger that's now putting everyone on edge. As we sit on the grass or at the picnic tables, munching on the miserable meal, Buckley calls for our attention and points to the melted piece of slag that used to be the Hub.

'Believe it or not, there's still life in this thing,' he tells us. 'This is a military-grade server, made for use in a forward base during battle, built to take a lot of punishment. The core hard drives are very well protected and Brother Mthembu tells me we can still access the archived data.

'But there's a time limit on this, because we can't plug the thing in. Everything around those drives, including the power source, was basically fused into a kind of shell by the fire and to try cutting through it would only cause further damage. It's running on its back-up battery, and that's going to go dead soon. However, we *do* still have wireless access. We don't have anything else with enough storage to download this amount of data to, which means there's only so much information we can save, so we have to *prioritise*.'

'Prioritise what?' Gemmy asks, chewing on his thumbnail. He's nervous. Gemmy's got issues with food, so I think he's seeing a little further ahead than the others. He's starting to get it. 'What are we looking for?'

'How to survive here until help arrives,' Buckley tells him. 'This island is hopelessly short of natural resources and the seas around us have been polluted and overfished. Even the birds don't stop off here as much as they used to. Put bluntly, there is very little to eat on the island.

'A number of the staff have experience in agriculture and botany, and even without guns, most of us can hunt, but we need all the additional information we can find about what we *can* eat out there in the wild and what we can't; what will grow best in this soil, how long it takes and what we need to do to make it happen. Anyone who has lived on this rock in the last hundred years has relied on supplies from somewhere else; supplies we no longer have, so we need to get busy figuring out how to keep ourselves fed out here.'

The gang of studes have a sullen, dejected air about them, maybe because they're just starting to feel the same thing I felt when I looked into that box of seeds. The threat of time. Our feelings are divided between the desperate, child-like need to see our parents again and the fury at being placed in this situation. This teenage resentment we're exuding is the wall we all put up; bad attitude is our first line of defence against harsh reality. Don't knock it – there's a reason evolution makes kids rebel against their parents. As far as our environment is concerned, we inherit their leftovers. My theory is, the young have to have someone else to blame for all their problems until their egos have formed well enough to take the hits themselves.

In this case, those self-centred defences can help balance the mounting dread at our situation with the righteous satisfaction of knowing this is all somebody else's fault. You'd be amazed at how much this can distract you from impending doom.

All that said, the scowls of my fellow studes have a petulant, shallow quality compared to the faces of the guardians around us. Once again, they've gathered round our flanks, a loose enclosure. The members of the Order already seem to be shifting into a different mind-set. These men and women who run the island, teach our classes and provide all our services, have all known hardship before; each one of them is a former soldier, a war veteran. It was a prerequisite for the job, along with regular psychological screening to monitor their mental health. I can only guess what atrocities they've faced, what traumas they've endured on their path to this point in their lives. As I study their faces, I see each of them has their own version of the same expression, calm but intent; an acceptance of the ordeal that's coming. We're slowly coming to a realization that they reached hours ago and they're waiting patiently for us to catch up.

'Do you all understand?' Buckley growls, jolting me out of my daze. 'We only have a limited time in which to use our main information resource before it *goes dead* and all that information is *lost.*'

I open my mouth to ask why we can't just download all of the Hub's files to our phones or tablets. But of course we can't. We did everything through storage on the cloud. Our phones and tablets have almost no storage capacity, a few gigabytes at the most, which will be quickly filled with large files such as photos or video. The massive capacity of the Hub's hard drives was only intended as a fail-safe for when the sat-link was down. Like the methane-powered heating system and generators, and the radios, and the emergency food supplies at the air base, those hard drives were nothing more than a back-up to tide us over until help arrived from the outside, in the *highly unlikely* event that things went wrong.

Everyone has already taken out their devices, connecting via the weak signal to the dying Hub. Supplied by the Order, these lumps are all we have. We weren't allowed bring our own phones, tablets or computers when we came to the island.

'Our number one priority is food we can either gather or catch immediately,' Buckley continues. 'Now, Brother Mthembu and Sister Adeyemi are going to set each of you a specific category of information to search for in the archives. We don't want to waste time duplicating work, so stick to the task assigned to you and *only* search for relevant information.

Brother Mthembu reckons we have a few hours at best before we lose the Hub.'

'What do we do with the information once we've found it?' Noddy asks, holding up his phone. 'Even if I'm only looking for the highlights, this thing will hardly hold anything. It'll be filled up in no time.'

'You'll need to clear off anything you can—' Buckley begins.

'We can record text on our censor chips too,' Duchess points out, tapping the side of her head. 'If you can read it off your screen, you can record it as text. You have about a gigabyte of storage in there.'

I wince at that. I have a couple of years of journal entries in mine already, and while text takes up hardly any space, I don't want my private stuff getting stored alongside something that could become a public resource for the island. Our chips are supposed to be private . . . up to a point. Besides, I've never backed it up online because you hear of hackers attacking the cloud all the time, so I hope Buckley doesn't ask me to make more room – I couldn't bear to delete it.

'Yes, we can do that, to save time,' he replies. 'But longer term, we'll still need another means of printing out whatever we have on the chips, and the only printer we had was in the off–.'

'We have paper!' I shout out excitedly, then shut my mouth, self-consciously turn down my volume control, and in a more sober tone, add: 'We have paper and pens. I brought them back from the base. Once the phones and chips are full, we can start writing this stuff down. Or summarising it, anyway.'

Everyone turns to look at me with a mixed assortment of expressions. Gazing furtively around, I can detect amusement, disbelief, confusion, complete lack of understanding, disgust and what could be genuine horror.

'If it comes to that, yes,' Buckley says, giving me a nod of appreciation. 'Save the information any way you can. It could be crucial to staying alive. When your devices are full, use your censor chips. But anything you record on the chips will have to be written down later.'

'*Written down?*' Smood exclaims. He looks around helplessly, as if needing confirmation that everyone else has heard the same astounding words he has. 'Written down with, like . . . a *pen*, you mean? Why?'

'Because this information has to be somewhere we can *all* read it. Each chip is powered by the electricity in your body,' Buckley says simply. 'If one of you dies, I won't be able to access your chip. Nobody else will be able to read that data. Only the Hub can power up a dead censor chip, so all the information that person gathered will be lost.'

There's utter silence in the pause that follows. That offhand remark took the wind out of everyone. We're all thinking the same thing: I have to write down the things in my head, *so that others can read it if I die*. Sh—*(deleted)*.

'Right, Duchess, Billy,' Buckley summons us. 'We have work do to do. Let's get started.'

Chapter Seven
An Invasion of Privacy

At Buckley's insistence, we begin the search with his quarters. The front door opens into a hallway, with a living-room to the right, the bedroom and bathroom to the left and a multi-purpose store room at the end of the hall, all painted in a simple apple white with bare, sand-coloured floorboards. Every residence in the village is a variation on this layout, though the décor and colour schemes are left to the occupants' tastes. Of all the guardians, Buckley is the only one who has as much living space as the students; a villa to himself with a small back garden, whose walls are just high enough to prevent someone seeing in from the upper windows of the monastery, which is set at the same level on the slope at the top of the village. The villa is in a key spot, with panoramic views, the hills behind and the harbour in front. The man appears to live like a Spartan, apart from the walls of bookshelves in every room except for the bathroom, mostly holding biographies, philosophy and psychology books or military histories. The windows are all open and it smells of the outside; foliage, sea air and smoke.

He watches patiently, following us into each room, but never standing close enough to be intimidating – not *quite*. Beside him, the boyish, unimposing figure of old Dr Karava stands silent, his delicate brown hands clasped in front of him. Duchess and I go through the principal's wardrobe and drawers, looking under his bed and beneath the mattress, and in the few other cupboards and compartments in the villa. When it looks like we're being half-hearted in our exploration, Buckley urges us to be more thorough, to take more time and satisfy ourselves that we've seen everything we need to.

It's uncomfortable. Apart from being our principal, Buckley is also our history teacher. Like most students, we don't regard our teachers as having lives much beyond their work; no hobbies or passions, romances or family. We tend to think their lives switch off after school. This is despite the fact that, even though the guardians have a separate area in the village where they can have some privacy, we all more or less live around each other all the time. Still, it's hard to think of Buckley as a . . . well, a *human being*.

Now I'm poking through his underwear drawer.

I could squirm with the awkwardness of it all; I slam the drawer shut harder than I mean to. In the living-room, there are photos on his desk; three children standing with a younger version of himself – I never knew he had a family, though the kids must be much older now. There are no photos of them as adults. In the white-tiled bathroom, there is little in the way of toiletries, but among the few containers we find haemorrhoid cream and anti-viral medication for herpes. Embarrassed, Duchess quickly puts them back in the cabinet.

'You better check the books,' he suggests gently. 'And gather any food you find. It has to go in the cart outside.'

There are a few oranges, a couple of mangoes in the small refrigerator in the living-room, a pack of salty crackers and a big bag of trail mix in a drawer in a sideboard. I take it out to the electric buggy that's waiting outside; a kind of golf cart on steroids, with chunky tyres and a pick-up-style flatbed on the back. I place the food in one of the crates on the flatbed, then come back in and throw a reluctant look at Duchess. We start picking books out at random, flicking through them, holding them out to see if anything drops from the pages. I'm supposed to represent all the students, to be sure the guardians are put through the same treatment my friends and I will face, but it feels pointless. The home is an extension of its owner, so defined by his character that, as we handle his possessions and furniture, it's as if we're putting our hands on the man himself. The thought makes me stop suddenly and stand up straight, moving out into the middle of the living-room, sticking my hands under my armpits. Journalists are meant to dig, I tell myself; curiosity is a good thing, when it's aimed in the right direction. But there are details of every person's life that they shouldn't have to share and I find myself disgusted by what's going on.

'Right, I think we're done,' Duchess says abruptly, without checking with me, though I don't feel like arguing. She slides a psychology book back onto a shelf over his desk and turns to direct her gaze at the guardians, elegant hands tidying her hair back into a tighter bun. 'Where to next?'

'I suppose we better do mine,' Dr Karava says, a note of resignation in his soft voice.

Set in the guardians' community, across the green from the students' villas, the doctor's quarters are different, busier, more cluttered and yet more open. An almighty stink hits us as we head inside, putrid, caustic to our nostrils and I have to stop myself recoiling in disgust. It's coming from the bedroom; we're breathing it in even as we walk into the hallway. It's th– *(deleted)* . . . Oh yeah, we can't talk about that now. I'd forgotten already, but Jesus, the smell of–*(deleted)* . . .

Karava has a close-lipped smile on his lined but lively face, wrinkling skin like that of a Mediterranean fisherman. He knows we're uncomfortable and is encouraging us to continue. It doesn't make things easier. He has real books too, though not as many as Buckley, and more novels, less non-fiction. Many of them are old, some with spines faded to cyan blue, bleached by daylight even though the bookcases, made of some dark, mottled wood, don't face the windows here.

I sniff the air, catching a fainter scent beneath the pervasive stink. Huh. The doctor smokes cigars. Smoking's supposed to be banned by the Order, but they must cut him some slack here. Buckley has to have known about it. We find a box of cigars in a drawer in the base of the couch.

I wince in pained sympathy as I hear the sound of–*(deleted)* .

. . Christ, I'm just mentioning th–*(deleted)*. Right, fine. Fine. Sometimes this damn chip can be a right uptight little rat's nipple. Bloody hell. What I *will* say, is that with the infirmary destroyed, Dr Karava has been treating patients in his own quarters. His bedroom is occupied and when we go in, it's– *(deleted)*. Right, okay, forget it.

We're both feeling clenched up after what we see in Karava's bed–*(deleted)* . . . Aw, now you're just making this sound perverted, you little micro-turd. Anyway, Duchess is as pale as I've ever seen her and I feel like throwing up. Both of us are close to tears and we'd probably be balling our eyes out if the two guardians weren't there, making us feel like we can't show weakness. If Noon was here, she'd know what to say to help prop me up, and wouldn't hesitate to say it, but she's not here, so that's that. We want these oldies to take us seriously, so we keep it together as best we can.

Again, we search the place out of a sense of duty to our friends, but we make a half-arsed job of it. I almost want to believe that Buckley's right, that it has to be a student, so it would save me from having to do any more of this. It's not even as if we know what to look for. What kind of clues would a saboteur leave? I feel like we're wasting our time. We're students in a teachers' home and we're glad when we finally leave.

It's only then that it occurs to me: Duchess and I have to do most of the work here. Sh–*(deleted)*! There are twenty-eight guardians to sixteen students. We have to search all of the guardians' quarters. Most of them live three or four to a villa, but each has a bedroom of their own. We're going to be at this *all day*. Less than an hour has passed and I'm feeling drained already; I've missed a night's sleep and the horrible awkwardness is making it feel all the more dragged out.

'Let's just get this done,' Duchess mutters to me. She can see the will's not in me to keep going. 'Let's not give the ba . . . uh . . .' She presses her lips together, her chip blocking the word. 'Let's not give them the satisfaction of seeing us fold. Okay?'

It's almost robotic, when we carry on from that point. We go through every room in every staff villa, working together, being methodical. Wary of missing something – or perhaps, of being suspected of missing things – we move along side by side, double-checking each other. We stop for a meagre lunch, more protein meals from the boathouse, then get back to it. By the end of the afternoon, we've been through every residence in the staff compound and we're mentally and physically numb, our bodies stiff with fatigue. Closing the door on Sister Noon's villa, we find Buckley and Karava waiting outside.

'Have you satisfied yourselves that we have nothing to hide?' Buckley asks.

'We've satisfied ourselves, as best we can, that you are not hiding anything in your quarters,' Duchess replies, because she's going to be a lawyer before she sets up her own business, becomes a style icon and then goes into politics, and she isn't about to give more ground than she absolutely has to. 'Your turn, Brother Buckley.'

And there's a restrained hostility in her voice that I feel too, as we submit to the two men, accepting our roles as passive witnesses as they prepare to prise open the cherished privacy of every student on the island.

Chapter Eight
The Shrine

We stroll away from the guardians' villas, down the road that runs parallel to the coast. The students' villas are ahead of us, clustered in a development of three crescent-shaped drives, surrounded by open lawns, lined with neatly pruned native shrubs and trees. The afternoon sun, high over my right shoulder, sears the white walls of the small houses, my tired eyes having to squint or look away. There are still some traces from the hurricane's passage across the island; broken branches on trees and missing roof tiles and solar panels, but the side of the development looking out across the slope towards the sea appears relatively untouched.

As the main road curves to the left, heading up the hill towards the ruins of the mon, following the edge of the green, the damage caused by the blast can be seen on the inland sides of the villas as we get closer to ground zero. Seen from a different angle, our homes show their hurt. The parts of the buildings facing the explosion are scarred, pock-marked by flying debris, the windows shattered, dark and ragged like sockets with the eyes gouged out, the villas blind to the scene of the disaster.

Overcome with a weary restlessness, I gaze out over the lawns and notice clusters of people at different points around the perimeter of the students' villas. In each group, there are three guardians and a couple of studes. It's a strange sight, forming a pattern I can't grasp at first, until I see others in one of the crescent roads too.

Of course . . . the studes are not allowed back into the villas before the searches have been carried out – they could interfere with any evidence that might be found there. The guardians have positioned themselves so they can see the buildings on every side, that way they can spot anyone trying to enter them. I wonder if this was part of their training when they became custodians of the island, because Buckley didn't give any order that I heard. The students have responded to this suspicion in kind, organising themselves so that they can watch the watchers. They don't trust the guardians either.

The guardians are armed now too, wearing belts holding pepper spray, shock batons and tasers. It's a graphic reminder that we're hunting a criminal, one who might be out to cause more harm to the Order. Or even *us*. If the searches turn up anything, someone's going to get stamped on. None of the oldies appear to have guns, but then it's possible there are no guns left on the island, given that the main weapons locker was in the monastery.

Duchess has agreed to start with her own quarters. I know how she feels; I want to get this over with too. The guardians have a cleaning rota, a crew of them storm through the villas every two weeks – it's not like they can expect *us* to do the heavy duty cleaning – but it's routine and we all know to put our private stuff away. This time, we don't get to hide anything before the invaders arrive. And the guardians have never exercised the right to root around in our storage spaces before.

I move up beside Dutch and Buckley leads us inside. They start in the living-room, stepping carefully over the broken glass swept to the edges of the floor. Dutch stands by the wide empty window and I stay beside her. Oddly, the breeze through the void feels cold on my back in a way that it wasn't outside. Duchess has the unruffled air of royalty waiting for tradesmen to carry out a job, but she takes my hand and squeezes it as the men start probing into her privacy. It's only then we realize how we let the guardians off easy when we searched their homes. We didn't treat our 'shepherds' with genuine suspicion; we allowed ourselves to be embarrassed into making a half-hearted effort.

And as we watch with withered, exhausted dismay, Buckley and Karava show us how professionals search a building.

The first thing the two men do is a walk-through. Then they video the entire place and take photographs of any points of interest. Once that's done, they divide each room into a grid and examine each imaginary square in turn. *They even sift through the broken glass,* in case it could be covering anything up.

They knew we didn't search the guardians' quarters this thoroughly and they didn't correct us, didn't give us any help.

It couldn't be more obvious that they're convinced it had to be one of the students who blew up the monastery. The idea that it could have been a guardian has already been dismissed. There's no need to investigate their own. Noddy's right to start checking up on them. We have to start looking into this ourselves, because they're not going to be fair about it . . . Huh, even I'm doing it now. 'We'. 'They'. Drawing lines between us. The thought leaves a bitter taste in my mouth and I find it hard to keep the scowl from my face.

Once they've done the groundwork, the two men start combing through all the furniture and accessories. Duchess hisses through her teeth as they unzip cushions, even slice open the fabric on the back of the couch and the two armchairs. Every drawer is meticulously examined, even the undersides. Every book is fingered through and held upside down to see if there's anything hidden in the pages. They find her diary in the drawer of her desk; I didn't know she kept a diary, an honest-to-God old-fashioned paper one. I suppose that way it's less likely to leak online. Buckley flicks through this too, and then tells her he's confiscating it for examination. She doesn't protest, but from the rigid tension of her body, I suspect she'd drive a knife through his heart right then if she could somehow explain it away later.

Like all of us, she has her own stash of food, which is taken out to the cart that has pulled up outside. We get whatever normal food we need from the village canteen, not just at mealtimes but whenever it suits; there are two expert chefs among the staff and a well run kitchen. So it's really just the indulgent snacks we keep in our villas. Our comfort food. Dutch's treats are not what I was expecting. I thought there'd be expensive delicacies, further evidence of her refined tastes, but it's mostly chocolate – good quality chocolate, of course – jellies, potato snacks, popcorn, soft drinks and the sweet balls she calls laddus, as well as a few of those cashew fudge things; Kaju Katli? Something like that, I can't remember.

We follow the two men into the bedroom, where they empty her laundry onto the floor, pawing through it before they check the basket itself. She winces as they take more photographs. With brusque, efficient movements, unashamed, they put her underwear back into the basket, along with her other clothes. I can see she's had her period recently. I'm offended for her, to see such private things handled by these old men. They strip the sheets from the bed, the slips from the pillows and run their hands over the pillows and mattresses for lumps. Karava searches her wardrobe while Buckley rifles through the two chests of drawers.

I can't help but be impressed by the variety of bras. I stick to picking ones that fit well, especially the sports bras I need for training or long runs. Duchess, on the other hand, has an extensive collection of brassieres – they deserve the full title – each one providing a different category of support, serving as another weapon in her social armoury. I arch an eyebrow at her when I see the number of padded ones she has, but I'm no match for her in the arched eyebrow department.

The cabinets and shelves in the bathroom contain enough cosmetics, skin and hair treatments to open up a new counter in our pharmacy. Karava takes the lid off each one and sniffs the contents. There are pills in different kinds of packets. Some are for period pain and one pack is for treating thrush. This time my scowl asserts itself with force. There are some things the men on this island just don't need to know. Between the razors, tweezers, scissors and depilatory creams, she has more products just for removing unwanted hair than I have toiletries in my whole bathroom.

As they finish up, she keeps it together, but I can see that the experience has left her feeling violated. She's been reminded that the control we think we have over our lives is little more than an illusion – one the guardians are normally careful to preserve. I'm feeling her hurt.

And now it's my turn. My villa is a few doors down from hers, less damaged by the explosion, with most of the windows still intact. This is it. Everyone is going to find out about the bloody shrine. Goddamn it.

Apart from that, I tell myself I don't have a whole lot to hide. I do wish I hadn't left so many socks on the floor, and that I'd changed my underwear a little bit more often after doing a run, maybe taken the clothes up to the laundrette more regularly between the visits from the cleaners. I keep my laundry basket in the bathroom rather than my bedroom. It really stinks compared to Duchess's. The exposure of all my bad habits and sloppy stuff is embarrassing, but I can take it. On reflection, I definitely should clean the tangled corkscrews of hair off my hairbrush more often – and out of the drain of the shower – but I can still cope with Karava examining my box of tampons and sniffing the cream for my athlete's foot.

I have to stifle a protest when they open up my mini-fridge and take out what few snacks I have left. Among them are three pieces of Dad's homemade maple nut toffee. This is not fair, *this is not fair* . . . that stuff's not just *food*, it's a piece of *home*. I always keep the last couple of chunks until the next package arrives. On the worst days, when the longing is so bad I can't bear it, I take that toffee out, cupping it in the warmth of my hands and breathing in the maple and pecan and caramel smell of it. It's my last link to home, it's my *magic*, and these creeps are taking it away from me as if it's just something people eat.

I don't cry. I suck up the misery, knowing everyone will be taking a hit today. I'm not going to be some little girl weeping for her mum and dad. And having seen the search process once already, I don't think I feel as eviscerated by it as Duchess did. That's what I tell myself anyway, as my intestines seem to squirm in my belly. I'm glad my journal is on the chip in my head; I don't know if Buckley can copy it from there without the software on the Hub.

Mostly though, I'm on edge because of the shrine.

Okay, here comes the pain. Christ on a bike, I wish this wasn't happening. When Buckley approaches the white cabinet over the small desk next to my bed, I take a deep breath and clasp my fingers together, clenching them in a tense knot, wincing as he swings the doors open.

Duchess blurts out a shriek, putting a hand to her mouth.

'Oh my *God*!' she gasps. 'I don't believe it!'

I can only peek through my fingers as she moves in for a closer look, her mouth gaping open in astonishment. Buckley, the ba–*(deleted)* . . . swine, moves out of the way so that *she can get a better look*. Maybe he's hoping to defuse the tension a bit or he actually wants me to become a complete social outcast, I don't know. Duchess does a theatrical twirl and puts her hands on her hips, tilting her head to one side.

'Well, we *have* been keeping secrets, haven't we?'

'Ah, Dutch . . . don't . . .'

'Our dear little Billy Goat's in love with Donny Benson!' she exclaims, clapping her hands together in delight. 'Oh my God, this is *priceless*!'

The little cabinet is packed full of photos, a few of them autographed, holograms, cherished concert tickets and other keepsakes, a collection to honour the achingly sweet, beautiful nightingale that is Donny Benson. Okay, so at a sweltering hot sixteen years old, his stardom at its peak, he can be found decorating bedroom walls around the world, idolised by girls in their early teens, but I've been a fan ever since he started posting his love songs on the web when he was nine. I felt he grew with me.

Unfortunately, his particular brand of heartfelt high school romance is considered utterly, face-meltingly uncool to anyone approaching college age. Given that I'm one of the younger ones on the island, there isn't a single other person within a thousand kilometres of here who will understand how I feel about him, so I've kept those feelings hidden. I put a hand to my throat, torn between loyalty and humiliation, gazing on the multiple images of his faultless face, peach-coloured skin, that warm smile and the earth-coloured eyes of a wise soul in a boy's body . . . And I know that this moment is the beginning of the end.

Duchess struggles to contain her smirk as she takes my hands in hers and gives me a solemn look of understanding.

'I'm going to help you get through this,' she tells me with exaggerated sincerity, clutching my hands to her chest. 'It's a *good thing*, that all this came out now. The earlier you carry out an intervention, the greater the chances of the success. I'll be with you in the struggle to free yourself from this terrible addiction. We *all* will.'

'Please, Dutch. Don't tell the others, okay? Come on . . .'

'If that's the way you want it,' she replied, suddenly serious as she puts her hands on my shoulders. 'Then I won't whisper a word to anyone . . .' The laughter finally bursts from her lips and she covers her mouth. 'Are you kidding? I'm telling *everyone*! You think I could keep this quiet? It's pure gold! This is *epic*!'

I must have an expression of cartoonish horror on my face, because she's suddenly seized by a fit of the giggles. At first, I'm really hurt, emotion filling me to the point where I'm almost trembling. I didn't cry over Dad's toffee, but I think it's going to break out of me now. Then she hugs me and kisses my cheek and has to clutch me to her as tears brim in her eyes from the laughter, which is issuing from her in undignified shrieks. Turning to stand with me, an arm around my shoulders, she's still giggling and I find myself smiling despite myself.

'He's a . . . a friend of a photographer friend of mine. Did . . . did I ever mention that?' she says, barely managing to get it out as she tries to breathe.

'Eh, no!' I say. Oh, *of course* she knows someone who knows him, but I'm amazed that she could have failed to bring this up in conversation in all the time I've been here. I don't want to sound too interested. 'Really?'

'Yeah. She's got, like, his private number and everything,' she takes a deep breath, the giggles subsiding. 'I don't want to burst any bubbles here, but he's a nose-picker.'

'What?' I murmur. 'Well . . . nobody's perfect.'

'Oh, I don't mean he has the odd poke up there. He's not clearing a blockage. It's a compulsion with him. As soon as he's out of the public eye, he's right in there, digging tunnels. Can't help himself. His manager bribes and blackmails people not to tell. Dude gets nose-bleeds and everything.'

'Yeah?' I'm trying not to sound bothered.

'I'm tellin' ya, he's a terror for it . . .'

'You're not going to–.'

'Sometimes he goes at it with two fingers at the same time . . .'

'I don't care . . .'

But I do care. It's too much. I'm going to crack.

'Snorting and digging, snorting and digging . . .'

Aw hell, now *I'm* starting to giggle. She turns to look at me, eyes locking onto mine. She grasps my shoulders again.

'I heard he's so addicted to snot, he's even got this special little *spoon*.'

My laugh breaks out like a scream, so loud, Buckley actually jumps. Dutch and I are clinging on to one another now, neither of us able to stand up straight on our own, bodies shaking with helpless fits of laughter. It takes a minute or two for us to get ourselves straight and when we do, I'm feeling better, emptied out, my body shedding tension as if I've loosened ropes that bound me. Duchess wipes her eyes, heaving breaths and sighing.

'God, thanks Billy. I needed that.'

'Glad you're finding this all so funny,' Buckley remarks.

She turns her head to spear him with a disdainful glare.

'Oh, lighten up, Buckley!'

Chapter Nine
A Waste of Resources

After my last few comfort snacks are loaded into the cart, we agree to take another break before the next house. We wander out to the green, where the watchful groups of studes and guardians loiter within easy view of the villas. Buckley has something to see to and he strides off towards his quarters.

'Wonder what he's up to now,' Duchess mutters.

I don't reply. With the giggles emptied out of me, it's like I've used up the last of my reserves. I'm feeling like I got trampled by a hippo, the aches and fatigue really dragging me down, and this whole mutual suspicion thing feels immensely dumb. We're in a pretty desperate situation and instead of trying to sort it out, we're poking through each other's undies, throwing accusations and following people around, hoping to catch them out. Yes, we've got a criminal among us, but . . . I dunno . . . it's like we're wasting valuable time and effort picking sides, like kids forming gangs and dividing up the playground, when there's more serious sh—*(deleted)* . . . crap to deal with.

Gemmy's standing with Noddy and Smood in one group off to our right, shadowing Brothers Mthembu and Nguyen. When he sees us, he comes hurrying over.

'Hey, Billy, can I have a word?' he says; there's a lightness in his tone that doesn't match his intense expression. Of all of us, Gemmy suffers most with mental health issues, and even though he's barely two years older than me, anxiety has already etched fine, permanent lines across his sensitive, South Asian features. 'Just wanted to ask you something.'

I nod and we walk a few metres off to the side, closer to the group he was hanging with. He's got his phone in his hand and I can see the screen. He's muted the sound, but the video's still playing; it's a slapstick dance, an obscene parody of a hit tune from a few months ago – one of millions of entertainment files backed up on the Hub. Maybe Gemmy felt he needed the laugh now, but it's not what Buckley told us to look for. Everyone's supposed to be doing searches for information on growing or finding food. I don't say anything about it. Gemmy's always had a brittleness to him, but he's in an especially delicate state now.

He's thin, but not skinny. He eats too much and too fast to be skinny, even if he doesn't keep most of it down. His voice has a rasping quality, an audible sign of the throat problems he gets sometimes. Up close, you can see the puffiness of his cheeks that creates a shadowy effect around those startling green eyes, framed by eyelashes a Bollywood star, male or female, would kill for. His good looks are further marred by eroded teeth, damaged by the acidic effects of repeated vomiting. He has faint calluses on the backs of his fingers too, from where they've rubbed repeatedly against his teeth.

There's a sour smell beneath the hint of mint on his breath.

'Look . . . I've got . . .' he starts to say, then chickens out, braces himself, gets his game face on and opens his mouth for another try. 'There's gear in my bathroom. Private things. It's . . . embarrassing. If there's anything . . .'

'I'll do what I can,' I tell him, though I'm not sure *what* I can do.

I don't ask him what I'm supposed to look for. He knows I know. The fact is, everyone on the island knows Gemmy suffers from bulimia, though he might be kidding himself that it's still a secret. It's where his name came from. He'd bolt down his dinner, swallowing a hefty meal so fast it barely touched the sides going down, then get up as soon as he was finished and say to one of us: 'Gemme a coffee, will ya?' and head off to the bathroom. He'd be gone a few minutes and come back smelling of breath freshener. I walked in on him once, by accident, which is why he's come to me now. I've already witnessed him kneeling in front of the toilet, with his fingers down his throat, a string of vomit hanging from his lower lip, turning and looking up with guilty anguish as I blundered in because he hadn't locked the door. So I've seen him at his worst, and much as I'd like to, I can never unsee it.

I want to tell him that he's got nothing to hide, because everyone knows anyway and nobody's really bothered. There's some awkwardness, but mostly just sympathy and a mute acceptance. Given our situation here, it's a wonder more of us aren't screwed up, seeing as–*(deleted)* . . . I'm just trying to–*(deleted)* . . . *Oh my God*, you bloody mute-happy, head-wrecking, arse pellet censor chip, son of a–*(deleted)*. Okay, so his head is messed up about food, so what? He's got an illness. He sees Karava for it, who's had training in psychology, and he's being monitored – *was* being monitored – by doctors on the mainland. Up until the last few weeks, he was probably better off here, where we all eat together most of the time and it's hard to pig out on junk too often, because there was one store and no takeaways. And I want to tell him everyone's got things we don't want the others to know, but I don't, because it won't comfort him. Nothing's ever as embarrassing as the cause of your *own* embarrassment, right?

'I'll do what I can,' I say again.

Gemmy doesn't look satisfied with this and he hovers beside me, hands shoved in his pockets, flicking furtive glances at me as I continue walking. I can see now that Smood isn't using his phone for bloody research either. He's on Share, the social media site. It can't be live, so he's just going through his old posts. He's seen all of these before, and he's using his last few hours on the Hub *to look at the same useless stuff again.*

I can't believe this. Why is nobody taking this seriously? Hasn't anybody seen the cart going round gathering up all the food we have left? Didn't they see *the box of seeds*? I mean, I know trying to research things we *need* might actually involve *reading*, but . . .

'Whatcha doing?' I ask innocently.

'Nuthin',' Smood replies, shrugging.

Like hell. The mug is checking his fan posts. There aren't many perks to being on this island, but there's no denying we're a privileged bunch. When the sat-link is actually working, our school programme means we have access to the best tutors in the world on any subject. We're known faces on Share, even if our access, while we had it, always had a two-week 'security' delay. And when we get home, we'll be given a guaranteed start in our choice of university or career, anywhere in the world. More than that, we'll be famous, which some of us aren't too crazy about – but others are only itching to plunge into the life of a celebrity.

Smood is one of those, and I don't think less of him for it. Okay, so he's a bit vain, but he's got a good heart, he's nice to people and he's smart and even though he'll play the game, he might actually use his fame to do some good. We all figure he'll be some kind of sports star and there are enough coaches trying to get hold of him – as much for the sponsorship deals he'll bring in as anything else – not to mention a whole load of multinational firms. They know can-do, charismatic CEO material when they see it. He's got a half-decent voice too, so maybe someone will give him singing lessons and package him as a rock star. The guy has a lot of options, that's all I'm saying.

Right now though, Smood's checking out the girls who

fawn over him. It must be addictive, I suppose, to scroll down through all that adulation, all those uninhibited offers. There'll be a mob of them waiting at the airport for him when he finally arrives back after his mother summons him home.

But you can't eat flattering words or teasing holograms. Mthembu and Nguyen are only a few metres away, so I keep my voice low.

'Shouldn't you be looking up–?'

But he interrupts me, shooting me a warning glance, his stare shifting immediately to the two guardians to see if I was heard.

'I'm just taking a break!' he mutters self-consciously, but not so guilty that he stops what he's doing. 'I need to take a load off, all right? What about it? You playing for the oldies now, or what?'

'Don't give me that!' I bark back at him. 'You *know* what's happening here!'

Noddy's standing beside him. I grab the phone from the lanky guy's hand. He's doing his own thing too, except he's not looking for entertainment. He snatches it back, angling his head and waving a finger, pale seawater eyes glowering out past blond eyelashes, to admonish me gently for being rude. Gemmy's still at my shoulder, all anxious tension, and he leans in closer to see. Noddy has some of the guardians' personnel files open. These are available to all the students – we're allowed see everything but the oldies' medical files. Noddy's looking for suspects; he's *investigating* . . .

'What's going on here?' Buckley says from behind us.

It gives us a start. Nobody heard him approach. How did he do that? He never used to do that before. The principal's eyes flick to Smood's screen, then Gemmy's, then see Noddy nonchalantly swipe his screen clear. Buckley holds up another phone.

'I found Nuke playing games on hers,' he sighs, holding up the device in a manner that suggests he doesn't even know what it is. His face has a weary, pained expression, the look of a parent whose patience has worn too thin. 'What do I have to do? *What do I have to do* to make you understand what we're facing here?'

Nobody answers, of course. We're teenagers; we're used to hearing pointless, rhetorical questions from our authority figures. Plaintive protests from old people are just part of the background noise in our world. Nobody says this either, because we can see there's some subtle change coming over him, as if he's shedding a sheath of translucent skin, snake-style, to reveal a harder, more toned version of the same creature.

'If you can't be trusted to focus on what's important,' he says in a chillingly calm voice, 'then we will *make* you focus. Mark this: As of now, there will be no more talk about sex, celebrities, sport, your devoted fans or any product of the entertainment industry.'

There is a chorus of truncated curses. The studes regard this as an outrageous breach of our rights. Buckley's not stopping us from *doing* any of this stuff, but cutting it from conversation will definitely dampen any enjoyment of it.

'What?' Smood snarls, stepping towards the older man, fists bunched. 'What kind of garbage is that? What have they got to do with anything! You're exceeding your authority, Buckley! We put up with all that other control freak bullsh– . . . uh . . . uh . . . all that other crap, but this is going too far.'

But Buckley has already done it. I can feel the new restrictions in my head. Perversely, my first reaction is relief. At least Duchess can't tell anyone about my shrine to Don– *(deleted)* . . . See? Cool. The relief fades as I realize the rest is not so good. This is really going to kill our banter. I can't even write the word 'Se–*(deleted)* . . . So . . . great. Just great. More blocks. If he keeps this up we'll all be bloody mutes by the time we leave the island. I think of my mum and dad again; about how they're not here. How nobody's come to check on us. We've been betrayed. There's no other word for it. Our parents have betrayed us all.

'Perhaps now you'll be able to keep your minds on the task at hand,' Buckley tells us. 'Now I'll thank you to do as I asked and search the Hub for information that will help us overcome this situation we're facing. We may only have hours left before the battery fails. Use that time well.'

He spins on his heel and walks purposefully towards

Duchess and Karava, who are waiting at the front door of Gemmy's villa. Grinding my teeth together, I hurry after Buckley. Gemmy follows for the first few metres, still wanting assurance from me. I wave impatiently at him and he pulls up, visibly fretting as he swivels and reluctantly heads back to the others.

'You're making a mistake,' I say, as I catch up with Buckley. 'Laying down another ban. You're just going to make things worse.'

'You have brought this on yourselves,' he retorts. 'If you're determined to act like children, then you force us to treat you like children.'

'Really? Did you *gag* your children when they didn't do what they were told? How'd that work out for you?'

He drops a grim glance on me and strides on. I nearly have to jog to keep up.

'Snide comments aren't helpful, Billy.'

'Well, I might as well get them in while I can. Who knows when you'll ban those too?'

'Very funny,' he grunts. 'So is that how *you* think we should use the last few hours of the Hub? Checking out pictures of girls, playing shoot-em-ups and watching pop videos?'

'Of course I don't! I'm only . . .' I stop talking for a moment. Nothing to do with the censor chip; I'm just stuck for words. An ordinary problem, but not one I suffer from very often. 'I think you're dividing us when we can't afford to be divided. You're making us into enemies.'

He stops abruptly, turning to face me and I'm forced to look up into his eyes, feeling as if I'm held in place by the grave weight of his expression.

'Is that how you see us – as enemies?' he asks.

He seems both hurt and implacable at one and the same time, and I see it in him then. The stressed soldier. Old armour is forming around him once again, covering up his weaknesses. He's shifting into war mode.

'That's not fair!' I exclaim. 'That's not fair. You know I can't talk to you properly about this and you know why. You and the Council have set it up that way. No, I don't think you're an enemy. You're not a *friend* either though, are you? You can't be. I know you even give Noon a hard time 'cos she's not a cold fish around me like the rest of you are. I'm just saying we need to work together, but that's not going to happen if you keep clamping down on us. It's oppression, Brother Buckley. That stuff you teach us about in history, remember?'

'There's a big difference between oppression and *discipline*,' he tells me. 'Believe me, I've seen enough of both. And until you all learn to discipline yourselves, yes, I will have to impose it upon you. Now if you're quite finished with your civil rights protest, young lady, we have to continue our work.'

Neither of us says another word until we join Duchess and Karava, who are still waiting for us at the door of Gemmy's villa. I ask if I can go in first with Karava, and Buckley agrees. He's well aware of Gemmy's problems. There's a faint hint of vomit in the bathroom, but it's not as bad as I was expecting. I spray some air freshener, give the toilet a good flush and pour some cleaner down it. The doctor watches as I gather the bottles and packs of pills from the cabinet; laxatives, diuretics and appetite suppressants. I'm surprised Gemmy's able to get some of this stuff past the security of the supply chain – this place is supposed to be locked down like a prison against banned substances. But like every human-made system, it's not perfect. Karava's in charge of our pharmacy and there's no way he's providing all of this to one person, so either Gemmy's getting other studes to ask for them on his behalf or he must be bribing one of the oldies to bring them in for him. Further proof that the members of the Order aren't as pure as they make themselves out to be. I put everything in a bag, take another glance around and am about to leave when Karava points to a large tube of depilatory cream.

'Bulimics develop more hair on their body,' he says softly. 'It's a reaction, to keep them warm when they're not taking in enough calories. He might not want people to know about that either.'

I add it to the collection, then go outside and put the bag beside the front door, catching Gemmy's eye to make sure he sees me do it. I'd say Gemmy's more worried about Duchess seeing what's in there than Buckley, but they both pretend not to notice as they head inside. It feels pointless, window dressing on a wooden building with dry rot, but from the relief on his face, it's helping him maintain the illusion, he can keep fooling himself that nobody knows. And I'm glad to do it. Sometimes, we need just a bit of self-deception to deal with the crap in life.

Gemmy has surprisingly little food in his home; I imagine his personal stash is almost used up after the supply ship failed to show up, and the new stress we've been under probably has him bingeing even more than usual. All that food wasted, gulped down and then thrown back up again.

The rest of the searches blur into a montage; similar rooms, similar vanities and personal issues and secrets and sources of shame or self-loathing. The various bans prevent me from listing them all and to be honest, I can't be arsed. Who cares about Smood's hair products and heat rash cream, or Nuke's black market collection of banned g–*(deleted)* . . . about Cheeks's love letters or her psoriasis, or Moose's waist-pinching girdles. After you've spent long enough wading through the hidden details of people's personal lives, it all becomes a mush of scenery that ceases to have any titillation or shock value. Several hours in and I want to wash off the pieces of sticky, ruptured skin of privacy that seem to cling to me. I'm craving a long shower and the luscious embrace of sleep.

It's nearly ten in the evening, the sun has submerged beneath the horizon, its last grasping beams of light clinging to the clouds with pinks and oranges before it finally sank, as if it wanted to stay and watch the searches to the end. We're down to the last few villas and I'm dead on my feet, my belly doing its best impression of a defensive dog, the heels of my hands having to continually push into my eyes to keep them from going bleary.

We open the door to Skip's villa and we're hardly into the living-room, when Buckley stops and tells us to wait. He surveys the room with one sweep and then back again, a movement that's almost robotic, smooth and economical, taking it all in. Then he turns to Karava.

'Have Skip brought in here immediately. And have Brother Mthembu bring me the records of his movements. I want to know everywhere he's been over the last four days.'

I'm kind of curious to know too. Because laid out on the coffee table in front of the couch, are print-outs of maps and satellite photos of the island, some fire-damaged electrical components and what appears to be a homemade radio set.

Chapter Ten
A Violation of the Rules

Everything about Brother Mthembu is long. He walks in, slightly stooped, ropey arms swinging, legs loping, body seeming to rock like a boat from all that swaying motion. He has a blue-black, long-jawed, pointy-chinned, mournful face, whose shape reminds me slightly of a crescent moon. Like many of the guardians, Mthembu bears scars on his soul from the things he has lived through, but that melancholic face is split occasionally by a sad smile that stretches wide, pushing the lines in his cheeks back nearly to his ears. He's not smiling now. Mthembu's one of the tech people – he's not in Noon's league, but he's not bad – and he's carrying a tablet, no doubt to show Buckley the course of Skip's movements around the island. Yeah, that's right; our movements can be tracked – another handy feature of the censor chip. Noon told me recently that, without the sat-link, the tracker can only show the general area we're in, accurate to a hundred square metres or so, but that's probably all Buckley needs.

This homemade radio is a major violation of the island's rules. Studes are not allowed have one of their own – all contact with the outside world has to be approved and monitored by the guardians. Even though this doesn't prove Skip's the saboteur – in fact, seeing as the saboteur stole a perfectly good radio from the air base, he'd have no need to try and make one – if they find out that Skip's managed to receive signals abou–*(deleted)* . . . It's just that, well, it could mea–*(deleted)*. . . oh, for Christ's sake . . . it just doesn't look good, that's all.

Skip follows Mthembu in, with Karava bringing up the rear. Duchess and I exchange looks. I have to be straight about this; if you asked me to pick the one stude on the island who fits the stereotype of a potential bomb-maker, it would be Skip. Surly to the point of belligerent, antisocial, but highly intelligent, he is gripped with an obsessive level of focus when he sets his mind to something. Skip keeps himself at arm's length from the rest of us and is the only one who's regularly, openly hostile towards the guardians.

It shows now, in his edgy body language, the restless way his upturned, East Asian brown eyes case the room and the wound-up sense you get from him that, at any instant, he might move with sudden speed and force. He walks right up to Buckley – right in his face – and for a moment, neither of them speak. Mthembu keeps his distance, but he's on the balls of his feet, ready to move too.

Whippet thin, with a sinewy strength, Skip is the only one who can give Smood a run for his money in sparring sessions on the mats and I'd struggle to beat either of them in a sprint (although long distance, none of them could catch me).

Skip's also the one person I've seen who writes in paper

notebooks. Apart from Duchess and her diary, of course. I'd be like that too, I suppose, except that the convenience of the censor chip has made me lazy. Whatever it is that he's writing all the time, it's secret enough to put in the extra effort to keep it offline and on paper.

'Whuh-whuh-whuh-what do you want?' he demands.

'I want you to explain this,' Buckley replies, gesturing to the things on the table.

'Buh-buh-buh-buh-bugger off!' Skip spits out.

However tough he might think he is, Skip would last no time at all against Mthembu or Buckley. There's a barely suppressed violence in his manner and I'm really hoping he's not going to start anything. I'm so weak and queasy, even *seeing* violence would probably knock me off my feet. Skip's skin is a beige kind of white – flushed now with defensive anger – under thin, straight, untidy black hair. His sharp-chinned face is set in pensive intent and there's a slight snarling twist of his thin-lipped mouth. The black and olive drab army surplus clothing helps him look like a proper nut among all the sun worshippers here.

'This is a serious situation,' Buckley repeats his order firmly. 'Take your time, compose yourself . . . but you *are* going to explain to me what you were doing here. '

For all his handy pro-guilt qualities, I just can't see Skip as a saboteur. He has no more motive to blow up the monastery than any of us – although I suspect you could say that about your average sociopathic school shooter – and I think all his hostility and rage stems from our isolation here on the island. It's possible he's simply being more open about how he feels, instead of buttoning it all up so he can get on with life, like the rest of us. Or maybe he's just taking a little longer to adjust; everyone feels it differently.

Skip is the most recent arrival to the island, walking off the ship less than six months ago. His name came from his stammer – he sometimes sounds like the recording of a song that's skipping. He told us he'd pretty much overcome the problem when he was younger, but now that he's found himself here, it's tying up his tongue again. The various bans on our speech and that seething frustration are probably a dynamite combination when your own brain *already* trips itself up as you try to express yourself.

Having your nickname remind you of it the whole time probably doesn't help either.

'I need an answer, Skip,' Buckley presses him.

'I was muh-muh-muh-making a radio,' he replies, his face twisting with the effort of forming the words.

'Oh, for goodness sake! You're not *allowed* have your own radio!' Buckley barks, exasperated. 'All your communications have to go through the Hub – you know that!'

'So suh-suh-suh-suh-spank me, buh-buh-baldy!' Skip retorts.

It's such a stupid, childish thing to say, I giggle and Dutch makes a snorting noise that sounds like she caught her laugh but only just managed to contain it. Buckley glowers at us, but keeps his attention on Skip.

'Some of these pieces, they're from the monastery,' he says, picking up a roll of copper wire. 'You stole these components from the site of the explosion.'

'Wuh-well, I needed some parts and you wuh-wuh-wuh weren't using them.'

'We'll discuss that in a minute,' Buckley adds, holding up the tablet Mthembu has handed to him. 'According to the tracker, you were also down at the air base two days ago.'

'I was out for wuh-wuh-wuh-walk. Or is . . . thuh . . . that not allowed either?'

Though his stammer is as bad as I've ever heard it, he's bashing on. When he hits a block you can see him trying to relax and get past it, but it looks almost painful, as if his mouth is fighting his brain to a standstill. It must be a bit like living your whole life with a malfunctioning censor chip. There's a thought that could give me nightmares.

Buckley turns to Duchess and me, giving Mthembu a nod.

'We'll have to carry on this interview in private,' he says. 'I need to unlock his chip or this will take forever. Duchess, Billy, thank you for your help. Please go with Dr Karava and Brother Mthembu and finish searching the last few villas. Once that's done, and Skip and I are finished here, we'll get everyone together again to discuss the food situation.'

'I really think someone should stay here with Skip,' Duchess declares, playing the lawyer role again. 'He has rights, Brother Buckley. You shouldn't be questioning him without witnesses present.'

I nod, because I agree, and because I'm dying to hear what will be said once Buckley unlocks Skip's chip. I imagine a fountain of unrestrained words vomited forth from him, the first of us who is finally, gleefully free to say whatever he wants.

'I know exactly what his rights are,' Buckley growls. 'And yours too. As principal, I am entitled to interview whom I want, when I want. I could quote the regulations at you, Duchess, but frankly, I don't *have* to. This is not a democracy and, as you well know, standard civil rights do not apply here. Brother Mthembu, please remove them from the room and carry on with the searches.'

And that's that. Gone is any pretence of normality – Buckley has put us in our place. Duchess is in a silent fury as we leave, but neither of us resist Mthembu as the long man gently ushers us out and waves us towards the nearest cluster of picnic tables. Night has well and truly enveloped the village; the familiar pools of light have come on across the green, though it's dark around the edges of the ruined mon – where the explosion took out all the lamps in the immediate vicinity.

'I need to run a diagnostic on the Hub,' Mthembu informs us, in his hushed, unhurried voice. 'It's on its last legs, I think. I'll be back in five minutes.'

Two of the tables are now stacked with all the food that's been taken from the villas, both ours and the guardians'. I want to have a closer look, and not just because my stomach is issuing gurgling rumbles of protest at the delayed delivery of its next load.

Instead, we're intercepted by Noddy, who's gazing over at Skip's villa, at the far end of the crescent-shaped road.

'What's going on?' he asks. 'Why did they call Skip in?'

'He was making his own *radio*,' Duchess announces. 'We don't know if he'd got it working, but he was doing something with maps of the island. And he took some electrical components from the site of the explosion. Buckley's questioning him now.'

Noddy, Smood, Gemmy, Nuke and a couple of others start asking more questions, but she doesn't have answers. That doesn't stop them using their imaginations, of course, and I listen to them making assumptions and accusations, a stuttering discussion with their censor chips causing hiccups and forced pauses, vague inferences having to serve as winding, diverted routes when straight statements hit the inevitable roadblocks. They're all ignoring me now, so I wander over to the loaded picnic tables, both of them kept under close watch by a team of six guardians. This is pretty much the last of our food. I'd bet money that Buckley told them to lay it out like this so we could have a good long look at it.

Food for thought. Ha ha ha.

Almost everyone on the island is of above average intelligence; every stude here is expensively educated and has been raised by ambitious, high-achieving parents to take care of themselves, anticipating a life of similar achievement. We understand nutrition. But the food we kept in our villas, unlike the meals we'd eat in the canteen, was composed almost entirely of treats and comfort grub. Carbs, fat and salt – at least we'd have the calories. Smood comes up beside me, a bitter smirk on his face as he looks at me gazing at the food.

'Well, I suppose you couldn't expect everyone to have secret stashes of fruit and vegetables,' he chuckles. He's nervous, and it comes through in his weak laugh.

A few months ago, we did a project in biology, part of which involved finding out how much a family of four would eat in different countries around the world. Noon, who teaches us some of our science, had us take a typical family from a wealthy nation as an example and we gathered that amount of food on these same tables. One week's worth of food for a family of four took up one table.

We only have *two tables* of food here, for the island's entire population of sixteen studes and twenty-eight guardians. Crisps, chocolate, marshmallows and jellies, soft drinks, individually packaged cake slices, cream-filled sponge fingers, liquorice allsorts and tortilla chips. A few other treats you'd only find in particular cultures. There are also packs of sugar-free chewing gum and peppermints which will do nothing but fool us into thinking we're eating . . . There are some decent foods too; fresh fruit, fruit juices, packs of dried fruit, a tiny amount of vegetables, bread in various forms. There's popcorn, which we kept as treats but at least it has some nutrition; packs of mixed nuts and salt crackers . . . but it's swamped by the junk food. I think we've already eaten all of the protein meals that had been stored in the boathouse, which might have been deliberate, to prevent people from getting 'hangry' while the guardians invaded our privacy.

As I stare at the collection on the tables, trying to ignore the way my mouth is watering, the pure *lust* I suddenly feel for this smorgasbord of artificially-enhanced tastes, straining to defy my body's almost overwhelming command to get eating. I wonder if this is how Gemmy feels when he loses his self-control. There's a dull cramp in my intestines, but I tell myself that I can't be that hungry – not yet.

I can't help noticing none of the cats are hanging round, looking for scraps, as they tend to do when we're eating. Perhaps they don't consider this stuff food.

I think about the box of seeds again. How long will they take to grow? We haven't planted anything yet, have we? Does anyone even know *how* to grow them? Although the guardians share the gardening duties in the village, how much do any of them know about farming?

Looming behind this anxiety is the shadowy mass of a

much greater fear, one I'm just not ready to raise my face to yet; the question of why no one sent a plane out to check on us as soon as we lost contact with the mainland. People should be wondering what's happened. *Why haven't they come for us?*

'We could starve to death,' I say, in a whisper so soft I don't think even Smood can hear.

'. . . I can't believe it's him,' Duchess is saying. 'Have you seen the way he dresses? It *can't* be him, it's too obvious. Too much of a cliché.'

'But he's a *type*,' Noddy argues. 'He's ticks all the boxes. That's how profiling works!'

'No, that's how *stereotyping* works,' Dutch retorts.

My jaw is trembling, though I have my lips pressed closed. Moving away from the lights, to a darker part of the lawn, I gaze out into the empty expanse of ocean, the rough-surfaced mirror offers an imperfect reflection of the spray of stars in the endless sky. The view has an awesome, powerful beauty that makes me feel small and lonely. My thoughts turn to our parents, who talked us into coming to this volcanic pimple of an island out in the butthole of nowhere. I take a long, trembling breath, my teeth chattering, hugging myself tightly. I don't understand why Mum and Dad haven't come, why *none* of our parents have come looking for us. Where *are* they? I wonder again if they have any idea what's happening to us . . . or if we've been left completely on our own.

Chapter Eleven
Evening on the Water

It's late, dark, and I'm too tired to go swimming. Even so, I join the others as they head for the lagoon. The thought of submerging my aching body in the cool of the sea has enough appeal to make up for the draining trudge down to the docks. It's one of the things we always try and get a good gang together for. Even Skip comes along most of the time, as he has tonight. On warm evenings, we make our way down to the beach for a night-swim, taking advantage of the low light and the fact that most of the guardians are off-duty, to chill and swim and sluice off the stress of the day. We can fool ourselves that we're beyond the parental gaze of the Order. Tonight, it's also a chance for Smood and some of the other studes to interrogate Dutch and me about what we saw in the villas.

'. . . I'm not asking you to name names,' Smood is saying to Duchess. 'I just want some grease, y'know? Spicy stuff. You *must* have seen something worth talking about!'

'Anything I saw was *private*,' she retorts. 'You get that, right? As in, none of your business?'

'Ah, you're no fun.'

'Oh yeah? That's not what you said last time we were down here.'

'No, I . . .' Smood's tone changes as he picks up on her cue.

'Are you . . . Are you wearing the same swimsuit?'

'You'll just have to wait and see, won't you?'

The gang follows the road that forks away from the main pier, curving right under the glow of elegant, sculpted, promenade-style sensor-lights that brighten as we walk into range of each one. The lagoon is not a natural feature of the island. A large, oval expanse of water, about the size of a football field, it's separated from the rest of the sea by a steel-reinforced rock wall made to look as if these boulders just happened to be tossed into place by the waves. There's a thin strip of beach along the inner edge, with various sets of gracefully designed steps, jetties, paths and diving platforms around the perimeter. There are floodlights, but they're normally left off. The lagoon lies to the west of the harbour, below the guardians' villas. On a good day, the water, between two and six metres deep, is as warm as the Caribbean. It's also, crucially, kept free of lethal jellyfish and the toxic algae that regularly builds up around the coast.

These blankets of growth are a relatively recent development in the life of the island, caused by rising sea temperatures. For several months every year, massive blooms of algae, a bright, acidic green, stinking like rotten eggs, surround the island, starving the waters of oxygen, and therefore fish, and making it unsafe for swimming and water sports. The stuff is pure poison. Which is why we have the lagoon, built to provide a safe place to dive in when we want more entertainment than the village's Olympic-sized swimming pool can offer.

We leave our towels on the boardwalk, kicking off our sandals and stripping down to our swimsuits or shorts. When we head across the beach for the water's edge, highlights twinkling on its opaque black surface as it's rippled by the faint breeze, I notice Moose has kept his t-shirt on. I wonder if he's wearing one of the girdles we saw in his villa.

At nineteen, he's one of the oldest and tallest here – shorter only then Noddy – a bulky build, and strong with it too. Maintaining our health is one of the priorities for the guardians, so Moose is one of the few who's overweight . . . I mean, he's not obese, but he's embarrassed about his muffin top and man boobs. Most of us are brown-skinned, but he and I are the darkest and he comes from a place where the colour of a person's skin used to be a big issue, what with th–*(deleted)* . . . Right, yeah – no politics. Asshat brain bug . . . Anyway, this inferiority complex is ingrained into Moose. Whenever he feels physically insecure, he hovers around me protectively, as if, y'know, us blacks have to look after each other. Now we're out among all these lithe, athletic bodies and he hangs with me and I figure I can let him do the big brother bit, if it makes him feel better. All I'm thinking is I hope he doesn't stare at Smood as much as I'm trying not to. That's another thing Moose and I have in common.

When we swim out towards the nearest raft, its infrared

sensors pick us up and a pattern of small lights activate on its under-surface, illuminating the water with an aquamarine glow. Duchess is the first to reach it, and pulls herself up onto its edge, arching her back and raking her dripping hair back off her face, knowing that everyone arriving after her can get a good long look. She's wearing a shimmering, dark silver one-piece that's split into what look like bands around her torso, revealing teasing glimpses of wet bronze skin. It's incredibly s– *(deleted)* . . . she loo–*(deleted)* . . . Oh yeah, all that's banned now too. Cheeks is the next up onto the raft; blonde, slim and graceful, with the cutest dimples. She's a paler version of Dutch in every way; our perpetual queen-in-waiting, always a little behind, a little less commanding than our statuesque pack leader.

Next up is Nuke; less of an attention-seeker, she just hates to be left out of things. With the body of a gymnast, she can catch the boys' eyes when she wants to, but I've never seen her show any of them particular attention. Or any of the girls, for that matter. She does enough to keep in with the crowd, while her snippy, slightly awkward manner ensures she'll never be at the centre of it. She lets her shoulder-length black hair fall across her broad, East Asian features, strands of hair sticking to her damp face as she leans back to coolly regard those still in the water.

More girls join them, though I stay in the water. This is how it normally starts out; the cool girls gathering on the raft, casual poses carefully positioned to show off what they have, slicked back wet hair and polished skin, looking down at the boys who swim around them, cracking jokes and trying to keep their attention.

'. . . No, seriously,' Cheeks is saying to Smood, eyeing him intently. 'What would you be willing to eat, to save yourself from starving?'

'I dunno,' Smood replies, resting a hand on Dutch's knee to hold himself still in the water. She doesn't push the hand away. 'What are my options?'

'Let's keep it relevant. It has to be something you can find on the island, but like . . . worst-case-scenario type of thing.'

'What, you mean like grass?'

'That's it? That's the worst thing you can think of?' Nuke says scornfully. 'Besides, you can't digest grass, bonehead, you're not a ruminant.'

'I'd be insulted if . . . if I knew what that meant.'

'Don't you *ever* listen in biology?' Nuke groans. 'You've only got one stomach. Eating grass would be pointless – you can't digest it. You might have the *brains* of a cow, but you've got the stomach of a human.'

'More like a dog! Have you ever seen him eat?' Cheeks scoffs. She waves her painted toenails at Noddy, those dimples of her always more prominent when she's giving a flirty smile. 'What about you, Nod? What's the worst thing you'd eat?'

'If I was hungry enough, I'd eat bugs,' Noddy tells her,

straight up, as he pinches her toes and uses them to pull himself closer to the raft. 'I don't care. Leaves, roots . . . Any animal I could find. To stay alive? What does it matter what it looks like? I'd eat maggots to stay alive.'

'Maggots? That is *so* gross!' Cheeks gags, shaking him free of her foot.

'Better gross than dead,' Noddy says, tilting his head in acceptance as he shrugs.

'Is that, like, your family motto?' Smood asks.

Noddy lunges at him and the two wrestle in the water, the cluster of girls watching in amusement. Not all of us take part in the ritual circling of the raft, but it's the core of the night-swim tradition. Skip represents our outer edge; with his goggles on, he's already on his way out to the next raft with smooth, strong strokes. He won't be gone long. Even he can't resist the pull of this scene; life in its pure, animal prime.

Part of me rebels against this archaic flaunting of female flesh and yet here I am, still looking on. Eventually, the formation will break up and people will pair off and retire to the beach, or we'll play sharks or our very hands-on brand of water polo.

'What about you, Billy?' Moose interrupts my thoughts, treading water close to me. 'What would you eat? I don't think I could eat meat, do you? I mean, killing an *animal* so you can *eat* it? I think I'd just puke. Maybe bugs, I don't know. I think I could eat worms . . . or fish. They don't *feel* anything, do they?

How about you? Where would you draw the line?'

Moose is a vegetarian, like most of the studes – like half the world now. I eat cloned meat, which is served on the island, and fish from time to time. I've never had free range meat, the kind that started off as a living animal. My family couldn't afford it when I was young and my parents would always have been against it anyway.

What's the worst thing I'd eat, if I was starving?

'I don't know,' I say at last. 'It's never been something I needed to think about. Nobody here has. I mean . . . let's face it; starvation isn't for the likes of us, is it?'

'Well, it wasn't until now,' he replies quietly.

No. Not until now.

Smood and Noddy's mock fight is over, Noddy has been dunked into submission, and my eyes are dragged over to where Smood is now leaning his perfectly formed chest and arms on the edge of the raft, gazing up at Duchess. She ruffles his hair as if he's some friendly mutt who's come up to her looking for attention.

We're beyond the reach of the lights of the boardwalk, so it's only the discreet raft-lamps under the water and the starlight that glistens over the wet, flowing shapes of the muscles of Smood's shoulders and back. Dutch, swanning over him like a siren drawing him to his doom, catches me looking and gives me a regal smile, our queen holding court. I grin back at her, even as I feel something brush against the toes of my right foot. At first, I think it's just Moose being playful, until I realize he's several metres away to my left.

My breath catches in my chest as I look down into the water and see a long, sinuous shape sweep past, silhouetted in the light from the raft.

Now, I've swum in water with creatures like sharks and lion jellyfish and been in a kayak when a humpback whale breached a few metres from me. I'm not prone to panic, but I want you to realize that right at this point, with everything that's happened, I'm not in my best mental state. Which may explain my reaction to the sight of a large, unidentified shape in the lagoon. Also, *nothing* is supposed to be able to get in past the sea wall, never mind a creature that size.

I scream like a little girl who's just locked herself in a dark closet and then start thrashing towards the raft.

Chapter Twelve
Predator

'There's . . . there's something in the water!' I shriek. 'Get out of the water!'

I'm swimming so badly and opening my mouth so wide as I inhale, that I swallow water and start choking, my strokes going from childlike to frantically-trying-not-to-drown. At first, some of the others laugh, I look that stupid. Then Smood and Moose head over to try and help. I stop flailing around, cough the water out of my throat and peer desperately around beneath me before I start swimming again, this time with more speed and less slapstick terror. Waving the two boys away from me, I snap at them.

'There's something in the water! Something big – could be a shark!'

Even as I say this, I'm hauling myself out, pushing between Dutch and Cheeks and scrambling to the middle of the raft. Under ordinary circumstances, my announcement would be met by exasperation, even sarcastic jeers. We live in the middle of an ocean and have been on enough sailing trips to understand a bit about normal shark behaviour. But nothing about the last couple of days has been normal. Our nerves are in shreds and the appearance of this wraith in the walled-off shelter of the lagoon makes no sense. In a frenzy of fear, all the studes in the water start powering at full speed for the raft.

We get everybody up onto its slick wooden surface except for Moose, who's further out, punching through the water towards us. I see the thing again, not far from him, a blurry torpedo shape, weaving slightly as it moves unhurriedly towards him.

'Moose, come on!' I howl. 'It's coming towards you! *Move it!*'

We're all shouting now, urging him on. The creature's on a perpendicular course and it's going to cut right across his path . . . It passes underneath him as he gets within a few metres of the raft and grasping hands drag him up and out of the water. We expect jaws lined with rows of teeth to snap closed as his feet clear the surface, but there's nothing. There are curses and exclamations, questions blurted out, anxious sobs and gasps of panicked breath.

'What is it? Does anybody know what it is?' Nuke asks.

'It's circling. Whatever it is, it wants *us*,' Duchess says. 'We need to call Buckley. Who's got a phone?'

There's a chorus of negatives, which is remarkable in itself. It's hard to imagine *all* of us coming onto the water without our phones.

'Goddamn it,' Dutch swears. 'The one time our damn lives depend on it . . .'

The raft isn't stable with this many people on it. Every time someone moves, it tips slightly or wobbles and my heart deals me a thump. We hold onto each other, those nearest the edges trying to pull in as far as they can. The warmth of the bodies around me makes me conscious of the chilling effect of the breeze. We can't stay here all night . . .

We can see just enough of the apparition to follow its progress. Its body flexes gracefully, lazily, moving in a steady, unerring path in almost an exact circle, though the raft isn't at its centre. Instead, each sweep brings it within a few metres of the raft's edge, close to where Moose climbed on, then its circuit takes it further out, where we lose sight of it again.

'What the hell are we going to do?'

Nobody answers. We huddle in the dark, watching for every sign of the creature.

'Wuh-wuh-wuh . . . wuh-why are you guys all up on the raft?' a voice calls to us from the darkness.

It's Skip, on his way back from the other raft, way out in the middle of the lagoon. There's some more soft cursing as we all realize we had completely forgotten about him. Embarrassment mixed with guilt. A few of the studes exchange glances; Skip, who'd made his own radio. Who'd been questioned at length about the explosion. The only one who'd been out on his own when the creature appeared . . .

'Skip, get out of the water!' Duchess shouts to him. 'There's something in there. We think it's a shark or something. You've got to–.'

'It's a drone!' Skip calls back, pushing his goggles up onto his face.

'What?'

He swims in closer, with no urgency in his strokes, then stops a couple of metres away.

'Couldn't you see it? It's a drone submarine. They must have had one in the lagoon the whole time and they never told us.'

There's a long pause. The shape come gliding in closer again and this time, a few at the closest edge who have goggles dip their faces into the water to get a more careful look.

'Balls, he's right,' Noddy says. 'It's a drone sub. It's doing circles because it's in a holding pattern. When the satellites went offline, the thing must have reset and now it's waiting for new instructions.'

We all relax – a bit. We're still freaked. The waters around the island are patrolled by dozens of these drone submarines, tasked with making sure nobody brings a boat or sub in near the coast without clearance from the Council. These things are state-of-the-art weapons platforms, hunter-killers, capable of taking out anything from a submerged swimmer to a warship. A small swarm of them could sink an aircraft carrier. This one is simply part of the many layers of security, in the air and sea, in place to protect us. We've seen these drones regularly while out sailing, we just didn't know there was one in here.

'How have we never seen it before?' Duchess asks.

'It might have a place under there where it can keep out

sight, a hide or something,' Noddy suggests. 'When it stopped receiving command signals, it came out and waited for a new contact. Hey, Skip! You should get out of the water anyway, man! I wouldn't take any chances with this sucker. If it's been cut off from its controllers, it might not be able to identify you. It might think you're an intruder.'

'Yeah, I've a question,' Skip snorts. 'If this thing can sink a buh-buh-buh . . . buh-*battleship*, wuh-what muh-makes you think you're suh-safe sitting on a *raft*?'

This gives us some pause for thought. I can almost hear the rolling eyes and the buttocks clenching in embarrassment.

'Awright . . . well, now I'm feeling a bit stupid,' Smood sighs.

He slips down into the water, still keeping a wary eye on the drone, which continues circling with what I can't help thinking of as shark-like grace. One by one, most of the others follow him, me included. The playful mood cannot be recaptured, however. Nobody feels comfortable with this submerged war machine, constantly circling us.

'This thing is really killing my buzz,' Cheeks comments. 'What the hell do we need a drone in here for anyway? It's not like anyone can get within a hundred klicks of this place.'

'Actually, someone did manage to sneak onto the island once,' Nuke tells her.

Heads snap up, all eyes suddenly fixed on her, where she sits casually on the edge of the raft, kicking her feet gently in the water. She has our immediate attention. I've never heard of intruders on the island before, and it looks like none of the others have either.

It's very possible that Nuke might know something the rest of us don't. Like me, she's only seventeen, but she's been in the programme longer than any of the other studes – about nine or ten years, I think. She already had her nickname when she arrived; we think it came from her taste for violent video games and her explosive temper, but it could also be becau– *(deleted)* . . . Bugger. She's been on this island for *three years*, and before that, she was with the juniors in th–*(deleted)* . . . Oh, for f-*(deleted)* . . . Nuts. Anyway, she's a veteran compared to everyone else here, and considering who her dad is, it's likely she could be in the programme for a few more years yet.

'Someone tried to get onto the island?' Duchess says sharply, in a voice that implies she should have been informed at the earliest opportunity. 'When did it happen?'

'Years ago, even before *I* was here,' Nuke says, seeming happy to have upstaged Dutch for once. 'I don't know the details. Some guy sent a team of special ops types; he wanted to try and take his daughter off the island without the Council knowing. The guardians caught them before they could get out again . . . dealt with them, y'know? But the Council hushed it all up. They didn't want word getting out that the place might not be secure.'

'Yeah? Then who told you?' Noddy asks.

'Someone who was here at the time,' Nuke replies airily. 'They're not around any more. But listen, it was told to me in confidence. You can't mention it to the oldies – if you do, I'll deny I ever told you.'

Oh, she's *really* milking this. Her face has an expression that's almost triumphant as she gazes sidelong at Dutch.

'I don't think our parents even know this,' Smood pipes up, a troubled frown on his face. 'My mom would've told me if she knew. Her people would have been all over it. This is serious.'

'This is a goddamn shambles is what it is!' Duchess exclaims. 'We've been suspecting each other of blowing up the mon . . .' She's careful not to glance at Skip as she says this, '. . . when it could have been someone from the outside? This changes everything! What if this isn't just about *one of us* being guilty? What if it *is* someone from the outside . . . and they're targeting *all* of us? What if we've been cut off because there's some major military operation being carried out against the island? For all we know, the Council could be receiving ransom demands right now.'

'But who would do that?' I ask. 'And why?'

'Why?' Dutch retorts, a look of disbelief on her face, instantly making me feel hopelessly innocent and naive. 'Why do you think, Billy? Because of *who we are*. Because of who *you* are. For some people, that's reason enough.'

Chapter Thirteen
In Hell

I wake up hungry the next morning and, as always, the first thing I do is look at the time on my phone. It confirms what the light is telling me, let in through the billowing curtains, the colour of terracotta, that cover the glassless window: it's not long after dawn, five thirty-five. I groan, knowing I won't get back to sleep. On reflex, I check for updates on my Share page. Since the sat-link failed, it only connects me to the other studes, through the Hub. Yes, we all live within a hundred metres of each other, and yes, we still keep in touch online. I can immediately see that two things have changed. My Share page is offline, as is the island's home page, which tells me that the Hub is probably dead.

The second bit of news is that Buckley has lifted the ban that prevents us talking about Brother Valtere. I know this, because I can now mention his name . . . and his screams, which I hear as soon as I wake up.

Duchess and I saw Valtere when we searched Karava's villa – but I was blocked from mentioning it at the time. The putrid stink in the place was coming from his flesh, destroyed by burns. When I read back on it now, it is *so weird* that something so massively important is just blanked from my description of the place. But then my journal is riddled with blind spots like that. Hopefully, one day when I get home, I'll be able to go back and fill in all the gaps . . . if I can even remember it all.

It feels obscene that I couldn't mention Valtere was lying right there in Karava's bedroom as we searched, as if he was some guilty secret. Here was a human being, suffering horribly, and I had to write about the room as if he wasn't there at all. He was almost entirely uncovered because he couldn't bear the pain of a sheet touching his burned skin and though I didn't stare too long, the sight was scorched into my memory as if someone had taken a branding iron to my brain. I've never seen, or smelled, someone with those kinds of injuries, not in real life. When the infirmary was destroyed, most of our drugs went up with it. A few people had various mild painkillers and sleeping tablets they could offer, but Valtere's throat was so damaged by inhaling super-heated air, that he can't swallow. Half the man's body has been burned so badly it's like charred meat and, though he's covered him in an antiseptic cream, Karava can't give him anything to ease the pain.

My villa is on the east edge of the green and Dr Karava's place is the nearest building on the west side. Just one of my windows was smashed in the explosion, the one in my bedroom, and the night was still warm enough to sleep in the room. But that window faces out toward the green. I could have slept on the couch, but I was half-paralysed with exhaustion and needed the comfort of my bed like a drowning woman needs air. I couldn't mention the screams yesterday because of the block, but even after we left Karava's, we could hear them on and off for most of the day, while we carried out the searches.

They continued on through the night; Valtere would fall silent just long enough for you to be lulled into the hope that he might stay unconscious, but before long the wailing would start again. The precious little sleep that I got between those agonised cries was consumed by the boiling acid of nightmares, abstract visions of hammer blows and burst eardrums, the terror of bones disintegrating, though painlessly, as if I could no longer feel anything, the peeling away of charred skin, fat and muscle. I eat and eat and eat trying to replace the flesh falling from my body, but I can't eat fast enough . . .

Sorry . . . drifted off in a daze there for a minute. My limbs, shoulders and neck are stiff, my ears and jaw are sore and because I ate less than usual yesterday, I'm already gagging for breakfast. It won't be served until seven; the rations are now set and the morsels we're allowed, portioned by calorie count, are to be released at specific hours. The times and amounts have been worked out so that the food will last us a week. After that, it'll be gone.

I throw my arm over my eyes to block out the light and try to curse, but I can't.

I hear another long, raw-throated wail. For an awful minute, I *hate* Valtere for his screaming. I despise him for making us listen to his torment. When someone dies, it's tragic, but it's over. Someone who is fatally maimed, as he has been, they drag you in as they suffer, sucking your emotions into their own. I'm shocked at myself for the thought, but there it is.

I'm suddenly overcome with remorse at my callousness – not that that makes me feel any better about myself.

I need to run. Taking a quick shower to rinse the last couple of days from my skin, I towel myself down, put a bobbin round my wrist, but leave my hair untied so it will dry in the air. I pull on some fresh underwear and a sports bra – I'm running low on undies, so I definitely have to bring some stuff up to the laundrette – slip on a singlet and shorts and then my socks and trainers. The mundane routine is shifting my body into gear and I'm feeling better already. I drink a glass of water before I leave, then I emerge into the crisp air of the morning, drawing in deep breaths of it through my nose, feeling it rouse my soul.

On the far side of the lawn, I see Buckley walking away from me, northwards into the treeline. He's carrying a recurve bow in his right hand, a quiver of arrows on his back and a bundle of wire loops that I presume are homemade snares. Good luck to him; I've spent enough time in those woods to know there's not a whole lot running round in there big enough to be worth hunting.

I start out across the green, intent on heading past the guardians' villas and up the mountain trail to the Perch, then maybe down around the far side of the hill. Dr Karava is standing outside his house, smoking a cigar. That's the first time I've ever seen him smoke openly. He's clearly in a what-the-hell type of mood. When he spots me, he waves me towards him and I reluctantly turn in his direction, loping over with an easy warm-up stride.

'Morning, Billy. Where are you going?' he asks, puffing on the cigar.

'I just thought I'd take a run up to the hill,' I say. 'How's Valtere?'

'Valtere is . . . well, you can hear how he is,' the doctor replied. 'I'm afraid he hasn't got much time left.' He carefully stubs the cigar out on the pavement in front of him and slips it into a metal tube he takes from the pocket of his green short-sleeved shirt. 'Billy, you can't go for long runs any more.'

'What?' I grunt, taken aback. 'What are you on about? Is *running* banned now too?'

'Of course not,' he sighs, putting the tube back in his pocket and clasping his hands together in front of him. 'But you have to start thinking about your energy levels. Energy is like money: you should never use more than you can afford . . . and we're *broke*. You're going to be living on a fraction of your minimum daily calorie intake; you can't waste calories on activities that aren't essential.'

'I can't *not* run!' I protest, almost scoffing at him at the very idea. 'That's pretty essential to me!'

'How's your head?' he asks, abruptly changing the subject. 'Any problems since you were knocked unconscious?'

'No. No, I've been fine. A bit stiff, but nothing worth talking about.'

'Good to hear. It's a lucky thing you weren't any closer when the place went up. Very late in the night to be out though, wasn't it? I suppose you were out for a run then too?'

'Yeah, well . . . I go when I feel the need. I couldn't sleep.'

'Of course. Anyway, please forget the run this morning. You'll be using enough energy later on,' he tells me. 'Brother Buckley will be putting everyone to work. If you need something to do until breakfast, I would be very grateful for your help. How about it?'

I shrug, giving in to his logic, and reluctantly follow him inside. The stench hits me as soon as I walk into the bedroom. Valtere is lying naked, uncovered, on the large single bed. His face is barely recognisable, a pulpy mass of blistered, scorched skin, oozing blood and pus, peeling back in places, or missing altogether, exposing bare muscle and bone. Much of the rest of his body is in the same state. Karava has done his best with whatever soothing creams he has left and a succession of cold wet towels, but it's hopeless. Valtere's moaning dully, hoarsely, as if exhausted from his marathon screaming sessions.

Tears well in my eyes and a sob blocks my throat. I'm going to throw up if I stay here, I have to get out. *I have to get out.*

'He's soiled himself,' Karava says. 'I need you to help roll him onto his side so I can clean him up.'

I want to tell him there's not a hope in hell of me going anywhere near that bed, I'm just not cut out for this nursing crap . . . but then I remember the hate I felt earlier, what a horrible human being I was for that short while, and the thought of it is unbearable now when I see what Valtere's going through – the guilt and the overwhelming sympathy is worse than the thought of touching that ruined flesh.

'Okay, I'll do it,' I mutter, swallowing to hold down the bile trying to rise up my throat.

'Thank you.' He hands me a pair of disposable gloves and I put them on.

'Burns can get infected, can't they?' I ask, remembering my first aid. 'Have you given him antibiotics?'

'No. I only have a couple of bottles left, and we'll need them,' Karava says as he shows me how to hold the injured man at the shoulder while he takes the hips. 'I can't use them for him. He'll die soon. Any medication I give him now would be a waste.'

I put the back of my hand to my mouth, feeling the vomit rise again, and then I stare at him, shocked by the ruthlessness of the statement. Karava gives me a helpless grimace and shrugs.

'Is he conscious?' I gulp down bile. 'Can he hear us?'

'I'm not sure how conscious he is, but he can't hear us,' the doctor says sadly. 'His eardrums were destroyed; he's deaf . . . and blind. His eyes are gone.'

'Oh my God.'

'I don't believe in God, my dear,' he says quietly. 'But I believe in *hell*. And Brother Valtere is in hell. Dying would be a mercy. I can't put him out of his misery, because there's still a slim chance that a hospital ship might show up in time to save his life and that is my first duty, though he might not want it saved. Even without the internal injuries, with most of his skin in this state, he'd probably never feel much again but near-constant pain.'

It's not right. The sheer, cruel unfairness of it is almost too much to bear.

'We have to find who did this,' I rasp.

'Yes, we do.'

He motions me to pull with him and we roll Valtere onto his side towards us. The patient whimpers, but that's all the protest we get out of him. It must be agony to be handled like this, so I can only imagine that he *is* unconscious. As I hold him in place, Karava takes up the towel under Valtere's buttocks, stained with a small bit of excrement, a putrid pool of yellowish brown slime, and then lays another clean towel down to replace the soiled one.

I go to shift my grip slightly and a thick piece of skin sticks to my palm and peels off. I flinch, let out a choked sob and nearly let go, but Karava reaches over to press my hands back into place.

'It's all right,' he says in a kind voice. 'It's all right. You're doing fine.'

After watching him in the role of the soldier yesterday, violating the privacy of our homes, coldly professional, I feel like I'm seeing the man I know again. He's a real old world type, is the doctor, formal in his manners, the politeness serving to make him seem a little bit removed from everyone, but always kind and considerate. I'm grateful that he's here with us and glad I can do something for him.

We roll the patient over onto his back again and he lies there, his faint breathing rattling slightly, sounding wet and uneven, as if he's on the point of drowning. I remember that lungs can fill with fluid if you come close to being suffocated by smoke.

There are pus-sticky pieces of Valtere's skin stuck to the gloves as I pull them off and drop the inside-out pieces of rubber in a bin set in the corner of the room. I flop down in the chair beside the bed, where Karava must have been keeping his vigil. The doctor looks shattered and I quickly stand up again, offering the seat. He nods his thanks and sits down carefully. His hands and knees tremble as he sinks into the chair.

'He was the first one who really talked to me, when I came here,' I say. 'You remember when I arrived, and I ran off into the hills?'

'Oh, I remember,' Karava says with a dry smile.

'When he finally found me, I was up a tree and wouldn't come down. Valtere climbed up and sat near me, just talking. Nothing stuff, really . . . telling me about the island and some of the characters . . . We were there for nearly an hour. Here's this guy in his fifties, he *must* have been uncomfortable, but he just sat there and talked and waited till I was ready to come down by myself . . .'

'Yes,' the doctor murmurs. 'He always had a kind heart.'

I rub my hands over my face, feeling drained. If I couldn't sleep with the sounds carrying across the green, it must have been utterly traumatic to sit here in the same room. I regard the doctor with renewed respect.

'Have you seen injuries like this before?'

'Yes, many times. And much worse. Though I had hoped never to see them again.'

'Much worse than *this*?' I can't keep the disbelief from my voice.

'Oh, yes. When I was deployed to the Middle East, as a medic, when I was much younger man – and later in Europe as an army surgeon. Injuries like this are common in war. Particularly when a city was bombed with incendiaries, we would see casualties with these kinds of injuries. For me, the worst was when they would bring in children. They would come in, burned and broken, like this, often missing limbs . . . We saw things most of us would spend the rest of our lives trying to forget. The bombing of civilians was, for me, the most monstrous aspect of war. But, of course, we must *not* forget. Forgetting allows it to happen all over again.'

I don't say anything. It's one thing to see old news reports and read about these things or see them reproduced in films. It's another thing to listen to someone who lived through the bad times, to be able to relate it to the devastated, pain-ravaged body right in front of you. It's one of the few things I can rarely get Noon to talk about. She's told me all kinds of daft or interesting things that happened while she was in the army, but hardly any of the dark stuff.

'Things are very different now,' Karava assures me. 'After everything that's changed, Billy, I can tell you, it's a better world out there for you than it was for me.'

I think about the lost sat-link, the failure of the supply ship to show, the fact that nobody has sent an aircraft to check on us.

'Is it still?' I wonder aloud.

'Is it still what?' he grunts.

'A better world.'

He sniffs, but doesn't reply. I wish he would. Even if it was to offer a reassuring lie.

'What about starvation?' I ask. 'Have you ever seen people

suffering from starvation? Dying from it?'

He gazes up at me, wearily, and there's grief in his eyes. I'm rousing memories now and I'm sorry I brought it up, but I can't help myself. I have to know.

'Isn't this a rather morbid topic of conversation, Billy? Why do you want to do this to yourself?'

'I don't think you even need to ask, Doctor. You'd ask if you were in my position, wouldn't you?'

'Yes . . . yes, I suppose I would,' he admits, blowing out his cheeks. 'And yes, I saw starvation. As soon as any war breaks out, people will go hungry – waging war costs vast amounts of money, money that gets sucked out of people's normal lives. That is a crime in itself. Again, you see it particularly in the cities in the conflict zones, where they are so reliant on food from outside . . . but most of the last wars were basically provoked by a shortage of water or food and the land that has them. Also, starvation of a population can be a weapon itself. The worst I saw was in the people who were liberated from the concentration camps. And in the refugee camps. They were often malnourished over months or even years . . . to the point where they were in a horrendous state, like the living dead, little more than skin and bone.

'But it can happen even in normal society too, you know. Poverty, mental health problems . . . even in the most prosperous societies, people can starve to death. Gemmy is a case in point. He's *already* malnourished. In normal circumstances, if his mental condition deteriorated any further, I'd order him to be removed from the island to a specialized clinic. He'd be risking starvation. Obviously, transport isn't an option for the foreseeable future, so I'm especially concerned about him now.'

'What happens? I mean . . . in your body. What happens to your body when you starve?'

'Billy . . .' he protests in mild exasperation. 'Really . . .'

'Come on, take a look at our situation, Doctor. I need facts, not mollycoddling.'

He snorts, but it's resignation rather than a dismissal. Lifting his bushy eyebrows in reluctant agreement, he nods and sits up straighter, his tone now that of a tutor, patient and keen to impart knowledge.

'The human body is extraordinarily well adapted to deal with hunger, assuming you're not suffering from dehydration too,' he begins, resting his clasped hands on his thin thighs. 'Your main fuel is glucose, which you get directly from your food. It goes to your liver and your muscles, while the fatty acids you take in get stored away as emergency back-up. As long as your glucose levels are okay, you feel hunky dory. That's the normal state, for most of us.

'When your glucose starts running low, just a few hours after eating, hunger kicks in and you get that "hangry" thing. After about six hours without eating, much of the glucose stores in your liver will be used up and you'll be getting seriously grouchy.'

'Like Skip, you mean? Maybe that's his problem – he just doesn't eat enough.'

'Ha! No, he's *consistently* grouchy. Perhaps understandably so, I suppose. Sating his hunger would do little to change his mood. Anyway, over the next twenty-four to forty-eight hours, your liver will start getting very strict with the glucose, because glucose is essential for brain function, so the liver has to stop feeding it to the rest of your body. At this point, the sirens are going off and you're feeling *real* need . . .'

'I think I'm getting that at the moment. I can't believe it's still nearly an hour to breakfast.'

'It's early days for us yet, Billy, though I suspect you're going to find our "breakfast" will be a meal hardly worthy of the word. To continue answering your morbid question: You'll struggle to concentrate on ordinary tasks, find it hard to think about anything other than food. Deprived of its normal fuel, your metabolism goes into emergency mode, a state called "ketosis". That's when it starts using ketone bodies from your fat rather than glucose. These are the last *safe* reserves you have.

'After about seventy-two hours without food, your body is now burning into its fat – great news if you want to lose weight! But the brain has started running on ketone bodies, and that's *bad* news, because there are some parts of your brain that just *cannot* operate without glucose.

'Can you substitute coffee?' I ask. 'Because sometimes I can get like that without coffee.'

'No, you can't substitute coffee for glucose. Anyway, as time goes on, your reserves are drained and your body now starts digesting your *muscles* for protein. This provides your brain with glucose again, but the rest of you is now paying the price. Your body is effectively *eating itself*. How long you can last now is a matter of how much fat you have to burn, how healthy you are, whether you have any underlying conditions that might make things worse. If you weren't malnourished when you started and your heart's in good shape, you'll probably last a few weeks, but it will be extremely unpleasant.'

'Right, well thanks for that . . .' I say, trying to bring the disturbing description to a close.

'A couple of weeks in,' Karava continues, clearly on a roll now, despite his earlier misgivings. '. . . and you won't experience the hunger pangs like you were. Your brain is starting to malfunction, you'll be feeiling sluggish, dizzy, weak . . . You can also become impulsive, irrational and aggressive. Your organs are beginning to shut down, along with your immune system. Most people die of infection, rather than actual starvation . . .'

'Okay, I think I've got the idea . . .'

'. . . Before that happens, your eyes could be affected – hunger strikers have been known to lose their eyesight – you could suffer from diarrhoea, skin rashes, the build-up of fluids in your body tissue, around the joints, making movement painful . . . ironically, you can get fungi infecting your throat, making it hard to swallow . . .'

'*All right!* Jesus, Doctor. Enough!' I throw my hands up as if to fend off the horrors he's throwing at me. 'I'm sorry I asked! I get it, okay? It's an awful way to die.'

'And it's not going to happen to *you*,' he insists. 'We will use what we have and we will forage, hunt and fish for more. Some of the guardians are already out there right now. In the meantime, we are going to start planting crops. Ours is not yet a hopeless situation, Billy. Far from it.'

'No, of course, I realize that. I was just . . . I don't know . . .'

'Considering the worst case scenario,' he supplies.

'Yeah, I suppose.'

Neither of us says anything for a minute. We both gaze at Valtere's ruined body, listening to his clogged, strained breathing, trying to ignore the stink of burned flesh.

'Would you mind staying for a while?' Karava asks. The thin, leathery brown skin of his angular face is slack with exhaustion. 'I'd like to take a nap, if I could, but he could pass at any time . . . someone should be here with him . . .'

'I'll stay.'

'Thank you, Billy. It's very good of you.'

And with that, he's asleep in seconds, his head sinking onto his chest. A rustling snore begins a couple of minutes later. I bring in another chair and a glass of water and settle in to sit and watch Valtere die. A lot goes through my head. Less than half an hour passes before the breathing stutters, falters and goes silent. I lean forward, holding my ear above his mouth, then shake Dr Karava's shoulder. He wakes awkwardly, then puts on a fresh pair of gloves, puts two fingers to Valtere's neck and goes still for a minute. Satisfied that there's no pulse, he pulls off the gloves, takes his phone from his pocket and notes the time. Then he reaches down to the end of the bed and pulls a clean white sheet over the corpse.

'Thank you for being here, Billy,' he says again. 'You should go and get your breakfast now.'

I let out a breath I didn't realize I was holding. I can't think of anything to say, so I shake a nod and turn towards the door. I'm wiping tears from eyes, and yet I feel lighter, as if all I'd come here to do was witness Valtere's death. A job done. It's a sickening thought, after the way I cursed his screams earlier. I'd always thought I was a better person than this.

'It's all right to feel relieved,' Karava calls after me, so I turn to look round. He gestures towards the shrouded shape on the bed. 'When we see someone suffering like this, it's all right to feel relieved when they pass. It doesn't make you unkind. It just means you were affected by his pain . . . and that's only human, after all. He'd have been glad you were here.'

I shrug, a completely inappropriate response, but the best I can manage in the situation. The doctor seems to understand, because he inclines his head and shrugs back. This profound exchange completed, I stride off towards the picnic tables, where breakfast is being served.

Chapter Fourteen
Rations

There's a soft hazy rain starting to fall, and Sister Adeyemi meets us at the picnic tables to tell us breakfast will be served in the gym. As we hustle into the large building, the mood of the studes is like Valtere's skin was until just a little while ago, red raw and tender, painfully exposed by hunger and by the rasping away of our privacy during the searches.

The gymnasium is the guardians' new headquarters. After the monastery, it was the next biggest building. It has one large multi-purpose space, comfortably fitting a basketball court, a few smaller meeting or classrooms, changing rooms and storerooms, so it makes sense to run things from there. I can see they've already repaired the radio mast as best they can and mounted it on the flat roof of the building. Now all we need is a radio to hook up to it. Oh . . . and someone to fly or sail close enough to us to communicate with.

This is nuts. Somebody has to come for us soon. How long can the Council leave us out here in this state? *Someone* must be coming for us.

There are tables and chairs set up on the wide mezzanine level, above the gym floor, a makeshift canteen that seems to mock us, half the space taken up with the exercise and weights machines that have been moved back against the far wall, once a way of using up excess energy, now demanding more than we can afford to spend. The scraping of the chairs' plastic-capped steel feet on the polished floor is loud in a room filled with hard surfaces under a high ceiling.

For some reason I can't define, I don't tell them about Valtere. It's almost as if I'm not completely sure he's dead, that I don't have the authority to say it out loud and make it official by telling everyone else. Or maybe I just feel it shouldn't be my job. Whatever the reason, I hold it inside; a dark little piece of pain waiting to be shared.

With the demise of the melted slag that was once the Hub, our phones are now next to useless, which isn't helping the sullen atmosphere. The most disruptive factor, however, is Buckley's latest block on subjects that pretty much formed the basis for most of the casual conversation at mealtimes. Every time any banter gets going now, it gets tripped up by the censor chips when we stumble over a forbidden topic. It's frustrating and irritating, exacerbating all the tetchy feelings brought on by what Karava would refer to as our dwindling glucose reserves.

Skip is the last of the studes to come up the stairs and he takes a seat at a table on his own. No one greets him, though that's not unusual, and the studied indifference we show towards him hides a burning curiosity. Buckley has said no more about what was found in Skip's villa, so everyone wants to know what he was up to . . . and most of all, whether he'd got that radio of his working and if he had managed to pick up any signals from the outside world. We're digital signal junkies in severe withdrawal now, but nobody comes out and asks because we can't imagine he'd give us a straight answer, even if his censor chip would let him. There *will* be questions though, you can count on that. We'll all want to talk to him at some point, one way or another. After the time I just spent with Valtere, I've got a *lot* of bloody questions.

Brother Nguyen carries bowls of breakfast upstairs, carefully stacked in red plastic boxes. He and Adeyemi place them on a table near the top of the steps. Adeyemi is one of the chefs and the island's dietician. Before serving the food, the small woman stands in front of us, her broad, burnished black face, showing just a shade of grief, her demeanour carefully controlled. She's heard about Valtere. Her strong square hands are clasped behind her back, which is unusual, because she's normally so expressive with them; thick, short-nailed fingers that move with such delicacy. Her file lists her age as forty-two, but with hardly a line on her face and a body shaped by unflinching discipline, she could be anywhere from thirty to fifty. Her eyes look very old right now.

'I regret to say that Brother Valtere has died of his injuries,' she says, her accent emphasising the round sounds, the drop of the deeper notes. 'The funeral will be held once Sister Noon and the others have returned. This is a tragic loss for all of us; he was a good friend and a noble man, kind and generous of spirit. I will miss him dearly, as I'm sure many of you will. If any of you need to talk to someone about this loss, please share your feelings with your friends. Doctor Karava is available to anyone who needs counselling.'

And then her face sets in a very different expression, grim but compassionate, perhaps a little apologetic. She gestures to the bowls of breakfast.

'Listen to me now. The food has been divided out fairly. Every bowl contains the same number of calories and as even a balance of nutrients as I could manage. There can be no seconds, no extras. Drinking water might help to ease the hunger pangs, but what you see is what there is and there is no more until this evening. The guardians will be eating the same quantities. I am sorry we cannot do more for you at this time. When you have finished, please remain here. Brother Buckley wishes to have a word with you.'

'When does he *not* wish have a word with us?' Smood snorts.

Adeyemi ignores the comment as she and Nguyen begin to hand out the bowls. The reactions of the first ones to receive their food tell me how bad it's going to be, but when I finally get mine, I feel a hollow dread sink into my guts. This is it, my only food until the evening; three jelly babies, a few pieces of popcorn, eight raisins and a small carrot stick.

'Wanna swap your jellies for a piece of chocolate?' Nuke whispers to me. 'I'm lactose intolerant.'

I look across the table, where she's holding her own meagre helping. Hers is much the same as mine, except that she has a single square of milk chocolate to my three jellies. We measure each other up like poker players, trying to assess each other's hand. Nuke's been on the island longer than any other stude and she's okay, but she has this way of always making you feel like you've caused her some offence and that you owe her because of it. I stare into her flat face, with its high, angular cheek bones that jut straight and wide, suspending taut, flushed, tanned cheeks beneath them. She has a small nose that's almost the exact same shape as mine, a full-lipped mouth and grey-brown, East Asian eyes that always have a faint look of wariness about them. She brushes a strand of black hair off her face and lifts her eyebrows to prompt an answer from me.

Three jellies for one square of chocolate. I'm thinking she'll get more sugar out of the trade, but chocolate has that extra fat and protein. I'm getting the better deal.

Also, it's *chocolate*.

I scoop the jellies out of the bowl and quickly pass them across the table, taking the chocolate from Nuke even as I draw the hand back. We're fast, but I'm pretty sure Adeyemi still spots us. The guardian doesn't say anything. Knowing her, she probably figures there's only so much she can do to keep us fed and any wheeler-dealing is our own damn business. I start nibbling, determined to make the morsels last as long as possible.

'Well, looking on the bright side, at least it's gluten-free, right?' Duchess remarks as she gazes despondently on her collection of dried fruit and popcorn.

I can see that Gemmy has a forlorn look on his face. And it's no wonder – he's finished his already. He only got handed his bowl a minute ago. Pushing back his chair with a harsh squeak, he stands up and heads away from the table.

'I swear, if he throws that up,' Smood mutters, 'I'm sending him down the toilet after it.'

But Gemmy's just going to refill his bottle from the drinking fountain.

I'm delaying, now that I've nothing left but the chocolate, trying to hold on for as long as possible, but in the end, I gnaw away at it like a squirrel with a nut, eating it in little scraping nips. I wipe my finger around the bowl to make sure I got every little crumb, and it's only then that I see Skip holding the last bit of his breakfast. It's a piece of Dad's maple nut toffee. *F–(deleted)* . . . I don't have the chocolate any more to trade. Would he just give it to me, if I explained what it was? One of the others might, but I don't know about Skip . . . I stand up suddenly, hardly aware I'm doing it, but he's already put the toffee in his mouth and started chewing. I nearly gag at the thought of that precious substance being mangled between his teeth, covered in his spit. I can't believe it – of all the people, why did it have to be him? *Why him?* I let out a whimper that causes Nuke and Duchess to stare up at me, wondering what's going on, but I don't care. Flopping back into my seat, I press my hands against my eyes so the others can't see my tears.

'Aw bloody hell!' Gemmy gasps. 'I only just realized. We've no *coffee*. How did I not cop that until now? How are we going to get by without coffee?'

From the exclamations and groans let out around us, it seems some of the others hadn't thought of this either. There's probably no tea either. Wiping my eyes, I can't help chuckling a bit and Gemmy puts his hands to his face in mock grief and yells out loud:

'We've no coffee! Oh my good Lord above, WE'VE NO COFFEE!'

With a scattering of laughs, a few others join in and the melodrama catches on. Buckley comes into the room as everyone is wailing and pulling at their hair, wiping imaginary tears from their eyes and doing their best ham-acted sobbing at the loss of their coffees, without which, life surely isn't worth living. He heaves a sigh and folds his arms to wait for us to finish.

Chapter Fifteen
Brother Earnest

The pathetic meal has left me feeling more hungry than I was, maybe because it forces me to accept that there's no more food coming any time soon. The rain has stopped its breathy hiss on the windows and we're told to go and dress in old, expendable clothes and to put on some sun cream. Fifteen minutes later, we're all loaded into three of the island's SUVs and driven up the road out of the village.

When we take the first right turn, running parallel with the coast again, I can feel the mood in the car change abruptly as we all realize where we're going. This road only leads to one place; Brother Earnest's house. None of us have been up there before, but I've glimpsed his house through the trees, as I'm sure some of the others have if, like me, they've spent much time exploring the island.

You can feel it in the car's cabin; anxiety, like an excess of static electricity in the air, so much so that you expect to get zapped by it if you should touch any metal surfaces. Brother Mthembu is driving and Nuke leans forward to get his attention.

'Is Brother Earnest going to be there?' she asks, an edge to her voice that could be trepidation or excitement.

I'm feeling that buzz too. This is something different; a

clear breach of the rules.

'Yes,' Mthembu replies. 'He'll be directing the work today.'

'But . . . he's not allowed contact with us. Has there been word of anything?' I ask, my voice tight in my throat. 'Did someone get through on the radio?'

'Eh, what?' he grunts, glancing round. 'No. No, Billy. Brother Buckley has suspended the no contact rule because he decided that Brother Earnest's involvement is necessary. It's the *farm*. We're going to do some work on the farm.'

I swear, you will never have seen such relief on a bunch of teenagers' faces as they're told they're being put to work in the fields. Hot damn, *Brother Earnest has a farm*. I knew he grew some kind of plants out here, but a farm means *food*. Things must not be as bad we thought. There's a new eagerness to peer ahead, everyone craning their necks for the first sign of crops, an orchard perhaps, or vegetable plots.

The road rises over a low saddle in the hills, lined with Norfolk pines, a stalwart type of tree with military posture, originally planted by the first colonists here to be used for the masts of ships when they matured. Over the hump of the hill, we then descend along a steep, winding route, following the corridor of trees towards the coast again. If the images evoked by the word 'farm' had us imagining a pastoral utopia of meadows full of grazing cattle and a landscape of corn and wheat, bordered by hedges of fruit bushes and apple trees, the reality of what we see as we approach Brother Earnest's property brings us back down to earth with an arse-bruising thump.

His villa is the same size as one of ours, and of the same design, with three out-buildings – two smaller than the villa, one larger – constructed in the same style, encircling a yard the size of a basketball court. The red tiled roofs and concrete walls, plastered in a rough, textured finish and painted white, look as if they could have been transported straight out of our village. Fake Mediterranean architecture designed for suburbia, the materials airlifted across the Atlantic to be assembled as an incongruously familiar home on a wild rock in the middle of the ocean. The development sits on the left edge of a wide open stretch of bare earth, littered with stones, mud-covered branches of trees and the dried stalks of dead plants; apparently uncultivated land that sweeps in a gentle, rolling slope, down to the rocky beach.

It's a little more than a hundred metres to the rocks down there, which appear to be piled with heaps of churned earth. This open area is about the same distance in width, a rough hectare of exposed ground, carved into jagged furrows by what looks like a flood of water that has since dried up. The area funnels into a cup-shaped treeline at the upper end, where the road leads in and I can see a stream curving away around the western edge, the opposite side to the buildings.

There's a group of guardians, maybe seven or eight of them, already here, unloading shovels, spades and other tools from the flatbed of a pick-up and moving around the out-buildings. Our three SUVs pull up on the drive outside the gates of the yard and we all climb out, looking around in confusion.

'Okay, I give up.' Smood is the first to speak. 'Where's the farm?'

'You're looking at it,' a voice replies.

Brother Earnest is standing at the door of his house. He's dressed in the usual short-sleeved fern-green shirt and a pair of khaki shorts. His bony face is formed of hard edges, as if it was beaten into shape on an anvil by an artless blacksmith, who then coated as much of it as he could with bristling, thick black hair. He has the trimmed back body of a career soldier, no wasted flesh, strength without bulk, and the roasted tan of a white man who has spent his life outdoors.

'This is what was left after the, eh . . . the hurricane came through,' he says, coming over to us, sweeping his arm out to the view. He speaks in reluctant grunts and his voice has a rasp to it, as if his vocal cords have dried from lack of use. 'This island is a lump of rock with a thin skin of earth, and, eh . . . what little soil it *has* is held in place by the pines, or eh . . . Mexican thorn, the mesquite trees you see on the lowlands, especially around the beaches. The stuff has roots like you wouldn't believe, eh . . . deep burrowers and tough as hell. It took me four years to get this much land to the point where it could take crops. Over the last couple of years, you lot have been eating some of the food I've grown here.'

His inscrutable face is betraying a hint of pride, mixed with a bullish need to justify himself, defensive perhaps, because we've invaded his cherished privacy at a time when his land is in ruin. I suppose it's a big-assed, agricultural version of unexpected guests arriving at your home to find your laundry all over the floor. Earnest is embarrassed at the state of his place. He's spent years creating a farm and has nothing but this mess to show for it when visitors finally come calling.

'When that last hurricane hit, we had the worst flooding and mudslides I've seen since I came here,' he continues. 'I'd just, eh . . . planted a new round of crops and a flood came down off the hill, followed the course of the stream through the trees and swept through here, destroying all the crops, undermining the ground and dragging most of the fertile soil with it.'

We all follow his gestures, imagining the violence of the water. We've all seen the effects of flooding on other parts of the island, but nothing as bad as this.

As far as I know, Earnest lives alone. He doesn't have the same responsibilities as the other guardians, but though we tend to talk about him as if he's some hostile old hermit, he does work with the rest of island's staff. It's only the studes he has to keep clear of. The other oldies are kept busy with their duties around the village, so it's not like there's been a team of labourers coming out here to work this land. If the Order had decided we needed a farm, they'd have shipped machines in here, crews of farmers, engineers and landscapers to do the job properly, efficiently, in the same way they created the village.

Instead, the island's creepiest guardian has been out here by himself, clearing the land, tilling it, laying fertiliser and planting seeds. We don't get to hear much about what he does day to day, but this can't be a task that he was ordered to carry out on his own. Or was it? Given his reas–*(deleted)* . . . that he's–*(deleted)* . . . oh, for the . . . just *let my mind go*, you itching little brain maggot! . . . It's . . . It's not as if he's here to be *punished*, is it? At least, not whe–*(deleted)* . . . But this . . . this is like he's sentenced himself to hard labour. Maybe it's driven by guilt.

And now he expects us to join him.

'We need food, so we need to get planting fast,' he goes on. 'Of the seeds we have from the stores, the, eh . . . the crops that will give us the quickest yields are radishes, turnips . . . spinach, eh . . . kale, beans and beets. Most of these can be harvested after about forty to sixty days.'

'Forty to sixty days?' Smood exclaims in dismay.

'. . . Before we can plant, we need to bring some of the soil from the bottom of the hill and spread it back over the ground up here.'

'We need to . . . what?' Noddy asks, his head tilted at an angle that suggests he must have misheard. 'What do you mean?'

From the guardian's impatient expression, it's clear that either he's not used to dealing with people our age – or he genuinely thinks Noddy's a bit slow.

'The *soil* we need to grow the *food* is piled up on the *rocks* down *there*,' Earnest repeats with excessive emphasis, his voice carrying more conviction as he starts giving instructions. 'We'll divide into three work parties; one will bring soil up, the second group will spread it, and the third will be digging a deeper ditch to channel the stream, to divert the water in case we get another flood. Once we have the first few rows laid out, we can start planting, but there were at least two more storms forecast over the next few weeks and we need to protect our crop.'

'You're joking, right?' Noddy scoffs. His head leans forward, eyes looking out from under his blond eyebrows, challenging the guardians' assertions. 'We're not f–. . . not frickin' *farm labourers*. I'm not digging any damn *holes*. The Council have abandoned us on this stupid rock and you're the ones who are paid to do a job here. Our welfare is *your* responsibility. We're in this f–. . . cocked-up situation because you and your organisation failed to prepare properly. *I'm not carrying any goddamn mud up a freakin' hill!*'

Judging by Earnest's pent-up manner, I reckon he's more used to dealing with soldiers he can order around, rather a bunch of teenagers who can simply refuse to work and tell him to go stuff himself. It's as if the man's making an exaggerated effort to be reasonable. But now, as he opens his mouth to bark a reply at Noddy, Mthembu speaks first.

'There will be guardians and students in each group,' he says in his slow, trundling voice, without addressing Noddy directly. The long man is standing off to the side, his corded arms folded. From his tone, I get the sense that he's not just answering Noddy, he's trying to manage Earnest's expectations in dealing with this gang of privileged teenagers. As in, don't expect too much. 'The brothers and sisters who are not here with us are out in the hills, trying to find food, a task that requires skills that none of you have yet . . .'

I notice that 'yet'. Like this fiasco is expected to go on long enough for us to *pick up* these skills. Good holy frickin' hell.

'The more everyone helps out with what needs to be done,' he continues, 'the more food we will all have to eat. It's that simple. Now, please listen: You're running on small rations and most of you are not used to this kind of work. Take it slow and steady, work at an easy pace. Drink plenty of water. Slow and steady, and you'll do fine.'

Earnest's jaw muscles twitch as he waits for Mthembu to finish, then he turns his head to stare at us for a few moments, as if he needs to reassess what he has in front of him.

'Right, let's get on with it,' he says. 'These crops won't plant themselves.'

Chapter Sixteen
Hard Graft

I stand up, leaning on my shovel and wipe my forearm across my brow, but both my arm and forehead are so covered by sweat, that all I feel is the slickness over my skin, its salty sting seeping down into my eyes. I rub the back of my work-glove across my face instead; it's already damp to the point of saturation, but it wipes away the worst of the sweat dripping from my eyebrows. My throat feels like leather and I pick up my water bottle from the ground and take another few sips. Tipping my head back makes me feel dizzy. The sun is bright and laser harsh, and though the guardians gave us boonie hats to wear, mine feels too hot to keep on over my thick hair. It's not as bad as the heat can be during summer on the island, but we've never laboured like this before and the air is so close and soft with humidity, I can feel the fuzz of it against my skin, hinting at another storm to come.

I'm at the bottom of the hill, on one corner, looking up at the gently sloping, rough, ruined ground, watching Smood push the wheelbarrow up the trail that runs down the left side of the field. I'd have to admit that he looks good, his toned, sun-kissed legs pumping hard, climbing that incline, and I think he's actually enjoying himself. I'm pretty sure he's never used a wheelbarrow before and I suppose this physical, mind-free work is satisfying in the same way routine exercise can be. Mthembu keeps telling him to slow down, take it easy, but that's not Smood's way. He always has to set the pace, make the rest of us keep up with his work rate. Without a decent amount of food to fuel those fine legs, we'll see how long that keeps up.

Duchess, Cheeks and Moose are working down here with me, loosening the muck, sifting the stones out of it and shovelling it into the barrows. Five more of the studes are further over to my right, near the other corner, forming a second team to move earth along the trail running up the far side. The rest of the gang are up near the top of the field, raking out the fresh earth into rows and tipping compost over it. I can see Gemmy up near the house; he's on his knees, scooping the compost into mounds with his hands, already planting seeds. I clench my teeth at the sight. We've been at it for about two hours and everyone else is feeling the strain, but Gemmy's getting off easy. Earnest has excused him from the heavy work on health grounds.

There are a dozen other guardians here, who are doing the more strenuous work of digging ditches and drainage channels around and down the length of the field, to carry floodwater away from our valuable crops. At the rate they're working, it looks like that operation could take three or four days to finish. I don't know how long it will take to get all the seeds planted.

There's a new tightness across my shoulders and the top of

my back, sore cords of tension, and more of it through my hands and forearms. Mthembu gave us all gloves, but I can still feel the rubbing burn of blisters coming up on my palms from handling the shovel. As I take deep breaths, waiting for Skip, on his way down with his empty barrow, I turn to scowl at Noddy, who's sitting with his back to me, on a boulder out on the beach, gazing out to sea through the heat-shimmering air. He has flat out refused to work, claiming this is the guardians' mess and they need to sort it out. Selfish, lazy asshat pillock.

Nuke's been making a drama of it too. She's as fit as any of us; with her gymnast's figure, strong thighs and shoulders, narrow, boyish hips, she's well able for this, but she's been complaining about one thing after another ever since we started. She was supposed to be doing the raking up at the top, but I can see her halfway along the trail, arguing with Earnest again. To give respect where it's due, if she's intimidated by him, she doesn't show it. I can't hear what she's saying, but she sure is lettin' rip at him. To hell with that crap. Everything's a problem with her. If she doesn't like it, let *her* come down and do some bloody digging. I'd happily prance about with a rake for a while.

Duchess is trying to pry a rock out of the muck. It became clear to me today that she's never used a shovel or spade before. I suppose her family has gardeners for that kind of thing. It took over an hour for her to stop treating her spade like a frickin' soup spoon. She's getting the hang of it now, but she's still being too delicate with it. Mum and Dad have been getting me out to work in the garden since I was eight or nine. We never grew vegetables; it was mostly about weeding and pruning and making the flowerbeds look nice before we'd have a slap-up lunch and sit out reading. It was something to do together at the weekends when Dad was home, so digging isn't new to me, but even I'm finding this hard graft. Duchess curses at the rock and drops her spade.

'Toilet break,' she says to Cheeks, who's next to her, then starts up the trail to the house.

That's her third toilet break in two hours, and she always heads up to the villa rather than going in the trees about twenty metres away. I'm getting very tired of her precious little ways.

I sigh out a breath and jam my shovel into the earth again. Skip's almost at the bottom of the hill and I need to have a heap of loose muck ready to shovel in. That means getting as many of the stones and rocks out of it as I can, and they're riddled through the compacted earth, making the digging awkward, every hard bang of the blade jolting through my tired arms, sometimes forcing me to bend down and use my gloved fingers to prise out a large one or pick out smaller bits. Earnest has drilled this into us: every piece of stone is useless weight, more load for the person pushing the barrow that will only have to be thrown aside when the earth is being spread on the vegetable beds. It's painfully frustrating work, but it has to be done, so I'm bloody doing it. I wish they'd let me have a go with the barrow, but Earnest says I'm not strong enough. He's an asshat too.

I think I might be getting hangry.

The need for food bites at the inside of my belly, making me groan, a weak shudder running through me. By the time Skip reaches me, I've still only got half a load for him. Moose and Cheeks are sifting stones and weeds out of other piles with their pitchforks, further along. Moose is struggling. He's carrying all the extra body weight and he's suffering even more than the rest of us in this heat. He and Cheeks throw Skip dirty looks, moving away from us as if they have something else to do, so Skip has time to sit down and wait while I load him up. With the others out of the way, I can finally put the question to him that I've been gagging to ask.

I try not to think about the piece of Dad's toffee he ate earlier, because it was like watching him chew on a piece of my home and that only makes me want to smack him across the head with my shovel.

Don't get personal. Just the facts, Billy. Just the facts.

'Hey,' I say in a low voice.

'Hey,' he says back, sitting down on a rock and shaking out tight arms.

'Buckley give you a hard time yesterday?' I ask.

'Not so muh-muh-muh-much,' he replies, eyeing me

warily. 'He's a puh-puh-puh-puh-pussycat really.'

I smile because it's almost funny and he deserves credit for the effort. Digging the blade of my shovel into the ground to stand it up, I rest my hands on my hips.

'The radio though, that was a pretty outrageous thing to do. Did you manage to get it working? Have you . . . heard anything? From outside, I mean?'

Skip lowers his head, his slightly slanted, cat-like eyes glaring up at me; it's almost as if I can see the defences coming up, the gates slamming shut.

'Did I puh-puh-puh-pick anything up from outside?' he snorts. 'You muh-muh-muh-muh-mean like something I didn't want anyone else to hear? Something that wuh-would muh-make me want to, say . . . *cut off our communications?* Is *that* what you muh-muh-mean, Billy?'

'No, I just meant–.'

'Did I hear suh-something that muh-muh-might make me want to buh-buh-buh-blow up the Hub and suh-suh-steal the spare radio? Like that, d'ya muh-mean?'

'Skip, I was just–.'

He stands up, bringing his face in close to mine, his whole posture threatening, but a look of polite inquiry on his face.

'Suh-suh-sorry, are you asking if I buh-buh-*burned Valtere to death*, or are you just making puh-polite conversation?'

When I don't answer him immediately, he pulls back again, his shoulders relaxing, his face crunching into a frustrated grimace, his fury no longer directed at me, but at the thoughts running through his head.

'I never got the radio fuh-finished,' he tells me. 'Buh-Buh-Buckley and Muh-Mthembu could suh-see that as soon as they wuh-wuh-wuh-walked in. I did take the electronic puh-parts from the muh-muh-mon, though. The puh-place was, well . . . a buh-bomb-site. I figured they wuh-wuh-wouldn't miss a few pieces.'

He falls silent, remembering it. When he speaks again, his voice is low, only for my ears. He's calmer and doesn't seem to stammer as badly now, his thoughts casting back to the night of the disaster.

'If the Hub was the main target, than whoever caused the explosion suh-suh-screwed up,' he says sourly. 'I think they only muh-meant to flood the Hub room with gas and cause a blaze in there . . . to wreck the radio and computers. They didn't muh-mean to destroy the whole buh-building.'

'What?' I say. 'How do you know?'

'I puh-puh-poked around in that room after the fire was put out, found the damage in the gas pipe where the leak suh-suh--suh-started. It was deliberate damage. Whatever flame was suh-suh-supposed to start the fire *didn't work*. The gas kept leaking out into the rest of the buh-buh-building. It ended up filling the whole puh-place before it was ignited buh-buh-by some spark or flame, muh-maybe just one of the candles in the muh-meditation room.

'The gas wuh-wuh-wuh-would have taken a long time to suh-spread, muh-maybe an hour or more. Valtere should have suh-smelled it and raised the alarm.'

Skip stares at me, his eyes hardening as they fix on mine.

'Noddy was right. Valtere died and now we're going to suh-*starve* buh-because the good brother was puh-passed out *drunk* when he was suh-supposed to be *on watch*.'

The violence comes over me before I even know what I'm doing. The trauma of watching Valtere's last breaths, the hunger, the horrible tension over the last couple of days, it all boils up inside me and I'm lunging at Skip, swinging my right fist at him. He's lucky – if I'd been holding my shovel, I'd have swung that instead. He flinches back instinctively, but my knuckles still catch him across the cheek. My left fist flails in for a second punch, but it's angry and wild and he knocks it aside. Grabbing my arm, he flings me away from him using my own momentum.

There's no way to know if he's done it on purpose or not, but I'm thrown forwards, my knees cracking painfully against the back edge of the wheelbarrow and then I'm flipping over it, the steel corner on the front scraping along my left arm and thudding against my ribs, my weight pulling the barrow over with me as I thump onto the ground and it tumbles over me, clanging against the back of my head.

I lie there stunned, wincing in pain and trying to curse, my chip suddenly making me stammer worse than Skip. He's standing over me, hands reaching for me, embarrassment and apology on his face. Then he's slammed aside as Smood crashes into him, tackling him to the ground. Moose and Noddy follow seconds later, all three of them pinning Skip with their knees, laying in punches to his head and torso.

'Wait!' I shout, getting up on my hands and knees, my head reeling woozily, the ribs on my left side feeling like they've got a hot metal strap clamped around them. 'Wait! Leave him alone! I started it! *Smood! Let him go!*'

Their blood is up and they're not stopping, so I stand up and land a sound kick up Smood's arse. He's surprised enough to look round.

'Get off him!' I shout. 'It's my fault – I started it!'

My three knights in shining armour finally pull themselves away, flopping back on the ground. After their labours this morning, that quick blast of aggression has emptied them out. Honestly . . . *boys*; any chance for a bit of righteous violence . . . I step past them and help Skip drag himself into a sitting position. He's got blood smeared around a split lip and running from one nostril, but otherwise he looks okay. Maybe he'll have a black eye too. He shrugs off my hands, pushes past me and grabs my shovel. Righting his wheelbarrow, he half-fills it with rushed, jagged movements and then sets off up the hill. I put my hands to my dirty, sweat-coated face, feeling my skin flushing hotly as I close my eyes, thinking I probably could have handled that better.

Ah, sod it. Nobody here is having a good day.

Cheeks is standing a few metres away, looking at the guys, flashing them a dimpled sneer and clapping her hands in that slow, sarcastic way she has. Though I'd have to agree that they charged in like clumsy young bulls, I can't help but feel grateful, and it occurs to me that Cheeks's cute, golden-tanned face with those well-crafted but prominent teeth, is looking particularly chipmunkish today, sitting atop her stick-thin body. In my severely hangry state, I'm about to voice this observation, when Smood takes a scan around and then waves the snarky cow over, coming up on his hunkers and leaning forward to the guys, his body language suggesting he's got some juicy bit of gossip to pass on. This is like oxygen to Cheeks, so she's over to us in seconds, crouching in close to Smood, her long bare leg brushing against his.

'Listen, Earnest has some *animals* up there,' Smood says in a near-whisper, even though the nearest other people are fifty metres away. 'There's some fenced-in areas behind the villa, in among the trees. I saw a few sheep, a goat, I think. I'm pretty sure I heard chickens too.'

Actually, I'd been aware of this already; I've heard the bleating of goats or sheep while I was out on my runs around the hills. I'd just never connected that awareness with my need to eat. It would be like considering eating one of the cats that live in the village.

'. . . That's gotta be a few days worth of meat for all of us right there,' Smood goes on. 'Wonder why they haven't mentioned it?'

I need a moment to take this in, but Moose asks the question before I can, the full, cushioned features of his deep brown face wrinkling in disgust.

'You mean eat meat . . . from an *animal*? You'd do that?'

I know that many of the studes are completely vegetarian, Moose being one of them. The rest of us will eat fish, and y'know . . . normal meat. The type that doesn't come from animals. I mean, it's one thing to eat cloned flesh grown in a tray in a factory – but only committed carnivores eat actual *mammals*. 'Walking' meat wouldn't be served on the island. And even assuming you'd want to chow down on the stuff, most ordinary people could never afford it. The thought of chewing on something that had been alive, that moved and breathed . . . something with eyes and a tongue, snaking veins and arteries, intestines and bones, bowels that passed dung . . . something that had a *brain* and *feelings* . . . . a body that would have to be butchered, the bones pulled apart at the joints, the organs cut out of it . . . I nearly gag right there, even as Moose says it.

'I've only eaten free range flesh three times in my whole life and I swore I'd never do it again,' Smood says simply. 'But I'd eat an animal rather than starve – I'd kill it myself, if I had to. Wouldn't you? When Noon comes back with fish, how many of you will say no? Seriously? We're only a couple of days in, and this could go on for weeks. How hungry are we going to get? How many of you will say no to the flesh of fish? Killing mammals is only one step further. There's no way the oldies can let us starve while there are animals to eat and I'm not going to say no to it when they do.'

It's hard to argue with that. After all, only a few decades ago, people ate the stuff every day. Animals were farmed in their masses, like crops, right to the point where the planet couldn't sustain it any more; domestic animals were being fed even as humans starved and most livestock farming just had stop. As the sea and environmental disasters claimed more land, the fields used for livestock had to be given over to growing crops. Most people either ate factory meat or became vegetarian. Walking meat became regarded as a sinful treat, only eaten regularly by the feckless rich and cold-blooded gourmets.

I'm sickened to be considering it, but for us, it could end up being a desperate measure and Smood's right: I'd eat animals rather than starve. Everybody has gone quiet, each one of us weighing up this new line of thought.

'So what about our cats?' Noddy asks abruptly. 'Would you eat a cat?'

'Whoah, man! Don't let Gemmy hear you say that!' Cheeks exclaims.

'Would you, though?' Noddy persists. 'Would you eat a cat?'

'Are you kidding?' Smood says, letting out a bitter laugh. 'This is *survival* we're talkin' about. Man, if things got bad enough, I'd eat *you!*'

Chapter Seventeen
The Stranger

We finish up for the day at around four in the afternoon and we're all done in. No one has anything to say as we're driven back to the village after our labours in the field. We're mucky, stiff and sore, but there's a feeling in the car of weary satisfaction – at least among the people who actually *did some work* – our bodies enjoying the stillness granted by real fatigue. We've grafted for hours and the knots of tension from the last few days have been exercised from our muscles. Though the team of studes and oldies got less than a quarter of the field planted, Earnest said it was enough to be getting on with and gave us a nod of grudging respect that we accepted as his best attempt at gushing praise.

As the electric SUV glides down the hill to the village, the only sound its chiming hum and the roll of the tyres, we get a clear view out into the bay, past the toxic green of the algae blooms, the open ocean a dazzling pearly grey in the light of a bright, but overcast sky. Moose, who's in the front seat jabs a finger at the sea.

'Hey, it's Noon! Noon's back!'

The boat, the *Santiago*, a handsome fifteen-metre schooner, is on its way into the harbour. Mthembu slows so we can all have a look from our high vantage point and I see that the two-masted boat is handling sluggishly, far too low in the water, that sleek hull dragging awkwardly despite still being under full sail. When they'd set out four days ago, Noon and the two guardians with her had been concerned about a slow leak they had been unable to fix. It appears the leak has been taking its toll. Mthembu drives on past the village to take us down to the dock. By the time we get there, the *Santiago's* sails are down and it's manoeuvring up to the pier under engine power. We jump from the car and mill around, waiting for the new arrivals. Eager hands grab the lines the sailors throw up, securing them to the dock cleats as the boat bumps against the rubber fenders along the concrete and stone wall.

We don't wait for an invitation, Smood leaps aboard, then Gemmy and then me. The polished woodwork above deck looks intact, but the engine is making an uncomfortable straining noise, before it's shut off. With the hatches open, we can hear the sound of someone down in the hold, sloshing through water. That means the leak has completely overwhelmed the bilge pumps. Not a good sign. Brother Sengupta appears from below, hefting a couple of shallow plastic boxes up onto the deck. Gemmy takes them off his hands. That'll be the fish, covered in crushed ice; I've *never* been so happy to see boxes of dead fish. Sister Thompson is finishing tying up the sails and Smood ducks under the boom to help. The guardians are in shorts and t-shirts under their compact, bright red life preservers, and I notice that Sengupta and Thompson both have their large fishing knives in sheaths strapped to their belts. I wouldn't have thought they'd be doing any fishing close to the island – there's not usually much to catch.

Noon, who was at the helm, smirks at me as I come up to her. Her thick, curly black hair hangs lankly, damp from sea-spray, around a face that's all flat planes, elegant but hard, like a cut crystal. She has a long, delicate nose, high cheekbones and thin lips, her white skin weathered and freckled, seamed with fine, shallow lines. Her eyes are the only rounded curves, almost circular, with irises so dark brown they look black. She's nearly a head taller than me, with wide shoulders for a woman, and the lean frame and upright posture of a career soldier.

'I was hoping you'd be gone by the time I got back,' she grunts.

'I was hoping you wouldn't come back,' I retort.

'I think you've got shorter while I was gone.'

'No, that's just your eyesight failing, you old bag.'

'My eyes are fine, thanks, they're just *watering* from the smell of *you*, ya little turd.'

'Like you'd know. You've got the biggest nose I've ever seen and you still can't smell past your own *breath*.'

This is how we relate to each other. You're just going to have to go with it. I'm bulging with emotion and I want to throw my arms around her and hug her, but we don't normally touch much and or make too big of a thing of our friendship when there are others around. I've missed her almost like I'm missing home and seeing her again makes me feel like everything is going to be all right after all. Noon will *make* it right – it's what she does.

'What the hell have you all been up to while I was away?' she asks. 'Why do you look like someone buried you up to your ears in muck? Is this why nobody's answering the bloody radio?'

I open my mouth and then close it again. Of course . . . she still doesn't know. Apart from the top of the low bell tower, the monastery is blocked from view if you approach the island around the headland to the east, as they've done today. She won't have been able to see the ruin until she reached the dock and could look up along the road, between the student villas and the gym. I'm trying to figure out what to tell her first when she lifts her gaze and finally sees what's left of the mon. Her face goes slack with shock.

'Holy shit!' she gasps, leaping over the rail onto the pier and taking some faltering steps toward the road. 'What the . . . Jesus, what happened?'

Sengupta and Thompson both let out curses and stare at the demolished building. A second SUV has pulled up and Duchess, Nuke, Noddy and a few others get out. Buckley is striding out the pier towards us, accompanied by some more guardians. Noon has the look of someone who's just been punched in the face. She gapes at the ruin and then casts her eyes around her, seeking answers.

'What the fuck *happened?*'

Buckley takes control of the situation, before all the studes can start smothering the new arrivals in different versions of the story. He wants to brief Noon on our latest dramatic change of circumstances himself, and he waves the other two guardians over to him. Everyone's distracted by this, but I'm a bit taken aback at Noon's lack of her composure – I was kind of expecting her to just take it all in and then start barking instructions – so as I study my mud-caked walking boots on the wooden deck, chewing my lip in dismay, I'm the only one who doesn't have their attention on Buckley and Noon when Sengupta brings someone else up from below.

We get three kinds of visitors to the island, apart from studes and guardians: Parents of studes, random dignitaries being given a tour, and the occasional gaggle of security-cleared personnel needed to support the guardians in their work here. The guy who emerges from the cabin of the *Santiago* does not fall into any of these categories. As sometimes happens, my mouth reacts before my manners do.

'Who the hell are you?'

I've obviously said this loud enough for everyone to hear, because they all turn round to look too. The man looks Hispanic, deeply tanned, and though he's small – not much taller than me – he looks strong and has the rough, calloused hands of a labourer, perhaps a fisherman. Despite seeming a bit beat up, he moves easily, loose-limbed, lightly built, but with long arms that give him an ape-like appearance. There isn't much of his thinning dark hair left on his head; what little remains there on the sides and back is shaved short.

Staring back at us, his deep-set, squinted eyes and a sunken stub of a nose fit into the prominent but rounded bone structure of a face that's both boyish and skull-like. He must be at least in his thirties, but his expressions don't seem like a mature man's, flickering instead between a sneery, ingratiating smile and a defensive grimace with the insecurity of a young brat who's been separated from his gang. His black fleece and grey work trousers are filthy and creased from long wear, stained with salt and sweat and engine oil. The top of his head and the upper surfaces of his face are sunburnt too. I'm thinking this guy was out on the sea longer than he'd intended to be. He pulls at his crotch, as if finding comfort from it – I don't think the gesture is aimed at us – and then gazes past us, taking in his surroundings.

I know it's unkind, but the thought that's foremost in my mind as I see this man is: Great, another mouth to feed. The last thing we needed was someone else to cut into our dwindling supply of food. And he looks in a worse state than any of us.

I notice Sengupta has his hand on the man's arm as he leads him to the rail, letting go only as the stranger climbs up onto the pier. Whoever he is, he's not meant to be here. Maybe he's even the reason Sengupta and Thompson are wearing their knives. Besides, I'm pretty sure we'd have heard if the *Santiago* was expected to pick up an extra passenger. The guy isn't comfortable with all the attention and I'm wondering if he even knows where he's just landed. He juts his chin out in greeting to us, giving us a flat smile as he grunts in a husky voice:

'Well. Here we all are!'

Skip is near the front of the group that have gathered on the pier and I could swear the man's eyes linger on him longer than the others. The stranger swivels, taking in the rest of them and then . . . yes, he looks back at Skip, almost as if he recognises him, his face opening in that way you do when you're about to say something to someone, and then hesitate. He doesn't speak, and when he catches me looking at him, he drops his eyes again.

I might be making too much of this. We're all kind of famous, in our weird way — some of us will even be serious celebrities when we get home — so it's very possible that he knows Skip's face; which would mean he realizes where he is. Still, he seems to be trying to hide his reaction, which has me wondering.

'This is Matthias Almeida,' Noon introduces him. Her voice is carefully neutral. Although she's not acting openly suspicious towards him, it's obvious she's treating him with caution. 'We pulled him off a sinking boat. Mister Almeida has a story to tell that might explain what's happened to our communications. He claims he was out alone on the vessel, but–.'

'We'll talk to him inside,' Buckley says sharply. 'Take him up to my villa. Ask Doctor Karava to join us, so he can check him over. It looks like he's been through quite an ordeal. All the students should take a break before dinner; you've worked hard today and you need to rest.'

'Whoa! Hold on a second, we need to know what's going on here!' Duchess speaks up, determination in her face and voice, the look in her eyes intense as she regards the stranger. 'We're not going anywhere. If he can tell us what's happening out in the world, we need to hear his story.'

'We'll tell you everything once he's been examined and we've spoken to him first,' Buckley says, in a voice like a written law. 'He's on the island without clearance, so he's not allowed any contact with you. This is now a security matter. Go back to your villas and rest. I'll call a meeting when we have information for you. Sister Thompson, Brother Mthembu, put Mister Almeida in a car and take him up to my villa. I'll be there shortly.'

And though Thompson and Mthembu don't touch the visitor, their body language is all business as they motion the studes out of the way and usher Alemeida towards the SUV. Once he's inside, Buckley turns to Noon.

'How did the fishing go?'

Noon nods toward the two crates Sengupta and Gemmy are loading into the back of the other car.

'That's it. There wasn't much to be had. We went fifty klicks beyond the exclusion zone and still didn't find squat. The waters are fished out. There's only so much you can catch with rods anyway. We'd need a trawler and nets to pull in anything in quantity. How much food did we lose? What's our supply situation?'

'Not good. I'll give you the details up at the house,' Buckley mutters. He glances at the crates. 'If those are full, that will maybe feed us for . . . I'd say it'll give us about another two days. Still . . . better than nothing. What about the radio? Did you pick anything up?'

'A couple of distant beacons, probably from buoys, and some garbled rubbish. Nothing coherent. I don't know if anyone heard our calls,' Noon replies. Her voice hints at more concern than she's showing. She glances at me, perhaps deciding how much she can say. 'There was nothing on the radar either. Not a single vessel, no aircraft, no drones . . . It's like goddamn limbo. No sign of the Council patrols. Look, you need to hear Almeida's story. If he's telling the truth, something big's going on out there.'

'Something big's going on back here too,' Buckley tells her. 'How's the boat? Could we sail some of our people out of here?'

'No, we barely made it home,' Noon says, shaking her head. 'The leak around the prop shaft is worse than ever and I don't have the parts here to fix it. I could patch it up again, but you wanna try and sail fifteen hundred klicks weighed down with all the bodies we can carry and the supplies they'd need, taking on water the whole way? Uh uh. With the winds this time of year, you're looking at a minimum ten-day trip. The last forecast we got said there were at least two more storms on the way. She'd never make it through those kinds of conditions.'

I'm soberly taking all this in. Noon's trip over the horizon, beyond the island's hundred-kilometre exclusion zone and out into the shipping lanes, had been a solid reason to hope that help would come for us. At the very least, we knew that once Noon became aware of the situation here, she could sail back to the mainland and fetch help the old fashioned way. Now we don't even have that. Great. Totally frickin' awesome. Sometimes, hope is a hairy-assed pig in a princess dress.

'That's that, then,' Buckley says. 'Well, at least we have a radio again . . . even if we can't *reach* anyone with it. I want you to take a look at the bomb-site this evening. In the meantime, we'd better go talk to Mister Almeida.'

Chapter Eighteen
Observation Post

The other studes and I are not allowed into Buckley's villa to hear what our new visitor, Matthias Almeida, has to say, but that doesn't mean there's no way to listen in. I can come clean about my guilty secret now, seeing as I've just been *found out* and Buckley knows the score about my little observation post (if you're reading this, Brother Buckley: Hey! How ya doin'?! Again, I'm really sorry about the whole invasion-of-your-privacy thing, but then you are *reading my journal*). So, having been caught with my pants down, so to speak, there's no reason not to post this whole episode now, is there? Godammit.

Anyway, we'll get to the bit where I'm nabbed in a few minutes. Let's do this in order:

As soon as Buckley and Noon head up the road towards his house, I hurry through the cluster of students' villas, then take a winding diagonal route which will bring me up to the green. Stopping off at my place, I quickly shove some laundry into a wicker basket and, carrying that, I walk casually up the road towards the laundry room, which is on the far side the monastery. I dump the basket on my shelf in the laundry, knowing I'll have the clothes back, freshly pressed by tomorrow evening. I'm one of the few studes who actually brings their own laundry up rather than waiting to have it collected. It gives me an excuse to walk up past the front entrance to the monastery and round the side. I have other excuses for this too, depending on the day.

It's weird being up here, because this is about where I would have been when the explosion happened. It's hard to remember details. The side door is facing me – or the the remains of the door*way*, at least – about twenty metres away. It was a sturdy fire-door, reinforced oak with a small window at face height. I get a moment of flashback as I look at the gaping hole that remains there. I see it again; Valtere, standing silhouetted in the doorway, already on fire, and the eruption of flame that consumes his body . . . when he woke up from his drunken sleep and smelled the gas he must have run for the nearest door, trying to ventilate the place before raising the alarm. All he managed to do was feed the inferno more oxygen. I shudder and move on.

I scoot to the back of the small utility building and reach under a thick section of juniper hedge. Taking out a cylindrical black plastic case about the size of my forearm, I check that no one can see me and duck through a small gap in the hedge. Hidden from sight of most of the village, I follow the line of the hedge for about thirty metres. From there, I slip through another gap to the rear of the mon, where a steel fire escape climbs the back of the building.

This back wall is one of the thickest in the mon and, as I'd noticed earlier, it's almost completely intact. The fire escape is still there, though the windows it led to on the top floor are all blown out, the roof above it gone, lying in piles of debris on the ground below. The steel steps and rails are covered in soot, so I try not to touch too much. Every brush against the powder-coated steel leaves incriminating black marks on my hands and clothing. It's a good thing I'm so mucky from the work in the field – hopefully that will make any other marks less noticeable, though I'm leaving clear footprints in the soot. The metal creaks with every step; I move as gently as I possibly can.

I notice the cats don't hang around here as they once did. Like the tables of artificial food, this lifeless place holds no appeal, particularly stinking as it does of burnt . . . everything.

Climbing in through the glassless window, I find myself still in daylight, with no ceiling, a stark glow against the dark shapes, the charred stumps of rafters jutting out like ribs above me. I'm keeping low, in case someone might look up this way. The doorway to my left opens into the bell tower and a flight of stone steps that spirals in right angles up one more storey to the where the bell used to be. The door is a wafer of brittle charcoal, hanging from melted hinges.

This is where it gets a bit . . . iffy.

The explosion blasted the top off the tower, so the steps end after two flights, letting out into open air. The steps and the walls are uneven in a way that they weren't before. The whole structure has been weakened, jolted out of shape by the impact of the explosion. The burnt, warped steel rail on the inside wall is loose on its mountings. It doesn't feel safe up here. A solid stone step shifts under my foot and I flinch, but force myself to move carefully on.

The corner of the stairwell that faces into the building is the worst damaged. More of the stone has fallen away than on the outside walls, a gaping hole that leaves the steps exposed on my right side, where I can see down into the ruins. With most of the upper storey gone, it's almost as if I'm looking at an open-topped model of the building. The damage looks even worse from up here. It's like some of the images I've seen of bombed cities, with devastated homes and businesses, apartment complexes opened up like dolls' houses, whole city blocks of buildings so concussed that they'll never be safe to occupy again. Whole landscapes of tottering walls and slowly collapsing roofs.

I think of Valtere, and of Karava's descriptions of the things he saw in the wars. The weapons that could do this to a building would reduce human bodies to pulp and pieces, burnt and shattered and stripped of all the things that make them recognisable as human beings. I've only been given the narrowest glimpse of that kind of destruction and it makes me shudder to the core.

The lower half of a window frame remains on the outer wall of the tower and through this, I can see Buckley's villa.

Crouching down so I won't be spotted, I open the case I'm carrying and take out the telescope, extending it fully. I quietly lay down the case and close it, then peer over the window ledge.

I used to do this by lying on the floor under the bell, which means I'm about two metres lower than I've been in the past – the bell and its floor are now somewhere in the mess below – but this actually gives me a better view in through the wide rear window of Buckley's living room. The problem is, I'd normally only do this at night, so the risk of being spotted is higher too. As I fold down in a crouching position, my guts make a churning, groaning sound and, in a hushed voice, I actually murmur at them to shut up. My stomach and I are starting to become like separate entities as I continually fail to respond to its protests. Trying to ignore the little stabs of hunger, I put the telescope to my eye, to see what I can see.

Buckley is in there, along with Noon, Almeida and Mthembu. Almeida and Buckley are sitting at the table, the others are standing. There's no sign of Karava, so maybe he's already examined the stranger, or he's going to do it after the 'interview'. Everyone's facing Almeida, who's doing most of the talking. I can see enough of Buckley and Noon's faces to make out what they're saying when they speak too.

I don't know how much you know about my background, so there are a couple of things I should mention here. Firstly, my mother is profoundly deaf. Her family couldn't afford implants for her until she was well into her teens; as a result, she's still more than comfortable using sign language to speak rather than using her mouth. There's only so much speech and language therapy can do for you that late in life. I grew up having conversations with her in sign. She also taught me to *lip read*, a skill we used in games when I was a kid. The fact that this skill is really useful for eavesdropping on people's private conversations only became apparent to me when Dad gave me a stern warning not to use it for eavesdropping on people's private conversations.

So here I am, 'listening' to the guardians and Almeida through a telescope. I can't always see their mouths, and I can't catch everything, so I'll do my best to fill in the holes as I go.

'. . . knew I recognised some of those kids,' the newcomer is saying. He's got a strong accent that distorts the shapes of his words a bit, but I can't tell where he's from. Accents are often defined by their vowel sounds and can be hard to identify just from reading lips. 'This is one of those islands . . . hey, this the *main* one, isn't it? These are all the—.'

'Yes,' Buckley says. 'You were going to tell us what happened to your boat.'

'Right, right.' Almeida nods and shrugs and adjusts his crotch. 'Well, with everything that was going on, the fighting got bad in town and this . . . this bunch of lunatics were claiming everything they could get their hands on, like they were, I dunno, fuckin' warlords or something. Like they could take what they wanted just because they had *guns*. I knew they'd take my boat too, if they could, so when things were going to hell in town, me and a couple of friends made it to the harbour and headed out. But–.'

'I'm sorry to interrupt, but you're going to have to explain,' Buckley cuts him off. 'Who were these people? What do you mean "everything that was going on"? What was the fighting about?'

Almeida stops for a minute, as if he's having to shift gear. With an expression of disbelief, or perhaps suspicion, he looks from Buckley, up to Noon and then glances at the others.

'What was it *about*?' he asks. Once again, that childish, gurning smirk stretched his mouth wide. 'You mean . . . haven't you heard what's going on?'

'Knock off the theatrics and tell him what you told me,' Noon snaps.

Almeida comes over all sullen, as if Noon just delivered his punch-line before he could finish telling his joke. He leans back in the chair, folds his arms and tilts his head as he regards Buckley.

'Just over, eh. . . three weeks ago, something . . . something happened. The news on the radio, they said someone released a computer virus or a worm or whatever they call it. That was while we were still getting any kind of news. It was a slow thing . . . spreading everywhere . . . hiding in the computer code.

Nobody knew about it until it switched on . . .' He pauses, his face furtively trying to gauge his audience, an exaggerated attempt to build suspense. 'It infected millions of computers. Maybe billions, I don't know. It crashed communications all over the world. I don't know much about computers, but this thing . . . it attacked the . . . the . . . the *language* used by the internet . . . or it used the language. I'm not sure how you'd describe it . . .

'From what he's told me, it was a cyber-attack on the communications satellites and the internet service providers simultaneously,' Noon says, running out of patience and taking over the narration. 'There have been plenty like it before, but nothing on this scale. This one has brought down most of the web. But the crucial bit here is that *they're afraid to bring those networks back online.* They haven't found a way yet to stop the worm from spreading further and causing more damage. They're trying to quarantine it, but it's *everywhere.* That's why the sat-link's down. Plus, you've got aircraft, ships, all of our drones . . . anything with a computer – which is almost everything – is a potential carrier of the worm, so it's all been disconnected. That's why nobody's been in touch with us.'

'But there are still other ways to reach us,' Buckley objects. 'Not *everything* requires a computer. Why not just go old school, analogue? Christ, I mean–.'

Noon holds up her hand, motions to Mthembu and nods at Almeida. Mthembu takes the newcomer out of the room.

Noon sits down in Almeida's chair.

'Think about this,' she says to the principal. 'The world's money is almost entirely digital. Nothing but information. Money that can't be transferred from one point to another is worthless. The financial world has just been set back over a hundred years. Over the last few weeks, a lot of very powerful governments and corporations have been realizing that all their digital money isn't worth the paper it's not printed on. Even the value of *paper* money will have changed hugely, because only a fraction of the money in the world is in the form of cash. It means nobody's getting paid wages. Credit and debit cards won't work. People won't be able to buy food or pay bills. Companies will fail, the banks could collapse. Governments will topple because of this. All because *communications* have broken down . . .'

I miss the next few words because as I'm reading this on their lips, I'm trembling, causing the scope to shake and the view to wobble. I manage to steady it by using my free hand to press the scope against the stone windowsill. It's not the situation they're describing that's getting me. It doesn't sound as if it could be real; I can't get my head around something so big. I'm shaking because we've been assuming it's only a matter of time before we'll get help from the outside world and I can see in Buckley and Noon's faces that the news of this disaster has changed everything. It's something that's completely out of their control, and these two people, who have an answer for every problem that arises on this island, who are responsible for our very lives . . . *they don't know what to do.*

'There's no money,' Noon says again. 'The only things that matter now are–.'

'Tangible things. Real things,' Buckley finishes for her. 'Food, water, land . . . the kinds of things that can be taken by force, that will be fought over when people get desperate. Fucking hell, Noon, there'll be chaos. The Council should have found a way to contact us as soon as this happened.'

'Maybe they *can*, but they're holding off,' Noon replies. 'If things are falling apart, there could be disputes over what to do with the students. The one thing we *do* know is that no ship or plane is allowed come near us unless it's been cleared by the Council and we don't know if the Council members are even able to *talk* to each other. Imagine the political situation, how fast it could be changing. We can't even be sure *who's in charge* there any more. Every one of them will have their hands full stopping their countries from descending into anarchy. You heard what was happening on Almeida's island. He wasn't exaggerating, Buck. I saw bullet holes in the side of his boat.'

Mthembu has come back in and sits down at the table. He's speaking now:

'Shit, if this is true, governments could be changing as we speak,' he says. 'So what does that mean for us? We can't even be sure who's *on* the Council any more. Who are we taking orders from?'

'Let's deal with one thing at a time here . . .' Buckley starts to say.

'This is an immediate problem, sir,' Mthembu cuts across him. 'Think about what would happen if one of these parents decided they were going to bypass the Council and just send out an aircraft or ship themselves to pick up their kid – assuming they can find any whose navigations systems haven't been bricked. What do we do? What if they *come in force*? Imagine what it could start!'

This is exactly what I've been thinking. As in; if all this is going down, why the hell haven't Mum and Dad sent someone to pick me up? But I get it now. Things are tense out there. Countries all over the world, huge military powers, barely holding it together, everyone feeling vulnerable, everyone afraid of what their neighbours might do. It's like one of those stand-offs in a film, where everyone's pointing guns at each other. The first person to do the wrong thing could set it all off. Nobody's going to make a move towards *this* island while all that's going on.

'It's easier for the Council to just steer clear of us until things have settled down,' Buckley mutters, his lips barely moving. 'They don't know what's happened here, that we have no food. As far as they know, we can easily last another month or two without new supplies, so they're just leaving us alone. As far as they know, our computers could still be clean too.

'The students must not learn about the conflict this is causing,' he adds, lifting his head. 'This is just the kind of destructive, half-assed story that ends up being sensationalised and passed mouth by mouth like a bloody disease. It must be made clear to all the staff that the students must not hear about the violence. They'll panic if they think there's a threat of war – and that panic must be avoided at all costs. We have to make them feel that they are still secure.

'At the same time, we also have to consider the possibility of a more immediate threat. If the Council fails to keep order, we could find ourselves facing an attack. Again, this must be kept from the students. Noon, you didn't see any sign of the patrol convoys. With all the high value targets here, somebody might be mad enough to have a go . . .'

Noon has turned her back to me. If she's talking, I can't tell. Mthembu has his hands up to his face, rubbing his eyes. I can't see his mouth either. Unconsciously, I shift forward, trying to get a better view. Buckley has his head down and it's harder to make out the shapes his mouth is making. I edge forward . . . just little further.

Just a little too far.

The damaged wall gives underneath me, stones, loosened by the blast, collapsing under my weight. As I fall outwards, I see it all in slow, painful detail. The expanse of hard, scorched concrete three storeys below. The telescope slipping from my hands, flipping end over end, the stone blocks I've pushed out tumbling with it. I hear it smash on the ground.

My upper torso, no longer supported by the toppling wall, drops with sickening suddenness into empty space, dragging my legs after it. I feel my body in free-fall for an instant before my grasping right hand flails out and clutches at stone and I manage to catch myself on something more solid, hanging precariously out over the long drop, my left hand braced against the vertical stones below me, holding me up. I try to move it up where I can grab hold of the wall near my waist, but I'm too far out. When I go to shift my hand, I feel myself start to slip forwards. F–*(deleted)* . . . Sh–*(deleted)* . . . Ah nuts! Give me a friggin' break! I feel a slight give in the remains of the wall I'm clinging to with my right hand. I try to change my grip but nearly fall. I can't pull myself back and I can barely stop myself from tipping forwards.

'Billy? *Billy!*' I hear someone shout, but I can't see who it is. 'Hold on!'

I've always thought that would be a stupid thing to say to someone in my position, but actually, now that I find myself here, the daftness of it is somewhat reassuring. As if I couldn't possibly fall, now that this cliché has been introduced. There are other people coming too, I catch glimpses of figures in guardian uniforms running towards me, but I really don't want to take my eyes off my hands. The telescope lies in pieces below me. Great, not only am I going to die, but I've been caught spying on Buckley too. There's more shouting, though my adrenaline-charged brain is tuning it out so I can concentrate entirely on sticking to the side of this building. I can hear clanging footsteps on the fire escape. They sound appropriately frantic. Good. Then my left hand slips abruptly down the wall, the jerk of my body dislodging the gritty, cement-coated block I was hanging on to with my right hand. I feel the lump of stone thud against my arm as it spins out into the air, then it bounces off my shoulder . . . and I'm gone.

There's an instant where I'm falling head-first, thrashing, screaming and I know I'm going to die.

I get a flash of confusion as I see people below me. The next sensation is like being hit full force with about six or seven arms, all over my body, all at once. It hurts like son of a b–*(deleted,* but it's not the being-totally-smashed-to-pulp-against-concrete I was expecting. I hear grunts and cries of pain and bodies fall over on top of me as I find myself sprawled on the ground. I'm badly winded and I've got pains everywhere but there's nothing that feels broken, bent the wrong way or split open, so I guess that's okay then.

I'm lying in a tangle of limbs with Brother Nguyen, Moose and Sister Adeyemi. Nguyen's round, acne-scarred face is crunched up in agony and from the way he's clutching his shoulder, I'd say it's either broken or dislocated. Adeyemi, like me, is gasping for breath and has a gash in her forehead that must have come from one of the falling stones. Moose is first to sit up, hugging his stocky body and groaning as he cradles an injured right wrist.

My eyes follow the wall up to the jagged gap I just fell from and I see Skip staring down at me. He must have been the one who came running up the fire escape. He could have moved a bit quicker. I gaze around at the others, stunned that they managed to catch me.

'Thanks,' I say, immediately conscious of how inadequate the word is. 'Thanks for saving my life.'

'Are you okay?' Adeyemi asks, getting stiffly to her knees.

'Yeah. Eh . . . a bit banged up, but I don't think anything's broken.'

'Okay then. Young lady, you are in *so* much trouble.'

Chapter Nineteen
Guilty as Charged

I am embarrassingly unhurt, unlike the people who absorbed the impact of my fall, so I'm brought before Buckley in prompt fashion. Mthembu and Almeida have left the villa, and my three human airbags have all been taken off to Doctor Karava to have their injuries treated. Adeyemi and Moose will be okay once they're bandaged up, and Nguyen has a dislocated shoulder that will need to be popped back in. At this point, people have got to be wondering if I can get through a whole day without being slammed onto the ground. Much more of this, and they'll start putting up health and safety signs wherever I go. 'Hard Hat Area'.

Skip's disappeared, I don't know where, so it's just me, Noon and Buckley. Three chairs have been pulled out from the table and we all sit, the two of them facing me. Noon looks concerned for me. Buckley . . . hell, I can't get any kind of reading on him. His face is like a castle gate, all hard straight lines made to stop you getting in.

'You're lucky you're small,' he growls.

'Yes,' I reply.

I don't have much to say for myself, being guilty as charged – or as about to be charged – and I'm feeling pretty sick about the others being hurt saving my scrawny ass from falling off a wobbly wall, so I'm staying quiet, writing this latest episode onto my chip while I wait for whatever barrage of anger, expressions of disappointment and morality lecturing that's coming down the track. Much to my surprise, Buckley cuts through all that and gets straight to the point.

'How long have you been spying on me?' he asks in a level voice.

I hesitate, wondering if there's an answer I could give that would seem reasonable.

'I was just up there trying to find out what was going on,' I start saying. 'I didn't–.'

He slams a fist down on the table next to him, making me jump, then opens his hand, as if forcing himself to relax it, his face working through the same process, the sudden burst of anger suppressed down to little more than a stern manner.

'I'm sorry,' he rasps quietly. 'That was unnecessary. Billy . . . I'm not an idiot. We've been curious about why you bring your laundry up yourself so often, when you know it'll be collected. It's not like you show any fondness for domestic chores. We've also seen you sneaking around the back of the monastery at night sometimes. We didn't know why, but we didn't pry, because you didn't seem to be doing any harm. A lot of the students need their private little hideouts – we allow for this, as part of trying to make life normal here.

'You were close to the mon when the explosion happened, and *still* I gave you the benefit of the doubt, frankly because I didn't think you had the callousness or the technical skills to engineer a piece of sabotage like that. But you acted with *familiarity* this afternoon. With an efficiency born of habit. You had the telescope concealed somewhere nearby – not in your villa, or I'd have seen it yesterday – and you knew you would have a clear view into my kitchen window from the bell tower. We hadn't been in the house long, so you must have found your observation point quickly and without hesitation. And you knew you'd have a close enough view, with the telescope you had ready, to read our lips. We know you can do that, because it's in your file. It's listed as a security concern.

'So I'll ask you again: how long have you been spying on me?'

I look at Noon, but there's no support coming from that direction. She might be the closest thing I have to a friend among the guardians, but she won't get in Buckley's way on this. I'm in the wrong here and we all know it.

'Why don't you read my journal and see for yourself?'

'Don't be disingenuous. You *know* I can read your journal whenever I want, as long as you keep recording it on your chip – so I'm not inclined to believe a word of what you write. Apart from the parts I can verify myself, it could be a complete work of bloody fantasy. Cut the bullshit and answer my question.'

I try and think of another lie, but I'm only kidding myself. Besides, he can go right to hell if he doesn't like what I've done. Noddy's been right about this all along. We're not on the same side here. We never could have been. I'm battered and mucky and exhausted and hunger is growing painful in my gut and making me dizzy and weak. I've had enough of him. I've had enough of this whole head-wrecking, soul-draining freakin' mind prison. To hell with him.

'About six months,' I tell him, scraping my teeth together. 'I was wandering around the mon one night when I couldn't sleep. I climbed up to the bell tower and saw you were out there.' I tilt my head towards his back garden. 'You were on your laptop, typing. I checked back at the same time over a few different nights and you were always there, like it was a habit. You had meetings in the kitchens sometimes too, when I could watch what you were saying, but mostly it was the work on the laptop. I realized if I had a telescope, I'd be able to read what you were typing, so I ordered one online.'

'Yes, I remember when you got it,' he says. 'You'd never shown any interest in astronomy before that. But I have my back to the house when I'm working in the garden. You wouldn't be able to see the screen.'

'You sit with your back to the *window*. I'm looking down from a high angle. At night, when the kitchen light is off, the screen's reflected in the window pane, clear as crystal.'

'And you can read text in mirror image?'

'It's not that hard.'

'A proper little secret agent, aren't you? From what I've

read, you haven't recorded any of this in your journal.'

'No, because I'm not an idiot either.'

He leans back in the chair, putting his hands behind his head, regarding me thoughtfully. Most of what I've managed to see on his computer is stuff on the banned list. Because the chip blocks me based on what I'm *intending* to say, if *someone else* is saying something that's banned, I can record it on my chip – it can transcribe from voices I hear. On the other hand, I can't just read something out and save it, because the intention is still there. Listening can be passive, but reading isn't. Buckley already knows that while I might be *aware* of any banned subject matter I've seen, I can't discuss it with anyone else. So now he's wondering if I've seen anything that might make me do something nuts, like, say, blowing up a building. Or helping someone else to blow it up. And *I'm* wondering if he has any specific information in mind. I tell ya, this convoluted crap would twist your brain into a knot if you let it.

'You heard . . . eh, *saw* what Almeida said? And Noon?'

I nod my head. I try not to look too shaken, but it has to be showing. I think about how hungry I am right now, focus on the gaping void in my belly, to distract my mind from the whole end-of-civilization-as-we-know-it deal. I really need to maintain my composure here.

'Everything that that man said, it's all rumour,' he tells me. 'Nothing's been confirmed. Don't start panicking over this, Billy. There has been no conflict that we know of for sure. We can only take this man's word for any of it and we don't know who he is, where he's from or what his motives are.'

'Noon seems to believe it's all true.'

'No,' Noon objects sharply, holding up her hands in a cautious gesture. 'No, I don't know either way, and the circumstances we found him in were suspicious. But we do have to allow for the possibility that he's telling the truth, so we can't *not* act on this information.'

'How were the circumstances suspicious?' I ask.

'Skip was in the bell tower,' Buckley says, ignoring my question. 'What was he doing up there?'

'As far as I know, he came running upstairs to try and stop me falling.'

'He wasn't there while you were watching us? What was he doing so close to the monastery? You're all supposed to be staying away from it – it's a crime scene.'

'I don't know. *You're* the guardians – aren't you supposed to keep track of everyone? Why don't you ask him yourself?'

'I will.'

Buckley's eyes fix on mine and I glare back at him, but I'm not in his league when it comes to intimidating stares. He can question me, read my journal, stop me from telling other people what I've seen, but he can't hurt me or force me to talk. I'm protected, because of who I am. We both know this, so his mind's whirring, working the angles.

'This casts an entirely different light on your part in all this,

Billy,' he says at last. 'Clearly, there's a deceitful side of you I hadn't fully appreciated before this. It seems I have to reassess your character. I can't trust you as I thought I could.'

'Yeah, I'd say that would be real problem for you . . . if you didn't already control every aspect of our lives. Still, we're in safe hands, right? Hey, what's for dinner today? *Sesame seeds?*'

'Yes, watch me wither under your teenage sarcasm,' he sighs, standing up and motioning me out of my chair. 'It's been a profoundly depressing day, Billy, and you've brought it to a new low. Mark this: you cannot discuss anything you've seen while spying on me. That includes anything said by Matthias Almeida.

'You can leave now.'

And, with one more block laid down on me, I walk out and slam the door behind me. He saw the tears in my eyes as I left, probably even the despair that was coming over me. I've been given a glimpse at the world collapsing beyond the horizon, at the prospect that help may not be coming for us, and I'm in a bad state; I needed him to be a teacher and I got a stone cold military dictator instead.

I'm f–*(deleted)* . . . freakin' terrified, I'm starving and I want my mum and dad.

Chapter Twenty
Rumour Control

My dinner that evening is a small cut of fresh sea bass and a few pieces of popcorn, with a single bit of liquorice for 'dessert'. I fill up the rest of the void with water. It's better than yesterday, because of the fish, but still woefully inadequate, especially after a day of hard labour. I lick my fingers and run them round the plate to ensure I get every last particle and bit of fish oil. I suck miserably on the liquorice, the sour-sweet taste soaking into my mouth, a poor substitute for a full belly. Despondently, I scan the table in case I missed any morsel that might have fallen from the plate. I glance down at the floor, but there's nothing there either. I notice Gemmy and Nuke doing the same thing and then I wonder who saw me. How long will it be before we start crawling around on the floor, looking for crumbs? Hunger can take real bites out of your self-respect.

Afterwards, Buckley appears in the gym where we're 'eating', to call another meeting. The crowd's all ears, because we'll finally get to hear Almeida's story. The others don't know that I've heard it already and, because of the block, I can't mention it to them. Still, at least everyone else is about to get their heads wrecked as badly as mine is.

'This is rumour control,' Buckley tells us. 'These are the

facts. Sister Noon and her crew discovered Mister Almeida after he'd been drifting for several days. He was half-starved, suffering from sunstroke and nearly dead from thirst. We've questioned him and he has explained how he came to be so close to the exclusion zone in a sinking boat. However, we have reason to believe that either he can't remember clearly because of his poor physical state, or he's not being straight with us.

'The story he's told us is riddled with half-truths and inconsistencies. Because of this, I am reluctant to let him speak to you directly.' Buckley gives me a judgemental look at this point, either to imply some comparison, or just remind me that I'm no longer considered part of the team. My face is like, *whatever*. Then he continues: 'What we can gather is that parts of the satellite network went down three weeks ago, due to a solar flare. As a result, communications have been disrupted and sections of the web are still offline. Which would explain what's happened to our sat-link.'

A *solar flare*? What the ever-living Christ in a fart-sack is he talking about? I go to shout out in protest, but my chip cuts me off. I try again and find myself blinking, attempting to remember what it was I wanted to say. Oh yeah. And of course I *can't* say it. I lift my head to listen to the rest of the bullology.

'The loss of the satellites has affected navigation too,' he adds. 'Which has no doubt contributed to the delays of our supply ship and possibly the aircraft too. There is no need to be alarmed. It is a massive *technical* failure, and that's *all* it is. But seeing as this was a freak, one-off event, and the world's leaders are all *united* in responding to it, I'm sure these communication problems will shortly be overcome, so we can expect contact from the Council at any time. I suspect tech support people all over the world will be making a fortune on overtime for the next few weeks. Mister Almeida, however, made the mistake of trying to take a boat out to sea last week with no GPS. Apparently his navigation skills weren't up to the task.'

Buckley gives a wry smile, and right at that moment, I hate the lying basket-head. I look around to see how this story is going down, and though most of the other studes seem to be taking it at face value, some are obviously sceptical. Noddy has a 'really?' tilt to his head and puts up his hand to ask a question, but Buckley waves him down. The principal's not finished talking.

'Now, because Mister Almeida has *not* been cleared by the Council to be on the island, he is not permitted any contact with you. And because he's still suffering from rather . . . *odd* delusions after his ordeal, I don't want you trying to speak to him either. We're facing a difficult situation and the last thing we need is garbled rumours floating round the village. So, mark this: None of you are to speak to Matthias Almeida.'

There are expressions of exasperation, dismay and anger at

this. Now that Buckley has hinted at 'odd delusions', *everyone* wants to talk to Almeida. And the number of things we can no longer say to each other is reaching the point where it would surely be simpler to lock us all in separate rooms and be done with it. Although it could be that a full lockdown is an option Buckley's considering for further down the line.

He sticks around to take some questions, but his answers are evasive or just plain blagging his way through, so the studes give up asking and he leaves. We stay in our seats, griping about this new turn of events.

'The whole world has been shut down by a solar flare?' Duchess snorts. 'Did anyone actually buy that crap?'

'No way!' Cheeks replies quickly, though I suspect she did buy that crap and is now embarrassed to admit it. 'What a lying turd!'

'What was he lying *about*, though?' Gemmy asks.

'I don't know, but I know crap when I smell it. I did work experience in a real estate office,' Duchess declares. 'Whatever is going on out there, it's the reason we're facing starvation – the reason the mon was destroyed. And we need to find out what it is.'

I just get up and leave. I'm bursting to tell them that I know the truth and it's so huge and important and I can't say a word about it. It's like being constipated or something and I think I'll cry from the frustration of it. I have to leave, because if they take a good look at me and suspect I know more than they do, they'll never leave me alone. This stinks. And I'm still so frickin' hungry.

I need to talk to Noon.

Chapter Twenty-One
Crime Scene Investigation

It's early evening and the sun has slumped onto the horizon, smeared by the humidity, though the blackened ruins of the monastery are lit up, as if caught in the instant of a camera flash, by dazzling work lights set on yellow tripod stands. Noon is in the comms room, where the Hub was once situated. The room is an eight- by eight-metre square, and it looks bigger now than before because it seems so much emptier, furnished only with the steel skeletons of desks and chairs, their more vulnerable parts claimed by the fire. The various computers, screens and other devices are little more than piles of melted plastic and circuitry. Everything's black or grey, and coated in soot and flakes and a dusting of ash. The floor, still lined with the fibrous remains of the carpet tiles, is littered with rubble and debris from the ceiling and walls that have fallen in on it. Noon's down on her hunkers, sifting through the ash and debris on the ground. Mthembu has let me onto the site with a stern warning not to touch anything. I think he feels sorry for me. He knows how it is between me and Noon, how she helps keep me sane, and he can see I'm in a bit of a state right now.

Noon glances up at me, sympathy in her eyes, then goes back to her work. This isn't her first bomb-site; before she joined the Order, she served as some kind of engineering expert in military intelligence. This is why Buckley left this work for her to do when she came back.

'Find anything new?' I ask her.

'I'm not supposed to let you in here,' she says. 'Brother Buckley has told us you're to be treated as a suspect.'

'Do you think I am? A suspect, I mean?'

'Girl, *everything* about you is suspect,' she quips. 'Your face is like someone stuck a bug's eyes on a spanked arse.'

I laugh and immediately feel better.

'At least I don't have an arse like a spanked bug.'

She laughs back, then it falters, she sighs and shakes her head.

'Actually, I . . . don't know what that means.'

'No, neither do I, really. So . . .' I gesture at the scene and search for a suitably cop-sounding phrase, but the best I can come up with is: 'What've we got?'

'Gas explosion,' she replies.

'No, really? Goddamn, Noon, you've cracked the case.'

'Look, I'm starting from scratch here, Billy Goat. We can't rush to conclusions. There has to be evidence for every assertion we make. It's funny, but the gas system was only supposed to be a back-up for a back-up. We have the generators in case the solar panels and windmills don't provide electricity, but they're so efficient, we've a surplus of power. The natural gas is for heat and cooking if the batteries *and the generators* fail. Apart from regular testing, we've rarely even used it.'

She points to a pipe at ankle-height along one wall. It's a few centimetres in diameter, and looks like it's made of some kind of rigid plastic. It's warped, but hasn't been melted by the fire.

'This was the source of the gas. There's a small hole in the pipe. Probably made with a bradawl or an ice-pick, maybe. It's possible the saboteur even hammered a nail in and pulled it out again. Very simple to do, once you know where the pipe is.'

She runs her latex-gloved hands along the wall, tracing from the corner where the Hub was to the doorway, stopping at the deep doorframe. She slides her fingers down to where the pipe bends at a right angle and disappears into the concrete floor, behind the charred skirting board. The hole in the pipe is near the doorframe.

'This whole room was sound-proofed, with acoustic panels behind the plasterboard, so the walls were *hollow*. This pipe was in behind the plasterboard too – the drywall's burnt up and fallen away, but you can see where it was. When it was still intact, you'd have to study the plans of the room to know exactly where the pipe was. Someone punched the hole through the drywall in precisely the right place, and into the pipe. It would have taken seconds. With all the people walking in and out of here every day, it could have been anyone.

'After they'd punctured the pipe, I think they must have

plugged the hole in the drywall, or somebody would surely have smelled the gas early on. That's the devious part. I think they plugged the hole in the soundproofing and let the pipe keep leaking gas undetected, contained within the hollow walls of the room. Because it was sealed in there, nobody caught the smell and the gas detectors didn't pick it up. Bit by bit, the sound-proofed walls filled with methane until the whole room was an inferno waiting to happen.'

'But how did they set it off?'

'I'm not sure yet. I've only started looking.'

'Skip reckons that the saboteur didn't mean to blow up the whole building. He thinks whoever it was meant to set fire to the comms room, but the . . . the . . . whatever was supposed to ignite the gas failed to work. The gas ended up spreading way further than it should have . . . it made a much bigger explosion.'

'He said that did he?' Noon murmurs, casting her eyes around the floor. 'I think he could be right. Anyway, I need to keep working here, Billy. You can hang around if you like, but don't touch anything, okay?'

'Yeah, sure.'

This is easier said than done, because there's stuff everywhere, and wherever I try to stand to keep out of her way, I'm stepping on something else. I watch her for a few minutes, asking more questions, until I think she's getting irritated with the distractions, then go quiet. I don't want her sending me away, because I'm starting to get scared again. I think it's the hunger, it makes any vulnerability worse. My stomach feels like it's folding in on itself. We've had dinner and I'm still coming to grips with the idea that I can't just get a snack from the canteen before a late-evening supper, that there isn't going to *be* a supper or some munchies to eat while watching a film tonight or just something I can grab from the cupboard or the fridge. There's no apple or a banana for a quick healthy bite. Every piece of food is now strictly controlled by Sister Adeyemi. There's nothing else coming until a breakfast that I know will depressingly, pathetically small.

My body knows there isn't some hefty feed in the foreseeable future and I'm overcome with a cold, shivery restlessness that has me constantly looking around in case there might be things near me that I wouldn't have eaten before, but would be willing to try now. I'm wondering can hunger cause panic attacks, because I've never had one before, and I feel like I might have one coming on. I try to breathe slower.

I see the remains of a long, thin picture frame jammed behind the steel wall of the unit that used to contain spare phones and tablets. Leaning on the counter-top, I tug the frame out to look at it. It won't come free at first, and I pull harder until it jerks out. A piece of slagged plastic scrapes up the wall along with it and bounces across the counter. I turn the frame until it's landscape instead of portrait.

It's not a picture, it's a quote, printed in some old script-like typeface. Most of it has been burnt beyond recognition, but I can make out the worlds: '. . . *to carry on a real war . . . with the children.*'

'Hey!' Noon exclaims at me, glancing up from where she's examining something just outside the door. 'I told you not to touch anything, you gimp!'

'Yeah, sorry,' I reply, with all the sincerity I can muster.

This frame had hung on the wall above the counter. It was a quote from Mahatma Gandhi: *'If we are to teach real peace in this world, and if we are to carry on a real war against war, we shall have to begin with the children.'*

That line is a real favourite of Buckley's. He has it up in a few places around the village. I regard the words sourly, then my eyes fall on the object that I pulled up with the frame. It's a phone. It's melted and misshapen, and it has two short pins, a few millimetres apart, sticking out of the back of it, but it's definitely a phone, with the typical featureless screen, though it has a slim metal casing instead of the near-indestructible, roll-up plastic ones we use. This is a type of phone we don't have on the island. Everyone, even the guardians, uses the same model, all of them provided for us and routed through the Hub. This one is a bit smaller and a slightly different shape, and rigid rather than foldable, I've seen the type before somewhere, though it wasn't melted at the time. This is someone's personal phone – and the use of personal phones is not permitted on the island.

'What've you got there?' Noon asks.

I hand it to her and she takes it, holding it up to the light. I tell her how I found it.

'This is our ignition device,' she says softly. 'Or it would have been, if it'd worked. But it didn't.' She touches the two pins in the back of the phone. 'Our sneaky little arsonist stuck the phone onto the wall, hidden behind the picture frame. Again, it would only have taken a few seconds. These pins were jammed through the plasterboard so they'd be sticking into the cavity in the wall, maybe gummed at the base with a sealant to make the holes airtight, to keep the gas in. *Then* the bastard punctured the pipe on the other side of the room. He could have just used it as a timer, but it was more likely a call. When he figured he'd waited long enough for the gas to fill the hollows in the soundproofing, he could make a call to this phone from a safe distance, causing a spark to leap between these pins and . . . boom.'

'What kind of range would the phone have?' I ask.

'It's not a satellite phone; you'd still have to use the island's network . . . somehow,' she replies, rubbing the back of her neck with her hand. 'The call would have to be made from somewhere on the island, or not more than a few hundred metres off-shore, within range of the phone masts. Sneaky! The arsonist was going to use the Hub to destroy the Hub. But if this phone *had* ignited the gas, it would have been blown to pieces. Instead, it just got melted in the fire. No, Skip was right – the saboteur messed up.'

Noon looks back towards the wall where the gas leak started. She raises her eyes to the evening sky, imagining the structure of the building as it once was.

'The gas kept leaking, expanding into the hollows, growing in pressure. If the explosion had been triggered then, the walls would have contained the worst of it; the comms room would have been destroyed, but the sprinkler system might have put the fire out before it spread further. Instead, the gas kept going, seeping out, up around the ceiling.' Noon has her hands up, moving them in what is almost a dance as she gestures in the directions the deadly methane took through the building. 'It spread out in all that open space above the ceiling panels in the corridors and gradually over most of the ground floor rooms. Natural gas has no smell. For safety, it's mixed with a chemical called mercaptan, to make it stink, so you'll know if it's leaking out somewhere. By the time it started spreading out through the ceiling, you'd start getting a whiff of it in the corridors. People coming and going might even have smelled it in places and just thought someone had farted. We never use the gas, so the possibility of a leak might not occur to you immediately.'

She lowers her hands and turns to face me.

'Once the gas had filled the spaces over the ceiling panels, this whole place had become a bomb waiting to go off. A single spark would be enough to do it. Valtere could still have prevented though. He must have been passed out, drunk, in the lounge. It happened a lot and I'm ashamed to say, we all covered for him. Nobody wanted to see him court-martialled. Buckley should never really have left him on watch on his own. Valt would have to be unconscious not to have noticed the smell by the time the explosion happened. When he *did* wake, he could hit the shut-off valve, opened the doors and windows and called for help. Instead, I think he set off the explosion.'

'What?' I blurt out.

It was one thing to hear Skip laying blame on Valtere – Skip's a belligerent, antisocial glute who'd want to see the attention deflected onto anyone but himself. Hearing Noon say it is an entirely different thing. She makes it real. She waves me out into the corridor; like the rest of the building, the hallway is little more than the blackened cadaver of the bright space it once was. She shows me the fire alarm button outside the comms room. It looks like the glass over the button was broken before it was deformed by the heat.

'I think he woke up, panicked and hit the fire alarm. Suddenly, electrical circuits close all over the building to sound the alarms.'

'Couldn't that just have broken in the blast? What makes you so sure it was him?'

'It's just a theory, so far.'

She's looking up again, her fingers snaking along the path the flames would have taken. It's almost a sensual movement, and there's a fascination in her eyes. That's the engineer in her, reducing this disaster to the patterns and forces of physics, seeing the beauty in the chaos of an explosion. 'It would only take one spark somewhere in the alarm circuit to ignite the gas. Ground zero seems to have been the games room – I'd say that was the first to go. The flames spread back across the ceiling, and that compressed, burning gas expands massively in a tiny fraction of a second. In that instant, standing on this spot, Valt would have heard a roar like a wild beast. It erupts out of that cramped space with an explosive power that devastates the areas below and blasts up through weak points in the floor above, tearing the sprinkler system apart. Every window and door is blown out, the force of the shockwave knocking out walls and slamming up into the roof above, causing it to collapse.'

'Valtere was found at the side door,' she continues, pointing down the hallway. 'He was probably hurled most of the way down the corridor by the blast, then dragged himself to the exit.'

Following her, I drift the twenty metres to the doorway. The wooden frame has been almost entirely ripped away, the door itself lying on the ground outside. I'm reminded of the broken door to the bunker at the air base, when we discovered the spare radio was missing. We gaze at the strong oak frame, the mangled steel hinges, at the solid wooden door, steel reinforced, all torn apart by the blast. I suffer a flashback, remembering how that force did the same thing to Valtere's body.

'Poor drunken idiot,' Noon breathes. 'He didn't stand a chance.'

'Buckley's convinced one of the students did this,' I mutter. 'Maybe Skip. What do you think?'

Noon regards me for a moment before replying, a hint of sympathy on her face, then turns her eyes back to the door.

'I'm keeping an open mind,' she says. 'But we have to catch the asshole who did this, and fast, because although this was very carefully thought through, cutting off our communications was only *half* a plan. This guy knows something about what's going on out in the world and when we find out what that is, it's going help us nail him. The Council could get back in touch with us at any time, so he—.'

'Or *she*.' I interject.

'. . . Or *she* only set this explosion to buy time to do something else. Whatever the hell is going on here, it's not finished by a long way.'

Chapter Twenty-Two
Parting Words

It's early afternoon, our third day without real food, and the hunger is like an illness taking over my body, emphasising every new ache and pain I've picked up, draining my strength and demanding more, a constant distraction from the other things we need to get done. All the boats that survived the recent hurricane are now out in the open ocean, beyond the harbour and the swathes of algae that enclose the coast. Although we had enough wind to get out here, the water has since gone dead, as chilly, flat and grey as slate under a glowering sky, the air calm, the stillness appropriate to the occasion, allowing us to sit with sails furled, motors switched off. The smaller craft form an arc around the port side of the *Santiago*, everyone aboard this little flotilla maintaining a respectful silence as Mthembu and Sengupta lift the end of the schooner's gangplank and slide Valtere's tarpaulin-wrapped corpse into the sea. The big boat is still lower than it should be in the water; when we sailed out to this point in the ocean, the schooner moved with a sluggish drag, as if weighed down with our collective grief. This island is a place of strained relationships, but Valtere was loved.

Buckley's oration carries across the water. He's going on about Valtere's life; his career in the French Foreign Legion, his love of teaching and of nature. And though I know it's disrespectful, I'm only half listening. I'm gazing at the shifting planes of light on the water, a shimmer of miserable greys, like different versions of the same crap mood, thinking of Brother Valt's wonky smile and the way his bald head got sunburned every summer. For a guy who loved the outdoors, he was rubbish at dressing for the weather.

A nauseous, pensive tension grips my body and I feel the need to cry welling up in my throat and behind my eyes, but it won't come out. At least my mascara stays intact. I'm not even sure why I felt the need for a touch of make-up; I'm not looking my best, I suppose, and it just always goes on with the dress. I think I was on autopilot as I got done up for the 'occasion'. I have my defiant hair bound up too, in a bun as tight as a cricket ball. We've all dressed soberly in dark colours – I opted for my multi-purpose little strapless black number, under a burgandy silk shawl. We do try to contrive reasons to dress up on a regular basis, but this serves me equally well for dinner parties, functions and funerals. The brown skin of my bare arms and legs has come up in goose-bumps in the cool sea air. Our formal outfits look slightly incongruous as we sit in the sailboats and rigid inflatables. I'm in flat black shoes because heels wouldn't work too well in the five-point-five-metre keelboat I'm sharing with Moose and Skip.

Skip. He seemed to be hanging close to me at the farm this morning and then jumped in here when he saw which boat I was choosing at the dock, which has me a bit weirded out. Duchess, Smood and Gemmy are in the next boat over, a nimble little sloop, not much bigger than our craft. I was heading down the dock towards them when they pulled out into the water before I could join them. I'm not sure if that was a snub or not.

We did a few more hours at the farm this morning. With empty stomachs and stiff bodies, the novelty's wearing off and more of the studes joined Noddy in his protest. Nobody was in the mood for work today, but first Cheeks, then Mumble sat down with him. Less than half an hour later, Spray and Keyboard did too. They all hung about on the rocks on the beach as the rest of us grafted. Smood shouted at them to do their bit, but they ignored him, calling on him to down tools and join the cause.

Duchess pointed out to Buckley that we'd now missed three days of school and asked what he was going to do about it. We still had our grades to think about. Absorbed in conversation with Brother Earnest, he hardly seemed to acknowledge the question, brushing her off with a curt reply. To my surprise, she left it at that and walked away to get on with spreading compost. She was making a good go of it, but I think she's suffering today. It's not like her to be so submissive.

Moose is stretched out on the deck over the prow, his meaty chin lying on the backs of his hands, his attention fixed on Buckley. Skip is sitting on the roof of the tiny cabin, listening to something on his earphones, which are hidden under his uncombed black hair. He's completely ignoring the eulogy, but I'm not about to start an argument about it. I'm in the stern, leaning over the gunwale, dangling my fingertips in the water. I wonder if there's a drone sub down there somewhere, watching us, listening to Buckley's warbling tones? Probably. What would it make of this? What kinds of thoughts would be darting through its uncurious brain? Voices waft over the water's surface like delicate vapours, barely audible; Duchess and Smood talking on the sloop behind me. They don't know I can hear them.

'. . . It's just an idea,' Smood is saying. 'The oldies are acting like they're still in control of everything, but they're *not*, are they? Buckley's getting more uptight by the day – I think he's losing his grip. We don't know who blew up the mon, or what else they might be planning to do. You just *know* Buckley's feeding us a line about what's going on out in the world. Something's gotta be wrong with that Almeida guy, the way they hauled him off like that. We're going to run out of chow and we don't know when help is coming. What are we supposed we do, Dutch? Wait till we're so starved we can't even goddamn *walk*? If we let it go too long, we could all end up dead. Think about it; what if nobody's coming? We have to do *something*!'

'Keep your voice down,' she replies. 'Still though, stealing the *Santiago*? Look at it . . . the thing can barely stay afloat.'

'Not *yet*, obviously,' he says in exasperation. 'We wait till Noon has it fixed up.'

'Even then, she says it won't make the journey out.'

'That's if they're trying to evacuate all the studes off the island. I'm talking about four, maybe five of us, enough to crew it in two watches. We pick the best sailors. It'd be tough, but we could do it.'

'What about supplies?' Duchess is objecting, but only because she's already working the problem. 'We'd have water, but what would we do for food?'

'Yeah, there's that. We'd have to break into the storeroom in the gym and take what we need. We could fish too. If we get the right winds, it's only a ten-day trip, maybe a bit longer. People have gone longer than that with no food at all.'

'Not sailing a sinking schooner fifteen-hundred klicks through *Atlantic storms* they haven't. I don't know about this Smood . . . who did you have in mind?'

'Me, you and Gemmy, of course . . . maybe Noddy, Turtle and Cheeks? Who do you think?'

'Cheeks? She can't sail worth a damn. Spray's the best sailor we've got.'

'Spray's a snitch,' Smood grunts. 'She'd go running to Buckley at the first whiff of what's going on.'

'What about Billy? She can handle herself on a boat.'

'Nah. She's not strong enough for the winds we'll be facing out there. We can't take everyone, Dutch. It can only be a few of us – that's the whole point.'

'Yeah, I suppose. What about . . .'

Their voices fade out slightly. I don't look at them, or react in any way that they might see, but I tell myself I'm not hurt by what they've said, just mildly irritated that they're thinking of stealing the only ocean-going boat we have. To be honest, I'm not feeling much about it at all. Maybe I'm just numb at the moment. It occurs to me after I've recorded this that I should warn Buckley about it. Or just leave it here in my journal where he might see it, if he's still reading up on me. One would require me bothering to go and let him know. The second would require me bothering to go back and delete what I've written. I can't be arsed to do either – that's as close as I come to making a decision about it.

I'm so absorbed in trying out-stare the ocean, I must have missed the signal to head back in. It's like the weather was waiting for us to be finished. A south-westerly picks up, causing a bit of chop in the water. I can hear motors start up and the whirring whumpf of sails being hauled up their masts. It's obvious nobody's in the mood to stay out, because all the boats are turning towards the harbour. Moose is up on his knees, hoisting the jib as Skip prepares the main sail. I could help, but it's a two-person job at the most, so I stay seated and leave them to it, resting my hand on the tiller.

By the time we reach the dock, the other boats are already moored, most of the studes and guardians walking slowly down the pier. We tie up at the wooden jetty that serves the smaller boats, sticking out at right angles from the stone pier. Moose holds out his hand to help me across – it's hard to step over the gap to the jetty in this form-fitting dress – but I wave him away. The big guy's got this old-world gentleman way about him that's charming most of the time, though all the girls reckon there's a thin seam of sexism under it all. Today, I think he's just being nice, but I'm not in the mood to be touched right now.

As I walk down the jetty, Skip stays a few paces behind me in a way that makes it feel like he's keeping up with me, without being too obvious about it. I think he wants to talk to me, and he's waiting until no one else is around. Which is making me curious. Moose is still down by the boat and I'm well behind the others who are heading up to the villas. I'm about to turn and face Skip when I spot Matthias Almeida, over on the boardwalk on the shore, walking between Sister Thompson and Brother Nguyen. His hands aren't bound or anything, so he doesn't *quite* look like a prisoner let out for exercise under guard. I'd say Thompson and Nguyen, left in charge of the visitor, just wanted to watch the funeral from the shore. They have weapons on their belts and their manner is different; that little bit more alert and deliberate in their movements. They look more like soldiers today. At the pace they're walking, I could speed up a little and just happen to reach the bottom of the pier at the same time as them.

Almeida glances over at me and from the way he's dropped his eyes away, I'd swear he's just had the same thought.

The other studes have gone on ahead, so they mustn't have seen him. They couldn't have ignored him. His presence is an anomaly, an event that distorts the fabric of our little community, tugging at our attention. He's a crude, leathery specimen, who seems at once uneducated and ignorant and yet has knowledge of the outside world that gives him massive stature in our eyes. After what I heard last night, I'm desperate to know more. Maybe he could give me some news about home. I'd give anything to hear something, anything . . . I've got a deep throbbing in my chest just thinking of Mum and Dad . . . I'm trying to put some distance between myself and Skip, so I can be alone when I intercept, then I glance back to see he's upped his pace too. Because of Buckley's ban, I can't even talk to Almeida, but he's drawing close and lifting his head, face expectant, as if ready to hurl some message across to me. I almost lift my arms out to him in anticipation . . .

'What have they told you?' he calls to me, his eyes barely visible through those squinted lids. 'What have that lot told you about what's going on out there?'

Oh balls, he's asking me a question. A bloody *question*. He doesn't know I can't answer him, I can't physically talk to him. And now he thinks I'm ignoring him. Sh–*(deleted)*. I try my best to say something to him and end up gaping at him as my mind goes blank and I mouth nothings, the motions of someone whose jaw has just clicked out. I can't even use hand gestures to tell him I can't talk. I try to appeal to him with my eyes, sending gawking signals like some inhibited dollybird hoping to be asked for a dance. This is precious time. *He has to tell me what he knows.* We only have seconds before the oldies interfere. Stop asking bloody questions and just *talk*, you pillock!

He's scowling at me in confusion, and it could be that he thinks I'm making faces at him, because he pulls his head back and up as if offended, his face contorts into a snarl. Maybe he's reading into this, like he's some coarse little islander and I'm a stuck-up, pampered kid who won't even dignify him with a reply.

'Get your head out o' your ass!' he barks, his accent some kind of Mediterranean mouthful I can't pin down, guttural and harsh. 'You gotta get outta here! They're lying to you! You hear me? Hey! You listening to me, you preppy little fart? You don't got a word to say? They're . . . Lying . . . To . . . You!'

As Thompson takes his arm and pulls him around to head back down the boardwalk, his last few words are shouted slowly, with heavy emphasis, as if he thinks I'm being wilfully dense.

That's *it*? That's all he's giving me? Fists clenched, I almost let out a roar in frustration. I watch them stride away and then turn to jog up the road – damn this *stupid* dress . . . and these shoes! – and straight to my villa, where I change into some shorts, t-shirt and my trainers, managing most of it without coming to a standing stop. Then I *really* run. Out across the green, past the guardians' villas, I find the mouth of a trail leading into the trees. I don't have a route in mind, I just need to get moving. This should take me to the Perch, but anywhere will do. I need pace and distance and to flush air through my lungs, feel the pumping of my legs.

I barely make it a hundred metres up the hill before I have to stop, gasping for breath, my chest tight, my lungs burning, the muscles of my calves cramping up. What the hell is *this* now? I've never failed to take this hill at speed. This time, it's like trying to run while carrying another me on my back.

'It's suh-suh-sort of your buh-buh-buh-body's way of telling you not to be suh-stupid,' a voice says from behind me, making me start.

Skip's standing there. He's breathing hard too, though not as badly as I am. He must have followed me the whole way. I'm instantly on guard. I don't think I believe he's the saboteur but he's followed me out here, caught me on my own. I remember what Noon said about the destruction of the mon. That it could only be half the plan. We're all still stuck here together. The saboteur has to be working on a way to get off the island. Was I wrong about Skip? I remember the way Almeida acted towards him when the newcomer first stepped off the boat – how I'd been convinced he'd recognised Skip.

Had I read too much into that? Or not enough?

'You could puh-puh- . . . probably keep running if you tried,' he says. 'But your suh-suh-suh-system's telling you not to. You don't have the energy for it.'

I want to snap something back at him, but I don't have the air for it. And I know he's right. What was it Karava said that time? 'Energy is like money: you should never use more than you can afford . . . and we're *broke*.' To think of all the time I worried about eating too much and now I don't have enough fuel in the tank for the type of run I do most mornings.

To my complete embarrassment, I burst into tears. Brilliant. Fifteen minutes ago I was all kitted out to be a picture of elegant grief on a frickin' sailboat and now I'm on the point of collapse after a toddler's run, heaving wheezing, snotty sobs in front of this stuttering glute.

He turns his face away, then sits down on a moss-covered log that lies by at the edge of the trail. It takes me a minute or two to compose myself. As my breathing slows and grows quieter, he starts talking.

'I suh-suh-suh-saw you up in the tower. You were using a telescope.'

'Yeah, what about it?'

'I've suh-suh-seen you up there before. Your muh-muh-muh-mum's deaf, isn't she? I've suh-suh-seen you talking to her in the mon. You can lip-read.'

I don't reply to that, so he continues on, lifting his face to look at me now.

'Buh-buh-buh . . . Buckley was in his kitchen with Noon when I went up the tower to help you. You were suh-suh-spying on them, right? And I'm guessing it's not the first time. Did you hear . . . *see* wuh-what Almeida suh-said? Wuh-wuh-wuh-what did you find out?'

I tilt my head and give him a pointed look that every stude would recognise.

'Oh,' he mutters, and deflates in disappointment, his head sinking onto his chest. 'Buh-buh-Buckley blocked you from talking about it, huh?'

I can't even give a nod, but we can all interpret each others' frustration with this stuff. When you're forbidden to speak about something, there's still an instinct there that allows you to read between the lines. Something more animal than language. I'm tense, edgy with suspicion now. So he's curious about Almeida. I suppose we all are, but it's not helping his case. Skip gazes out through the gaps in the foliage of the tall, straight Norfolk pines that line the hillside. The textured plain of the sea is visible beyond, the grey touched now by a blue sheen.

'Remember wuh-wuh-when I came here first?' he says. 'I fuh-freaked out. As suh-soon as they let me out on muh-my own, I ran to the harbour . . . grabbed a buh-buh-buh . . . boat and muh-motored out into the bay.'

'Yeah,' I reply with a chuckle. 'We all thought you'd

actually chickened out – that you were trying to get back on the ship. I mean, I did a runner too when I got here, but I never tried to get off the island!'

'I wuh-wasn't really trying,' he sighs. 'They'd have taken me buh-buh-buh-back, though, if I'd wuh-wanted. It was an . . . an Asian Federation ship, not a Council vessel. They'd have taken me straight buh-back to my dad if I'd wanted, no argument.'

I'm staring at him. He knows it too, although he's not meeting my eyes. He's fully aware of what he's done, and he's holding on to see how I'll react. Slowly, I sit down on the log, about a metre away from him.

'How did you do that?' I ask softly.

'What?'

'You *know* what, you gimp! You just said *where you were from.*'

'What, you mean the . . . . Asian Federation? That's not where I'm from. That's a whole bunch of countries, I just–.'

'Whoah, whoah, don't brush this off! You mentioned one of the *powers*. We can't do that – it's blocked. You just beat the chip. How did you to do that? Can you say what country you're from?'

He swivels to face me, his eyes fixed on mine. He takes a deep breath.

'I-am-from-Japan,' he says, the words seeming to rush out of his mouth. 'Part-of-the-Asian-Federation . . . wuh-wuh-wuh . . . wuh-with-China-Korea-and-others.'

I lean back, my mouth hanging open. This is one of the *very first* blocks every one of us has programmed into our chip. We all know where everyone's from, but outside of history or geography class, we can't talk about nations or international relations of any kind. Certainly no politics, no alliances between nations. We can discuss small, day-to-day things in our lives at home, yes, but nothing to do with our countries as a whole; including even *naming* the country. It's one of the core blocks, and Skip just defied it. No, he just blew it out of the water. Questions flood my brain, but he sees the barrage coming and holds up his hand.

'It's my suh-stammer,' he tells me. 'I get a natural buh-block . . . get tripped up on suh-suh-certain sounds. "S" and "B" are the worst, buh-but I've got a load of them. When I was young, I was a really bad case . . . At fuh-first, I tried to just *avoid* the sounds, to speak without them . . . tried to find other words for things, but you end up thinking so much about it, that it makes things worse. You twist yourself into knots. I did speech and language therapy for a couple of years, and as puh-puh . . . part of overcoming the blocks, I learned to stop being afraid of the difficult suh-sounds and just *go* for it. You don't worry about other people's reactions to your suh-stammer, the embarrassment of that . . . that *waiting*. That just messes you up. Suh-so you just *speak* and to hell with it if you suh-suh-stumble a bit. It's like having to jump across a wide gap between two buildings and . . . and instead of creeping up to look over the edge, I had to just suh-suh-stride up to it and . . . jump. I got to the puh-point where I hardly stammered at all. But I can't think too far ahead about wuh-what I'm going to say. I can't give speeches or read out loud much, or I suh-suh-start tripping up again.

'Anyway, the suh-suh-censor chip must use a similar part of the buh-buh-buh . . . brain that causes the stammer, or whatever. I can do the same thing with a buh-ban, just run at it and jump across, but it's *a lot harder*. I can suh-say things in bursts, like I just did, buh-but nothing much longer than that. It's too hard to fuh-focus on suh-suh-saying stuff and thinking ahead at the same time. Like now, it was easier having you ask questions I can answer, instead of just coming out and suh-saying it.'

'Wow,' I snort. 'That's, like, the most I've ever heard you speak. Do the oldies know about this?'

'Huh! Yeah, Buh-Buckley found out eventually. Heard me mentioning it to my puh-parents. Not much he can do about it though. And he knows it's hard for me, and I don't talk to the others much anyway.'

I'm blown away. I'm thinking about all the things we could talk about, all the stuff I could add to my journal . . . I can write down anything he says. That's one of the loopholes in the blocks.

'Why did you never tell anyone before this?' I ask.

He shrugs, screwing up his face in a non-committal

expression.

'I don't . . . really *like* many of these suh-stuck-up, entitled shitheads.' (even as he says this, I relish his use of that word and wish I could use it myself. God, I miss swearing properly.). 'I mean, sure, my dad is who he is, buh-but he almost ended up in the job by accident. We wuh-weren't part of some rich elite, like most of these jerks – he came up through the military. And yeah, I agreed to come here, I'm a believer in the whole thing, I really am, but . . . well, if the others knew I could do this, they'd all wuh-want me to *talk* more. I'd end up like a side-show performer. Buh-buh-before I came to this suh-stinkin' rock, I could talk almost completely without a stammer. Now listen to muh-muh-muh-me. It's freakin' puh-painful.'

I nod, understanding. There are topics we can all talk about that skirt the edges of the chip's bans, that aren't quite blocked, but are related to subjects that are. We avoid those too, most of the time, because it's awkward to talk about them and you pause and stutter like someone speaking in a foreign language. In the end, it's easier to not discuss them at all, than to look uncool. I notice that the more we talk, the less he's stammering. Is that a sign he's more at ease with me?

'Why are you telling *me*, then?' I ask.

'Because you're all right. You're less of a puh-puh-privileged glute. And because you were spying on Buckley. You heard some of what Almeida said, suh-so I thought . . .'

'You thought you could get me to trust you, by sharing your secret. And then I'd tell you what I knew in return.'

'Yeah, suh-sort of.'

'But I can't. You know I can't.'

'Yeah. Yeah, I know,' he says, looking off into the distance. 'Suh-something bad has happened out there, Billy, and the oldies aren't telling us wuh-what's going on. And I think . . . whoever blew up the mon heard about it before the rest of us. You heard or . . . suh-saw some of what Almeida said. And . . . you want to tell me, but you can't, am I right?'

I can't even nod. I can't communicate about it in any coherent way, but I want *so much* to tell him what Almeida told Noon and the guardians and he can read the strain, the suppression on my face; my eyes widen slightly, my jaw sets as my teeth press together, the muscles tighten in my cheeks. He notes all of this, nodding to me.

'Okay, that's a yes. Wuh-wait. How about . . . can we do "yes or no" like this? No, we can't really. I can just suh-suh-see . . .' He waves his hand towards me. '. . . this, like you're ready to burst . . . Okay. We can just do "Yes" then. No reaction at all means "No". Right? You up for this?'

I nod, though I find even that difficult. He composes himself, as if preparing to read my mind, which in a way, I suppose, he is. He locks eyes with me.

'Has there . . . has there been a war?'

I don't react.

'Okay, well that's a good thing, I suh-suppose. Right. Has there . . . has there been some kind of massive natural disaster? Lots of destruction, maybe?'

'That's such a crap way to ask a question. Keep your phrasing clear, you monkey.'

'Suh-sorry, okay. Has there buh-buh-been a massive natural disaster?'

No reaction.

'Right . . . so . . . That story about the solar flare is bullshit. Eh, did . . . did one country suh-start the problem?'

I don't react, because I don't know.

'No. Or at least you don't know. Okay,' he breathes. 'Is the suh-sat-link failure part of the buh-buh-big problem out there?' He registers my reaction. 'Right. Yes. That means it could be global, maybe . . . maybe something technological. Is that failure worldwide . . . ?'

It takes us a few more minutes of this kind of trial and error interrogation, but eventually, he knows as much as I do about the situation in the outside world. He works out some of it from my answers, but then he can extrapolate from that and figure the rest out on his own.

Out there, way over the horizon, the world as we know it is starting to come undone. It gives me a chill, thinking about it, trying to define it in my mind so that I can respond to Skip's questions. The sheer mass of its significance rises up inside me as I lead him there, with 'yes or no' options, but I can't talk about it, can't get it out and tell him how it's making me feel. And it's like trying to puke your guts up with your jaw wired shut.

He stares at me in sympathy, knowing what I must be going through. I expect he's felt a milder version of this for most of his life. That must really suck.

'Is that everything you heard?' he asks, finally. 'The virus, the collapse of the wuh-wuh-web and the suh-satellite network . . . the . . . the . . . the complete buh-buh-buh . . . buh-breakdown of communications, how digital muh-muh-money has become wuh-worthless . . . and that's . . . that's affected the value of *everything*, and it's causing chaos, right? Is that it? Is that all you can tell me?'

That's it. Once he's had my final answer, we both relax. I'm sweating, drained, feeling like I've run a ten-kay race.

'That's why the suh-saboteur wrecked our radios,' he murmurs. 'He or she is connected to this in some way. They know suh-something about this virus. If we can find out more about wuh-what's happened *out there*, we might figure out wuh-what's going on *here* – who destroyed the monastery and killed Valtere. Goddamn it, why wuh-won't the oldies just let us *talk*?'

Why? That's a daft question. We both know why. Because the guardians can't have us working out who the traitor is before *they* do. Above all else, they must keep control. It's the whole point, it's why we're here. Their job, under 'normal' circumstances, is to remove us from the wider world, to control us, so that they can keep us beyond the reach of our parents. And it's almost certainly that control that the saboteur is trying to escape.

'We should wuh-work together like this,' he says. 'Find suh-some way to get close to Almeida. I can't say much to him, buh-buh-because of the buh-block – I could get a few words out fast, but I can't *ask* him much. Hold a conversation. It's just too hard. It's nuts, y'know? We could be suh-standing right in front of him right now and we couldn't suh-suh-suh-speak to him.'

'There's something I found out a while back,' I tell him, speaking quickly now, excited at the possibilities, to have someone to talk this out with. 'We can *write down* anything we hear someone else says – *anything*, whether it's banned or not. As long as you're writing as you hear it and try not to think about it. Not everybody knows. If you can *say* it, I can *write* it . . . Maybe you and me . . . we could . . . we could find a way to get close to Almeida. He won't know what information we need and we might only get a few minutes, so we could have some questions written out for him to read. That way, we can get him to tell us what we need to know . . .'

'Yeah, yeah, that's wuh-what we'll do,' Skip mutters. 'The guardians are watching him all the time, but if we could get to him somehow . . .'

His voice tails off as he thinks and he goes quiet, gazing

down at the short, scrubby grass that separates the log from the trail. I use the lull in conversation to start getting all this down in my journal. It helps order my thoughts too, having to put it in writing. I've already got the banned stuff Skip's said. I normally find the longer I leave that kind of thing, the harder it gets; it's as if, as time passes, they become more my words than someone else's and I can no longer use them.

I'm stuck into the writing when he asks, abruptly:

'Wuh-what are you thinking about, when your fuh-face goes like that?'

'Goes like what?' I retort.

'Like that, how it just wuh-was. Like this . . .' He puts on an expression that resembles someone on the point of sneezing; eyes half-closed, mouth hanging open as if on the verge of expelling something. Real dopey lookin'. 'Like that.'

'I was *not* doing that!' I snap at him.

'Sure you were. You do it all the time. The others call it your "zombie face".'

'Who does?'

'Well . . . everybody, really. What were you thinking about?'

Now I can feel my cheeks burning. Oh. My. God. Was that happening every time? *Every time?*

'I was updating my journal,' I wheeze. 'I keep a journal on my chip. I was just writing up what we were talking about.'

'You keep your journal on your suh-*censor chip*?' Skip

exclaims incredulously. 'Where *Buckley* can read it? What are you, an idiot? Wuh-why would you do that?'

'It's just . . . easy,' I say weakly.

'But you're not writing *this* down, are you? You're going to delete that stuff now, right?'

'Yeah, sure. I'll do it right away . . .'

'Woah! You're muh-making that damn face *again*! Billy, for fuh-fuh . . . sake, suh-stop writing!'

I'm hardly listening to him because I'm trying to think of all the times I recorded on the chip while other people were around me. It's impossible to say, but it was *every day*. Several times a day. Normally only a few short sentences, but sometimes I wrote for whole minutes at a time. With that look on my face. And nobody said anything before this.

'Oh my God. I can't believe this. Oh my God.'

'What, that you've been doing the face thing in front of everyone?' he says with a chuckle. 'Yeah, that's a buh-buh . . . buh-bummer.'

If he's just going to stutter his way through stupidly unhelpful crap like that, I wish he'd shut up and move on. I think I'm going to start balling again.

'Oh my God.'

I'm spared further mortification by the sudden cry that slices through the crisp air of the forest, cutting off my thoughts. It's female, I think, and I'm more sure of that when we hear another moments later. It sounds like someone's being hurt. Skip throws one glance my way and then stands up, hurrying into the trees in the direction of the noise. I hesitate for a moment before following him. There's something about the voice . . .

We creep hurriedly forward, taking care where to place our feet. Skip's as nimble as I am, but he's heavier and makes that much more noise. My eyes search the ground for any useful, club-sized stick, but I'm not seeing anything I can pull up without breaking it off, a crack that would give away my presence. Quiet, just stay quiet. Get up there and see what's going on. There's another voice, lower than the first, grunting with effort. The female voice gasps out another cry, louder this time, and is quickly stifled. This is it then, more violence on our sheltered little isle. The sounds are harsh, animalistic in the rustling hush of the forest. A breath of cool wind blows over the sweat on my skin and I shiver slightly, woefully aware that I'm weaker than I was only a few days ago. I flex my hands, thinking of the martial arts training we do every week, and if I'm going to have to use it. If it'll be any use. Confident as I might be, I'm grateful that Skip is here. He's stronger, and a better fighter than me. I've never been more conscious that I'm the smallest person on the island.

We're getting closer to the sound when Skip drops into the long grass, behind a mound of Mexican thorn. He waves at me to do the same. I get down and crawl up beside him, following his gaze where he's peering through the gnarled stems at what's ahead. The first thing I notice is that there are pieces of clothing draped over a fallen tree. The broad trunk lies at an angle, propped on the rotting remains of two other trees. One set of clothes is a guardian's uniform; a short-sleeved green shirt and khaki shorts. The other clothes are civvies, there's a patch of blue and white visible under the uniform, which means one of the two figures is probably a student.

We can't see much of the people beyond the trunk, just the lower legs of one and the back and top of the head of the other, but it's pretty clear what they're doing. And no, nobody's hurting anyone. It's definitely a guardian and a student, though; this is a *serious* breach of the island's rules.

They're ha–*(deleted)* . . . they're do–*(deleted)* . . . they're b– *(deleted)* . . . Ah, nuts.

'Say what they're doing,' I whisper to Skip.

'What?' he replies, his voice barely louder than a breath.

'Let's try this thing,' I press him. 'It'd be good practise. Say what they're doing, so I can record it.'

'Will you suh-suh-stop writing down everything we're doing!' his voice is too loud through his clenched teeth as he glances anxiously back at the couple, but they're too busy to hear us. 'Wuh-what is it with you? Is it like a . . . a . . . a compulsive thing or what?'

'Just *say* it!' I growl eagerly.

'No!'

'Are you blushing? You are! You're blushing! Aw, man . . .

like, really? Are you shy about this stuff?'

'No, I'm not! I'm just . . . This is . . . Just, shut up!'

'Aw, that's so sweet. But seriously, just say it so I can get it down, huh?'

'Let's get out of here,' he says, turning to crawl away.

'But we could wait to see . . .'

'It's none of our buh-business, Billy!' he hisses at me. 'Or do you just not *get* that concept? Get your nose out of it and leave them be. It's nothing to do with us.'

When he puts it like that, I feel embarrassed about it – and a bit pervy. I'm not always sensitive enough about where to draw the line on the whole privacy thing. He's right; this one, I should let go. If anything, I'm a bit jealous of them. On the day we drop Valtere's body into the sea, who can blame two people doing all they can to grasp life and hold on?

On knees and elbows, I start to creep away after Skip. Yeah, I suppose we all have our secrets. I have my shrine and my journal, he has his radio and his way of beating the block. And whoever's busy behind that tree has . . . well, you get the idea. But one by one, we're all becoming exposed, aren't we? It's a small island and we're all living on top of each other. And sooner or later, we're going to find out which of us is a murderer.

Chapter Twenty-Three
Lost Time

(Unreadable File)

(Unreadable File)

(Unreadable File)

(File Restore Failed)

(Searching . . .)

Oh, for fu–*(deleted)*. Where has my text gone?

Chapter Twenty-Four
A State of Shock

Two weeks lost. I can't believe it. Wincing, I touch the singed pair of puncture marks in my neck, over my left shoulder, but the sting of those is nothing compared to this gaping wound left in my journal. Two weeks worth of the file has been corrupted. It's gone. I asked Noon if anything could be done, but she reckons it's lost forever. I would have lost more if the chip didn't automatically compartmentalise large files. I close my eyes, scrolling back . . . The most recent entry I can find is . . . the day I met Skip in the woods and we did our Peeping Tom bit. Everything since then has been scrambled into gibberish by the electric shock I just got. This frickin' pigeon-wart, mushy-pea piece of crap they've put in my head; it couldn't even take a bit of an electrical jolt.

God, I'll never be able to fill those two weeks in again. Two weeks of growing desperation and dread, minutes stretching out like hours as the hunger grew worse. Unable to concentrate on schoolwork or read anything at length; even struggling to keep focussed on a conversation because of the writhing tangle of barbed wire cramps where my guts and stomach should have been, then even that pain began to fade as the days continued to pass, a loss of sensation as my muscles weakened; shivery, sore and awkward, as if they'd been removed from my bones, everything disassembled, and then reattached with poor quality, second-hand ligaments and sinews. Everything took more effort, even staying awake, even thinking.

I missed my period, but Noon told me that was just another effect of starvation. The body temporarily shuts down anything non-essential. Despite the fact I was spared the cramps, that upset me more than I expected. I suppose having babies is a liability when your body hasn't even enough food for itself. I captured all these wonderful little nuggets as time went on, recording the sensations, the minute-by-minute experience of slowly starving.

I haven't given up hope of help coming or of our crops being harvested – Christ on a bike, the *work* we put into those, I got all that down too – but I wanted to come out of this with something I could share with the world when we got back. *If* we got back. *When* we got back. When. I imagined the interviews, the requests for my story, the recognition of our ordeal, the shock of it, and the big questions it would make the world ask . . . I'd have it all here, ready for an audience that would hang on my every word. I'll never be able to remember all those little details I wrote down every day. They're gone from my head, emptied out by the writing process, forgotten by my glucose-deprived brain . . . and now they're gone from the chip too.

Fu–*(deleted)* . . . Oh yeah, of *course* the little fart pip still remembers how to block my *bad language.*

I'm in my bedroom; the window has been fixed, a new pane of glass fitted and everything cleaned up. I was lucky; some people only got boards over theirs, as there wasn't much spare glass in the stores. The repairs are old news, but my original mentions of them are gone too, so I need to set the scene. I'm sitting up in my bed, dressed only in a vest and shorts. It's early morning and Karava has just been in to check on me. My body feels as if it's recently been crushed in a vice because a couple of hours ago, I had tens of thousand volts punch through my body, which snapped me like a whip and dropped me to the floor hard enough to whack my head and give me a concussion. *Another* concussion. Karava says if I keep hurling my head at the ground as I have been, I'm sure to perfect my technique and might soon be able to teach classes. The smart-arse.

My vision is blurry, my brain feels like it's learning to swim at the deep end of the pool and I want to throw up, but it'll only be a dry gag, because there's nothing in my stomach.

On the positive side, it's the first time in weeks that I haven't felt hungry.

Okay, wind it back a bit. I need to fill in some blanks here if all this is going to make any sense. Early this morning, at about four, I was up and wandering round. In one of life's cruel twists, the flipside to feeling so done in all the time is that I can't sleep properly. So I get up and go for a walk. Slowly.

And not very far. The smell of the algae was coming in off the sea that morning and the sludgy, rotten egg stink of it distracted my mind from other things, so I let it draw me down to the harbour.

I turned left and strolled along the boardwalk, gazing out at the way the first dawn light picked out the low-lying shapes of the boats in flat, Cubist planes of orange, amber and yellow, as if my view of the world only made sense if I looked at it from a certain angle. I expected to bump into one of the guardians somewhere down this way. Seeing as the *Santiago* is now the only boat we have fit for the open ocean, Buckley has posted armed sentries on the boathouse ever since the schooner was moved in there with its masts lowered, and lifted out of the water so Noon could work on it. They took the radio out too; it's up in the gym storeroom with the food, with a minimum of six guards in and around the building.

Everything's been getting more 'secure'. Half the guardians carry weapons now – non-lethal, of course. As I said to Smood when he tried to help fight the fire, they can't risk damaging the merchandise. You can see the difference in the guardians' manner too; more blunt, less affable. They give curt replies to questions; they're as helpful as before, but it's civil and efficient. The ones who are normally friendly have lost their warmth. Even Noon hasn't had much time for me lately. More and more, we are made to feel as if the island is on a war footing and our custodians have shifted into a different mode.

So there I was, drifting slowly along the boardwalk, already tired from the exercise, wondering if I'd gone too far, worried that the walk back to my place, back up the hill, would be an uncomfortable strain. I'll admit that this wasn't the first time I'd ended up down here and I swear it wasn't out of any dastardly plan to try and steal the boat, or even to try and catch someone else trying to steal the boat. I was there that night because of insomnia and the mind-smothering smell of the algae and some mild curiosity about why there was no sentry out where the boardwalk passed over the concrete apron in front the boathouses. The closer of the buildings is wrecked, its front wall and its roof missing. While the one holding the *Santiago* has some damage too, it's still standing. The steel shutter was down over the wide main door facing the ramp to the water, so I peered into the shadows along the duck-egg blue expanse of the near wall, trying to see if the side door was open. The light over the door was out. It had been working the day before. I know, because I was there at the same time last night. Like I said, insomnia. And . . . just a little curiosity, maybe.

I was halfway along the path down the side of the building, eyes still on the door, feeling just a little bit creeped out, when I tripped over something lying on the ground. I fell, landing on a large, hard, humped shape, my hands stretched out in front me, scraping the heels of my palms on the concrete path. My face smacked against soft warm skin. So, not something.

Someone. Brother Nguyen. Still breathing, still alive, but with blood on the side of his face from a small wound above his temple. From this position, I could see the side door of the boathouse was standing open. I could see the searchlight motion of a torch beyond the doorway, could hear furtive scuffling inside.

I got to my feet, not making a sound, breath caught in my chest, hoping they hadn't heard me fall. There should have been another guard. If Nguyen was down, then the other one was either involved, or had been taken out too. These were serious guys, professional soldiers. Nguyen had served for years as a paratrooper, jumping into war-zones to fight behind enemy lines. He was one of our martial arts instructors. Guys like him wouldn't get caught out easily. I tried to breathe more normally, because I was starting to feel light-headed. Whoever had broken in there was *way* out of my league . . . I quickly formulated a wily plan to sneak back to the boardwalk, then sprint away as fast as I could, screaming out for help at the top of my voice.

Keeping my eyes on the door, I walked slowly backwards, fingers brushing along the rough surface of the wall, feeling for the corner, where I'd turn and start running. The bushes along the landward side of the boardwalk would provide enough cover in case they, I dunno, *shot* at me with something.

Then I saw the torchlight flicker out through the doorway for a second, just as my fingers reached the end of the wall. I pivoted to bolt away down the boardwalk, only to have a gloved hand clamp across my face and shove my head back against the wall. Someone who'd been standing behind me. There were two of them. *Two of them.* Even as I felt the thud of the impact against the back of my skull, I punched out wildly, knocking the hand away with my left and catching my attacker's nose a lucky jab with my right. It probably hurt them enough to make them really mad. Ramming past them, I tried to make it out onto the boardwalk.

'Help! HELP!' I shrieked. 'I'm at the boathouse! HELP! HEL–!'

Which is when the darts hit, embedding themselves where my left shoulder meets my neck. My body was jerked into a rigid spasm, thousands of volts flowing through the two wires attached by barbs sticking into my skin. My brain got scrambled, my thoughts went haywire as my jaw clamped closed and breath gurgled up my throat and through my clenched teeth. It could only have been a few seconds, but it felt like I could see the sun sailing up over the horizon.

I fell; a hooked fish thrown onto the deck of a boat. I don't know if my head hit the wall or the ground or both. Experience has taught me that you can't trust your memory where loss of consciousness is concerned. But there were two of them at the boathouse – I remember that.

And they robbed me of two weeks of my *journal* with that goddamned taser, the ba–*(deleted)*.

Chapter Twenty-Five
Urging Caution

It's seven in the morning and I'm not feeling much better. Sister Adeyemi brings me breakfast in bed. I'd feel spoiled, if it didn't consist of a glass of water, quarter of a boiled egg and half a steamed potato. The spud's not even in a particularly good state and there isn't butter, salt or gravy to have with it. Adeyemi's still wearing a small bandage on her forehead from the time I fell out of the wrecked bell tower, bringing some chunks of rock with me, and landed on top of her. She's healing slowly.

The egg came from one of Earnest's chickens and that morsel, even without any kind of seasoning, tastes like pure heaven. The birds are getting old, but he has four that still lay every couple of days. The potatoes are from a sack from his last harvest that he found at the back of his shed. He'd been keeping some for seed and had forgotten about them. They weren't in great condition, tentacle-like shoots curling out of them, their flesh turning spongy and grey, but Adeyemi told us they were edible, and that was enough. Even cooked, this one has a texture like raw fish and an acrid aftertaste.

It occurs to me that there have been people who lived almost entirely on these for long periods of their lives. I can only imagine the misery of that. A couple of weeks of this is bad enough. We've planted a lot of potato seeds, but also other vegetables that grow faster and will be ready for harvest sooner. Of all the vegetables, however, the potato offers the most nutrition per square metre of ground needed to grow it. It's the poor man's superfood, so if you've a limited space to grow crops that will be your only source of nutrition, you grow spuds.

We don't expect to be left hanging that long. Help will come for us, eventually – we all still have faith in that, in our parents and the Council.

I'm rubbing the last of the food around the inside of my mouth, holding off swallowing for as long as possible. Then I lick the plate, though there's nothing but damp, grainy residue and a few fragments of skin left on it.

It's funny what your brain can dredge up when your focus changes. During the 1840s famine in Ir-*(deleted)*, they *prayed* for the health of potatoes . . . and for four years in succession, they watched their crops rot, turning to black slime in the ground, as the people slowly starved to death while rich landowners used armed police and soldiers to keep and export the other crops that grew with no problem at all, untouched by the blight. A million people died, trying to survive on less food than we're each getting on the island. I've never appreciated the horror of that before now. It always felt like the type of thing that happened to other people. Other *kinds* of people. It feels frighteningly real now. What an ignorant gimp I was.

Trying to shift my mind from such morbid musings, I think of that film, *The Martian*, where the guy grows potatoes using the sterile soil of Mars and the stored excrement left by his crew, wise-cracking away about the wonders of science as he faces starvation on a dead planet. That's how I want to be, the positive problem-solver. And really I would be, I swear, if I wasn't so profoundly depressed.

We're still a few weeks away from being able to harvest the first of our vegetable crops, but we're not totally without resources on the island. The sailors have been managing to catch the odd fish further out past the algae blooms, though the stuff has probably rendered any shellfish along the shoreline toxic. It helpfully killed off the turtles that used to come ashore every year too. There are no guns left on the island, or so the oldies tell us, but Thompson and Buckley are both archers. Their bows were, thankfully, kept in the gym, so they weren't destroyed in the blast. They've been out most days, hunting birds. You know how much flesh you get off the average bird on this island, the likes of terns, sparrows or petrels? Sweet bugger all, as it turns out. But it all helps, I suppose.

All the poisons and engineered diseases used years ago to keep the place free of vermin and irritating bugs, pretty much wiped out most of the small animals, pollinating insects and even some of the less enduring plant life. Apparently, environmental concerns were secondary to creating our idyllic little holiday village.

'Hey you!' Noon pokes her head round the door.

'Hey you back. Did you actually ring the doorbell, or just walk into my house?'

'No, I just walked in. How's the brain?'

'Dislocated,' I reply.

'Maybe stop using it as a basketball.'

'Oh, you're so funny, I forgot to laugh.'

She comes in and sits down on the edge of the bed. Nodding towards the plate, she asks:

'Breakfast in bed, you pampered little princess! Enjoy the potato?'

'It was outstanding. Like a party in my mouth. No . . . actually . . . it tasted like your face looks. What's going on out there? I can hear shouting.'

'Family conference. Buckley's reading the riot act and there's some protesting going on. We reckon you just stopped someone stealing the boat with all your yelling this morning, and it's hard to believe two students could overcome two armed guardians, so we're in full-on conspiracy mode. Everyone's a suspect − except you. Personally, I think you could well be orchestrating all these crimes, but they won't listen to me. Anyway, Duchess and Smood are trying to give our principal the third degree right back at him. Duchess thinks there could be a gang of traitors at work here, or a team of soldiers on the island, while Buckley is ready to go on the warpath against the studes. And believe me, that is something you *don't* want to see. If that happens, it'll be the end of his warm, cuddly persona.'

'This is still his warm, cuddly persona?'

'Girl, you have no idea. Of all the Council's isolation sites, this has the highest priority,' Noon says, her face and tone turning serious. 'Every military power in the world follows what goes on here – or at least, they did while we were still in contact with the world. The pressure on the principal is enormous. You think they'd give that job to anyone but the hardest nut on the planet? He's doing his best to stay humane and reasonable – your welfare is his first concern – but sooner or later, he's going to put us in lockdown. And at that point, you stop being students and become *prisoners*. No discussions, no protests, no freedom of movement. Censor chips turned up to the max. You're upset about losing two weeks of writing? He could delete your entire journal if he wants to. You know this, Billy. You had to learn about the martial law conditions before you came here; if he chooses to, he can exercise complete control over you. You can be confined to your villas, locked in, allowed out for meals and exercise only.

'I need you to do something for me – seriously now. I need you to remind the others of all this, when you're talking to them. Tell them not to push their luck. They need to crank it down a notch, before Buckley decides he's got no choice. You don't want him declaring a lockdown.'

'That sounds like a threat, Noon,' I mutter.

'He has to keep control,' she replies, as she stands up. 'By any means necessary. We have traitors on the island and he'll find them, you can count on that. But don't put him in a position where he has to go hardcore on you guys, Billy Goat. It won't be pleasant. Also . . . you're still recording everything, yeah?'

'What, you want me to stop my writing too?'

'No.'

She takes out her phone and opens it up, a rolled-up plastic one like mine, except hers comes with more power and memory. I know the guardians have apps for various jobs they do on the island, so I'm not surprised when she holds the phone up and then stares at a point on the left side of my head.

'Your chip is still transmitting your locator signal, though without the GPS, the position is so vague it's not much use to anyone here. And I'm pretty sure Buckley can still *read* what's on the chip, but I can't be sure. His is the only chip that can read all the others and it might have lost that function when the Hub went offline. But anyway, no, I don't want you to stop writing. Keep it up, and make it as complete a story as you can. Maybe stay in your villa, keep out of trouble for a while and write things up. I think the day'll come when we're going to need a full account of what went on here. So, keep writing. Although . . . you haven't put down anything that might antagonise him, have you?'

'Eh . . . no, no. I don't . . . think so . . .' I cough. 'There's not a whole lot I *can* say. If Buckley keeps adding to our bans, I'll have nothing left to write *with* except punctuation.'

'Well, now *there's* a fine challenge for any aspiring author,' she replies, grinning. 'Anyway, just don't got giving him any reason to delete the whole thing.'

'Oh yeah, sure.'

Noon's heading out the door when something occurs to her and she swivels to look back at me.

'Hey, you know you can use flashbacks, right?'

'What do you mean?'

'Well . . . Buckley's added a whole load of new blocks lately, but you still have all the text you wrote *before* each ban – a couple of years' worth of it, yeah? That hasn't been affected. You can still read those words. And you can also copy and paste those older sections of your text into other places in the journal. I don't mean single words or phrases – you can't go writing new sentences with it or it'll set the chip off – but if you use a big enough excerpt, technically, you're not saying anything *new* if you paste it in, so it's not covered by the block. You know, like flashbacks.'

'Holy sh–.' *(deleted)*

'Yeah, you still can't use it to swear, either. Listen, remember what I said, okay? Talk to the others. Buckley's on the edge. Don't go doing anything to push him over it.'

'Like what?'

'Like . . . anything. Just, be good.'

As I watch her leave, I wonder if it's possible she's forgotten she's on an island full of teenagers. Be good? Yeah, right.

Chapter Twenty-Six
Bad Omen

Okay, let's try this out – a flashback. Something that can give some context for our story here and, maybe, taking us back to the start of this mess might help me get my head around some of the stuff that's happened since. I find the scene I'm looking for, copy the text and figure this is as good a place as any to paste it in. So let's take a look back about three weeks before the explosion in the monastery, when we were enduring the last few hours of the worst hurricane the island had seen in decades . . .

The mon stands strong against the battering it's taking from winds with the strength of the gods. Rain lashes in, almost horizontally, a deluge with a noise like sizzling oil. We've all been moved into our HQ so that the guardians can keep a closer eye on us, and because Buckley has concerns about the integrity of the villas. Some of the oldies' homes, those closest to the shore, have already taken damage to their roofs, and a number of windows have been smashed too, despite the shutters. Ceramic roof tiles and sections of solar panel fly through the air like shrapnel, prompting stern warnings from our principal not to venture outside. Debris smacks against the walls and the shutters of the monastery, but this is the third day of the ordeal and we no longer flinch at the impacts.

On the slope above the mon, the wind turbines groan and the trees bend under the storm's onslaught; the sounds of branches snapping like bones breaking, are barely audible in the roar of the wind through the forest. It's easy to imagine the trees bracing themselves in ranks for strength, suffering casualties around the edges of their formation as they bunch up and scream their battle-cries against their old enemy.

I'm in our small meditation room, sitting cross-legged in one of the armchairs with my tablet propped up on my knees. The candles are the only source of light around me, comforting against the background noise of the wind and rain, making the glow from the screen seem flat and cold by comparison. I'm online, talking to Mum. She started nattering as soon as I called, filling me in on the latest from home, but she's beating around the bush about something and I know it. I wish she'd get to the point, because I want her to say her piece so I know I'll have her full attention for what *I'm* bursting to tell *her*.

We are almost completely silent; we're conversing, as we normally do, in a mixture of sign and lip-reading, our hands and faces animated, shape-shifting, conveying more than you can do with words alone. With her implants, Mum can hear almost as well as me, but she always says deaf is as much a culture as a disability – she was raised by deaf parents – and she's encouraged these skills since I was a baby.

'. . . I know the supply ship has been turned back,' she signs, anxiety tightening lines into her forehead and cheeks, her smooth skin darker than mine, with that elegant bone structure she failed to pass on to me. 'They've assured us they'll send another one out as soon as the weather calms down. Is there anything else you need?'

'I'm almost out of toffee,' I reply.

'Well, we can't have that!' she makes an expression of abject horror. 'We'll send some immediately – maybe your dad can despatch an aircraft carrier. Listen . . . there's something I've been meaning to say to you. There are good things happening here; we're achieving a lot and . . . and . . . the party's asked your dad to stay on for another year.'

I rock back, staring at my mum's face in shock. My hands fail me for a moment.

'*What?!*' I finally manage.

'I know it's a lot to ask, but . . .'

'No, no, no!' I sign ferociously at her. 'No! I've been in this . . . this . . . prison colony for over two years, I still have another ten months to go and you want me to stay for *another year*? No way! *No way!*'

'Honey, you should see what we're getting done!' she pleads with me. 'People are rallying around your father – we're making a real difference here. We're back trading with Europe, London's almost been entirely reclaimed and we have support from Ireland and Scotland now too–.'

'I'm not doing it!' I cut her off, fury on my face and in the frantic motions of my hands. 'Mum, I *saw* them! That's why I called! I saw Buckley and Earnest and some of the others doing a . . . a fuckin' *rehearsal*, as if a Sanction had just been declared. They were running through it like . . . like . . . like it was a bloody *fire drill*!'

It's one of the concessions we're granted in the way the censor chips work; we can talk about anything we want if we're in private conversation with our parents. Mum has pulled up short, blood draining from her face.

'What do you mean?' she asks. 'Nothing's happening anywhere. There's been no threat of a Sanction.'

'Yeah, but they still have to *train* for it, don't they?' I rage at her, tears in my eyes. If I was using my voice I'd break down sobbing, but I'm spared that. 'So they can be ready, y'know . . . for the day when the . . . the *call* comes through. You don't know what it's *like* here. Nobody can talk about it, because they won't let us, but that makes it *worse*. And every time we see Earnest show up or . . . or even if Buckley gets called into the comms room, we think the Sanction's been ordered and . . . and . . . Listen, when the eye of the storm passed over yesterday, I went out for a run, past the guardians' villas and I saw them acting it out . . .'

'Oh my God, I'm sorry sweetheart! You're never supposed to see that!'

She's on the verge of crying now too, but I have no

sympathy for her. She's not here; she doesn't have to live in this place, cut off from the rest of the world. What's she got to cry about?

'You know you're safe, right?' she signs, tears on her cheeks now. 'Nobody's going to do anything–.'

I hold up my hand to stop her right there. I've had enough.

'I'll finish the term, but then I'm coming home,' I declare, every centimetre of my body language making it clear I'm not for turning. 'Tell Dad I'm sorry, but I'm not putting up with this for another year. Oh . . . yeah, and as if things weren't bad enough, Buckley added a new ban the other day.'

'Oh, those stupid censor chips! What is it this time?'

'He says he's had enough of us swearing at the guardians and that we can't use obscenities any more. He's put a block on swearing . . . I mean any *real* swearing.'

'Wow,' Mum signs with mock seriousness. 'Are you . . . Are you even *capable* of talking without swearing?'

'Oh, ha ha . . .'

The screen just freezes. I try to refresh and nothing happens. A notice comes up saying the signal has been lost. I throw my hands up, growling in exasperation. Goddamn it. God *damn* it! I think I really *am* going to start crying now. Fu-*(deleted)* this whole twisted pantomime of a boarding school on this bloody island in the lonely butthole of nowhere. Ten more months. I don't know how I'm going to last.

I hear Noon, speaking in a low voice out in the hallway.

She'll be able to sort this.

'. . . No, nothing's happened here yet,' she's saying. 'We still have a signal. Everyone's okay here for now. Yeah, I *know* what it means. Yeah, thanks for the heads-up. I'll . . . I'll see what I can do to–.'

I jump up and swing open the door. She's just to one side of it and reacts with a start as I appear suddenly behind her. Clutching her phone to her chest like a kid caught stealing biscuits, she smacks me softly across the head.

'Damn it, Billy! I didn't know you were in there – you scared the shit out of me! What, were you sitting in there finding your inner child or . . . doing drugs or . . . or doing drugs with your inner child or . . . what were you up to?'

'I was signing with Mum,' I tell her, then hold up the tablet. 'I got cut off.'

'Yeah, satellite coverage has gone down,' she says, ending the call and slipping her phone into her pocket. 'I just heard.'

'But I heard you say we still had a signal.'

'Not *our* coverage – Britain's. They're losing contact with the satellites over Europe. Our comms are still working. Nobody knows what the problem is yet. Don't worry, it'll get sorted out.'

She reaches out, her fingers touching my cheek, catching a tear that has just run down from my eye. It's a tender gesture, hardly a brush against my skin, but it does more for me than words could right now.

'You okay?'

'It's Dad,' I reply. 'He . . . He"s been asked to stay on another year.'

'Aw, nuts. Are you ever going to get out of here and leave me in peace?'

We hear a distant ripping noise and then a tumultuous crash from outside, which sends us running to the end of the corridor. The shutters are down over the big glass doors, but the steel shutters have horizontal slots that you can peer through, their hardened plastic now smeared with rain. Valtere's already there, having come out of the games room at the same time. His fleshy, broken-veined face is screwed up in a grimace, one hand rubbing the side of his balding head.

'The boathouse,' he groans, jerking his chin in the direction of the harbour. 'The roof just got torn off. It's a fucking mess . . . !'

We can't see the harbour beyond the student villas, but the boathouse is further off to the left, visible through a thin copse of storm-tossed palm trees. The crash we heard was the *Orca*, our big catamaran and one of the island's only two ocean-going boats. It's been lifted out of the mangled boathouse and thrown over the building's back wall, breaking one of the hulls in half. We watch it rock like a see-saw over the wall, almost as if it's trying to clamber over it, and then the wind flips it into the covered swimming pool a few metres behind the wall.

'If that gets picked up again, it could take out another

building,' Valtere mutters. 'Look at the boathouse! *Putain de merde*! We could lose the *Santiago* too.'

'No, it's strapped down on the lift, it should be okay unless it's hit by something,' Noon replies.

Damn. We've already lost a few of our smaller boats, but the *Orca* was our sweetest ride for longer cruises. A large section of the boathouse roof has landed on the grass, breaking apart as it flops across the lawn that lies between the swimming pool and the road. It must have dragged half the contents of the building's attic with it when it was torn off, because it's spewing crates, boxes, bundles and other debris every time the wind shunts it forward.

One long crate rolls out and is caught by the wind, lifted off the lawn and hurled towards us. It somersaults across the ground, splitting under the bashing impacts as it bounces, becoming misshapen and ragged, and I see the polished surface of the dark wood, the handles on the sides. When the lid wrenches off and flies away, the ivory-white, cushioned interior becomes visible, before the whole thing disappears from sight and smashes against the side of the monastery.

Not a crate. A coffin, that had been stored in the attic of the boathouse. Nobody says anything. I shouldn't find it as shocking as I do. After all, the island is supposed to be completely self-sufficient for long periods of time if needs be. It's all part of the isolation the Council aims to achieve for us. Send a bunch of people to live on an island for long enough, eventually, you're going to need a coffin, right? Maybe more than one.

'I think we only had one of those left,' Noon says. 'Let's hope nobody dies any time soon.'

'No skin off my nose,' Valtere says with a chuckle. 'I want to be buried at sea.'

Chapter Twenty-Seven
Seeing Things

My head is a bit of a mess after reading through the storm scene again. The memories it's woken up are bitter and sharp, juddering with intensity; I'm seeing those events again, but with the new perspective forced on them by what's happened to us over the last few days.

It's given me a lot to think about. Stuff I don't want to write down just yet.

After splicing the scene into my journal, I read it through a few more times, trimming it to fit. Then I stay in bed for most of the day, head melted, wondering how the world's scientists are coming along with their research into suspended animation, because that's just what I could do with about now. Nobody bothers with me apart from Karava, who knocks on my bedroom door at around midday to check on me, waking me up from a bad dream where I kept getting electrical shocks as I tried to escape from a burning building. I jerk awake, crying out and find him waving apologetically at me. Once I've convinced him I'm lucid enough to utter mild curses in an articulate fashion, he lets me go back to sleep. I make a note on my chip to remind people I have a bell by my front door, so maybe they could stop just walking into my bedroom.

What feels like moments later, Skip is shaking me awake.

'I have a doorbell! Get out!' I blurt out, in a state of semi-consciousness. Then: 'Wait. Have you got any food?'

'No, I'm here to–.'

'Then get out!'

'Come on, get up! Wuh-wuh-we haven't much time!'

He shakes me again and I growl and sit up, glaring at him with the fury of the roughly roused. Part of it is embarrassment too. We've spent a lot of time together over the last couple of weeks and I won't say we're go–*(deleted)* . . . I mean, it's maybe the star-*(deleted)* . . . I do kind of li–*(deleted)*. Goddammit! It's not like we've *done* any–*(deleted)*. Anyway, now he's here, sitting on my bed. I can see the mirror on my wardrobe; I have the imprint of my fingers on my face where I've been lying on my hand, and my hair looks like I got dragged backwards through a bush. Not that he looks much better. He was lean to begin with, and nearly three weeks of malnourishment has taken kilos off him. His cheekbones are more prominent, there are dark circles under his eyes and his face looks all grey and drawn, emphasised by his feathery black fringe. He's agitated, making an impatient expression as he jerks his head towards the door.

'What?' I snap at him.

'Earnest is up at Buh-Buh-Buh-Buckley's,' he says simply. 'Wuh-wuh-we've got our chance.'

Two minutes later, I'm dressed, my hair reined in and bound up in a pony-tail. I'm more energised than I've felt in ages (apart from that the time early this morning, when somebody plugged me into a high-voltage battery). With Brother Earnest up here, Almeida could be alone at the farm. This might be our chance to get him talking. Tilting back my bedside locker, I pull out the sheet of paper taped to the underside.

It took us nearly an hour to get our questions down on paper, because they're about things that either I'm specifically blocked from mentioning or we're both blocked from talking about. And, of course, all the way along, we were working against the ban that forbids us to communicate with Almeida. Which meant we were working against our own brains. Ever tried to lose weight by dieting, or try to remember something you've forgotten, or quit a bad habit? It's *hard* to get past your own brain.

But I can write down anything that anyone else says and Skip can say blocked things out loud, though it takes great effort and focus.

Through a rather contorted process we devised around the 'loopholes' we've found, we worked out what we wanted to ask Almeida, then Skip spoke the questions out loud and I wrote them down. It wasn't easy. He was barely able to blurt out a few words at a time and each one took a number of goes before I was able to get it down in an intelligible sentence. We figure we'll be pressed for time, so we aimed for a short intro and the five questions that will get us the most relevant information. Nice and big in black marker, I've written:

'The guardians won't tell us what you've told them. We have chips in our heads that stop us from talking to you. Please answer these questions:

'1. Where did you come from?

'2. What can you tell us about what's happened to the web and the satellites?

'3. Have any war crimes been committed? And if so, by whom?

'4. What questions have the guardians asked you?

'5. What else can you tell us?'

It's not exactly an exhaustive list, but we're hoping for long responses and we think Skip can spit out a few more questions depending on how Almeida answers. As I read over it once again, I think about what Noon said, about not doing anything to antagonise Buckley, and I wonder if this is the kind of thing she was talking about.

I think it could be. Actually, I think it's probably *exactly* what she had in mind.

But still . . . you know. Whatever. I'm seventeen; consequences are what other people worry about. I pull open the curtains and am surprised by the gloom outside. Low, anvil-grey clouds pile up against each other in the sky.

'What the hell? How long did I sleep? What . . . what *time* is it?'

'It's nearly fuh-fuh-four,' he replies. 'Buh-buh-buh . . . but

273

there's wuh-weather coming in. The wuh-wind's getting up too, so wrap up.'

He's not kidding. I'm struck by the chill when we head outside and I'm glad for the thick fleece hoodie I've put on, but almost immediately regret not bringing a jacket too. Skip's only in a hoodie and combats, so I didn't think I'd need one. With my energy levels so low, I've been feeling the cold much more lately, and walking or running as far as the farm is out of the question these days, so we're going to cycle, which will warm me up, and we'll be more sheltered once we get into the trees.

The wind shoves us with rough gusts as we jump on our mountain bikes, making it hard to keep our balance. And even though it's at our backs, coming in off the sea, we can barely cope with with this gentle slope as we cycle up towards the woods. A few weeks ago, we'd have done it without thinking about it.

The village is quiet now, nobody else is out, the elements persuading everyone to stay indoors. Our hunger is taking its toll on the maintenance of the place. The grass hasn't been cut; the kerbs, verges and flowerbeds haven't been weeded. Some of the damage to the trees and buildings left by the hurricane remains unfixed. Buckley has suspended all non-essential work to enable the guardians to rest more and save energy. It's not long before I realize we should have taken electric bikes. Though I've always taken pride in cycling under my own steam, I click down through the gears as the incline increases, standing up to pump the pedals, already feeling short of breath.

Once we pass into the trees, we do an acute right turn off the road and up a trail, facing into the wind now. This hill was a challenge, back when we did cycle races along this trail, but in our weakened state, it's become impossible to pedal up. We swing ourselves off the bikes and push them up the hill. Even with the exercise, my body is stiffening up with the cold. I should have brought gloves. I *never* wear gloves at this time of year. I'm shivering already, the wind seeming to slice right through the fabric of my clothes, fingers of chill on my skin. I'm seriously starting to wonder if I'll even make it to the farm.

Where the trail reaches the shoulder of the hill, it corners, the zig turning to a zag that heads up along the short ridge. There's an open spot here, an observation point with a bench that looks out on the view beyond, taking in the village, the wind turbines and the harbour below them. You can normally see the ocean out to the horizon, but today the view fades away into the scudding mess of low cloud. There's a slight, hunched figure sitting on the bench, his back to us, with three of the cats weaving around him, a black-and-white and a tabby arching their bodies against his legs, and a ginger on the back of the bench, at his shoulder, licking at the fingers of his upraised hand. As we walk up, we see that it's Gemmy. He doesn't turn, though we're so close, he must have heard us approach.

'Gemmy?' I say to him. 'Hey man, are you okay?'

He doesn't look okay. He's shivering, his head hanging heavily over his chest, his shoulders slumped, arms tucked against his body, his thighs pressed tightly together. In the last couple of weeks, his face has seemed to collapse, his brown skin becoming bloodless, his once chubby cheeks caving into gaunt hollows, his eyes gazing, with a stunned expression, out of sunken pits. His limbs are skeletal, the knuckles of his hands and the bones of his wrists painfully swollen, the clothes hanging crumpled on him as if he was nothing more than a wire frame with a human head stuck on the top. If I'm cold, he must be absolutely *freezing*, and yet he's sitting out here, in the full force of that piercing sea wind.

Then I see what he has in his hands. Shreds of meat, probably from the dinner yesterday, when we shared the flesh of the frigatebird that Thompson had shot down with an arrow. For my meal, I got a piece the size of my finger, along with a quarter of a damp potato.

'Gemmy . . . Are you . . . are you *feeding the cats*?'

He doesn't answer, so I come around to sit down beside him. Skip stays standing, hovering at my shoulder as I lean closer to Gemmy.

'Gemmy, hey,' I say gently. 'Man, seriously, you can't feed the cats. You've got to eat your food. They can hunt. It's why they're here. You *need* that food.'

He finally seems to notice my presence and looks up. His eyes scare me. They're too wide and it's as if something has gone from him and left the door open behind it.

'We have to show them we can still be kind,' he says in a weak, rasping voice.

'Show who, the cats?' I ask.

'No . . . no, the ones . . . the ones who are watching it all,' he gestures with an old man's motion at the trees behind us. 'They're observing us. To see if we can stay human. Humane. We have to . . . have to . . . show them we can still be kind no matter . . . no matter how bad things get.'

'Gemmy, I don't understand. Who are you talking about?'

He shakes his head at me as if we've been through this many times and I refuse to see reason.

'It's part of the experiment,' he says. 'The sabotage, the . . . the starvation, that guy arriving from out on the sea, the soldiers on the island . . .'

'What soldiers on the island?' Skip asks.

'It's all to . . . to modify our behaviour, test our responses,' Gemmy continues, ignoring the question. 'Even the guardians are guinea pigs, right along with us. They don't know what's going on, but I figured it out . . . I figured it out . . .'

He's rocking back and forth now, staring straight ahead, holding the ginger tom on his lap and stroking its back. He's shivering violently.

'Gemmy, I'm not sure what you're saying,' I tell him,

glancing back at Skip. 'What did you figure out?'

'This place isn't real!' he wheezes. 'This island, the sea . . . even the sky. They're all . . . all *artificial*. It's a giant . . . giant psychological experiment. Our parents don't know we're here. The Council hasn't told them the truth. Why would a man like your dad leave you here, Billy . . . let this happen to you?'

'You . . . you heard about the communications,' I stammer. 'Gemmy, it's just . . . they don't know we're starving . . .'

'They *can't* know the truth. Nobody's telling them,' he insists. 'My mum's back in Canberra, all that power at her command and she doesn't even know her son is *missing*. I've probably been replaced with a . . . a copy or something. A clone maybe. Or they're faking recordings of me, to make her believe I'm okay. You think Smood's mother would . . . would stand for this? If she knew what was happening we'd have the fuckin' Navy SEALs coming up the beach. There'd be stealth bombers flying overhead. Or Duchess? You think that Indian trillionaire, the most powerful man in the world, would let this happen to his precious princess?

'You and the others are so . . . so blinkered. You reckon it's just one saboteur who blew up our supplies and now the guardians can't find the bastard who did it. Just one guy – the legendary lone gunman right? Only now you find out there's *two* of them. Or you're like Duchess, believing there's some squad of soldiers who've infiltrated the island to . . . kidnap us or . . . or . . . help the traitor. This is all a . . . a narrative that we've been made to believe. Everything that's happening here is being *manipulated* – every little detail. We've been fed a line and we've all fallen for it. This whole place has been built under some dome somewhere and made to look like an island. Everything's controlled, even the weather. This wind . . . this cold we're feeling? They're *making* this cold. We were handed over to the bloody United World Council like sacrificial lambs because that's what our parents were told to do to earn their precious seats and now *they haven't a clue what's really going on here.*'

He's raving, but we feel compelled to listen, because he's saying things that he shouldn't be capable of saying. I've never seen anything like this before. Either he's so malnourished that it's affecting the working of his censor chip, or he's become so unhinged, his brain is unable to monitor its own speech any more. Either way, he has us transfixed, babbling facts mixed with paranoid delusions that we know can't be true, but seeming so convinced of them that I'm actually starting to question what I know about this place. Now *I'm* starting to feel paranoid.

'. . . But I've seen the soldiers in the trees, watching us,' he goes on, his voice croaking, strained. '*They* know. Almeida's part of it too. They're making sure we don't go too far astray, that . . . that we don't look behind the scenery and see how this place has been made. It's an experiment and the scientists will do whatever they want to us until they get their results.'

'Gemmy . . .' Skip sighs, shaking his head. Even he's hugging himself against the cold now. 'It's not some big conspiracy. Come on, man, I muh-mean . . . you know wuh-wuh-why we're here. Who needs to muh-muh-make up stories about this? There's no experiment—.'

'That's why it's so brilliant! Nobody would believe it could be done to *us*! We're supposed to be untouchable!' He turns to stare right at me, a feverish intensity in his eyes. 'And after everything they've done to us, d'you think they can ever let people find out? They can never let us off this island. They can't risk the world finding out what they did. We have to *die* here.'

I look up at Skip, and the same dismay I feel is written all over his face. We can't leave Gemmy here. The poor demented sod won't even make it down the hill in this state – if it even occurred to him to try. If he stays up here, he could die of exposure before someone else finds him. Maybe we can still make it over to the farm afterwards, but I'm feeling exhausted already.

'Come on, Gemmy,' I say to him in my best social worker's voice. 'Let's get you home, eh? It's pretty cold out here; me and Skip could do with warming up with a cup of . . . y'know . . . hot water . . .'

Skip helps him up off the bench, draping Gemmy's arm over his shoulders to support him. Skip's hardly in prime shape, but I can tell by his posture that there's no weight in our friend's emaciated body.

'. . . I think they're trying to make . . . make us turn . . . turn on each other,' Gemmy's saying, his speech broken by the chattering of his teeth. 'That's the aim; to make us turn nasty. You wa–. . . watch Smood and . . . and Noddy and . . . the others. They'll fall for it. They'll get angry and . . . they'll lash out. We have to defy those bastards out there, Billy. Prove them wrong. We have to show them we can be *kind*, no matter how bad it gets.'

'You're right, Gemmy,' I try to assure him, reaching out and gripping his hand. 'You're right.'

He lunges at me, nearly slipping from Skip's grasp. I can't tell if he's crying or if it's just those red-rimmed eyes watering in the bite of the wind.

'*We have to show them we can be kind*!' he wails. 'It's all we have left! Otherwise, what good are we? What good are we?'

I nod to him, fixing a look of grim assertion on my face, showing him I'm ready to stand shoulder to shoulder with him, flaunting my determination to defy those watchers in the woods. He's too weak to walk far, so we get him up onto my bike and walk either side of him, wheeling him between us, with Skip taking his bike with his free hand. I shake my head helplessly, overcome with pity for this deranged soul, a sympathy that's woven through with creeping seams of fear. Because he's got to me. He's got me wondering if maybe someone, somewhere is sitting in judgement on us.

And if there is one single, hard fact that led to the founding of our little colony, it's that the world is tragically short of kindness.

Chapter Twenty-Eight
Fragile Life

The rain falls thickly, with a forceful weight that dislodges loose earth and soaks deep into the once-firm ground of the field, reducing the earth to mud. As we haul ourselves out of the SUVs, Earnest, Mthembu and Nguyen pass out shovels, spades and picks. Though it's still a couple of hours before sunset, a murky darkness has settled over the island, the sun's glow smothered behind a roiling mass of cloud. There are battery-powered work-lights set up wherever solid ground can be found, the rain slashing the beams of light into ribbons.

The island has been caught under the very edge of a hurricane that's passing to our south-west. It had been forecast weeks ago, but Noon and Buckley had hoped it would skirt us without incident. It didn't. The wind is nothing like the strength of the storm that steamrolled over us last time, but it has brought a deluge that has lasted for over a day and keeps on coming.

Noon has been trying to pull me aside to talk to me about something, but I'm in no mood for it. She seems frustrated that I'm avoiding her. I'm trying not to think about her at all.

From the start of the rain, Earnest kept watch on the field and our fragile newborn seedlings, anxiously gauging the effectiveness of the new drainage channels. Earlier this afternoon, a team of ten guardians went out and started deepening those channels, but even then, they've been overwhelmed. Now we're all being called in, even Matthias Almeida, who I can see labouring under the watchful eye of Thompson, halfway down the slope, the pair digging a new trough. This rain could mean our deaths if we lose these crops. I've never been so conscious of the destructive power of the weather . . . and how the outside world has abandoned us to the merciless elements.

The strongest guardians are working closest to the dangerous areas. Smood, Moose and a couple of others join them, even Noddy, trying to clear the muck out of the troughs that have been cut down through the field, to divert the new streams rushing down the slope, in the form of three torrents and a number of smaller runs. They've already swept away about a quarter of the crop. The earth is treacherous to walk on, slippery and crumbling, pure liquid in places. The channel that ran down the middle of the field is fast becoming a river as tonnes of rainwater flow down off the hills above us. As I watch, a section of ground collapses on my side of this churning water, disintegrating and carried away in the current and Sengupta is taken with it, crying out as he's rolled under the water. I put my hand to my mouth, then start down towards him, but Mthembu stops me, and heads down himself. Almeida is plunging through muddy slop further down to try and intercept the flailing guardian. I see Sengupta dig his feet in where the stream gets shallower and haul himself out, though it takes all his formidable strength to fight against the flow. Then Mthembu and Almeida are there, their arms stretching out, gripping the other man's hands and dragging him onto firmer ground.

'Billy!' Earnest shouts at me over the noise of the elements. 'Come on, stop gawking and get stuck in!'

The smallest and weakest of us have been set to work saving as many of the seedlings as we can. Anywhere that the mud has started to slip, but it's still safe to walk across, we're on our knees with trowels, digging up the delicate, precious plants and placing them in wheelbarrows, which have covers strapped over them. I've got Cheeks working on one side of me and Gemmy on the other. He seems to have recovered a bit from the breakdown he suffered up on the trail yesterday, but his movements are still feeble and I'm surprised Karava let him come out here. He's barely lucid, gazing at the new life in his hands with a wistful compassion.

Cheeks is crying as she fingers the feathery leaves of a plant. Her fanatical personal grooming regime has been increasingly neglected over the last while; depression has set in and all airs and graces have been lost. Now she tenderly removes each tiny turnip plant and carefully places it in the barrow, as if it were some trembling, injured animal.

It's almost how I feel too. It takes me a few tries to figure out how deep each plant's roots go and how to preserve most of them. Hunger knuckles my guts, but it has lost its claws, the pangs little more than a dull ache. Even though I have gardening gloves on, my fingers are already cold and starting to go numb. The small shoots feel desperately fragile; the thumb-sized nubbins of turnip would have meant nothing to me only a few weeks ago – I didn't even *like* turnip – and now I see each one as a means of living just a little bit longer. They are precious capsules of life and we have to save every one we can. We toil in the rain, kneeling in mud, gently spooning up each plant with our trowels, placing them in plastic crates and bringing them to the barrow, stacking them with exaggerated care. Mucky clay clings to my gloves, making my hands all the more clumsy. As each wheelbarrow is filled, Skip or Nuke hauls it up the hill to the sheds.

The rain is so loud on the hood of my waterproof that I don't hear the shouts at first. My brain registers the urgency before I can make out any words. I raise my head in alarm, eyes searching the drenched darkness for the cause of the cries I'm hearing. Further up the slope, I see figures scattering away from the middle of the field, bolting for the sides. Then I hear the sound, growing louder until it's nearly drowning out the noise of the rain; a sludgy, grinding, tossing, roaring sound. Something giant is coming down through the forest.

A huge Norfolk pine crashes out onto the field, horizontal, lying on its side on a flood of mud, brush and rocky debris. Its foliage has been almost completely torn off, leaving only the jagged, broken spikes of its branches and the long straight trunk, nearly fifty metres of it, which comes out of the treeline like a battering ram, only to turn side-on as the flood spreads out across the open space. I blurt out a censored curse and run to my right, towards the edge of the field. I grab the shoulder of Gemmy's jacket as I pass him, he's still staring, and drag him at a stumbling sprint, slipping and staggering across the swampy earth. I don't even look towards the tree until it's tumbled past behind me and floodwater is sloshing across my feet and still I run, Gemmy struggling after me.

I stop and turn round and Cheeks slams headlong into me, knocking all three of us off our feet. I shove her off, watching the tree roll like some kind of medieval siege engine, the flood itself losing force across the wide space, but the pine, now under its own momentum careens onward. At least two people are crushed beneath it, maybe three, it's hard to see in the madness and the gloom, with mud plastered on my face. I hear shrieks stopped short. I think one of them was Mthembu. The tree keeps going, each end of it bouncing in turn, swinging round and finally rocking to a halt on the beach.

'Billy!' Cheeks calls to me, panic in her voice. 'Billy! Help!'

She's on her knees, leaning over Gemmy, who's clutching his chest, his back arching, his face contorted in agony. He twists round to glare at me, then his eyes screw shut and he gurgles a growl and his body goes slack.

'I think he's having a heart attack!' Cheeks gasps. 'Help

me!'

We're all trained in CPR. She puts her hands on his chest, starts compressions, rocking from her hips with her elbows locked. I clear the mud from around his mouth and nose, tip his head back, pinch his nose closed, waiting for her to pause and then breathe hard into his mouth. One, two. She starts pushing down again. A few rounds and we get into a rhythm. It won't be like in the films. Gemmy isn't going to wake up. His starved heart is not going to spontaneously restart. All we're doing is keeping oxygen going to his brain until someone can bring a defibrillator and jump-start his pump. Can we even give him an electric jolt when we're all soaking wet? Don't think. Breathe. One . . . two . . .

I don't feel the cold or the rain any more; I'm focussed on his face, centimetres from mine, his slack skin, scrawny neck, blue lips, his teeth, worn down by stomach acid, and grey tongue. I'm reading his body, searching for any sign that we're succeeding, that we have a chance. He doesn't feel like a living body. He's a limp mass of muscle and bone, run through with a mind-bogglingly complicated mass of tubes. We're pumping a bellows through dead meat and I'm crying and begging him to hold on, because hearing is the last sense to go before someone loses consciousness.

Don't think. Breathe. One . . . two . . .

Chapter Twenty-Nine
Loss

The worst of the flooding is over and we've done what we can. We've saved about half the crop and the drainage is now under control. The fallen tree must have been holding back a natural reservoir of floodwater, because once the big wave came through, what followed became a more manageable flow. We'd already had 'dinner', so there's no more food coming until the morning and I'm feeling completely hollowed out, a faltering automaton, wobbling on my feet as we trudge towards shelter from the lashing rain. Incredibly, some of the guardians stay out in it, working, but Buckley sends the students into Earnest's house.

It's the same size and layout as Buckley's, though it's suffered a lot more wear and tear, reflecting the fact that it's effectively a farmhouse. The storeroom at the back, which has only a single, tiny window, has recently been fitted with two secure locks. We take a quick peek inside. There's a narrow, steel-framed army bed, a chair, and a small desk in there. This must be where Almeida is kept when they need him under lock and key.

Earnest has an approach to maintenance that's all practical and gives little consideration to aesthetics. His fixes ain't pretty. Much of his furniture looks beaten up, a lot of it pretty raw, even homemade. The shelves are constructed out of wooden crates and scaffolding poles. It's rough and homely and dry and warm and none of us really care much about how it looks. We don't care much about anything right now.

The short couch and two armchairs are quickly claimed by Duchess, Cheeks, Noddy and Spray. The one difference between this house and all of ours is that it has a fireplace, with logs and kindling in two big baskets beside it and a box of lighter blocks. Caked in mud, shivering and wet, desperate for more warmth, I start putting a fire together. Smood offers to help, but I wave him away – I've seen him trying to light campfires and I haven't the patience for that nonsense. Nuke opens a drawer in a pine dresser and finds a box of matches, tossing them to me. The firewood is dry and well seasoned and it only takes me a couple of minutes to get a decent blaze going. Anyone who didn't get a seat has plonked themselves on the floor in front, using the legs of those behind them or each other's bodies for support. We are a mass of frightened animals, huddling for comfort. I wedge myself between Moose and Skip and rub the heels of my hands against my freezing cheeks, my eyes feeling like they're bulging swollen from all the crying I've done.

Gemmy, Mthembu and Thompson are dead.

We feel each death differently. Gemmy was one of us, part of us. We knew he was weak, that his bulimia had taken its toll long before the real starvation set in. Obviously, it had left his heart in a bad state and the strain of the last few weeks had finished what his mental illness had started. Even so, he was like us and it turned out he wasn't immortal, like we all assumed we were and now the reaper has brushed past us, exhaling its chilly breath on all our skins, making us feel the limits to our lives. We'll grieve eventually, but right now we're in shock, terrified at the closeness of his death. He may have been further along the road of starvation, but it's a road we've all found ourselves on now. Gemmy has shown us our impending future.

Sister Thompson was one of the cold ones; civil and helpful, but always keeping a professional distance. She was here to do a job and didn't want to get attached, protecting herself emotionally from the possible cost of growing too close to us. But of the three fatalities, her body suffered the worst damage and most of us saw it before she was covered up. The tonnes of rolling tree, protruding with spike-like branches, had mashed her up pretty badly. She lived for a few minutes afterwards and I can still hear her failing breathing through crushed ribs and lungs.

Despite his sombre manner, Mthembu was an uncle to us. He took us seriously, didn't talk down to us or treat us like children, while at the same time, we always felt like he had our backs when we needed him. The man's oversized smile was a reward of warmth, his damaged soul giving him a tenderness completely at odds with the horrific war-zone he'd been brought up in, first as a child soldier, then mercenary, then professional soldier and peacekeeper, then brought here at Karava's recommendation to take responsibility for a bunch of teenagers who knew him only as the kind, loping geek with the torture scars on his legs and back, the obsession for model planes and quirky gadgets. Unlike Thompson and most of the others, he left himself open. His life was the absolute opposite of ours and yet this gem of a man empathised with us more than anyone except Noon.

It is a small mercy that he died instantly, his head smashed to a pulp, a branch impaling his chest. The bodies were carried away, hidden quickly from our eyes. Not quickly enough. A couple of others were injured too, though Gemmy was the only student casualty.

'Hey. Hey . . . you've got your writing fuh-face on again,' Skip whispers to me.

I immediately stop recording and straighten up the dumb expression on my face.

'What did you say?' Duchess pipes up from over my shoulder, where she's sitting on the couch.

Oh f-*(deleted)*, I write, unable to help myself.

'Nothing,' Skip says stupidly.

'Did you say "writing face"?' she presses him.

'No . . . I suh-suh-suh-said she had her . . . her "vapid" face on again.'

Oh my God, he's a crap liar. I don't know why. All he has

to do is sit and stammer while he thinks up the right thing to say, the idiot. I'd thump him if it wouldn't look even more guilty.

'No, no, I heard you – you said "writing" face,' Dutch repeats firmly, making sure everyone can hear. 'Is that what you're doing when you do that zombie face thing, Billy? Are you *writing*? Are you keeping a *journal*?'

'On your chip?' Noddy adds from the armchair off to my left, tilting his head forward, like a dog pointing at a hidden bird. From where he's sitting, he can get a clear view of my face. 'Are you writing your freakin' journal on the censor chip that Buckley can *read*?'

I open my mouth to deny it, but my expression betrays me. I'm emotionally and physically drained. I've no fight left in me. I can't even start mounting a defence. Noddy collapses back in his chair, grimacing in disgust. Some of the others are giving me the same look.

'Oh my God, you *are*!' Duchess explodes, throwing her hands towards me. 'I don't believe it! Are you writing down the stuff we say? Have you been doing that the whole time?'

'Not everything . . .' I start to say, getting to my feet because I'm feeling the atmosphere change around me. I move forward to stand by the fire.

'You mean Buckley's been able to read anything we said when we were around you?' Noddy snarls.

'No, I don't write down *everything*–.' I protest.

'Are you writing down what we're saying right now?' Duchess presses me.

'No! No way!' I exclaim. Skip gives me a dubious look, which he can take and stick right up his skinny arse. 'Besides; since when did any of you care about privacy? Up until a few weeks ago, you stuck every minute of your lives, every thought you had on Share. You still would if you could. You want the whole world looking at you. You *love* it! At least when I write something down, I keep it to myself.'

'Yeah, so it'll be seen by just you and *Buckley* and anyone *he* wants to show,' Noddy snaps. 'I share what I choose to share, not what you decide you want to report on. You're a freakin' snitch!'

'I am not!'

'Goddammit, Billy, I trusted you . . .' Duchess says, shaking her head.

That hurts more than Noddy's accusations, more than any of the hostile glares I'm getting from the others. Call me an arse-licker, but I don't want to lose Dutch's approval. I care what she thinks of me. I don't want to–.

'Hey, what's he doing out there on his own?' Nuke barks, interrupting my thoughts.

She's been standing by the window behind Dutch's armchair, peering out at the last few guardians at work in the bubbles of light scattered around the field. Eager for a change in subject, I move over beside her and gaze out into the darkness. From here, we can see down the slope of the field, but also into the small yard formed by the house and the out-buildings, illuminated by lights on the walls. Nuke nods her head towards Almeida, who's just walked past into the yard, carrying a bundle of shovels. Though he should be under guard, the nearest oldie is Earnest, a good forty metres away, staring at one of the new channels in the earth.

Almeida opens the door of the shed opposite and carries the shovels inside. A few seconds later, he's back out again. If he sees the gang of studes ogling him through the window, he doesn't react.

'Why isn't someone watching him?' Duchess asks, leaning in from behind me.

'Muh-muh-maybe they don't consider him a threat,' Skip suggests.

'How can they be so certain?' Noddy snorts. 'We don't know anything about him. Not for sure. He could be anyone.'

Almeida has gone into another shed, the next one along. We all stare like rabbits in the headlights at the door that's been left ajar, as if expecting him to come out holding a rocket launcher or something.

'They're just letting him root around in the sheds,' Duchess remarks in disbelief. 'Earnest is, like . . . giving him the run of the place. Is this what they call *security*? What kind of tools can he get at in there? They might as well *hand* him a *weapon*, for God's sake. I can't believe this. We're virtually on our knees here; the world's forgotten about us, our comms are down, our drone defences are offline, we've lost three guardians, we're all weak with hunger . . . we couldn't be any more vulnerable – and they're letting the only stranger on the island walk around without an armed guard? What the hell? They're supposed to be professionals!'

'What can he do?' I ask. 'We're already as isolated as we can get. If he does anything to us, he'd get screwed over too.'

'Who says he's working alone?' Duchess says, turning on me. 'I mean, Noon just happens to come across a lone guy on a sinking boat just outside our exclusion zone? What are the chances of that? Something stinks about that guy. Look at us – look at what we represent. There are a lot of people who'd see us as a dream target. Maybe that's what the sabotage has been about all along. And now this? What if he's a scout for an assault team coming in off a submarine . . . or some kind of . . . of suicide bomber?'

'I'm pretty sure the drones would still attack any sub that came anywhere near the coast without clearance,' Noddy points out. 'And Almeida didn't have any bombs with him when Noon and the others found him.'

'He doesn't *need* bombs. Terrorists are trained in all sorts of crazy stuff. He could make a weapon out of a damn box-cutter, or a car or . . . or the kind of tools or chemicals you'd keep in a *farm shed*!' She points out the window. 'And I'll say it again: what if he's not working alone? It's been weeks and

Noon and the others haven't turned up a damn thing on whoever blew up the monastery. What's going on there? These people are supposed to protect us! What the hell's going to come at us next?'

We stare at the shed door, waiting to see what kind of horrific threat will emerge. Almeida comes out carrying a small sack.

'That's feed for the chickens,' Nuke remarks.

'Hey . . . could we . . . could we *eat* that?' Moose asks.

'Forget the damn chickenfeed,' Smood says. 'We should be eating the *chickens*!'

'The chickens are laying eggs for us, bonehead,' Moose points out.

'Right, sure. We get . . . what? Half a dozen eggs a week? Eight, maybe?' Smood snorts in derision. 'Okay, let's spare the dried up old birds for a while. What about the sheep? Or the goat? Why are we starving while there are animals to eat? What's up with that? Earnest gets to have his little hobby farm up here while we go hungry? We're scraping by on pieces of egg and some rotten potatoes! Gemmy's *dead*! He's dead! He's dead because he was starving – and the rest of us could go the same way while there's *meat* walking around back there, waiting for us to eat it!'

'Maybe they're holding on in case help doesn't come,' Nuke says. 'It could be they're not sure how long this could keep going on. They're doing their best, I think. They can't be sure what's going on out there in the world. And we just lost half the crops . . . Maybe . . . Maybe they're holding on to the animals for when things get really bad.'

It's a bit weird hearing Nuke be . . . positive. It's like our little apocalypse has made her see the best in people.

'We're starving, Nuke! Gemmy's dead!' Smood growls at her. 'How bad do things have to get?'

'Buckley hasn't told us half of what Almeida knows,' Duchess declares. 'We need to find out what's going on, and this could be our chance – while the guardians aren't around. We have to catch him on his own and get some answers out of him.'

'How do we do that when we can't even talk to him?' Smood asks. 'We're blocked; we can't say a word to the guy. What are we gonna do? Make funny faces at him in the hope the floodgates open? Get real!'

Duchess is stung by the remark, but she doesn't retort. She's not the only one seething over this, though. The gang's pent-up frustration is an electrical charge in the air, looking for release. I wish I could tell them what I know about what's happening over the horizon. Not that I think it would make things better, but a bit of information might earth the charge that's building up. I can't though, can I? I've been gagged.

I shoot a glance at Skip. He knows now, and Buckley hasn't blocked *him* from talking about it. *He* could tell them. He shakes his head. We've already discussed this. We've agreed to keep our heads low, not to draw the oldies' attention. We're not letting anyone else in on what we know, in case they blow our chance to reach Almeida. And if we tried to approach our new arrival now, with everyone else in tow, in the mood they're in, it'll be like leading a lynch mob. We need to get to him when we're on our own, keep things calm.

I remember what Noon said about Buckley being so close to instigating martial law. It's vital we don't do anything to push our principal over the edge and cause a lockdown before we can get some answers to our questions. We have to play it cool . . .

'Right, I'm gonna go out there and kill the goat,' Smood announces. 'Who's with me?'

A few of the guys give enthusiastic rumbles of approval as he strides into the kitchenette, pulls a carving knife from the block of knives on the counter, and heads for the door. Noddy and Cheeks follow him out; the rest of the group wait a few seconds and then scramble after them.

Ah, nuts.

Chapter Thirty
An Act of Violence

Earnest's modest farm has four aging chickens, three sheep and a goat – not exactly a cornucopia, but my mouth is watering despite my misgivings. I've never eaten walking meat and I really don't want this happening, but damn . . . I can just *taste* that flesh. The rain is as heavy as ever, rattling on the hood of my waterproof and I'm missing the heat of that fire already. The chickens are in a wood and wire run behind the sheds and the sheep and goat are in a fenced enclosure further in, backing onto the trees.

As we hurry through the gap between the house and the shed at the end of the yard, we pass Almeida, who looks up warily. Duchess tries to speak to him, but can hardly get a word out, muted by the censor chip and her own brain. Stifled, she scowls bitterly and then jogs on to catch up with Smood. She needs to be up the front, leading the herd, not following.

When they reach the gate of the enclosure, a one-point-five-metre-high wooden fence with chain-link nailed to the inside, Smood, Noddy and Cheeks let themselves in, carefully closing the gate behind them. The only light is from two lamps on the back wall of the shed over my right shoulder. Duchess watches the action intently, something alive in her eyes that I haven't seen in a long time.

'Smood, hey . . . I don't know about this,' Moose calls out. 'This doesn't feel right.'

'You're a vegetarian, Moose, it's not gonna feel right,' Smood replies, his gaze fixed on the goat. 'Let's see how those principles hold up in front of some juicy, roasted meat, huh?'

'Stop!' Almeida shouts from behind me, hustling through the rain to catch up with us. 'Wait, wait! Look kids, I don't know what's going on here, but you really need to think this through—.'

Duchess pivots round and hits him. The sudden violence startles everyone. Like all of us, Dutch has had years of martial arts training, so she knows how to hit and he's caught flatfooted, still walking forwards as she drives the heel of her hand into the bridge of his nose. His head snaps back and blood starts flowing from both nostrils. He grunts and shakes himself like a dog, then leans forward to snort blood on the ground, never taking his eyes off her. If he's shocked, it doesn't show. His expression has gone flat, unreadable. Dangerous. Dutch doesn't say a word – *can't* say a word – she just glares at him, daring him to come at her.

'That's how it is, eh?' he croaks. 'Off you go, then. Carve your meat. I'm gonna get in outta this rain.'

He walks away and I think maybe this is my chance. I have our questions on the sheet, folded up in the inside pocket of my jacket. I could go after him . . . instead, I turn to look back at the enclosure, captivated, watching Smood, Noddy and Cheeks trying to corner the goat. I don't know why they don't opt for one of the sheep, which are the same size. Maybe it's something about the goat's nature. It's a little scoundrel, asking for trouble. Maybe that makes them feel less guilty about what they're about to do. I wonder if any of them give a thought to where I got my nickname, but I'm feeling pretty weird about it now.

Although the animal's small, its blunted horns barely higher than crotch level, it's nimble and deceptively strong. The muddy ground is slippery, making everyone's movements stiff-legged and clumsy. Smood reaches out for the goat, but it wriggles free, only to have its back leg caught by Cheeks. It kicks back, it's free hoof thumping her in the ribs, and it breaks from her grasp. Noddy dives for it and it swerves past him, so he ends up sprawled in the mud. He struggles to his feet. The three studes are shattered, tired and weak from hunger, but desperation is giving them energy.

After some more scrambling around, a few more nasty kicks and some spectacular falls, Smood manages to get his arm around the goat's head. Noddy and Cheeks quickly pile on, holding it down. It's still thrashing wildly and Smood manages to cut the edge of his own hand trying to get the carving knife to the animal's neck. Cursing in gurgling growls, he slashes its throat. He must have missed the artery, because there's flowing blood, but no spurt and the goat's still wriggling, screeching in pain and terror, a horrible noise that makes me shiver. It almost sounds human. It takes two more deep cuts with the knife before blood finally sprays out onto the muck like a hosepipe under pressure and the goat's struggles start growing weaker. Noddy and Cheeks look sick – victorious, but sick. Smood has the glow of elation on his face, eyes wide, his skin pale and spattered with mud and blood. He's breathless, panting, teeth bared, though he doesn't seem sure how to process what he's feeling. I can see the realization grow on him. He has taken a life . . . and something has lit up inside him.

Cheeks is first on her feet. She swivels away from the others and throws up what little food she has in her stomach. She's still that girl who cried over the seedlings, after all. I'd wondered where she'd gone for those few vicious minutes. Noddy gets up too, gazing at his hands, rubbing them together. Smood is having some kind of moment of baptism, standing straight, staring up into the rain, letting it wash over him, rinsing off the blood and dirt, the goat's corpse held in his left hand by a thick tuft of its coarse hair.

'What have you done?' a voice roars from behind me. *'What have you done?!'*

Earnest strides past, wrenching open the gate and slamming it closed behind him. He's left a wake of clear space through the students standing outside and now he storms right up to Smood. Cheeks steps into his path, a hand raised to try and reason with him. He punches her in the solar plexus and she doubles up and is shoved out of the way. Noddy charges at him and is stopped short when Earnest jabs stiff fingers into the soft flesh of his throat. The guardian then sweeps his feet out from under him, the stude landing flat on his back. Earnest stamps on his thigh to make sure the younger man stays down, hardly breaking stride as he does so.

Smood's blood is up, mania in his wide eyes as he tosses the dead goat aside and points the knife at Earnest.

'Back off, you old fart!' he snarls. 'Things are going to change around here. We've had enough of your crap. You're going to hand over all this meat and you're going to tell us everything we want to know. It's time you clowns learned your place!'

'What, you're all manned up now, are you?' Earnest rasps, casting a bitter look at the goat's corpse, then raising his eyes to Smood. 'You cut a small, defenceless animal's throat and now you're all stone-cold killer, is that it? All right, come on then, boy; let's see what you can do with that blade.'

It's all the goading Smood needs. He lunges at Earnest, who responds with swift, efficient movements, his right hand touching Smood's wrist, deflecting the strike and sweeping the knife arm up. Then, sliding in with his left hand, Earnest catches the wrist in a lock, twisting the hand back painfully against the arm. Still holding the knife hand with his left, Earnest blocks a flailing punch from Smood's other hand, then delivers three wicked strikes with his right fist, to the ribs, sternum and face. Smood's head jerks under the impact. Earnest hooks his heel behind Smood's right knee and stands on it, forcing the stude to kneel. A twist of the wrist-lock causes Smood to cry out and drop the knife.

Smood is groggy, struggling to breathe after being winded by the body blows. With his left hand, Earnest grabs the boy's hair and pulls his head back, then the guardian lifts his right arm so that Smood is staring straight up at the elbow that's about to slam down and smash the bones in his face.

'Earnest!' Buckley bellows, rushing into the enclosure. 'That's enough!

Earnest hesitates, but he raises his elbow further in readiness. Buckley seizes him in an armlock, pulling the man's face close in to his.

'Have you lost your mind! Let him go!'

'Look what he did!' Earnest growls. 'And then he came at me with the knife!'

'I said that's *enough*, Brother Earnest! Stand down, goddammit! That's an order!'

It's almost as if he has to forcefully will his hand to release Smood's hair, but Earnest bites on his lip and lets Smood fall backwards into the mud, the younger man stunned and suddenly feeble. Buckley lets go of Earnest. His expression is grim, his glare sweeping slowly across us, meeting each person's eyes, the disgust evident on his face and in his voice as he speaks.

'Has this night not been bad enough? How much do we have to lose before you realize we are all in this together? We're trying to keep you *alive*, you fools! Go back to your homes. You're all in shock. Go back and think about what's happened here tonight. Tomorrow, we will see how much we can recover from this mess. Go home!'

As we come out through the yard, we find the SUVs are waiting for us, lights on, engines running. Noon is standing by the side of the leading one. My head is melted, a mess with all the stuff that's been roiling around in my brain and I really don't want to talk to her right now. I have to, soon . . . but I just can't right now. I go to get into another car, which surprises her. She catches my eye, nods towards the others behind me and shakes her head in dismay. Yeah, I know. We screwed up. But I can only handle one drama at a time – we can face whatever Buckley throws at us tomorrow. Right now, I've got to sleep before I fall on my face.

Chapter Thirty-One
Animals

I'm eating meat. Real, free range meat. The kind that was a living creature, jumping around, breathing and bleating until yesterday. I crush the soft, oily fibres of barbecued flesh between my molars and feel those juices run down my throat; it's like I'm absorbing pure life force from the animal. Unable to suppress it, I shudder with guilty pleasure.

All around me are the sounds of people experiencing the same thing. Nobody talks. There are quiet chewing noises, low moans and breathy sighs and throaty groans. Most of the others have finished theirs; some wolfed it down and now mope in disappointment. We haven't been given much. The rations are still tight and Adeyemi has warned us that our stomachs will have shrunk, so we can't eat much anyway. She estimates, with these portions, we'll get about three meals for all of us out of the goat. I'm determined to get every squeeze of pleasure out of this, to make it last as long as I possibly can.

We've been told Buckley wants to talk to us after breakfast. We know he's on the warpath after last night, so we're not expecting good news. It doesn't matter right now. For now, I'm a goddess feeding on the flesh of mortals.

Licking my upper lip, I fork up the last piece of meat, gazing at it with utter lust. Lifting it to my mouth, I caress it with the very tip of my tongue, teasing myself with it. The last touch before the last bite before I masticate ('chew' is too brief, too impotent a word) and then it's gone. I moan in anticipation of it being over.

Skip is sitting across the table from me. He's finished and now he's staring at me, an intrigued smile on his face. I grin back before sliding the meat between my lips. We're all feeling good. There's a real intensity in his gaze as I grind the meat into pulp between my teeth and swallow.

'Muh-muh-muh-meet me,' he says in a hushed voice.

'Huh?'

'Meet me. In the woods, where we suh-suh-saw the other two that time. When I followed you. Meet me up there.'

I lock eyes with him and feel a low throb of energy in the pit of my belly. There's a different kind of hunger in him now and I'm feeling it too. I'm about to answer when Buckley and Noon come up the stairs. We're about to get our lecture. I can't be bothered with that, but I want to talk to Noon afterwards. Now, while I'm feeling strong. While I can work up the nerve. She walks past my table, giving me a friendly nod. I can't muster enough warmth to respond and I don't want to. Her expression shifts slightly when she meets my glare. My teeth are clenched shut, my mouth compressed into a scowl. They're only small signs of hate, but she picks up on them and I think she's a little hurt as she walks on. Let her be hurt.

'Hey, what's up with you?' Skip asks, looking from me up to Noon and then back at me. 'Billy? What's up? Wuh-wuh-what was that? It was like . . . like you wuh-were trying to kill her with your eyes. I thought you and Noon were tight?'

'Yeah, well . . . we've got some stuff to work out,' I say through my teeth. 'Where were we?'

'We were going to muh-meet . . . up in the woods,' he reminds me, hopefully, hungrily.

Yes. We absolutely are. Actually, I think that's *just* what I need.

'Yeah,' I say simply, biting my lip and then giving him a sly smile. 'Okay.'

'I'm not staying for Buh-Buh-Buckley's suh-sermon,' he tells me. 'You can if you wuh-want.'

'I've got something to do. Meet you after. Twenty minutes.'

'Right then.'

He gets up, adjusts the sagging waistband of his combats and heads towards the stairs. Buckley calls after him, but he ignores the principal and is gone, down the stairs and out of sight.

'All right, all of you,' Buckley sighs. 'I'll keep this short.'

'So we should be done before dinner?' Smood pipes up, and gets a few sniggers.

Buckley responds with a flat smile. He pauses, stretching out the silence until it starts to become awkward.

'We lost three of our people last night,' he begins. 'You

have all been traumatised by that. But that loss doesn't excuse what happened afterwards.' He gives Smood an especially chilly stare. 'You must understand that we have very little to work with on the island. That includes the few animals left on Brother Earnest's farm. Until we're sure that help is on its way, we have to think long term. That means we avoid doing anything that reduces our options for the future. Once an animal is dead, that leaves us with one less resource. One less option. We must think through every action that affects our future. There can be no more thoughtless, impulsive acts, like the one last night. Is that clear?'

'No.' Duchess says bluntly, her chair scraping back as she stands up to face him down. 'No, it's not. We're getting tired of you lot just laying down the law here.' There are murmurs of agreement from the others around me as she continues. 'We all agreed to come to this island. We *volunteered*. We submitted to your authority for the benefit of our parents and our homes. But that situation has changed a bit, hasn't it? Our safety is entirely your responsibility. You're a bit upset about last night? Really? We're a bit browned off ourselves. Because *you're not doing your bloody job*, Buckley! Why are we starving when there are animals to eat? Why won't you tell us what Almeida has told you? What's going on out in the world that you won't let us know, Buckley? And what we *really* want to hear, what's *seriously* bugging us, is *why the hell you haven't found the freakin' traitor yet?*'

'Enough!' Buckley roars, the sheer volume of his voice sending a tremor through us. He's never shouted like this before. His face is rigid with restrained fury. 'I have had *enough*! Yes, you're right; your safety is the responsibility of the Order. My responsibility. That means, for your own good, you do *what* I say, *when* I say it. And if I feel that you won't cooperate, then I will put this island on lockdown. You'll be locked into your villas. Is that what you want? To be separated from each other, put in isolation? You want to give up your right to walk around freely? If that's what it takes to keep you from hurting each other, or preventing my people from doing their jobs, then that's what I'll do.

'From this point on, I don't want to hear another fucking word of complaint or protest. You will occupy yourselves with your normal activities and let us get on with our jobs. So, mark this: You are now blocked from criticizing the staff, or objecting to, or questioning our work in any way.'

I'm gobsmacked. Stupid as it might sound, my first concern is how much I won't be able to put in my journal. What kind of thing counts as 'criticizing'? He's letting our own brains decide for us and he *knows* he's being vague. We could end up being completely unable to talk to the guardians in any meaningful way. And as for thrashing things out with Noon about her 'work' . . . how the hell will I be able to do that now?

Even Noon is looking at the principal in shock – she mustn't have known this was coming. Buckley can't be serious.

There is an immediate outcry, given extra urgency by the fact that we don't know what we'll be able to say in the next few seconds. Some people start cursing and insulting the guardians. Others just shout their objections. Duchess, Smood and Noddy begin to argue their points, but Dutch puts a hand out to the other two to be quiet. They need one voice, to be heard above the others. She waves at the rest of us, waits until everyone has fallen silent.

'Brother Buckley,' she says in an even voice, holding her hands up as if trying to placate a snarling animal. 'Please, you can't do this. You can't . . . gag us like this. What does that even mean, to "criticize" your work? How are we going to be able to talk to you? We *have* to able to discuss problems with you. What if we need to tell you about some issue or threat and we can't, because it's critical of something you've done? There's already so much we can't say. We have to be able to speak our minds . . .'

'As I have told you before, this is not a democracy,' Buckley growls at her. 'This block will stay in place until I'm convinced you're all ready to play on the same team. Our survival on this island demands unity. You can either engage with that willingly, or I'll enforce it.'

I can feel the block come into place. I want to write down all kinds of crap about our fasci–*(deleted)* . . . our Naz–*(deleted)* . . . Goddamn it . . . about our *beloved* principal, but it's not happening. The guardians are now shielded from any criticism and we can only guess what the boundaries are on that definition. It's probably different for each of us.

I had a friend back home once who was hyper-sensitive. She could find an insult in any compliment and criticism in every question you asked her, no matter how innocent. I ended up being unable to talk to her at all because I'd start anticipating it; I never knew when she'd take offence, or act hurt or embarrassed. It became unbearable to be around her. I'm now finding I can't say anything about the block itself, however, because it's Buckley's work.

How the holy hell am I going to tell this story now?

Chapter Thirty-Two
Taking Chances

A muted anger has settled over the mezzanine level. I'm next to the rail overlooking the gym floor. I can't bring myself to look at Buckley as he carries on to the second point on his agenda. Even so, he gets our full attention with his next few words:

'The *Santiago* has now been repaired and is as seaworthy as we can make her. Sister Noon is not convinced that the boat will make the journey to the mainland, but we have decided to make the attempt. We think that a small crew could at least make it to the shipping lanes, where there's a chance of being picked up by a commercial vessel.'

There's a lingering pause as if he's waiting for a reaction, and is almost surprised when there isn't one immediately. What can we say that won't count as 'critical'? They want to send a leaking, slowly-sinking boat out into the middle of the Atlantic to try and find help. Our imaginations are already filling in the blanks. It's interesting that I've even managed to write this much down. Maybe if I'm just . . . observing facts enough, I can get through the block? But still nobody says anything. It's our own hesitation that prevents us. Nobody likes being tripped up by their censor chip, so everyone's thinking about how to phrase a response. It's a weird situation, as if somebody's turned down our volume so they can listen to another sound somewhere else.

'Noon didn't meet any ships out there last time,' Noddy says carefully. He's pointing out a fact, but not raising any objection. 'Almeida's boat was the only one she saw.'

'Two weeks have passed since then. We're confident that there'll be more traffic this time round,' Buckley replies. 'Sister Noon will be in command again. Sister Noon, do you want to take this?'

'I know what you're all thinking,' Noon says to us. 'And no, I don't consider this a suicide mission. I wouldn't be doing it if I thought they were impossible odds. Maybe you think this means we're desperate, that we've given up hope of help arriving. No, we haven't. This is just another angle we're going to try, to speed up the process. We're talking about one of the busiest shipping lanes in the world. Even with what's happened out there, we'll last long enough to for someone to find us.'

'What *has* happened out there?' Duchess seizes the chance to ask.

Like Noddy, she's cautious about her wording, even her tone. No criticism is implied, no blame asserted. The question sounds like innocent curiosity. Even so, when Noon goes to answer, it's Buckley who cuts in:

'As I explained before, Mister Almeida told us the world's communications and navigation satellites were damaged by a solar flare. This has caused great difficulties, but the world is united in responding to the crisis. Mister Almeida had not heard any reports of any major conflict. I can assure you there has been no word of war crimes being committed. There's no need to be alarmed, but it must be a tense time out there, so we believe the Council are keeping us out of it. They don't know we're in trouble here. If they did, they'd be rushing to help.'

The same story as before, and it receives the same reaction – though less vocal this time. Buckley tells us the boat is being taken from the boathouse and Noon, Sengupta and Sister Frisch will set off as early as possible today. Then he wraps things up and heads for the stairs. I'm out of my seat seconds later, hoping to catch Noon on her own. I'm torn over what to do; part of me wants to grab her by the scruff of her neck and shout questions in her face; part of me wants to plead with her not to go. No matter how my feelings have changed for her, I can't bear the thought of her suffering a lonely death, swallowed by the sea.

That's assuming I can manage to say anything at all. *Wanting* to is a whole other thing to *being able* to. She and Buckley are still walking together as they leave the building, talking in low voices as they make for Buckley's house. My steps falter, still hoping Noon will split off and go her own way. It doesn't happen.

My attention is drawn by the mouth-watering smell coming

off the gas barbecue on the lawn near the door of the gym. My stomach makes animal sounds and urges me to get closer. I can't, because there's an armed group of guardians forming a cordon around Adeyemi, who's cooking up the rest of the goat. She has skinned and butchered it and, having served us our meal, is now preparing to feed the staff. There is still a sizeable portion of the carcass left, though it lies in pieces under some plastic sheeting on the bench beside her – enough to recognise it as a once-living creature.

The meat is considered enough of a temptation for the studes that Adeyemi has no less than eight armed sentries ensuring we keep our distance. I can't talk to Noon now, so it's time to go and meet Skip and do things we're not allowed talk about.

It's only then that I see Earnest. He's just arrived in his SUV and now he's walking with tentative steps towards Adeyemi. His hatchet-job of a face is haggard and he's gazing at her with a profound sorrow in his shadowed eyes. The man is distraught. I realize it's not Adeyemi he's looking at – it's the goat. There are tears running down his face, which he quickly, self-consciously brushes away. Brother Earnest, the scariest man on the island, is crying for a goat.

He catches me looking, scowls, and wipes at his face again. Then he hurries off in the same direction as Buckley and Noon. I watch him go, a little bit touched at this barely-revealed, tender side of the fearsome guardian. It's probably the gradual starvation I've been suffering, affecting the glucose levels in my brain and all that, but I'm slow to spot the opportunity.

Brother Earnest is here, now, and has gone to talk to Buckley. That means that Almeida is probably alone at the farmhouse, where he's kept locked in a room when Earnest isn't there. Almeida is alone. I have the sheet of questions folded up in the back pocket of my shorts. I should run and get Skip, but that would waste valuable time. And with my fitness as it is, I don't know if I have the stamina for both distances. No, I've got to do this now, while I have the chance – we might not get another one. Skip will have to wait. On his own. Up in the woods.

Oh, he's going to *hate* me for this.

Two minutes later, I'm on my bike, heading for the trail that will take me over the hills to the farm.

Chapter Thirty-Three
Mercy Killing

The electric bikes have been locked up to stop us wandering off very far, so I'm on my mountain bike again. I have to push it up most of the first hill. Whatever extra energy I'm due from my meat breakfast has yet to hit my muscles, which feel weak and stringy. I pedal as hard as I can down the steep decline, using the momentum to get me most of the way up the next slope. The backs of my calves and the tops of my thighs, particularly those forks of flesh right above my knees, are burning within minutes. My knees and ankles hurt. The adrenaline that had me pumped up, triggered by my excitement, has worn off, leaving me shaky and cold. I forgot how exposed parts of this trail are to the ocean's wind. I become chilled through so easily now. I can't breathe fast enough. I'm feeling sick, breathless and light-headed, the world swims around me for a moment and I start wobbling on the bike as I get close to the top of the next hill.

Swerving off the trail, I manage to skid to a halt before I hit a tree. I stagger sideways off the bike, barely keeping my balance. Reaching out, I stumble forwards to the trunk of the tree and puke my guts up. Despite the painful heaving, there's not much to come out.

Aw frickin' hell, there goes the *meat*.

It's the hunger. I spent more energy than I could afford and my body's overwhelmed. In a moment of despair, I wonder if I should try and pick out the biggest chunks of the vomit and eat them, dog-like, to save those precious calories, but I can't bring myself to do it. Maybe if my stomach was in a stronger state. With my hands splayed as if I'm on a high wire, I sink down to my knees, a feeble movement, narrowly avoiding the vomit, then I carefully roll over onto my back. Even as the world seems to turn into a carousel around me, I can appreciate the irony of me lying here on my back in the grass in a breathless daze having made the tough decision to leave Skip waiting among different trees on another hill.

Just . . . just need to close my eyes. Give me a minute here . . .

. . . That was longer than a minute.

I sit up with a start, looking up at the sky. How long have I been lying here? Did I . . . Did I *fall asleep*? Aw, nuts! I check the time on my chip. It's quarter past eight. Nearly an hour lost. Some hardcore action chick I am – falling asleep on the ground, on my way to complete my mission. Get up, you gimp!

I stand up shakily, my legs still feeling weak. I'm at a low peak in the path, ahead of a dip and another climb to a point that looks off the section of high cliff we call Thelma's Leap. Beyond that, partly hidden by the trees on the downward slope, lies the farm. From the Leap, it's all downhill to

Earnest's place. Maybe he's not back yet. I could still have a chance.

I hear bleating from the trail ahead of me and blink slowly, going still to try and lock onto the sound. Yes. Bleating sheep. Balls – Earnest *did* come back. And now he must be bringing the animals to the village. I think he must be using the walk to say an emotional goodbye, or something, because it would be simpler just to drive them over in his truck. Getting on my bike, I start heading down the trail, seeing him appear at the crest of the hill ahead of me as I swoop down into the dip and start driving the pedals hard to climb towards him. He's waving the three sheep on with what looks like a small stick and in his left hand, he's holding a cloth bag that's twitching and jerking about. He must have the chickens in there.

I'm about forty metres away when he reaches Thelma's Leap and stops, turning to gaze out at the sea. The sheep seize the opportunity to nibble some of the grass, probably flavoured by the salt in the sea wind. It's a small enough area up there and it's a drop of sixty or seventy metres to the rocks and surf below, though I suppose sheep know well enough to stay away from a cliff edge. Earnest takes a long look at the bag of birds in his hand, his face expressionless. There's something about the way he does it that makes my heart, already struggling from the uphill cycle, take a sickening lurch . . .

Earnest flings the bag out into the air and watches it fall

tumbling into the churning, tossing water below.

I want to scream words at him, but I can't. I can't question or criticize. I can't object in any way, uttering incoherent sounds as my exhaled noises are scrambled into gibberish. I have no breath, no volume, and if he hears me, he shows no sign of it.

That's not a stick he's holding, it's a gun. An old-style, six-shot revolver. He has a gun. He has a *gun* and Buckley and Thompson have been using *bows and arrows* to hunt . . . I know, even as I see it, why that gun hasn't been used for hunting. But now Earnest is herding the sheep closer to the edge, barking sounds at them, firm but fond, reluctant but resolved . . .

'Earnest!' I gasp, finally reaching the top of the slope, only metres from him.

He raises the revolver and fires it, an explosion of sound. The sheep, terrified, leap away from the noise in panic. Out into the void; thin, bony legs flailing, squeals erupting from their small mouths. They screech all the way to the rocks below, where gravity breaks their bodies over the stone and waves crash over them, spreading their blood and spilled organs, shoving clumsily at their shattered remains.

I swing myself off the bike, letting it clatter to the ground as I totter up beside Earnest, who has his left hand up to his face, remorse creasing his features. The revolver dangles loosely from his right hand. All the things I want to say about what he's done and I can't. The words pile up behind my face, their exit blocked and I'm bursting with the frustration of it, the shock of what I've seen. Tears flow down my cheeks and I feel like I'm choking. We stand there long enough to see the waves drag the corpses away and then Earnest looks down at me, eyes like flint, as if noticing me for the first time.

'Billy,' he says hoarsely. 'What are you doing here?'

I hardly hear him. I'm wheezing and my heart is pounding so hard I can feel the pulse in my head. My eyes . . . my eyes are fixed on the gun in his hand. I spin round, grab my bike and start down the slope, pedalling as fast as my worn out legs can manage. Because I've been so wrong. I've been a blind idiot and now it might be too late to do anything about it. It feels like an age before I'm out of sight of Earnest. Feeling his glare on me, I spend the entire time until I reach the cover of the trees, wondering if he's going to put a bullet in my back.

Chapter Thirty-Four
Finding Your Way Back

It's not long before I just don't have the wind for cycling, so I have to get off the bike and walk again. Thanks to the rather strained convenience of the chip in my head, I can write while I walk. I'm so gagged by blocks, there's not much I *can* write – it's getting so I can't even remember all the things we're not allowed say. So, recalling Noon's advice, I search back through my text. I can use flashbacks to get round the bans. Go back to move forward. Ah – here's what I've been looking for, from about a year ago, before the hurricane, before the block on swearing, even before Skip arrived on the island. Here's the thing:

Checking the clock on my chip, I'm making good time, reaching the crest of the hill, going like shit off a shovel and still feeling strong. It's early morning on a crisp, clear day, promising heat later, but right now, the cool air and gentle breeze are perfect for running. My breathing is easy, a fresh sweat coats my skin and life flushes through my limbs. That first bit of stiffness in my legs ahead of a long run has been flexed out, I'm revved up and ready for the kilometres of hills ahead.

The trail to the Perch is a lovely surface, beaten gravel and clay, not quite as hard a road and just rough enough to be interesting. I can go across this stuff like there's a rocket up my arse, and I want to cut at least ten seconds off my time along this stretch and I feel like I can do it today.

The Perch is a high observation point above a steep, sweeping slope that gives the best view out over the village, the harbour, the lagoon and out to the sea beyond. By unspoken agreement, the guardians steer clear of it, leaving it as a private gathering place for the studes. There's a circle of scorched, smoke-stained rocks in the middle of the clearing for a campfire, rugged wooden picnic tables, deck chairs and loungers, as well as cylindrical chunks of log for sitting by the fire. Off to one side of the clearing, just under the edge of the trees, there's even a small, open-fronted shelter with a cast-iron stove tucked in at the back and firewood stacked in the shade of one wall.

We often come up here on clear evenings, bringing musical instruments, bags of snacks and stuff to cook over the fire and pretend we're just a gang of friends from a normal town, kicking back, shootin' the shit in the woods. We sing songs and argue, read poetry and stories aloud and have swearing matches and joke and cuddle up under fleece blankets when the night gets cold. The Perch has given us some of our best moments on the island.

There's only one person here as I run past along the track this morning. It's Nuke, sitting at one of the picnic tables. I intend to just give her a wave and keep on running, but when she spots me she flinches in fright and grabs something off the table, slipping it onto her lap where I can't see it. Okay . . . It's not just the furtive movement, it's everything about her posture, her expression that just screams '*wrong*'.

Shit on a stick. So much for cutting a slice off my time. Still, I'd better stop and see what's got her knickers in a twist. It's not just curiosity – I'm concerned too. I can be like that, you know. Nuke is sitting side-on to me; her eyes betray a dread of having to explain herself and she looks away before swivelling slightly to greet me, still concealing the thing on her lap. Her whole body language looks closed off, defensive, and at the same time there's this air of defeat about her. Her black, straight hair is lank and greasy, half hanging from the pony-tail it's tied into, strands of it everywhere. Her East Asian eyes are red raw from crying, her flat-boned cheeks are puffy, seeming even broader than usual.

'Do you mind?' she says sharply, but with more dismay than aggression. 'I came up here for a bit of privacy. Anyway, don't feel like you have to stop running just for me.'

'Are you okay?' I ask, trying to ease down my breathing. ''Cos you don't look okay.'

'I'm fine. Just leave me alone.'

I should do that. Whatever this is, it's none of my business. And yet, as I look at her, I think there's part of her that wants me to stick around. That's the overwhelming thing I'm getting off her. Indecision. She's balancing on the fence of some big choice she has to make. Like maybe I could influence her one way or the other and she's not sure if she wants that or not. I hang there for a minute and she doesn't push it.

'Let me just get my breath back and I'll go,' I say, blowing my cheeks out and leaning my hands on my thighs.

Though she doesn't buy my breathlessness – she knows how far I can run – she doesn't object either. After thirty seconds or so, she's fumbling with that thing in her lap, as if trying to draw my attention to it without being obvious about it. I go to the other end of the bench, put my foot up and start bending my knee into a deep stretch.

'What you got there?'

'Nothing.'

She's waiting now, though. I can tell. The way she's picking at the weathered surface of the table with the fingernail of her right hand, her left hand clumsily shielding the object. I meet her eyes and she holds my gaze for a few seconds before looking away. I sit down, waiting again for her to tell me to piss off. She doesn't. I pause for a few seconds, and then reach out and take her left hand, gently moving it off her lap.

It's a gun. A large calibre revolver, with a polished steel finish and a knurled, fine-grained wood in the handle – some kind of antique six-shooter, in perfect condition. It can't be hers; there's no way any stude would be allowed bring their own gun onto the island. The Order's firearms are all stored in the weapons locker in the mon and it is kept extremely locked. But it's the only place I can imagine she could have got hold of one. Guns are controlled more carefully than anything on this very carefully controlled island.

From the way she's acting, I'm guessing she didn't come up here for a spot of target practise.

'Is this loaded?' I ask.

'Of course. Not much good without *bullets* in it, is it?'

'What's going on, Nuke?'

She smiles a contorted smile, snorts slightly and caresses the gun's cylinder.

'Just working some things out,' she says in a sad, dreamy voice.

I sit there, not saying anything. Give her a silence to fill. It's something good journalists know how to do. A trade skill.

'You ever been in love, Billy?' she inquires casually.

'I don't think so, I . . . No, not properly. It hasn't really come up yet.'

'I've been in love,' she tells me. 'A lot of people might think it's not the real thing. That it's just like, y'know . . . an infatuation, but it's not . . . it wasn't. It *was* the real thing.'

'Sure, I can understand that.'

'I've been here so long, you know? I don't get to go home as often as the rest of you. I hardly even remember what it's like.'

We've all wondered about this, how it is for Nuke. None of

us get to go home very often – once a year for a week or so if we're lucky. It's generally discouraged, because most people say it can make the homesickness worse. But Nuke almost never gets out. And she's been in the programme longer than any of us. She's nineteen and she came here when she was fourteen, the youngest age they can take on this island. Before that she was with the juniors on th–*(deleted)* . . . on another island. She's been in the programme for *nine years*, and it doesn't look like her dad's going anywhere just yet, so she could be here for a few more years still. She must be completely institutionalised by now – she hardly knows any other life. Some of the other studes think she won't even want to leave, when her time comes.

And now she's in love with someone on the island . . . and from all the evidence in front of me, it's not going well.

'I thought he loved me,' she says, her face adopting a childlike frown, someone who wants to be *seen* to be thinking hard. 'I really did think he felt the same way. But now I know he doesn't. I told him up straight up how I felt and . . . and he was . . . very . . . *understanding*.'

There are tears again, tight little ones, barely bulging over her lower lids, as if these are all her worn out eyes can muster.

'Who are we talking about here?' I ask.

She shoots me a suspicious glance then, her gaze hardening suddenly. I'm reminded of how vicious she can be in martial arts training. She's one of those people who can hurt without restraint when her blood is up.

'You think I'm going to tell you, Billy?' she whispers, her expression relaxing slightly, as she carefully places the gun on the table. 'It's embarrassing. I don't want anyone to know.'

'Okay, sure. I don't need to know. You want to talk about it, maybe? Leaving his name out of it?'

'*Talk about it*? What would you know about anything, Billy Goat?' she snaps harshly. 'You've hardly been here a *year*. You still don't understand shit about this place. And it's not like anything's going to happen to *you*, is it? Daddy's precious little princess, ain't ya? Nobody's going to let anything happen to *you*!'

She starts sobbing. Ragged, hoarse, gluey, ugly sobs; the type you never want other people to see. I let my right hand rest on her left and she clutches it so hard I think she might start breaking bones. And as she cries, I just stay there, not saying anything. My mind cranks out possibilities; I try and figure out who she might be talking about. The studes do try each other out, of course, play the field, and she's had flings, but I've never noticed her paying anyone any particular attention. I can't think of anyone who's especially affectionate towards her either. She's difficult, for the most part; prickly, with a quick temper, easy to offend and yet caustic in her remarks about others. While she can be funny and there's a rather cold, agile sensuality that some find attractive, I don't know anyone I could say she was close with.

She's calming down, rubbing her face on her sleeve. I can tell she doesn't want to look at me. I put my hand on the revolver.

'Listen, why don't we put this thing back where you got it?' I suggest. 'Whatever's going on, it's not worth this, is it?'

'You can't take it!' she blurts out, grabbing my wrist. 'Look, I know this was . . . this was stupid. Maybe . . . maybe I was just . . . I dunno . . . just thinking things through. I wasn't going to *do* anything . . .' She gives a slightly hysterical laugh, that sends a shiver through me, her face suddenly manic. 'But you can't take it! If they find out I stole it, they'll find out *how*. He doesn't know, but I . . . I used *him* to get it. If you hand it back in, everyone will know who it is! I couldn't bear it, Billy. Let . . . let me put it back. I swear, that's all I'll do. I'll put it back.'

She's looking calmer now, her eyes pleading with me. I'm not convinced she's down off the ledge, but she has one foot back on the windowsill. I'm seventeen years old – I'm not cut out for this shit. Suicide counselling isn't exactly the kind of thing we cover in personal development class. I've done what I can and I'm terrified I'm going to keep talking and say the absolute wrong thing and end up fighting to stop her from sticking that gun up into the roof of her mouth. She needs professional help. I'll drop a hint to Doctor Karava as soon as I can come up with some excuse to see him.

I flick the release on the side of the gun, flipping the

cylinder out, and tip the cartridges onto the table-top. Checking that it's empty, I snap it back into place and lay the weapon on the table. I put the cartridges in the pocket of my shorts.

'Got any more rounds?' I ask.

'You mean *spares*?' she mutters. 'What would I need them for? What kind of moron would I be if I needed more than *six bullets* to shoot myself in the head?'

It's such a serious moment, a life on the very edge of the abyss, and my laugh catches me by surprise. I slap my hand over my mouth, stifling it, hoping it won't upset her. It has the opposite effect. She sniggers, a little string of spit flying out of her mouth. She makes this pathetic little 'Oh!' sound, and starts giggling. Wiping her mouth on her sleeve, she thumps me on the shoulder. Then we both crease up in fits of laughter, releasing the painful tension that has built up. It lasts less than a minute, petering out as we both stare at the gun. I push it back towards her.

'Don't let the bastards get you down,' I tell her, touching her hand again. 'Any of them.'

She sniffs and nods, picking up the weapon.

'I'll put it back. But you can't tell anyone, Billy. *Anyone.* Please. Promise me you won't.'

'I promise,' I say. 'I won't tell a soul.'

And maybe I'm being a complete idiotic twat . . . but I don't.

Chapter Thirty-Five
Fools Rush In

You've got that, right? Yeah, it's *that* gun. That's the revolver Brother Earnest used to run the sheep off the cliff. It didn't burn up in the monastery with all the firearms in the weapons locker, because it's his personal weapon. He's the only one on the island allowed to have one and he keeps it in his *house*.

And Nuke knew where to find it, over a year ago.

This blows everything wide open. I have been so bloody stupid. I've missed signs that were so totally obvious. It's got to be the starvation, messing up my brain chemistry. Now, I try to put my thoughts into some kind of order. Writing's good for that.

When Skip and I saw the two people in the woods, the girl *could* have been Nuke. The muted sounds of her voice. Her skin was the right colour, the flash of dark hair that I saw. We knew the other person was a guardian, but that was about it. I was curious enough to want to see more, but Skip talked me out of it.

I'm guessing Earnest ended up falling in love with Nuke after all. You see, I have a confession to make here. I've been lying in my journal. Well . . . by omission, anyway. I've been withholding evidence.

When I was attacked at the boathouse, I recognised Nuke.

She was the one I fought with in the dark and I saw her face, if only for an instant. I didn't dare tell anyone, didn't even put it in the journal, because I didn't know who to trust. She and her partner took out two armed, veteran soldiers. Whoever she was working with was seriously dangerous – a professional. It had to be one of the guardians and there was no way of knowing which one. It might even have been *Buckley*. I shared the knowledge with Skip later, but that was as far as I took it. I was paranoid. If Nuke or her partner knew I'd recognised her at the boathouse, they'd probably try and kill me. I had to find out which guardian she was working with.

Nuke's guilt made sense for the explosion at the monastery too. Of all the studes, she was at the greatest risk from what was happening out in the world. Because of who her dad was, she was the most likely to b–*(deleted)* . . . to ge–*(deleted)* . . . Sod it, never mind.

I missed things. The eagerness Nuke showed the first time we were taken to the farm. She didn't show the same fear as the rest of us when I saw her arguing with Earnest. The familiarity she demonstrated when we were in his house, knowing which drawer held the matches for the fire. The way she defended the guardians for not butchering the animals.

I missed all that early stuff because I wasn't looking properly. Then later, I thought I'd figured out who Nuke's partner was. It's all I've been thinking about for the last couple of days. I've been remembering the night of the storm, when I was talking to Mum.

It's ironic, because it was Noon's suggestion that made me use that scene as a flashback. It made me recall the moment when I interrupted Noon while she was talking on the phone – the one she quickly hid when I came through the door. It wasn't one of the island's phones, it was a personal device. Illegal. I didn't think it was a big deal at the time, and in all the drama since, I'd forgotten all about it. *But it was the same type of phone the saboteur used to try and detonate the gas in the comms room.* Reading back over that scene made me recall it . . . and ever since, I've been absolutely convinced that Noon was the traitor.

This isn't her 'doing her job'. I can criticize this. She didn't do herself any favours. She all but blamed Valtere for the explosion, saying he'd set it off by triggering the fire alarm. It was as if she *needed* someone other than the traitor to take the blame for her friend's death, but I saw Valtere at the side door of the mon at the moment of the blast. He was nowhere near the switch for the fire alarm. She figured the sabotage out so fast, and then the search for the traitor seemed to stall completely. Yes, she made sure she had an airtight alibi; she was well out of range, in the middle of the Atlantic at the time of the explosion. But she could easily have used the phone as a simple timer, instead of calling it to trigger the detonation.

And then, of course, she knew she would be the one to lead the crew of the *Santiago* again, when it came time for someone to sail away from the island.

I was so clever; sickened though I was by my friend's guilt, I had her all figured out. She was working with Nuke to isolate us from the outside world long enough for the two of them to get off the island. I was certain of it.

The only thing I couldn't work out was *why*. Why did she do all this? Did she and Nuke have some close relationship I didn't know about? Were they lo–*(deleted)* . . . Oh, for Christ's sake . . . And yes, okay, part of me was jealous at the thought of it, but only because how could I not know about them? I thought I knew Noon better than anyone else on the island. This didn't fit. She's a true believer, absolutely loyal to the Order, has devoted herself entirely to the cause. It simply didn't make sense for her to betray everything she knew to help *Nuke*.

I held off telling Buckley everything, or even putting this in my journal, because I wanted to talk to Noon first. Even if she killed me for figuring it out, I just had to know why she'd done it. She'd broken my frickin' heart.

Except I've been wrong this whole time.

Nuke and *Earnest*. Damn. I've gotta find Buckley . . .

I hear a whining sound then, and look up to see one of the guardians' buggies coming towards me, its small base and chunky tyres allowing it to follow the narrow trail in a way that the SUVs can't. There's another buggy behind it. They're being driven by studes, nine of them in two groups, riding on the powerful little vehicles. Nuke's not among them. These buggies are only for the guardians' use, so it looks like we're in full-on rebellion now. It's all change here on the island.

Smood's at the wheel of the lead buggy, with Duchess at his side. They pull up beside me.

'We heard a gunshot,' Duchess says to me. 'Have you seen anything?'

'Earnest just killed the animals,' I tell her. 'Drove them off the Leap.'

'What?' Smood snarls. 'What about the meat?'

'Gone,' I reply. 'They went into the sea.'

'That's it . . . That's *it*! I'm gonna kill this vegan scumbag!'

'Yeah, 'cos that went really well last time you tried it,' I sigh. 'Listen, I think Earnest and Nuke are the ones who blew up the monastery. They're the traitors. Turn around, we have to go and tell Buckley.'

'To hell with that!' Smood snarls. 'We're going after Earnest. Buckley can catch up!'

'Earnest has a *gun*!' I snap at him. 'And we are *way* out of our depth. We need help!'

'We'll deal with it,' he retorts.

He gestures at the extra bodies behind him – most of them guys, looking like they're all fired up for a fight. Smood thinks his reinforcements are going to be enough. I think Earnest is capable of murdering the lot of them. I turn to Duchess. Even as I do, I can see it's no good trying to reason with her – she's all up for it as well. I cans see the laser heat of the fanatic in her gaze. They're going to tackle Earnest on their own.

'You coming?' she asks, her tone daring me to refuse.

They're not thinking straight. This isn't some kids' mystery or a Hollywood thriller, some frickin' rough-and-tumble adventure. Earnest is a professional killer who wants off this rock and will put down anyone who gets in his way. A bunch of half-starved kids isn't likely to pose much of a problem for him. I lean my bike against a tree and squeeze in on the shallow seat beside Duchess. No, I absolutely don't want to take on the most frightening man on the island, armed and on his own turf, but I don't want my friends getting killed either.

As we set off, I wonder if Skip is still waiting for me up in the woods, behind the Perch. I'm feeling really guilty about that now. If I do manage to live through this, he's probably never going to speak to me again.

Chapter Thirty-Six
Savagery

In the rugged, four-wheel-drive buggies, it takes us less than ten minutes to reach the farm. Smood, Duchess and their followers arrive bristling, ready for battle, but there's no sign of Earnest or his vehicle. All the rage that has built up against him staggers with nothing solid to push against; frustrated, the mob are lost for a direction with no one to fight.

'Almeida,' Duchess says.

They storm into the house. The room where Almeida sleeps is locked from the outside. Though there are no keys for the two locks, a barrage of kicks from three of the guys smashes the door open in seconds. I attempt to follow the mob in, but there's barely room for everyone to fit. I can only stand behind those at the back, up on my tiptoes to try and see what's going on.

Almeida is up on his feet, his back against the wall, caught between the bed on his right and the small desk on his left. He's looking frightened. Shocked at having his door kicked in, he can sense the violence in these people in front of him.

'Wha . . . wha . . what's going on?' he stammers. 'What do you want?'

But of course, no one can answer him. No one can talk to him.

'Nnngah!' Duchess tries, her face screwed up in effort. 'Gaaaannggggheeeh . . .!'

She stops, embarrassed and enraged, her entire body trembling. Almeida shakes his head in confusion.

'What it is?' There's a tremor of fear in his voice now. 'I don't understand . . .'

He still doesn't know. The guardians haven't told him that we can't talk to him. He goes to step forward, but Smood growls and shoves him back against the wall. Then he pushes the man again, even though the guy's got nowhere to go. Almeida's quaking now.

'I don't know what you want! *What do you want?*'

I wish he'd stop asking questions we can't answer. The others are right on the edge here. He has to start talking or it's going to–. Oh, for Christ's sake . . . *Questions.*

'Wait!' I call to the others, reaching for the sheet of paper in my shorts pocket. 'I've go–.'

I'm stopped short by the censor chip. It won't even let me say that – that I've got questions we can ask him. I can't even try to communicate with him verbally, but I have them *written down.* He only has to *see* them to understand. And the censor chip controls the language centre of my brain; I can't even sign, but I *can* just hold up my hands. I only have to show him . . .

I'm trying to shove through the press of bodies when Duchess turns to Smood, her voice tight through tense jaws:

'Make. Him. Talk.'

It's as if Smood is let off a leash. His first punch smashes into the side of Almeida's face, the older man's head unable to back away from it because of the wall behind him. Almeida, already stunned, tries to fight back, strong, ape-like arms raised to guard his head, punching back at Smood.

'Stop!' I scream at them. 'Stop! Will you *look*! Please! I have ques– . . . uh!'

I'm cut off again, waving the sheet of paper like a mad woman and it's like I'm not even there. Nobody can see anything but the violence now.

The others pile in, six different arms jabbing in at the man, getting in each other's way, some hitting, others scraping off or even thumping into the wall behind him. Almeida is crying out, squealing in fear and pain, begging them to stop in a voice that can barely form words around burst lips and broken teeth.

'Dutch, please! Please make them stop!' I wail at her, my voice ragged with sobs now.

Almeida is still squalling, his outbursts spraying blood on his attackers and the smell of it fills the air around us. Smood grabs him by the head, pulling him down, kneeing him repeatedly in the face. Almeida is forced to the ground, where the mob start kicking him; there's hardly room to move, but they're stamping on his limbs, his groin, his ribs and his head. I hear bones breaking.

'Dutch! Please, stop them! Duchess!'

'Kill him! Kill him! *Kill him!*' Dutch shrieks.

'Itssch . . . the . . . Sshaaaapaneese kish!' Almeida screeches. 'Pweeeese! Pweeeese! Itsssch the Sshaaaapaneese kish!

'Wait! What did he say?' Duchess shouts. 'Stop! Stop, hold on! Stop! What did he say?'

The beating eases off until she can make herself heard and pull them back out of the way. Almeida is sobbing through mouthfuls of blood and fragments of teeth, his tanned face battered beyond recognition. He can only move one arm and both his legs look misshapen. His chest moves fitfully, shattered ribs clicking their sharp edges against each other. He gazes up into Dutch's beautiful face, eyes pleading for mercy.

'Juh Sshaaaapaneese kish . . .' he spits. 'You . . . wantsch juh Sshaaaapaneese kish.'

The Japanese kid? Is that what he's saying? The words turn my heart cold. No, I think. No, no, no! Not that. Please, not that.

'Uh?' Duchess prompts him, managing a clumsy nod, her glare every bit as intense as a few moments ago, but compassion in her expression now too. 'Billy, shut up with the crying, you goddamned baby, I can't hear a word he's saying . . .'

Almeida sees her softened expression and it gives him hope. He takes a few tortured breaths, steeling himself for his next sentence.

'Assshuns Feddsshh . . .tacked ship. Bwishish ship. Asshuns tacked ship. Shharted . . . war.'

The words are barely intelligible, but we can make them out. They're words that change things for us; each one thudding into place with the weight of a concrete block.

The Asian Federation attacked a British ship. They started a war.

'Yesssh. Shhharted . . . war,' Almeida gurgles eagerly, as he sees we understand. Moaning in pain, he manages to repeat the last phrase, knowing what it means to us. 'Shhharted uh war.'

You can almost feel the temperature drop suddenly in the room. 'Started a war'; it's a phrase that carries a particular dread on this island. It has special relevance for us.

'Skip,' Smood snarls. 'It was *Skip* the whole time.'

And it's worse because Skip's country has declared war on *mine*. They attacked one of *our* ships. I shouldn't even be able to write this, but I figure I'm in shock. I'm not thinking straight. Maybe, like Gemmy towards the end, I've started losing my mind. Everyone's eyes have turned on me. My head reels. Those fools out there, out in the world . . . they've gone and done it. That's what this was about all along.

'No,' I say. 'This isn't right.'

It can't be. I shake my head vigorously at them, denying it as forcefully as I can. Even hearing this news, I can't believe Skip is the traitor. I don't think he could know something like this, that he could be trying to escape the island, and manage to hide it from me. And what about Earnest and Nuke? What does *their* treachery mean now? I gaze down at the sheet of paper in my hands. The questions are there, smeared in blood – defaced, but readable. We could still use them to get more out of Almeida. First though, we have to get him to Karava. His breathing doesn't sound good; wet, rattling and irregular. He needs help, fast. How the hell are Duchess and Smood going to explain this?

But, of course, they're way past that.

'We have to find Skip,' Duchess declares, moving like a lioness, ferocious and pure, pushing me aside as she heads for the door. 'Let's find the little turd and put an end to this mess.'

They all hustle out, moving as a pack, their minds already focussed on their new prey. I want to rush after them, try and reason with them, but first I kneel down by Almeida's side, trying to pull him over into the recovery position to clear his throat and ease his breathing. The movement only causes him more pain from his broken ribs and collarbone.

Taking his bloodied hand, I open my mouth to tell him how sorry I am, that I'm going to get him help. I want him to know that I care about what's happened to him, that I'll try to make it right . . . Nothing comes out. Even now, I'm prevented from saying anything. I curse Buckley with all the words I can't say out loud, that I can't write down.

One of the injured man's eyes is swollen closed while the

other is haemorrhaging, bright red seeping around the white. Almeida locks his eye on mine, as if he wants to tell me something more. I lean in closer, waiting for him and . . . there's nothing. He's not making a sound. He's not even breathing. His pupil is wide open and he's not blinking. He doesn't give off a last sigh or death rattle, there's no sudden stiffening and then going slack. One second he's there, then his body is empty meat.

I roughly scuff the tears from my face and lean back, letting my head tilt backwards, staring at the ceiling and feeling an overwhelming exhaustion come over me. A dizziness sways me and I could quite comfortably collapse and stay there for some time. Then my chin sinks down onto my chest and I'm forced to gaze upon the damaged body of this man we hardly knew – a man my friends have beaten to death.

Skip.

I have to find Skip before the others can, or they're going to do the same to him.

Chapter Thirty-Seven
Exit Strategy

I have one chance; that Skip has stayed at the place we were supposed to meet. Nearly two hours have passed since we left the gym after eating the goat – it seems like I've lost the whole day, somewhere in there, so I'm not holding out much hope he' still there. I managed to catch a lift on the second buggy because a few of the guys wanted to clean the blood off their faces and hands before heading off. Maybe they didn't want to show up back at the village looking like utter maniacs, I dunno. I leave my bike where it is as we pass it – the state I'm in, I'd never be able to keep up with the buggy.

Now we're coming back down the road towards the student villas and I'm trying to work out how I can separate myself from the rest so I can get up to the place in the woods without anyone seeing me. After that? Well, we have to get off the island. There's nothing else we can do. Both the students *and* the guardians will be after Skip now. Nothing about this is making sense to me and my glucose-starved brain might just be misfiring too much to deal with it all. One thing is clear: there's nowhere for us to go but out to sea. Skip can't stay here. I'm thinking, if the *Santiago* is back in the water, we might be able to figure out how to steal it . . .

'What the hell is goin' on?' Noddy exclaims.

He's sitting beside Cheeks, who's driving. They're both staring out towards the harbour. The rest of us look to where they're pointing and see the *Santiago*, its sails still down, the boat moving under engine power. I feel a massive cavity in my chest, suddenly caught for breath as if the vessel is drawing it from me as it creeps away into the distance, curving round the east coast of the island. Noon has gone . . . she went without even saying goodbye . . . and after the way I treated her last time I saw her. And now the boat is gone too . . . I think I'm going to cry again.

Sister Adeyemi is running across the lawn. Smood's buggy gets past her, but she waves our one down, striding out in front of us to force Cheeks to stop.

'Get out of that damn vehicle!' she roars, a shock baton in one hand, a can of pepper spray in the other. 'As of now, this island is in lockdown! Each one of you is to return to your villa and remain there until Brother Buckley comes to speak to you–.'

'Who's on the boat?' Noddy cuts across her. 'Is it Skip?'

'Brother Earnest and Nuke have stolen the *Santiago*,' Adeyemi snaps at him. 'They killed Sister Frisch and Brother Sengupta and shot four others to take the boat. They sabotaged the three ribs too, so that nobody could catch up with them.'

'Skip will be with them, I'd bet my life on it,' Noddy says. 'He's the goddamn traitor, Adeyemi! We have to get one of those ribs working . . .'

The guardian is still standing in front of the buggy, so all the studes simply spread out and rush past her, taking the chance that she won't use her weapons on one of them as they run the last few hundred metres down to the harbour. Hissing with frustration, she jumps behind the wheel of the buggy and I just manage to dismount before she drives off after them.

I watch them all heading down the hill. Through no cunning of my own, I seem to have found myself free to go and find Skip. I'm still convinced he's not involved with Earnest and Nuke. I don't waste time celebrating my good fortune; waiting until the others have disappeared along the boardwalk beyond the villas, I turn and start jogging across the lawn, up towards the path into the woods.

A run that would once have taken me an easy five minutes takes more than ten, my jog little more than walking pace. All that training doesn't count for much when your body is running on fumes. To my amazement, Skip is still waiting there, sitting on the fallen tree, over two hours after he walked out of the gym. He stands up to greet me and I'm too out of breath to speak at first, stumbling into his arms and clinging to him as if we're both about to fall off the Earth.

'You . . . waited!' I pant. 'I can't . . . can't believe you waited!'

'I wuh-wuh-was ssh-sh-sure you'd come,' he replies, his mouth tucked into my neck where it meets my right shoulder.

'I figured it wuh-would be worth wuh . . . wuh-waiting for.'

'Oh my God, you are such a *boy*! Still, you're here . . . you're here.'

My breathing starts to ease its way down from the crisis level it reached on the rush up the hill.

'Wuh-wuh-what's wrong?' he asks. 'What's happened?'

'Earnest and Nuke are the traitors,' I tell him. 'The others went looking for Earnest. They found Almeida instead. They . . .'

I fail to finish the sentence. It's not the chip this time, it's the emotion choking me, getting in the way when I can't afford to be silent.

'They killed Almeida, Skip.'

'They *what*?!'

The initial surge of relief I felt when I found him is dissipating like vapour, leaving me shivery cold. How can I tell him what's going to happen to him? I just can't bear to do it . . . in fact, I'm *physically unable* to do it. I'm prevented by that very first block that's placed on our speech when we arrive on the island. Because it's the reason we're here and I absolutely cannot talk about it – but maybe Skip can. This is spiralling down steadily into a freakin' horror story and now he'll have to do this for me, find the way into my mind to work out for himself what's happened . . .

'We have to do the . . . that thing,' I tell him, freeing myself from his embrace, moving a step back and then taking his

349

hands in mine. Drawing in a deep breath I force myself to become calm. 'You have to say it for me, because I can't. You have to ask me questions.'

It must be written all over my face, the terror that's building inside me, only barely contained. He sees it in me and now he's starting to feel it too. He can tell by the way I'm looking at him. I think . . . I'm *sure* he can sense *my fear for him*. Skip nods, gulps and fixes his eyes on mine. Questions. Composing his thoughts for a moment, he blows out through tight lips and nods again.

'Okay . . . Right, okay. Let's suh-suh-suh . . . suh-start then,' he stammers, constricted by a tense throat. 'This is to do with me, isn't it?'

My whole body nearly convulses, my urge to tell him is so strong, and so painfully suppressed.

'Right. Heh! Got that one, I think,' he says, and he chuckles humourlessly. There's a quaver in his voice as he puts the next question to me:

'Have . . . have the guardians received the order for a suh-suh-Sanction? No? Okay, well that's something, at least, huh? Okay . . . eh . . . eh . . .'

He desperately needs to know, but he doesn't *want* to know. I press my lips together, silently pleading with him to keep going.

'. . . Almeida,' I manage to blurt out. 'Almeida, he told us something before he died. About . . . about outside.'

Skip takes another shaky breath.

'Has . . . has suh-suh-suh-something happened that will *trigger* a suh-suh-suh . . . suh-Sanction?'

Again, I flinch visibly in response as the chip stops me from answering. He turns pale.

'Has the *Federation* . . . has my *father* committed an act of war?' he wheezes.

When he sees my reaction he whimpers and looks as if he's about to faint. I'm still holding his hands and I support him as he sits down on the trunk of the fallen tree. He lets go of me and hangs his head down between his knees, trembling violently.

'I can't buh-buh-buh-believe it!' he moans. 'This can't buh-be right! I can't believe he'd do it. I didn't think it was possible. The buh-buh . . . buh-bastard! The only reason I agreed to be a fuh-fuh-fucking *hostage* for him, to come to this shit-heap of an island was because I never thought he'd be *insane* enough to start a *war*. I come here and . . . and he gets to be Puh-Puh-President of the whole Asian Federation. He said he was going to make the world a buh-buh-better place! I can't believe this! He started a fucking *war*, that asshole! Oh my God, they're going to *execute* me, Billy! They're going to take me to Earnest.'

'Earnest is gone.'

'Then they'll get someone *else* to be the . . . the fuh-fuh-fucking executioner, won't they?' he screeches at me. 'Fuck, Buckley will probably do it himself! What difference does it

351

make who puts the *buh-buh . . . buh-bullet* in my head? What does that matter?'

I look over my shoulder, anxiously wishing he'd keep his voice down.

'We can't stay here,' I say. 'They'll be out searching for you. We need to get out of here.'

'And . . . and go *where?*' Skip blurts out in near-hysterical exasperation, glaring at me as if I'm an idiot. 'We're on an *island*! Where can we go? That's why they keep us here. So when some dickhead fires missiles at his neighbour and the suh-suh-suh . . . suh-Sanction is ordered, there's nowhere for us to escape to.'

'I'm not giving up!' I growl at him. 'We've gotta steal a boat. Get off the island.'

'Yeah . . . and go where? It doesn't matter wuh-wuh-where I go.' He's sobbing now, the despair flushing through him like bloody drain cleaner, destroying his spirit. 'Every country in the world is buh-buh-bound by the law. No matter where I try and escape to, the death sentence still stands. They'll hunt me down wherever I go. I'm a fuh-fucking dead man.'

I'm so hurt by his words, stabbed by them, that I swing at him, catching him across the face with my open right hand. His head snaps to the side and he stares back at me, stunned. I'll confess, the result is satisfying enough that I hit him again on the other side to make sure I have his attention. Then I kneel down in front of him and take his burning face in my hands and I kiss him.

'I don't care who comes after us. Or that we have nowhere to go,' I say slowly and firmly, my mouth centimetres from his. 'You'll stay alive as long as you can, until the world remembers we're here. We can't know for sure what's happened out there – what might have changed. Everything could be different. To hell with Buckley and all the others. We're going to run as fast and as far as we can and stay alive as long as we can. We're going to *live*, you hear me? Cos' that's all there is, Skip. Now stop your bleating and start moving.'

'Hmph,' he sniffs, leaning his brow against mine. 'Tough little goat, ain't ya?'

'Shut up and start running,' I reply.

Chapter Thirty-Eight
Being Tracked

Despite my defiant words, it's not long before I'm doing little more than staggering through the woods, attempting to keep up with Skip. My lungs feel like someone's trying to wring them out, my joints ache and my muscles have all the suppleness of dried chewing gum. I've noticed lately that I'm getting rashes wherever my skin rubs, like my armpits or my crotch and they're really stinging now. I feel emptied out and I'm not going to make it much further – I just don't have anything left in the tank. We need food, water and a place to hide.

We follow the less-travelled paths through the forest. After twenty minutes, Skip hooks his arm around me, my right arm draped over his shoulders, and I'm not too proud to accept his help. After all, he's been resting for the last couple of hours while I ran around watching our community tear itself a part. He's almost carrying me by the time we reach the downhill slope towards the deserted air base. It's a steep path down and I groan as my knees struggle with the strain of it.

The bunker's storerooms were emptied of food, but there are other things there we can use. Our plan is to stay here just long enough to put a couple of packs together and then head on. The door has been fixed, nailed shut with a couple of boards. Skip lowers me down to sit with my back to the wall, next to the door. Looking round, he finds a rusted steel bar lying nearby and levers the boards off.

'Keep watch,' he tells me, before venturing inside. 'Take a rest. I'll get what we need.'

I try to stay alert, I really do. It's just that my brain seems to have turned to liquid and the world has a watery, drugged quality, solid shapes oozing colour like leaking containers. It's actually quite cool. The sensation makes the pains in my body seem less intense than they were. Even so, the ground is very hard under my buttocks; I'm a whole lot bonier than I was a few weeks ago. I imagine the pain as a fire, twin rockets that are about to lift my near-weightless body up off the ground. I wonder how far out to sea I could get, hovering like this . . .

'Girl, you are a pretty useless sentry, you know that?' a voice says.

A dark shape stands over me, blotting out the sun. Too tall to be Skip. Thick, curly black hair. It's Noon.

'Hey, Noon!' I give a drunken laugh. 'You're in the middle of my sky! Get it? You're Noon . . .'

'Yeah Billy, I get it, you're hilarious. Starving to death is doing wonders for your wit. Come on, get up. We need to go.'

Skip appears at the door; the steel bar's in his hands and he's ready to use it.

'You can stay if you want,' Noon says to him, unfazed by the sight of the weapon, 'or you can come with us. I'm not bothered either way.'

'You're going to help us escape?' I ask, as she pulls me to my feet.

'I'm going to help *you* escape,' she replies. 'What Skip does is up to him.'

'But he's the one they're after,' I say. My head is still groggy. It's really hard to think. 'They're going to exe— . . . uh . . exe- . . . aw, balls.'

'Execute him,' Noon finishes for me. 'No, they're not. Right now, Buckley has his hands full bringing the studes back under control, but even when he does, he won't carry out a Sanction without the order from the Council. And Skip won't be executed anyway.' She leans in close to me, gazing into my poorly-focussed eyes. '*His* father wasn't the one who started a war. *Your* father did. I've done everything I can to stop word of it reaching the island over these last few weeks, but we're running out of time, Billy. We've stayed too long already. Any time now, that order is going to come through when the sat-link comes back online, or they get a plane close enough to use the radio.

'And when it does, they're going to kill you.'

Chapter Thirty-Nine
Confession

Noon's right; I'm a useless sentry. She managed to drive an SUV onto the airfield without me even hearing it. Now we're riding with her, me in the passenger seat, Skip sitting behind me, both of us jolting back and forth as she steers the vehicle up a track that's barely wide enough for the car to fit between the trunks of the mast-like pines that loom over us.

'How did you find us?' I ask groggily.

She points at my head.

'Your chip still acts as a tracking device,' she says, gesturing to the phone in its mount on the dashboard. 'You nearly blew it, Billy. I tried to tell you to stay put. I needed you to keep out of trouble until I had everything ready. At the moment, I'm blocking all the other guardians from finding both of you, but once they realize that, the game's up. They'll work out what I've been doing the whole time and I'll be hunted along with you.

'You buh-buh-blew up the monastery,' Skip says.

'Yes,' she replies.

'You killed Valtere,' I add sourly.

'Yes,' she says again, grimacing and breathing out through her teeth. 'I . . . I didn't plan for that to happen. The fire was only supposed to take out the comms room. I knew Valt would be on duty, but I figured he'd be all boozed up and dozing on the couch in the games room, as usual. I made a mistake with the detonator somehow. It didn't go off when it was supposed to. Look, Valt was my friend. I'll be dealing with that one for the rest of my life, but it's a price I can accept. He was an old soldier who was slowly drinking himself to death. He'd caused enough collateral damage in his life, I can tell you. He was no angel.'

'You still murdered him,' I mutter, scowling. 'Did you cut us off from the satellites too?'

'No, no. That virus you heard about is the real deal. Pretty apocalyptic stuff, it seems. I'm amazed we've been out of contact for so long.'

I lean back against the seat, my body settling as if it's made out of drying concrete. Instead of feeling several kilos lighter than I've been in years, I imagine the car sagging under the weight of my dread.

'So what's going on here, Noon?'

She stares out through the windscreen. The light goes from bright to gloom in flickering green washes, the thick foliage above us blocking out the sun, then letting stark beams of it through that dazzle the eyes, the trunks like dark bars against the sky where it shows through. Noon doesn't answer at first; I don't think she's going to answer at all, and then she starts talking, still looking ahead, never meeting my gaze.

'I was a committed to the Neutral Order, heart and mind,'

she says. 'I really did believe in what we were doing here. You're too young to have known the world before . . . Look, I was born in Syria – I'm old enough to remember the war there. I was eight years old during the worst of the bombings, the Siege of Aleppo. I saw my family get killed by government forces when we tried to flee the country . . . but I got out in the end. You'd think I'd have run in the opposite direction from any more of that hell. I got adopted by this American couple . . . both of them had served in the military, so when I finished school, I ended up in the army myself–.'

'You've told me all this before,' I say impatiently. 'It doesn't explain *why* . . .'

'I'm getting to that!' she snaps at me. For the first time that I've ever seen, Noon looks visibly distressed. 'Look, I'm in the middle of screwing up everything the Order has achieved, and completely fucking up my life! I'm just trying to explain . . . *why*, okay? I need you to understand – and I know how hard it's been for all of you, not being able to talk about this. Oh, and I know you're recording this, you've got your writing face on.'

I throw a sour glance at Skip and he shrugs.

'So . . . it's . . .' Noon throws her hands up. 'Consider this a confession.

'I was . . . I was in the army; infantry, then engineering, then intelligence. I think I wanted to *understand* the nature of it – of war. Sometimes I wonder if I was actually drawn back to that shit I'd witnessed when I was a kid. Like some abuse victim who ends up being an abuser, as if I'd already been programmed with it. And it just seemed to be getting worse. We'd bollocksed up our climate. The world was fighting over basic stuff like farmland, food and water. The more desperate things became, the more people turned to extremist leaders . . . these power-hungry maniacs who preached small-minded nationalism and racism and just escalated things further; a conflict in one place would trigger another one next door.

'And I was in the middle of it all, transferring from one unit to the next, moving with the mayhem, following it like one of those lunatic storm-chasers, searching for the perfect tornado. I kept looking for a righteous fight and the more I understood things, the less justice I found. And I caused my share of harm too, I'll tell you that.

'When you're fighting in a city, you know how you clear a building, one room at a time? I mean, if you can't just demolish the whole damn place with artillery. What you do, is you shout a warning into each room to come out with their hands up, then throw a grenade in if they don't. You don't risk your life going in first, so you can be shot by whoever's in there. One room after another, you shout, toss a grenade, check the room after the explosion, and move on to the next one. Sometimes you don't even shout the warning. Sometimes the people you kill aren't enemies. They're just . . . just normal people, hiding away in their homes behind doors they're too scared to open.

'But you can justify it all, you see, because you're at *war*. The word has a unique kind of magic to it. It's a license to commit any atrocity. I could murder a human being, the worst crime you can commit, and it wouldn't be a crime, because it's a *war*. You might think what we do on this island is monstrous, but you have to understand, I've seen *thousands* die – hundreds of them children. We were facing one climate disaster after another, each one bringing more conflict over . . . dwindling resources, basic stuff. And it got to the point where some serious people started saying we were facing the collapse of civilization.

'And just when things were at their most desperate, the United World Council was created. Here was a proposal to *end war* in our lifetimes – and I listened. Billions of us listened. It was decided that the governments of the world would no longer recognise the state of war. Where military force and the law was concerned, there would only be peacekeeping and war crimes.

'Any country that engaged in illegal military action could be completely isolated, made a pariah nation until they complied once more. Elected leaders would sit together on this council with massive, combined democratic legal power . . .'

I stay quiet and let her talk. I know all this, of course; it's just that I've never been able to put it down in my journal before. It's just history to me, but she *lived* through it. So I let her talk, trusting her to get to the damn point in her own time.

'A position on the UWC came with extraordinary power, so it was decided that if you wanted to take a seat, you had to have a personal stake in its decisions, and in the actions of your country. So you had to be a parent, and your eldest child had to be under twenty-five,' she continues. 'And . . . and you had to offer your firstborn child as a hostage – a child with whom you had a verified relationship. This was the Firstborn Policy . . . and they created the Neutral Order to enforce it. The guardians of the peace.'

'And in the event of your country being the first to commit an act of war, your child would be put to death. That was the basic idea of it. If you started a war, your child was the first to die.'

Noon is driving faster now, the trail a little wider. She wrenches the wheel to the right, the SUV nearly tipping over as it banks around a steep turn.

'You can bet it divided people!' Noon snorts. 'Some thought it was barbaric, others, like me, thought it made complete sense. We'd watched too many politicians order armies into conflict zones, while never suffering the consequences of their decisions. Executing a child made more sense than nations having stand-offs with nuclear weapons, pushing us to the brink of World War Three. Threaten one life instead of wiping out millions? For me, that's not even a *decision*. It's one of the reasons the Order recruits war veterans.'

We're high up on the extinct volcano that forms the centre of the island, in forest that skirts the bare ridges of rock that make up the north-west third of the land. She seems to know where she's going, but I can't for the life of me figure out where that might be. There's nothing much on this side of the island; just the wild landscape and the deserted ruins of a few houses that belonged to some of the original inhabitants, before they abandoned the place decades ago. We've only ever come out this way for walks, cycles and camping trips.

'I joined the Neutral Order pretty much as soon as it was established, one of the first,' Noon goes on. 'A true believer. The Order sent me here. Of all the isolation sites, this one was the most important. We took the children of the most powerful world leaders. It was a rocky ride in the early days – it took a while for everything to work out. We were nearly five years setting it up, but after the first couple of executions, everyone realized this was how it was going to be. We weren't messing around. But it worked.'

She slams the heel of her hand against the steering wheel.

'*It worked*! The world has gone over ten years without a major conflict. People got a taste for peace. It's given us a chance to do so much! We've solved so many problems . . . we've dragged civilization back from the brink. And what's even more incredible is that, for people your age, this is *your normal*. You've no idea of the scale of that achievement. For me, it was worth the cost.'

'But . . . then I met *you*, see? And . . . I grew to love you, Billy. I'd never had children of my own, so . . . for the first time I truly understood *why* the Firstborn Policy worked. I understood the utter strength of that bond. And then I got a phone call, that time during the hurricane. It was an old friend in British Intelligence. He warned me what was coming, and I knew I couldn't go through with another execution.

'What I'm trying to tell you is, I absolutely believe in the system. I understand its importance as well as anyone – better than most. And now . . . now I've found that none of that counts for anything. No matter how necessary it is to keep order in the world, I can't let them kill you.'

'But why is Billy being Suh-Sanctioned?' Skip asks, his voice jarred by the car's bouncing motion. 'Wuh-wuh-what happened?'

'The virus that's brought down the world's communications?' Noon tells us. 'It was the British. It was all about money, an AI cyber-attack that targeted the Asian Federation's economy, their banking industry . . . but the thing *spread*. It went *everywhere*. That intelligence operation couldn't have happened without your father's approval, Billy. Maybe he was stupid and didn't think it would count as an act of war, or maybe he thought he could get away with it and never be found out, but either way he's going down for it.

'The virus was transmitted from a British spy ship in the South China Sea. That was the ship the Federation's air force sank. Almeida was just a civilian; he only knew what he saw on the news, which is why he named Skip. But the air-strike was an act of defence – they were trying to prevent the transmission of the virus. They were too late. This is all on the Brits. Billy's father's government is responsible for everything.

'As soon as it happened, my contact called to warn me, told me it would only be a matter of time before the truth of the operation came out and then the Sanction would be ordered. Ever since that night, I've been trying to keep us isolated from the world until I could get you off the island. I had to finish the repairs to the *Santiago* and wait for that second big storm to pass or we'd never have made it. I've pushed our luck too far already – now we have to get out of here.'

I have my face in my hands, shaking my head. This is all too much to take in. Thoughts bellow in my head, too loud and crowded to hold inside, so now I'm groaning under the pressure of it. Dad, Dad, you almighty, treacherous idiot, what have you done? *What have you done?* And Noon too, acting out of some noble intent, but people have died because her. Because of my dad. Because of me. How . . . how can this ever be made right?

'Earnest and Nuke took the Suh-Suh-*Santiago*,' Skip points out. 'What are you going to do now? And if it's buh-been you doing this shit all along, why did *they* make a run for it?'

'They didn't know any more than the rest of you,' Noon tells him. 'But North Korea's been threatening other countries with its nuclear weapons, like, forever. And Nuke's had to listen to all of it; living in fear that, one day, her dad is going to finally lose his mind completely and push that fucking button. It's one of the reasons we control what you lot can see on the news, to save you from hearing too much of that crap. When the comms went down, Nuke assumed her dad had gone and done it. And Earnest is devoted to her. He'd do anything for her – and he did. Given what *I've* done, I suppose I can't blame him, even if they did steal our only chance of getting out of here.'

'It's over now, though, isn't it?' I rasp. My whole body feels clenched with tense emotion. 'If the *Santiago's* gone?'

She gives me a twisting smile and squeezes my hand.

'Not exactly,' she replies.

And even as she says this, we emerge from the woods on the north-east side of the island. I'm surprised to see how high the sun is in the sky, torn-cotton stratus clouds scattered sparsely across an airbrushed blue. I realize it's not even midday. I thought it was late evening. It's so quiet over this side, the sun warming our faces, we could be out on our way to the start of a trek or a picnic on the coast. We're heading down a gentle slope through banks of Mexican thorn erupting out of thick tufts of weathered grass, the island's forested bulk rising ever steeper behind us. In a small cove, partly hidden by a copse of trees, we see the distinctive shape of a schooner, its sails furled, the vessel moored and waiting. It's the *Santiago*.

Chapter Forty
Departure

Noon pulls the car up to the narrow concrete jetty that juts out into the cove. As she gets out, she takes a gun, *Earnest's* gun, from the pocket of the car door, shoving it into her waistband. There's a derelict old wood and stone cabin, a simple two-room place, set back from the pebble beach. The hovel's walls and roof have been scoured the colour of ash by the abrasive sea wind. Noon leads us inside. There's little in here apart from some pieces of wooden and steel furniture so old and worn they look like they washed in on the tide. With a crowbar, she tears up a couple of floorboards and points to the plastic-wrapped packages and containers hidden in the space beneath the floor.

'I don't get it; how is the boat here?' I ask her.

'I'll explain in a minute. Give me a hand.'

'Is this . . . Is this *food?*' I stare in disbelief at the bundles she's pulling out.

'Yeah. I stole it from the stores before I set the bomb in the monastery,' she replies. 'I was counting on the fire causing enough damage that all this stuff wouldn't be noticed missing until we'd gone. Think I overshot a bit on that one . . .'

'Yeah, no kidding,' Skip grunts.

'If Skip is serious about coming, we'll have to stretch it out for three of us, but we should be okay,' Noon says. 'It has to last us two weeks, minimum. We need to head north, rather than east. Much longer trip.'

'I thought the *boat* wouldn't last that long?' I say. 'Isn't there a leak around the propeller shaft? You said it wouldn't even last ten days on the water.'

'Yeah, I kind of lied about that,' she tells me, shrugging. 'I did have the parts to fix it. I just didn't want to risk anyone else taking it out. I replaced the rotor, coupling and seals this morning. This baby will sail around the world if we need it to.'

'Bloody hell, Noon. You . . . you did all this for *me*? I mean . . . Couldn't you have–?'

'Billy, do you want to die?'

'No.'

'Then do as you're told. Just get the supplies on board. I'll be back in a second.'

After a few seconds of looking at each other in consternation, Skip and I start pulling the bundles out of the floor. When we come out of the cabin with our arms full of packages, we find her up on the deck of the boat, dragging something out and down the gangplank.

It's Earnest. There can be no mistaking the fact that he's dead. There's a stab wound in his side and his throat is slashed open.

'No, before you ask, there was no other way,' Noon assures me coldly as she dumps the body on the jetty. 'I can handle myself, but guys like Earnest, Buckley and some of the others, they're a whole other level of dangerous. Someone like this, you get one chance to take him by surprise and be damn sure you make the most of it.'

She trots back up on deck and then she's hauling Nuke down. Nuke's face is bruised, but she's alive, her wrists and ankles bound with duct tape, her mouth gagged with it too. I guess she was a little easier to handle – or maybe Noon was a bit more reluctant to finish her off.

'I was under the deck, working on the prop shaft when they stole the boat,' Noon explains, lowering Nuke to the concrete with more care than she'd shown to Earnest's corpse. 'So I just let them take it, then I took it from them. Saved me having to deal with the other guardians. I didn't have a gun. I already had an electric bike stashed at that cabin, so as soon as I'd docked, I went back to the village to look for you. But of course, you'd already scarpered. Always the Billy Goat.'

I'm still staring at Earnest's dead body.

'Would you have killed the others too?' I ask shakily.

She glances at me, tilts her head from side to side.

'Not if I could help it.'

I feel on the verge of throwing up. I probably would if I had anything to puke. My head's spinning again, I get wobbly and have to sit down on the ground beside Nuke, who's lying on her front. She glares up at me with savage eyes. I think she'd sink her teeth into my throat, if I gave her the chance. I almost want to apologise to her, though I'm not entirely sure who's done more harm to who.

'Billy, go get on buh-buh. . . board,' Skip tells me, shoving his packages under the rail and onto the boat, then picking up mine. 'We'll get the rest of the suh-stuff. You take a few minutes, get yourself together. We can muh-manage.'

'You're sure you want to come with us?' I wheeze.

'Yeah,' he drawls casually. 'This puh-puh-place is getting old, y'know? I need a change of suh-suh-scene.'

I hold my hand out to him and he takes it and clasps it for a few seconds before letting go.

'Get on board,' he says again. 'I won't be long.'

I do as he says and drag my starved and bony arse up the gangplank. More out of habit than need, I start checking the boat over in preparation for getting underway. On the control panel at the helm, I look over the fuel, electrics, test the lights and make sure the batteries are charged. I know Noon will have done all this; she's been planning this trip for weeks, but my brain is barely trundling through conscious thought, so I'm operating on autopilot.

Going aft to ensure the emergency kit is in its locker, I'm dimly aware of Skip bringing on the last of the supplies and piling them by the hatch between me and the helm. It occurs to me that this feeling I have of my senses fading is down to hunger and I should find an energy drink or bar to eat. I want to be able to help with the sails when we get out of the cove.

Noon's shouting about something. Skip rushes past me and I have to lower myself onto a seat, my free-floating brain objecting to the sudden change in direction as I turn to see what he's doing. He's up at the helm, turning the key on the control panel. What's happening? Are we going without Noon?

The engine rumbles under my feet, the vibration thrumming up through the soles of my shoes. The gangplank's already been pulled up and I swivel back to see Noon untying the lines from the rusted steel rings on the jetty. She throws the ropes over the railing even as the schooner starts pulling away. Glancing back, an expression of fearful resolve on her face, she leaps for the side of the boat, feet nimbly catching the edge of the deck as she grabs hold of the rail.

Then, as she swings her leg over the rail, an arrow pierces her neck.

My senses suddenly snap back into life; in that instant, I take it all in. It's Buckley, having just got out of an SUV that's pulled up beside Noon's. Even as others jump from the car, he's pulled out his bow, nocked an arrow and taken a shot. And it's frighteningly accurate, given that he had mere seconds to take aim. The arrow punches through the side of Noon's neck, from back to front and she loses her grip on the rail. I'm on my feet in a heartbeat, lunging across the few metres to her, catching her arm before she can fall off the side of the boat. Yanking her close, I get my arms around her chest and clumsily haul her over and onto the deck.

I immediately drop down beside her, thinking Buckley will take another shot, but instead, he's charging up the jetty. Behind him, I see Nguyen, Adeyemi and a couple of other guardians running to catch up. They won't make it before the boat clears the small pier. But Buckley might. He comes on like a frickin' Olympic sprinter, pounding towards us, scarily fast. Skip has the throttle full forward now, the engines churning up the water behind us, but the schooner's not a speedboat – it's not exactly quick off the line. We're still passing the end of the jetty when Buckley tosses down his bow and hurls himself across the water. He jumps twice the distance Noon did only seconds before, grabbing the rail and catching himself on the side just as she did.

I have moments to react. My first instinct is to try and knock him off while he's still hanging from the rail, but I stop myself. If I get within reach of him, he'll make short work of me. I stumble backwards instead, slipping on blood and falling over Noon's inert body. Buckley vaults over the rail and lands on the deck, panting for breath. He spares me a baleful glance and starts towards Skip, intent on taking control of the boat and turning us around.

He stops short at the sound of the double click as I pull back the hammer on Earnest's revolver, cocking it. My entire body is trembling, the barrel wobbling so much I must look comical, but I've got his attention. Noon still had the gun tucked into her waistband. I'm really hoping she reloaded it after Earnest used it on the guards at the harbour.

Up on one knee, right hand cupped in my left, I take a deep breath and force myself to go still, relaxing enough to steady my aim. My heart feels like some boxer is using it for a speedbag. Buckley regards me with eyes that have seen the very worst that humans can do to each other and has done some of it himself. He's not in the least bit scared that I'm pointing a gun at him; he's using this long, long moment to compose himself. To become calm again. He will soon have everything back under control.

'And what are you doing to do with that, Billy?' he asks me, compassion in his voice.

I shake my head, rising slowly to my feet, keeping my aim on him. How has it come to this? An innocent seventeen-year-old girl, pointing a gun at a man she once liked and still respects, a man who has devoted himself to preventing war. I want to explain myself, to argue with him, reason with him. But even as I'm forming the thoughts in my head, I know that I'll fail to express them – choked by the censor chip, my own brain will betray me. My words will be cut off at the throat. He has left me with nothing to say. And if I give him a chance him to do *anything*, he'll get this gun off me, I'm certain of that.

In the end, in the roar of that moment, the violence comes easily.

I pull the trigger, over and over, firing into the centre of his chest. He doesn't even try to avoid the shots. He can't believe what's happened. Shock opens up his face, his eyes and mouth widened, the breath thumped out of him. After six shots, the hammer clicks on an empty chamber, then another. He topples back and collapses onto the deck. Sickeningly dead. I let my arms drop, the gun hanging by my side, staring down at the damage I've done. There's this sensation of numb stillness, as if my body is waiting for the slamming emotional impact it knows is coming.

I've just killed a man.

I'm not given much time to dwell on it. Noon coughs and cries out. I drop back down onto one knee, laying the smoking gun on the deck. I knew she was still alive when I pulled her over the rail, but assumed it was a fatal wound. Now she's pawing at her shoulder, teeth gritted in agony, head twisted up and back as if it's trying to get away from the arrow that's embedded in the side of her neck.

'Oh my God, Noon! Are you okay?'

'What . . . what kind of suh- . . . stupid question it that?' she snarls, her voice gurgling, her breath coming in painful fits. 'I've got a fucking arrow in my neck! It's . . . it's not a good look. Now li. . . listen, I can't tell. Is . . . Is there much blood?'

'It's pretty messy, but I don't think it hit the artery,' I tell her. 'What do you want me to do?'

'Get the first aid kit – you're going to have to help me cut the head off this and pull it out. And tell Skip to head north.

374

I'll take over when I can.'

'I . . . killed Buckley,' I say, my voice cracking.

'I know,' she replies weakly, raising a hand to touch my cheek. 'He drove you to it, Billy. We all did. We *all* did. It's a shitty deal and I'm really sorry for the horror we've brought down on you. Now . . . stop your whinging and get me the bloody first aid kit. I've a fucking arrow in my neck.'

Chapter Forty-One
Final Words

For the first time in the weeks, I've eaten a proper meal. My belly is uncomfortably full and I feel mildly ill. Noon let us eat as much as we could, cautioning us that, in our state, we would only manage a fraction of what once was normal. Even though we'd need to ration our supplies, we also needed to get our strength up for the voyage ahead.

I'm in the galley now, peering out the porthole at the setting sun, which smoulders across the undersides of the clouds, as if there's a raging battle just over the horizon. It makes me wonder what we're going to find when we get back to the world. I'm still amazed that Skip came along, and knowing he's here for me is doing a lot to help me cope with all this, but he's not the one everyone's going to be hunting. He could cut loose at any time and go home. The reality of my situation is only slowly sinking in. Wherever I go, I'll be under sentence of death. I could be on the run for the rest of my life.

'How am I going to do it?' I ask Noon, who's laying some surgical instruments out on the galley table. 'I'll be hiding forever. Is that even possible, to stay hidden for years? Noon? What am I going to do?'

'Don't get ahead of yourself,' she says, picking up a device that resembles a small screwdriver with a tiny claw on the end.

Her voice has a horrible rasp to it. 'The world will have changed. We don't know how it'll be different. We can't even be sure if the Council still exists. I have friends who can help us out once we reach land. We're going to be dealing with a lot of unknowns, but . . . well, that's how life is anyway. We'll deal with it.'

She has two pieces of gauze taped over the entry and exit wounds on her neck. I had to stitch them up for her, under her direction. Not the grossest thing I've ever done, but close. Soon, she'll have to return the favour. The slight motion of the sea is a constant now, rhythmic, almost in time with my breath. Skip is at the helm, up on deck, guiding the boat along under engine power to keep it as still as he can on the gentle swell. Noon needs things to be steady when she goes inside my head. After everything that's happened, you'd think there'd be other things to be depressed about – you know; starving for weeks, being sentenced to death, killing another human being . . . instead, *this* is the thing that's getting me down.

'You okay?' she asks, her instruments at the ready.

'What kind of stupid question is that?' I retort, mimicking her tone.

'We can't leave it in there, Billy. When the satellites come back online, it can be used to track you. We have to destroy it.'

She means my censor chip. It has to come out. She'll have to remove Skip's too, and he can't wait. As he says, it might be the size of a pea, but it'll be a load of weight of his mind. We'll finally be able to say whatever we want again. You'd think I'd be happy about it.

'Of . . . of course I want it gone. The thing's a curse; it's just, y'know . . . it's also my *journal*, Noon. I mean, I'm going to lose everything.'

'Should've bloody written it down the normal way, shouldn't you?'

'Yeah, that's really helpful. Thanks for caring. You even told me to keep writing, remember? To make it as complete a story as I could.'

'I was hoping it would keep you busy, make you stay out trouble until I was ready to sail.'

'Didn't work, did it?'

She shrugs. I know she understands. She may be hardcore, but she's sensitive enough to get what I'm feeling. It's just that we don't have any choice.

Although . . .

'Do you have to *destroy* it?' I ask.

'Why?' she regards me suspiciously. 'What did you have in mind?'

The brain surgery is, fortunately, pretty straightforward. When the surgeons implanted the chip, they made sure it would be a routine matter to take it out again. Noon injects the left side of my scalp with a local anaesthetic that numbs the area behind my temple, just ahead of the top of my ear. Taking a scalpel, she makes a small cut, dabbing the blood away with a piece of gauze. She has exposed the top of a titanium screw lodged in my skull, its head flush with the bone, a few millimetres in diameter. The screw is plugging a short titanium tube that goes through the side wall of my skull. She just unscrews the plug and she now has access to the part of my brain known as 'Broca's area'. I have one of these complex bundles of nerves on each side, key to producing language, but the one on my left side is dominant, so that's where the chip has been implanted. I shiver as I see the screw come out. Noon puts it carefully in a sterile aluminium dish.

I don't know if I'm ready for this. The censor chip has been the bane of my life, but my journal has kept me sane through more than two years of surreal existence. Once she removes it, it'll be as if this part of my life is officially over.

'You've got the bottle ready?' I ask for the fifth time.

'Yes,' she assures me, patiently. She knows how insecure I'm feeling.

I can't keep the chip, I do understand that. It runs on the electricity in my body, but the tracker has a temporary back-up battery that will keep it transmitting for a few days after it's been removed from my head. That's why Noon had intended to destroy it, or just drop it overboard. We don't have any way of downloading my journal . . . and I can't bear the thought of years of writing being lost forever.

So I came up with a compromise, one Noon thinks will actually help give us a head start. We're going to put it in a bottle and drop *that* overboard. That tiny, lonely signal will float away with the currents while we put reins on the wind and let them sweep us away in a different direction. If someone does track the signal, all they'll find is a rugged, insulated plastic water bottle. And a microchip containing the journal of a girl who, with any luck, will have completely disappeared.

I hope someone does save it from the sea. Perhaps they'll release it online or publish it some other way and I might find it, years from now, and read it again. My long lost message in a bottle. I wipe tears from my eyes and see Noon looking at me, the little screwdriver tool in her hand. Its micro-pincers will slide painlessly into my brain and retrieve the censor chip. In less than a minute, I'll be able to speak completely freely again.

'Time to wrap things up,' she says tenderly. 'You ready?'

I nod, sniffing and rubbing my eyes on my sleeve. She fits the tool into the titanium socket in the side of my head and I have a shuddering sensation of pain/pleasure that has nothing to do with the pincers that are, even now, extending in through my skull. Unlike most other parts of the body, the brain doesn't have any pain receptors. It cannot feel pain. It's all in my mind, perhaps the mental equivalent of using the tip of a knife to dig out a splinter.

'We're going to be okay, Billy,' Noon tells me.

'I know,' I reply.

Out of the corner of my eye, I see this formidable woman, her fingers pressed against the side of my head to hold it still, staring at me with the intense emotion that has brought us to this point, a violent escape from our bizarre home. I see her bite her lip; she gives me one last look, needing me to be ready, to accept this.

'Yes,' I say.

With one last touch of her fingertips, the chip is seized, and she prepares to pull years of written thoughts from my brain.

And the story is over.

CUT OFF AT THE THROAT

OISÍN MCGANN